Tommy Storm

Alan Healy was born in Dublin and his life has taken many directions including jobs at Goldman Sachs in London and in a brick factory in South Africa before his life-long passion for writing culminated with his first novel – *Tommy Storm.* He self-published a first edition of the book in 2006 in Ireland. He now lives, happily married, back in Dublin.

A J HEALY

TOMMY STORM

Quercus

First published in Great Britain in 2006 by Enow Ltd
This editon first published in 2008 by

Quercus
21 Bloomsbury Square
London
WC1A 2NS

A CIP catalogue reference for this book is available
from the British Library

ISBN 978 1 84724 425 3

10 9 8 7 6 5 4 3 2 1

Designed and typeset by Rook Books, London
Printed and bound in England by Clays Ltd, St Ives plc.

For Mum

THE LOW-DOWN

If you're someone who just wants to know the story and wants to know it fast, then feel free to skip the footnotes and the boxes of information (like the one below) throughout the book.

Nosey Parkers of the World Unite

On the other hand, if you're the kind of person who'd like to know as much as possible about the world of Tommy Storm, then the footnotes, the boxes and the Extra Bits at the end of the book are for you.

1

THE BEGINNING OF (FUTURE) HISTORY

2096 could've been a very ordinary year on Earth . . .

* Over 50,000 people – a pretty average number – reported seeing a bird in the sky, even though all birds had been extinct for many years.
* The Grand Council raised some taxes and lowered others, thus ensuring people stayed as confused as ever.
* The President of Earth, Guttly Randolph, remained popular in the polls despite the tabloids claiming (incorrectly) that he was having a romance with Helena Jadely, a fellow Councillor.
* And Earth's Deputy President, Elsorr Maudlin, killed a traffic warden while showing off his sword skills, but escaped punishment because it was 'an accident'.

Yes, 2096 could've been quite unremarkable had a certain round object not fallen through Earth's atmosphere, shot down a chimney and landed in the centre of the Grand Council Hall.

Guttly Randolph, Elsorr Maudlin, Helena Jadely and the other Councillors looked on in amazement as the small sphere broke open and the invitation was revealed . . .

Inter-stellar Invitation

Earth Date: March, 2096

Dear President of Earth,

Greetings.

We, the MilkyFed, are delighted to invite five Earth children to a training school on a space-station in the centre of the Milky Way. The training will prepare participants for a vital mission that is too dangerous and too secret for us to divulge. Many different species of space-people will take part and we hope that Earthlings will be represented.

At the end of this training, a final group of five people – of differing species – will be selected from the entire group of space-people for the mission.

Children rather than adults are required for two reasons:

1 Everyone will have to be rigorously trained once they reach the space-station and children are better at learning and adapting to new things than adults.

2 Adults can be quite disagreeable.

Yours expectantly,

Lord
Beardedmoustachedwiseface-oh

Lord Beardedmoustachedwiseface-oh

R. S. V. P.

(strictly within 22 days – include the names of 'The Five' and their hat sizes if they are to attend)

2

THE WILCHESTER ACADEMY FOR YOUNGER ADULTS

Tommy Storm hated two things about himself when he was a kid.

The first was his stutter – which would go into overdrive whenever he became angry or upset.

The second was possibly worse . . .

Towards the end of the 21st century, spiky hair was in fashion for boys. 'In fashion' meant that of the 3.5 billion boys on Earth aged six to sixteen, approximately 3,499,999,999 had spiky hair. But no matter what Tommy tried – gel, melted marshmallows, super-glue – his efforts always ended in failure.

You see, much to his disgust, Tommy Storm was the only boy on Earth whose hair wouldn't spike.

Two days after the Inter-Stellar Invitation landed in the Grand Council Hall, Tommy found himself in an infuriating situation.

Felkor Stagwitch wasn't the tallest boy in the class, but he was definitely the strongest. In fact, he was possibly the strongest boy in all of the Wilchester Academy for Younger Adults. He could run faster than anyone, he packed a punch

3

that could knock out a mule and he had a laugh that set itself apart from everybody else's. It sounded like a dog being kicked. Repeatedly. Felkor was laughing now as he watched the red computer-pad float higher and higher towards the ceiling of the blue-marbled classroom. He pointed his sabre-beam a little to the left and the computer-pad dodged to the left.

'G-g-g-g-g-give it b-b-back,' cried Tommy, but this only made Felkor laugh even harder. 'All my w-w-w-w-work is on it.'

Again the peal of laughter like a dog being kicked and the computer-pad soared higher – towards the floating spotlights high above the classroom. Just then, someone shouted something about Tommy's hair, making all the other kids laugh hard.

'P-p-p-p-please, Felkor,' Tommy pleaded, the top of his head only just reaching the maddening boy's shoulder.

Felkor aimed his tractor-beam sabre yet higher. 'G-g-g-g-give me b-b-back my computer-p-p-p-pad,' he mimicked. Then he laughed his piercing laugh. 'Darky's gonna cry now, innit?'

Felkor often called Tommy *Darky*. Indeed, Felkor could've called a snowman *Darky* since his skin was so white that he sometimes looked almost light blue (not that he'd ever seen a snowman in real life). He had blond hair (spiky of course) and very, very light blue eyes. The other detail to remember about Felkor was that he would fart whenever he got scared or nervous – although few of his classmates knew this because he always managed to blame someone else for the smell of rotten Brussels sprouts.

Felkor wasn't the only classmate who called Tommy names. The freckly kids called him *Dusky*, the kids of Oriental origin claimed he was Latino, the Latinos said his eyes were half-Oriental, and some of the very dark kids called him *Pasty*. One kid had laughed at him one day and called

4

him a *mongrel*. If Tommy could've asked his parents it might've helped, but he knew nothing about them. Not even that their names were Lola and Errol.

At this moment, however, his parents were the last thing on his mind. He'd just spent two hours, under test conditions, writing an essay on 'The Great Climate Enhancement' into his precious computer-pad (also known as a *CP*). Miss Gideon would be returning to class at any moment and would want to see everyone's work. Famed for her high-pitched scream, and three-time winner of the *World's-Strictest-Teacher®* award, she wasn't someone you wanted to cross.

Felkor's laugh and grating words pierced through all Tommy's thoughts. 'Darky's gonna cry.'

Tommy pointed his own sabre-beam at his CP, but Felkor had a Royce Turbo Tractor Beam VVS sabre (*VVS* standing for *Very Very Strong*) – Tommy had a Mega Minor NVS model (you can make your own guess what *NVS* stands for).

Realizing he had no chance against Felkor's sabre and hearing the laughter of other classmates, Tommy aimed his sabre at the platinum-plated duster on the teacher's desk. It was at this moment that Miss Gideon stepped into the room and witnessed an act of 'pure evil'. Her prized duster – the one she'd been presented with upon winning her record-breaking, third *World's-Strictest-Teacher®* title – yes, that very duster flashed through the air, hit Felkor's belly (sending him into a heap on the floor) and bounced onto a corner of marble, sustaining a long, ugly scratch. Felkor dropped his sabre-beam, releasing Tommy's CP from its grip.

And so it was, that a high-pitched scream rang out across the class – heard by everyone in the school – as a red CP obeyed the law of gravity and smashed into little pieces across Miss Gideon's desk.

5

'The Sun Won't Come Out Tomorrow!'
(7-times voted Earth's most annoying song)

In 2096, it was 34°C throughout planet Earth at *all* times. The sky was never visible through the permanent layer of clouds, it drizzled constantly and there was no wind. (Unsurprisingly, weather forecasters found it difficult to make a living.)

3

THE CHOOSING

Let me take you back briefly to the day that the Inter-Stellar Invitation splattered onto Earth . . .

Once the twelve members of Earth's Grand Council had read and digested its meaning, Guttly pleaded with The Council to accept the invitation. He was supported in the debate by Helena Jadely.

'This is an opportunity for us to extend the hand of friendship to other people in the Milky Way,' she said.

'But how can we send five children to some unknown place?' said a Councillor. 'It could be very dangerous.'

'The MilkyFed could destroy Earth at any time,' said another.

'Exactly,' replied Helena. 'So why don't we send a Grand Council member with the children? Then, if things get too dangerous, the Councillor could withdraw the children from the training school and bring them back to Earth.'

The strongest opponent of the invitation was the Deputy President, Elsorr Maudlin, who had an intense dislike of space-people, preferring to refer to them as 'alien monsters'. (He almost always voted against Guttly's recommendations – some said this was due to the fact that Guttly had beaten him in the Presidential election years earlier.)

Milkyfeddy star ate my hamster
(headline from *The Cloud* – a newspaper hostile to
the MilkyFed)

The MilkyFed consisted of four solar systems in the Milky Way
that had sustained intelligent life for millions of years. In 2082,
the MilkyFed sent a video message to Earth, introducing itself.
Subsequently, Earth received invitations to join the MilkyFed –
but always refused.

Extra Bits no. 1, page 415, gives more info on the relationship
between Earth and the MilkyFed.

Eventually, despite Elsorr's protests, the Grand Council
voted to accept the invitation by a majority of eleven to one.
Five children would be chosen to represent Earth on the
MilkyFed space-station and a Grand Council member would
accompany them. Guttly would choose one of the children
and the Grand Council would choose the other four.

Two weeks later, Guttly Randolph was standing on a
platform before the Grand Council members.

He was bald as an eagle (a bald-headed one, that is),
although wild silver hair bushed over both ears and spilled
into his thick, finger's-length beard. Despite the widespread
availability of anti-baldness pills, he stubbornly refused to
alter his appearance – which surely cost him the chance of
appearing in many soft-drink commercials as previous
Presidents had done. Like all the Councillors, the old man
wore a white cloak, draped around his body like a gown.

Guttly twirled a large ruby ring on his right index finger
then raised his arms to hush the dignitaries seated around the

Majestic Table. 'So now our job is to choose the five children who will represent our planet within the Milky Way and beyond.'

The Councillors had been briefed for days by a team of researchers who'd made continuous presentations, promoting various children from around the world.

There was the kid who was double-jointed all over. Double-jointed elbows, double-jointed knees and even a double-jointed chin. Or the girl who could speak three different words at once. When you listened, it sounded as if she was speaking gobbledegook, but if you recorded her speech and separated it into three, she was having three intelligent conversations at once. This could be very useful on an intergalactic space-station, some believed.

Helena Jadely especially remembered the boy who only ate things that began with the letter B. This would've been quite restrictive, except that he could eat *anything* beginning with the letter B. *Bread* and *barbed-wire sandwiches* were one thing (OK, so they were two things), but *bottoms*, *buildings* and *battleships* were quite another. This eating skill could be quite useful, some contended, if the boy were sent far into space where normal food rations ran quite low. Maybe he could feed on a black hole if he got particularly hungry. (It should be stressed that he only ate things that began with the letter B in the English language, as English was almost the only language spoken on Earth at this time. This little fellow's digestive system could've benefited greatly if he spoke Gaelic or even Hungarian – there being many additional things beginning with the letter B in these languages.)

Guttly Randolph stood back and let the appointed Councillors come to the platform one at a time. Within fifteen minutes, three children had been decided upon. They were:

1 **Egbert 'Sugar Floyd' Fitchly** (age 11½) – a boy who talked very, very fast and could convey more information in a minute than most people can in an hour.

2 **ZsaZsa Vavannus** (age 11¾) – supposedly the best girl in the world at art-o-pathy[1] (I'll explain later).

3 **Anjel*eek!* Jalfrezi** (age 11) – a girl who could scream louder than anyone on the planet (it was thought she could be useful in emergencies).

It was at this point that Elsorr Maudlin raised his objections to the whole project. He stood up, pulled his sword from its hilt and stabbed it loudly into the Majestic Table.

'I object! Co-operating with stinking MilkyFederans – pah! I'm not letting *one* child embark on this stupid space project.'

Unlike anyone else on the Council, Elsorr insisted on wearing an ornamental sword – to represent his 'duty of defence to planet Earth'. Elsorr had mullet-styled black hair, a pointy nose, angular cheekbones and a yellowy complexion that made you wonder if he had jaundice. No one was sure of the colour of his eyes as they were shadowed by a prominent forehead and thick eyebrows.

'Sit down, Elsorr. Put a plug in it,' said Helena Jadely.

Guttly tried to suppress a smile. Elsorr scowled, straining to remove his sword from the Table.

Helena was in charge of intra-planetary harmony issues on Earth and had crossed sabres many times with Elsorr. At thirty-seven years of age, she was one of the youngest-ever female Councillors, but this never daunted her.

'Thank you, Elsorr,' said Guttly. 'Your objections can have

---

1 Some historians claim that the fact her father was a very influential businessman just might have swayed some Councillors to vote for her.

no effect. We're sending five kids and that's it!' Once more, the bearded President of Earth twirled the ruby ring – the Presidential Insignia – around his finger.

Elsorr fell backwards as he wrenched his sword free from the Table. Recovering his balance, he smiled sarcastically at Guttly. 'Hah . . . ! I've got two words for you, oh mighty Guttly . . . *Filibuster*.'

'Isn't that *one* word?' asked a Councillor.

It took a number of Councillors to hold Guttly back as he stepped forward, red-faced, towards Elsorr. His voice came out strangulated with anger. 'You short-sighted – You . . . ! You . . . !'

Elsorr broke into laughter, the meeting broke into loud disarray and Guttly felt a small palpitation sting through his heart (strangely, it always seemed worse around Elsorr).

In case you're wondering . . . According to long-established rules, any Councillor could delay actions and decisions of the Council by putting their feet on the Majestic Table, putting their fingers in their ears and repeatedly uttering the word 'filibuster'. By having a tube inserted into his stomach to accept food and using his ability to talk in his sleep, Elsorr had once managed to delay a vote (on the world-wide banning of wigs) by almost three months. If Elsorr could filibuster for just two weeks, Earth would miss the deadline for the MilkyFed invitation.

It took over half an hour before order was restored, the room was hushed and Elsorr was once again addressing the gathering. 'I'd like everyone here to know,' he said, 'that I'm not an unreasonable man.'

This caused angry mumbles among some Councillors, but Elsorr continued and raised his voice above the noise. 'I do not necessarily want to frustrate the will of this Council or the will of our people. I will *not* object to sending five kids on this fanciful space-station project, on two conditions.'

11

Once again the Councillors broke into an angry hubbub, until Guttly raised his hands to quiet them. No one had noticed his right hand gently rubbing his breast. 'What are your conditions, Elsorr?'

Elsorr grabbed a candle from a nearby ledge, tossed it in the air and swished his sword in a flurry of movement – the candle floated to the ground in a shower of salami-thin slices.

'I don't like candles,' he said. 'Especially bendy ones . . . Sorry, what was I saying?'

'Your conditions,' said Guttly, trying to be patient. Elsorr liked to show off his swordsmanship at every opportunity.

'Oh, yes!' replied the jaundiced-faced man. 'Quite simple, really . . . First, I want to choose one child to go on this mission.'

A general nodding of heads and positive murmuring gave Guttly the signal. 'Agreed,' he said. 'And the other condition?'

'I want complete freedom, no appeals, no nothing, to choose which elder accompanies the children on their trip to, and on, their initial training in, the Intergalactic Space-station.'

This left the Councillors a little puzzled, but after a time they nodded their assent towards Guttly.

'Agreed.'

'I have your word on that, Guttly? Your word in front of the Grand Council?' Elsorr asked these questions dramatically. As if to emphasize a point.

'You have my word,' replied Guttly, still rubbing his chest.

The Council agreed to reconvene in a few days to hear Elsorr's nominations. However, to save time, it was decided that Guttly should nominate the fourth child immediately. Guttly moved to the raised platform and thought once more of the child he'd chosen. He'd pondered long and hard over the last thirteen days and now his mind was made up.

'Fellow Councillors,' he said. 'The child I have chosen to represent Earth on this mission is currently studying in a school known as the Wilchester Academy for Younger Adults.'

4

THE CELEBRATION

The Wilchester Academy for Younger Adults (known to most as plain Wilchester) was a boarding school established in 2063 and was therefore one of the oldest schools in existence towards the end of the 21st century. Unusually for a school at this time, Wilchester wasn't housed in a floating building or in a floating city. It was built on the top of a dormant volcano.

Each year at Wilchester had its living quarters on a single floor of the school building, and each floor was split into two dorms (male and female). Tommy's year was permanently housed on the uppermost floor, which was smaller than others, so one person was required to stay in the loft above. Every year since he'd been at Wilchester, Tommy's classmates had voted for him to take the loft-room.

This particular morning, at 6.53 a.m., the sea (as ever) lapped against the edges of the old volcano and then a square of blackness 101 metres up switched to a warm yellow glow. Inside, Tommy Storm smacked his alarm clock and groaned . . .

Five minutes later he was showered, dressed and examining the mirror with a grimace. That stupid mass of hair lay lank upon his head. Not even a trace of anything sticking up. Perhaps today, he hoped. He opened a drawer and removed a parcel.

This, he thought, must be my last chance. My last chance

to fit in and not to feel so . . . so . . . so . . . Well, so different and stupid-looking.

He'd saved for months for this, sent away his order and it had only arrived last night. Through the door of his room, he heard the sound of boys and girls laughing and talking below as they made their way to the Great Dining Hall. They're moving a little early, he thought. Breakfast never started until 7.15 and it wasn't yet 7.00 a.m.

He ripped the paper off the parcel, revealing a white, toothpaste-like tube, emboldened with an orange logo: *ITDDINEW* (short for, *If This Doesn't Do It Nothing Ever Will*). On the other side of the tube were the words, *Danger – Very Very Very Sticky*.

Feeling a strange nervousness, Tommy opened the cap and squeezed a blob of the substance into his hand. Stripy light and dark green, and emitting a low hum, it felt remarkably like earwax (which he'd tried twice before) as he massaged it through his hair. Gradually, the humming faded and it was time to peek in the mirror.

The smiling face that looked back was exactly what he'd hoped for. Dark hair standing proudly. 'You know, you don't look too bad, Tommy Storm,' he said to the mirror. 'You don't look half bad.'

He was about to join the others for breakfast (it was already 7.12 a.m.) when he paused. Was this what happiness felt like? He wasn't sure, but something felt good deep within his tummy. He'd even spoken without stuttering, but then he could always do that on his own. But maybe today he could do it outside, in front of others. Yes, he thought. Now that my hair looks so . . . so . . . *NORMAL*, I'll be able to do it.

Everything in the Dining Hall was fashioned in grey marble and reflected a cheerless sheen from fluorescent lights overhead. At the top of the Hall was a raised platform. Teachers sat up here during meals, keeping an eye on the pupils below. The Hall's walls were festooned with large floating screens that usually played images and boomed out instructions, reminding pupils of various rules, competitions taking place or newly invented rude words that were forbidden at Wilchester.

As Tommy left his room, unbeknownst to him, 499 students were standing, staring up at the platform in the Dining Hall. Behind them, 499 CPs were stacked on a large table, leaving everyone's hands free to clap and wave. But no one was clapping or waving. Everyone was standing motionless, paralysed with wonder. In front of them, Mr Withers was talking into a floating microphone, a bank of teachers seated behind him. Not one of these people noticed a boy descending at the back of the Hall, on a lift-panel, through a gap in the ceiling.

The three seconds it took to reach the floor were enough for Tommy to register surprise, fear and excitement.

Surprise, because he could think of no reason why everyone should be gathered so early this morning. Tommy was well used to his classmates disconnecting the information screen in his room, but even so, there'd never been a before-breakfast assembly in the whole time he'd been at Wilchester.

The fear arrived when he realized that he was the only person not already at the assembly. He'd already incurred the wrath of Miss Gideon for the smashed CP and scratched duster incident. A week's detention had been his punishment and Miss Gideon had awarded him an F for his exam essay on the Great Climate Enhancement. Alarmingly, this result, along with that of all his classmates, had been relayed to the central

16

data bank of the Grand Council to help them in assessing (for some unknown reason) the ability of all students throughout the world. (He'd also incurred the wrath of Felkor who'd twice since punched him in the stomach, leaving him retching for breath on each occasion.)

Lastly, the tingle of excitement was because Tommy reckoned that everyone would turn to look at him. Now, finally, with his extra-spiky hair, he could look everyone in the eye.

Mr Withers, the headmaster, seemed to be enjoying this assembly. The old man had wispy grey hair that fell to his shoulders, framing a wrinkled face. One of his eyes always remained fixed in the same position so that whenever he looked down to read something with his good eye, he could still keep a watchful gaze over everyone listening. His oversized glasses magnified the effect, making you think of a giant drunken fish looking out of a goldfish bowl. (Two pupils were once expelled for scrawling 'Googly Eyes' on a dorm wall, though the nickname remained frequently – if quietly – used by most students.)

'And so,' Mr Withers announced to the gathering, 'the Grand Council had to choose five children to represent Earth on this mission – which involves an . . . intergalactic space-station.' The words 'intergalactic space-station' were uttered as if they were very rude words that shouldn't be uttered in polite company. The old fellow cleared his throat nervously, then continued quickly. 'It should be stressed that only the most gifted, most celebrated children could be chosen.'

Tommy tiptoed forward from the back of the Hall. All the students were transfixed by the old headmaster's words – there weren't even paper fexa-cetters flying in the air. This was highly irregular. What was going on?

If Tommy had realized that his hair was beginning to wilt, he'd have been more careful about tiptoeing into the assembly.

But he didn't know. He still thought he looked 'normal'. And once he stepped off the lift-panel and heard Old Withers mentioning an intergalactic space-station, he became entranced.

Space? For some unknown reason, Tommy had always dreamed about travelling into space. It had a strange pull on him. He felt that Earth was like a little hut, with all its windows covered in cotton wool. There must be something huge and unknown out there. And the unknown was more exciting than frightening. You see, due to Earth's constant cloud cover, Tommy didn't even know that space is black and that the stars look white. If truth be told, he imagined space as being like a giant beanbag – Earth being just one bean alongside millions of other planets all squished very closely together.

'We are all in the gutter, but some of us are looking at the clouds.'
(from *Fanny's Windy Lady* (2092) – a play by Tim-Id Oscar)

After the Great Climate Enhancement, adults believed that children had enough difficulty adapting to floating cities without worrying about huge things like space. The clouds had blotted out the stars for a reason. And once the space-people of the Milky Way contacted Earthlings, adults felt that it was even more important to keep all talk of space hush-hush. Children would be frightened to death if they learned that intelligent beings existed beyond Earth.

'Therefore,' continued Withers, 'I am very proud to announce that one person has been chosen from the Wilchester Academy of Young Adults to join four other children who have been chosen from amongst all the children on Earth. Now, I hope that none of you will be scared when I say this, but this expedition is going to involve a place called *space*.'

He paused for breath, relishing the hush and the tinge of fear in the room.

' . . . So, with no further ado, let me say that I know you will all be pleased and I know you will all be proud, when I tell you that this person is in fact a boy. And that the name of this boy is'

CRASH! KERBLASH! KITTISSHH!

Old Googly Eyes stopped mid-sentence and 499 faces turned to stare at the back of the Hall. There, lying on the ground, was a boy with lank dark hair falling about his head and a pile of broken CPs all around him.

A chorus of angry voices rose from the assembly.

'The idiot's broken our CPs.'

'He just walked straight into the table. Idiot! Knocked 'em all over.'

'What a moron!'

'The fellow with the stupid hair and the stutter – look what he's done.'

Tommy tried to stand up. 'I'm s-s-s-s-s-sorry,' he mumbled, before slipping on a CP and landing once more on his back.

The cries got louder. Tommy recognized Felkor Stagwitch's voice through the crowd. 'Hey, look! What's that green stuff dripping from his hair? It looks like a giant bogey, innit. Must be. Tommy Storm's got boogers in his hair!'

A chant of 'Boogers! Boogers!' rose from the crowd and, above the throng, Tommy could hear the sound of a dog being kicked. That laugh. Felkor was enjoying himself even more than usual.

Before the group could move forward and attack the boy who'd destroyed their CPs, Mr Withers bellowed into the microphone.

'SILENCE! Silence! Stay where you are. That boy will be dealt with later. *Severely* dealt with . . . Now, I still have to announce the name of the boy who will make us all proud here at Wilchester. The boy who has been chosen from billions.'

The chant of 'Boogers!' died and the 499 faces forgot about the stupid wretch struggling to stand up amidst the scattering of shattered CPs.

The happy feeling in Tommy's tummy was gone, but he didn't feel as bad as expected. It was weird. Maybe Withers' words about space had something to do with the odd feeling. The very thought of space filled him with a strange sense of hope. A hope that could lift him above the wreckage of the CPs, the disaster of green floppy hair and having everyone – everyone – yelling 'Boogers!' at him.

One boy from this school, he thought. One boy to travel into space. Imagine. Imagine . . . How wonderful to escape this dreadful place.

He closed his eyes and made a wish. If there was anything above the clouds, if there was anything out there watching over him, if somehow his mother or father could hear him calling, then surely his wish would be answered. He felt a pulse of strength swell momentarily through his veins. There he was – just a speck of dust in the expanse of the universe, sending out a pure, honest wish.

'Please let it be me,' he pleaded silently.

Old Withers cleared his throat and Tommy opened his eyes. Was it really possible that someone could get his message far, far out in space and somehow alter his destiny? He felt oddly composed. What was this? Confidence? But he never felt confident. Maybe this was the power of someone responding out in space. Could it really be his mother or father responding? Hardly. Lola and Errol were names he'd still never heard. The empty feeling in his tummy turned to butterflies.

Please let it be me.

Again, old Googly Eyes cleared his throat, savouring his role in the moment of drama. He opened his arms – his gnarled, veiny fingers outstretched. 'I am very pleased to announce that the boy who will be representing Earth from this school is . . .'

He paused – his good eye looking out over the crowd, his bad eye locked on the floating monitor before him. There was an audible intake of breath from 499 expectant faces. Behind them all, a young boy pressed forward onto his knees, clenched his hands together and closed his eyes. *Please. Please.*

Withers waited for absolute silence before he spoke again. 'The boy who will be representing Earth from this school is . . . Felkor Stagwitch.'

A great cheer rose from the mass of children and filled the vast hall. It echoed across the ceiling, around the tables and past the miserable figure kneeling, hands clenched, upon a pile of ruined CPs.

Smiling and beaming, Felkor Stagwitch was carried over the heads of 498 children by 996 excited arms. 'Felkor! Felkor! Felkor!' The chant grew louder and louder: 498 cheering children, delirious that one of them had been chosen. Felkor cleared his throat and tried to think of a speech that would convey to everyone how great he really was. He had time to think, because it took some minutes before the cheering and chanting died to such a level that he could make himself heard.

21

5

THE WORST WEEK

The five chosen children were expected to set off in an Earth spaceship and rendezvous with a MilkyFed craft somewhere near the Moon. (This was because an Earth spaceship would take thousands of years to reach the Intergalactic Space-station now located towards the centre of the Milky Way, whereas the MilkyFed craft could make the journey in under three hours.)

Felkor Stagwitch heard the news about being chosen as one of The Five (as they were now being termed around the globe) on a Friday, exactly one week before The Five were due to fly towards the Moon. Within a few hours, he'd packed his bags, returned to the Great Dining Hall for some more celebratory speeches and then he was whisked away to a secret location for training. The training took place in close proximity to a large rocket – the very one that would take The Five on their initial journey.

After Felkor left, Wilchester returned to some form of normality – although classes remained suspended for the day. The pupils who wished they'd been chosen instead of Felkor began to revise their opinion. Representing Earth on a mission sounded a bit scary and the secrecy surrounding everything was a little sinister. No, they were relieved that they hadn't been chosen . . .

Gradually, everyone dispersed from the Dining Hall to

hang out in the upstairs corridors and do a lot of running, yelling and any other forbidden things they could come up with (the teachers were all at a long lunch with Old Withers to celebrate the choosing of Wilchester).

From his room, Tommy Storm could hear the sound of laughing and shrieking below – every now and again a wild yell of *Cauliflower!*[2] would soar above the revelry. He felt so miserable, he was almost glad that his punishment for breaking all the CPs was to be locked in his loft-room for a week. 'Solitary confinement,' Old Withers had called it. He'd get no food, except for one tray of bread and water slipped through a cat-flap in the door each evening. The power to the information screen hovering against the bedroom wall was cut off and a block was put on all other communication devices. Mr Withers had called it 'a lenient punishment' and Miss Gideon agreed. She even promised to revise his test result down to an F minus, saying this would be communicated to the Grand Council in case they were still interested in receiving test results.

Two days into his punishment – on Sunday afternoon – Tommy was feeling so dejected that he thought about trying to climb out the window that looked over the sea. For the first time he could remember, he let a tear escape his eyes and it rolled slowly down his cheek.

If I jumped to my death, then they'd be sorry, he thought. Then they'd regret locking me up.

But then he realized he was just being silly. Self-indulgent. So he clenched something deep within himself, forced the tears to stop and gave up all ideas of jumping.

2 The yell was part of a game which is described in *Extra Bits no. 2*, page 420

If truth be told, he wasn't sure if it was the loneliness that made him despair or the final realization that his hair would never spike. Perhaps it was his stutter.

On Monday and Tuesday, he sat alone in his bedroom, tried to stop feeling miserable and, instead, felt jealous of Felkor.

Imagine going on an adventure with no boundaries and no limits. Everything new to your eyes . . . Wondrous . . .

By Wednesday, he was trying to banish such thoughts from his mind. 'Silly, childish fantasies!' he exclaimed. 'You're a *loser*, Tommy Storm, and you'll never amount to anything.'

On Thursday morning, he realized that he might've been too negative on Wednesday. Why, didn't things always turn out for the best? And even if everyone treated him badly, he told himself, 'I'll show them. I'll defy them and I'll amount to something some day.'

By the afternoon, he was starving and beginning to doubt the morning's positive thoughts. He felt sure of nothing. Maybe his classmates were right. Perhaps he really was a freak.

So he stood in front of the mirror, ignoring his awful hair, and promised to himself: 'Whatever happens, however bad things get in the future, *I'll never give up*. Whatever happens, *I'll always try and do my best*.'

Swearing that solemn oath made him feel as if he'd achieved something. It meant that it didn't matter if he was weird. So what if he was a freak?

And then he got out of bed, stepped over the six empty trays and took a shower.

Some time in the evening, just when he was expecting the seventh tray to appear, the door clicked and swung open. It was Mr Withers, looking very serious – as if someone had

24

died or as if he'd just discovered that all his clothes had been see-through for many years. He spoke quickly and sternly.

'You've got five minutes to pack your bags and say good-bye to this place.'

~ 6 ~

A New President

The Great Climate Enhancement happened earlier in the 21st century. Over twenty-five years, sea-levels soared, leaving only the highest mountain peaks visible. All wars stopped (since who'd bother invading a land that would be under-water in a matter of years?) and everyone started constructing tall – and I mean *TALL* – (water-tight) buildings. Trouble was, these buildings took for ever to construct, they weren't very stable and there was nowhere to put a garden shed.

These problems were solved when a young kid, Denise LeMenise, suggested floating buildings. As she explained in her Nobel Prize acceptance speech: 'The idea came to me in the bath, after attaching a rubber duck to the chain on the end of the bathplug.'

And so, thousands of floating buildings were produced, some the size of Bangladesh. Great dome structures were erected over groups of these buildings and together they became known as floating cities. Wars started up again when various groups began arguing about who had the biggest or flashiest floating city. After much bickering, it was agreed that floating cities could not name themselves after historical countries or continents and, instead, they compromised and named themselves after different types of cheese.

For many kids studying history in 2096, it was hard to believe that a little bit of pollution – a few chimneys here, a few cars there – had actually caused Earth's climate to change irrevocably (and had turned Pongy into a respectable name for a city). But sadly, it was so.

On Thursday morning, while Tommy Storm was stuck in his room wondering if he'd been too negative the day before, the Grand Council reconvened – exactly a week since their last meeting. Guttly brought the meeting to order and got straight to the point.

'So, Elsorr. We're all here because of you. Because of you and your two conditions. One, you choose a child, and two, you choose an elder to . . . whatever.'

'I get to choose an elder,' said Elsorr, 'to accompany The Five to the MilkyFed space-station and then to stay with The Five throughout their training.'

'Yes, yes,' said Guttly.

He had a suspicion that Elsorr was going to nominate himself to accompany The Five in order to sabotage the mission and stir up talk on Earth of a possible war with the MilkyFed (in which case, the Grand Council might look for a more aggressive leader and replace Guttly with Elsorr).

However, at this moment, Guttly remained calm because he'd foreseen Elsorr's move and he'd arranged two things with the MilkyFed:

1 Elsorr would be confined to his quarters as much as possible while on the space-station.
2 Three MilkyFed guards would keep Elsorr under constant supervision.

It seemed unlikely, therefore, that Elsorr could cause strife between Earth and the MilkyFed, no matter how hard he tried. And so Guttly smiled contentedly. 'Alright, Elsorr. Let us know your choices.'

Elsorr stood up and the large floating screen above the Councillors sprang to life. A tiny picture appeared, then grew and grew until it filled the screen. The picture was of Guttly Randolph coming sixth in the annual Grand Council Egg and Spoon Race.

'Very funny,' said Guttly. 'I never knew you liked me so much, Elsorr.'

'Oh, well I do,' said Elsorr drawing his sword and removing a block of cheddar from his top pocket. 'I think you're *delightful* . . . So delightful, I've chosen *you* to accompany The Five.'

The other Councillors leapt to their feet – voices erupting. Elsorr sat quietly and smiled. Guttly looked ashen. He felt a mild heart palpitation coming on. 'You can't mean that,' he said. 'I'm the President. I can't—'

The Councillors calmed, keen to hear the exchange.

'I seem to remember that you gave your word,' said Elsorr, cutting a corner of cheese with his sword and putting it into his mouth.

You probably don't realize it, but as Guttly came from the city of Cheddar, this was a most insulting act – worse even than throwing a glove at someone in the 17th century or mooning at a teacher in the 20th.

The Councillors nodded reluctantly at Elsorr's words. Eventually, Guttly stepped off the platform and sat at the Majestic Table, his head bowed. After a while he spoke.

'I have never broken my word and I will not start now. But I know your game, Elsorr . . . With me off the planet, you become *acting* President.' Elsorr just smiled. Guttly continued. 'But I'll only be gone for six months or so and then I'll be back, Elsorr. Then I'll be back. Six months as President. That's all you'll have.'

The old man started to twist the ruby ring off his finger. For a time no one spoke. Only Elsorr smiled. It was Guttly who broke the silence. 'And the child? Who do you choose?'

Elsorr walked to the Presidential Platform with the block of cheddar on the end of his sword and telepathically raised the platform so he could look down on everyone (and not have to share the cheese). 'I don't like the Milky Way Confederation,' he said. 'I don't like others meddling in our business.'

Helena Jadely shouted up from the Table. 'They're not meddling. We can learn from them. We should all learn to live together.'

'Ha!' sneered Elsorr. 'You're so pathetic, you'll be offering to give us all wuggle-hugs next.' Some of the Councillors laughed. After a pause, Elsorr continued. 'Are you all so foolish that you don't see? They plan to conquer us. They want to rule us.'

'If they wanted to conquer us, they could do it in five minutes,' shouted Helena.

'Shut up!' Elsorr shouted back. 'I'm not here to debate. I'm here to tell you who I've chosen as the fifth child.' The room fell silent again. 'As I was saying, I don't like the MilkyFed and I don't want to help with any of their schemes . . . I'm still against this ridiculous mission of theirs.'

The screen high above the room started to flash pictures of broken CPs and then a bright blinking F minus, followed by a vision of 499 faces laughing and jeering – chanting 'Boogers!' repeatedly. Then the voices faded and Elsorr resumed his speech.

'I've chosen the worst-performing child I could find. This boy is a disgrace to children, a disgrace to humanity and he will likely disgrace our planet on this ill-conceived MilkyFed mission. He eats alone, he has no friends and he had the worst test result of any child on Earth in the recent census we performed. I give you the world's worst child and my choice for this mission.'

As Elsorr finished off the cheddar, the large screen filled with an image of Tommy Storm. The picture had been taken by a miniature camera embedded in one of the trays slipped under Tommy's loft door. The picture was from Sunday morning, when Tommy had briefly thought about jumping out his window. But the Councillors didn't know this. They just saw a miserable-looking boy with a large tear rolling down his cheek. What's worse, his hair lay lank across his head.

Even Guttly felt a pang of despair as he gently rubbed his chest. This boy is going to let us all down, he thought. This boy is going to ruin everything.

> 'You could've changed your socks!'
> (popular post-wuggle-hug 'joke')
>
> Wuggle-hugs are generally performed in weightless conditions as both people remain vertical, but only one is 'upside-down'. You therefore hug 'top-to-tail' – and pray that the other person has showered recently. Wuggle-hugs are a popular form of greeting amongst top MilkyFed diplomats.

30

— 7 —

SPACE PREPARATIONS

On a Friday morning, two hours before they were due to climb into a rocket and blast into the unknown, ZsaZsa Vavannus (pronounced, *JjahJjah*), Egbert 'Sugar Floyd' Fitchly, Anjel*eek!* Jalfrezi, Felkor Stagwitch and Tommy Storm were sitting in a room that was totally yellow – each with a computer-pad before them and an antenna on their head. The room resembled a tilted box with the floor and ceiling sloping down and sideways (supposedly, to teach people to fight gravity).

Basil Bakewell, the instructor, had a scrawny body, a mousey face and the neatest side parting you've ever seen in a head of brown hair. His suction-pad boots had the advantage of enabling him to stand at the same angle as the floor and the disadvantage that they made his legs look like straws.

'Listen *up*,' he cried (in a squeaky voice). 'This is the *final* ranking test of the *week* . . . You have been awarded *point*s for the *forward roll* test, the loud *screaming* contest and for the *sheep* impression competition.'

'The sheep impression competition was stupid, innit.'

Basil Bakewell pretended not to hear Felkor's comment. 'When we *hand* you over to the *MilkyFed*, we will be in a position to *rank* you from *best* to *worst* – from *one* to *five*.'

In case you hadn't noticed, Basil Bakewell rarely uttered a sentence without stressing one or more words in an effort to make them seem of 'life-or-death' importance.

'E-e-e-e-e-e-excuse m-m-m-m-me.'

'*What?*'

'This is m-m-my f-f-f-f-f-first—'

'Your *first* test? Yes of *course* it is. You're *six* days late.' The instructor glared at Tommy. 'You will be ranked on this test *alone.*'

''S'not fair!' said Felkor. It was the first time Tommy had ever agreed with him.

'The rules *cannot* be changed,' said the instructor.

'If he does well in this test, 's'not fair if he's ranked higher than me.'

'Nor me,' said another voice.

'*Anyone* who's not happy with the *rules* can leave *now*. We'll find a *replacement* for you.'

This was quite a threat, as the family of each kid who went to the MilkyFed training school would receive the equivalent of $2 million (in today's money) – although this wouldn't apply to Tommy since he had no family.

The financial offer was made by the Grand Council when the parents of the chosen children threatened to prevent their kids from going on the expedition – because they were 'worried about the hygiene standards of the MilkyFed training school and the nature of the Dangerous Mission that some kids would be chosen for.' The Grand Council guaranteed that the final mission would 'probably not be dangerous', that all kids would shower at least once a week and that the family of each kid who completed the MilkyFed training would receive $2 million. The parents were so satisfied with this response that they convinced their kids the expedition would be fun and would make them famous. They also made promises such as, 'I'll never make you do homework again.'

Basil Bakewell looked pleased with himself and with the silence. '*OK*,' he said. 'As you all *know*, this test is called *Mercy Mercy Art-o-pathy*. The antenna on your head is *linked* to your computer-pad, so if you draw a shape in your *mind*, it will appear *on-screen*.'

'Tell us something we don't know!' said Felkor. (In 2096, all school kids practised art-o-pathy – see *Extra Bits no. 2*, page 419)

Bakewell made a squeaky sound of irritation and then continued: 'I will start the *music* in a moment and *then* you have to draw a large circle and colour it *in*.'

'Man, circles are so uncool,' said Egbert Fitchly. 'Can I draw a triangle instead?'

'Certainly *not!*' Bakewell took a number of deep breaths, cleared his throat like a choirboy and resumed his speech. 'Marks will be *awarded* for the level of *imagination* used in *matching* the colours to the music, while marks will be *deducted* for colouring *outside* the circle and for any *inaccuracies* in the circle itself.'

'Why are we doing this silly test?' someone asked.

Strangely, Bakewell seemed pleased with the question.

'*Imagine* that you have to *defuse* a bomb to *save* a city. And the bomb could go off at *any* time if you make a *mistake*. And *all the while*, aliens are prodding you with things that make you go *Oooohh*.'

Anje*leek!* screamed, making Basil Bakewell jump. 'I don't like bombs,' she said. 'Or things that make me go *Oooohh*.'

'*Don't* worry. There are *no* bombs involved – I'm just *saying* that this particular test *could* be seen as preparation for such a *scenario* – if it were *ever* to happen – and it *probably* wouldn't ever happen.'

Anje*leek!* looked relieved.

'Excuse me, darlingk,' said ZsaZsa. 'I don't like this *copper*-coloured antenna. Silver goes so much better with my complexion.'

Bakewell ignored her. 'You all have *twenty-nine* minutes to complete the test,' he said. Then he clicked his fingers and three different pieces of music started playing at the same time.

Tommy started drawing a circle on the screen, which was fine at first – he'd done lots of ordinary art-o-pathy at school. However, he was having trouble balancing on his chair because it only had two legs – and the steep incline didn't help. If he set his new suction-pad boots on the floor it only seemed to make matters worse, so he ended up kneeling on the chair and holding on to the CP. He was halfway through the circle when something tickled him in the ribs. It made him laugh and his circle went all funny. He looked around but saw nothing.

I must've imagined it . . .

But when he erased his creation and started redrawing, the same thing happened again. Twice more, he erased and restarted the circle – each time he was tickled in a spot that made his circle go all wonky. Even when he tried to block the tickling out, he couldn't get his colouring right. The three pieces of music sounded so awful that he could come up with no inspiration. So he just scribbled in some purple.

The other four kept laughing too, as though they were being tickled (Anjel*eek!* more screaming than laughing), but from the look of their CP screens, they were coping much better.

Tommy's problem lay in three factors.

One was the test itself. He hadn't been told about the tickling (which was the *Mercy Mercy* aspect of the test) and, also, in regular art-o-pathy only one piece of music is played at a time. (The other four had received six days' training on how to combat the tickles and on how to deal with three pieces of music playing simultaneously – the trick is to focus on just one of the three pieces and colour in based on that.)

Two, he was very, very tired. This was mainly because the previous night he couldn't get comfortable with the arm-restraints and headrest (you'll see what I mean later).

Three, he just wasn't concentrating . . . Everything about the last fifteen hours had been so extraordinary. How could anyone be expected to concentrate given what had happened in such a short period of time?

There was the packing in under five minutes, followed by the hurried walk to the fexa-cetter landing-pad to the west of the Wilchester building (used by visiting rich parents). In a pained tone, Mr Withers explained that Tommy was to be the final member of The Five. There was an accusing quality to Withers' voice that made it sound like Withers thought this was all a practical joke dreamed up by Tommy himself. Maybe this was why the headmaster was anxious to avoid any other pupils as they hurried to the landing-pad. There were no speeches, no cheers and no congratulations. Tommy was spirited out of the school as though he were a criminal.

I should mention here that the Grand Council managed to get Elsorr to concede that Tommy's participation in the mission wouldn't be publicized. Almost nobody on Earth should know the name or the details of the embarrassing fifth boy chosen.

Tommy waved at Withers from the rising fexa-cetter, but the old man was already disappearing down a set of steps. (A fexa-cetter, by the way, is a starfish-shaped aircraft that takes off and lands like a helicopter. It's made of the same material as the black box found in early 21st century airplanes – so fexa-cetters almost always survive crashes.)

There were three people inside the fexa-cetter, all dressed

from head to toe in military uniform – yellow with purple polka-dots. Their visored helmets meant that Tommy couldn't see their faces and they were clearly under orders not to speak to him. They flew through the night, over-flying many great-domed cities, including Feta, Camembert, Smelly, Cheddar and E-Zee-Singles.

Who Cut the Cheese?

The city of Smelly tried on numerous occasions to name itself WhoCutThe, but this was always vetoed by the Grand Council. E-Zee-Singles was a relatively poor area and the location for many cheap TV documentaries that featured ordinary people in night-clubs on holidays behaving like demented chimpanzees.

Tommy sat in quiet bewilderment until they started to descend upon a white, non-domed city. As his ears began to pop, he noticed gleaming towers with the letters N-U-T-S painted on them. (When NASA and other space agencies merged in 2044, they became NUTS – Nations Undertaking Travel into Space. The name stuck, despite the later abolition of country names.)

The fexa-cetter came in to land by a conical building and, as soon as the engines died, Tommy was whisked inside. Immediately, the heavy doors to the outside world slammed shut. Tommy expected to see the military men beside him, but they'd stepped back before the doors closed – probably already flying off to Camembert, LowFatSpreadable or some other more hospitable metropolis.

Tommy looked about and found himself standing on a wide ledge about the size of a large dinner table. Above him, the walls on all sides rose high, maybe sixty metres, until they met each other in a point. A flea standing just inside a witch's (white) hat and looking upwards might've been confronted with a similar view. For a moment, Tommy felt very small – until he peered over the ledge. Then he felt really, really tiny. The conical walls kept spreading outwards as they fell away, far below ground (or sea) level. About a mile below, they met a giant circle that was purple in colour, except for a tiny blue dot left of centre.

Before he could fully take this in, the ledge started to move – downwards. It was dropping vertically and picking up speed. Tommy felt his stomach rise to meet the sinking feeling in his throat. It felt like being on a hurtling roller-coaster that had just come off the rails. The purple circle was growing fast and yet time seemed to slow down within his brain. He knew how a flea flying towards an oncoming (purple) train must feel. Twenty seconds after it started moving, the ledge came to a standstill just off the purple ground.

'Mr Storm, I presume?' The voice was deep and gravelly and came from behind. Tommy turned to see a bald-headed man, clad in white robes with a finger's-length grey beard. Tommy nodded. 'You know you're six days late?' Before he could reply the old man broke into a half-smile. 'Well, late or not, you're welcome . . . My name is Guttly . . . Guttly Randolph. And I will be accompanying you and the other four on your journey.'

The bearded man extended his arm, stood on one leg and Tommy shook his hand rather formally, quickly standing on one leg also. (Shaking hands while standing on *two* legs – the 'two-leg salute' – was considered extremely rude in 2096.) Tommy couldn't help noticing a mark on one of Guttly's fingers, a smooth groove, as if, perhaps, a well-worn ring was missing. There was an air of strength about the man that gave Tommy an odd feeling of safety.

'H-h-h-h-h–hello.' Tommy's greeting came out softer than expected and seemed to be swallowed by the enormity of the witch's hat.

The words of the old man boomed back at him and, in contrast to his own faltering stutter, they seemed to fill the entire building. 'Speak up, little man! Don't be afraid to express yourself. You are now one of our five ambassadors. A chosen one. So seize this chance. Seize it. And don't let fear destroy it.'

Tommy wasn't quite sure how he was meant to react to this outburst. He'd perfected an extremely loud fake belch during his six days in solitary confinement, but he felt almost certain *that* wouldn't be the appropriate response. Before he could think of anything to say, the large man uttered: 'You have nothing to fear but fear itself . . . Nothing, I say.'

Guttly let this point resonate and looked deeply into Tommy's eyes. Tommy wished he could think of something clever to say – at the same time feeling that the old man must be seeing untold evidence of past and present fear in his eyes. Just when he thought that Guttly must've seen something terrible – why else would he stare at him for so long? – the old man whipped around and started walking away.

Oh, no, thought Tommy. He's realized they've made a terrible mistake. I'm not really one of The Five.

If Tommy had felt any fear since Old Withers had told him to pack his bags, then this was it. The fear that everything was just one big misunderstanding and that he'd have to return to Wilchester and maybe receive another week of solitary confinement for his troubles. Already, on half a dozen occasions he'd expected one of the fexa-cetter pilots to suddenly peer closely into a screen and shake his head. 'Oh, no!' the pilot would exclaim, 'we've made a terrible mistake! It's

Tommy *Stork* we were supposed to collect.' Or maybe Jonny Storm or Timmy Chorm or Ronny Stern.

'Well, come on. Let's get moving.' The old man was standing on a white table-sized panel that Tommy hadn't noticed and his words jolted Tommy from his fears. 'You've a lot to catch up on.'

Tommy followed Guttly onto the lift-panel. As their knees sank below the purple floor, Tommy looked across and saw something that looked like a metallic blue bottle standing upright in the distance. *How had he not noticed it when talking to Guttly?* This was the blue dot he'd seen earlier from up above. Although he'd never seen a spacecraft before, the image of the NUTS rocket sent a shiver of expectation – or maybe trepidation – through his body.

The lift-panel descended numerous floors before it came to a halt and Tommy and Guttly stepped out into a corridor – the walls, ceiling and floor of which were all covered in a flowery green carpet. A low humming sound filled the air – like a hundred rhinos in conference.

'That'll be the oxygen system,' said Guttly, guessing Tommy's thoughts. 'We're a long way under sea-level.'

They walked in silence until they reached a shiny metal door. It opened and Tommy followed Guttly inside. Here, the floor, walls and ceiling were covered in flowery *blue* carpet. A sofa and floating coffee table sat opposite a floating screen. Against one wall, Tommy noticed arm-restraints and a headrest. Guttly must've seen the alarm crossing his face.

'That's for sleeping in,' said the large man. 'Apparently, you've got to learn to sleep standing up – in case you need to do it in space . . . Can't say that I can do it yet, mind you – keep getting a crick in my neck.' He motioned to the couch. 'Please. Take a seat.'

Tommy sat down and suddenly felt very tired and hungry. He'd never even received his tray of bread and water for dinner back in Wilchester. It must've been after midnight, and only a few hours ago he thought he was going to spend the night as usual in Wilchester's loft. This was all so much to take in.

'I'm sorry I have to leave you so soon after your arrival,' said Guttly. 'I have many important affairs of state to attend to before our journey into space tomorrow. You must be hungry?'

Tommy nodded. The coffee table sank below the floor, then reappeared with an empty plate, an empty bowl, an empty glass, some cutlery, a jug of water and four very slim plastic sachets.

'You should start getting used to space-food,' continued the portly man. He noted the boy's blank look. 'Just add water to the contents of each sachet . . . When you're done, turn on the information screen over there. It will fill you in on the training so far. Then try and get some sleep – standing up. Tomorrow's a big day.'

Guttly walked towards the door, then thought of something and turned to the rather bewildered boy sitting on the couch. 'You're not going to let us down, Mr Storm, are you?'

Tommy wasn't quite sure what Guttly meant. Was he talking about the food sachets or about sleeping standing up? Before he could answer, the old fellow turned and walked out the door.

'Th-th-th-th-thank you M-M-M-Mr R-R-R-R-R-Randolph.' Tommy didn't think Guttly heard him before the door closed and the bearded man was gone. And suddenly he was all alone. All alone in this strange and funny place.

Tommy ate a bit of the food. It wasn't very good, but extreme hunger can do strange things to you. (At Wilchester it was rumoured that a student had once eaten a booger sandwich after three weeks trapped in a cupboard. *Ughhh!*)

When Tommy added water, the first sachet turned into something resembling mushy peas. The second tasted like eating a tube of toothpaste. The third, like liquorice spaghetti with a cough-mixture sauce. The fourth sachet was a drink that tasted of cod-liver oil. Tommy could stomach everything but this, so he ended up drinking the last of the water from the jug to quench his thirst.

Feeling more awake (but a little queasy), Tommy flicked on the information screen and settled into the sofa as though to watch a movie. He wished he had some popcorn and a large glass of *Choke* (very like cola, except it's even darker and 3.8 times as fizzy). The screen sprang to life with an image of Guttly's face.

'Welcome to the NUTS space training and launch-pad building.' Images of children appeared on the screen. 'Out of 11.4 billion children, you are one of five chosen to represent Earth on the MilkyFed Intergalactic Space-station.'

Those of you who are brilliant at maths and predicting the future (or else just read ahead to the end of this paragraph) will know that this 11.4 billion consisted of all people on Earth aged between one second and $17^{3/4}$ years who were 'fully potty-trained' according to international regulations.

The old man continued: 'The next voice you will hear is that of the chief NUTS instructor, Basil Bakewell.' Guttly's face disappeared and the screen went fuzzy.

'So far, the training for *this* mission has been *very* strenuous.' This new voice was quite squeaky – how a loud, highly strung mouse might speak. 'We don't *know* if you'll be able to stand *up* in the MilkyFed space-station, so forward rolls might be your *only* mode of travel.'

Suddenly, there were images of four children doing lots of forward rolls – up to fifty in a row. Three of the kids started going wonky after about thirty rolls, but one kid kept in a straight line for the whole fifty, despite being blasted occasionally by a fire-hose. It was only when this kid jumped up with his hands in the air, that Tommy recognized the face of Felkor Stagwitch.

The screen then showed each of the four kids, in turn, yelling as loudly as possible while suspended upside-down.

'Loud yelling can be a *vital* form of communication in dangerous situations,' the voice explained. 'And the next test is the very *serious* art of sheep impersonation.'

Each of the four kids then did a sequence of sheep impressions with ranking points appearing in a box above their heads. Tommy disagreed with the judges who awarded Felkor top marks – he would've plumped for Egbert Fitchly who sounded like a drunk billy goat trapped in a washing-machine.

'*We* believe,' said the squeaky voice, 'that the people of the MilkyFed sound very like *sheep* when they speak in their own language and so this aspect of the training is *extremely* important.'

Before you start doing your own sheep impressions, please understand that NUTS was very wrong here (see Extra Bits no. 1, page 415 for a full explanation).

Tommy was so tired that he stopped watching the film halfway through the explanation of performing art-o-pathy to three pieces of music played at once. He hooked his arms into the arm-restraints in the wall and stood for a while with his head flopped back onto the headrest. As soon as he did so, the lights in the room dimmed. With the screen off, he could hear once more the sound of a hundred rhinos in conference, reminding everyone how far below sea-level they were.

'What a strange day,' he mused. But the thought of space made him smile as he settled down to sleep.

Basil Bakewell looked very cross. He was assessing the marks awarded to The Five for the Mercy Mercy Art-o-pathy test.

He approached the girl next to Tommy. 'ZsaZsa Vavannus, you have scored highest with *minus* 1,340 points.'

ZsaZsa had coiffed (dyed) blonde hair in a long bob and golden skin (due to fake tan). Her white teeth glinted, her violet eyes shone (due to tinted contact lenses) and her long painted nails glistened pinkly. She feigned joy and surprise, as though she'd just won an Oscar.

'Me?? Darlingk, I can hardly believe it!'

Next, Bakewell approached Felkor, awarding him second place. Then he went up to a dark-haired girl with mocha skin. 'Anjel*eek!* Jalfrezi, you came *third* with minus 2,003 points.'

The girl yelled so loudly in response that Bakewell sustained a brief nosebleed. As the mousey instructor held back his head and searched for a tissue, Tommy noticed how skinny Anjel*eek!* was. Only her orange sari prevented her from looking like one of those stick drawings with a round head on top. Even so, she had a pretty face with furtive chocolate eyes that looked out from beneath a high beehive. (Girls had much more leeway than boys when it came to hair-styles – yet 72.4% of girls under sixteen had their hair in a beehive in 2096.)

Once his nosebleed stopped, Basil approached Egbert 'Sugar Floyd' Fitchly, awarding him fourth place with a score of minus 2,873. The boy's charcoal eyes betrayed his disappointment. 'My uncle could have you totally assassinated,' he said quickly (which wasn't true).

Lastly, Bakewell turned scornfully to Tommy, who'd scored minus 4,923 – not far from the lowest possible score. 'You let the tickles *disrupt* you every time,' he squeaked.

'That shows *poor* concentration and a *lack* of willpower.'

If Tommy had watched the end of the training video before going to sleep, he would've known that the other four had trained all week on performing art-o-pathy Under-Tickle-Conditions (here, the CP is programmed to send telepathic tickles back to the user through the antenna). The secret is to perform the art-o-pathy between tickles and the thing to know (which Tommy didn't) is that you cannot be tickled while holding your breath. It's a difficult skill to master because being tickled makes you short of breath – so you can only work in short bursts.

'Least that stupid test's over,' said Felkor, ripping the antenna off his head. 'Feel like I've run twenty kilometres.'

'Well, darlingk, I feel like I've run *thirty* kilometres,' said ZsaZsa in a proud voice.

Felkor looked stung. 'When I said twenty, that wasn't countin' the twenty before that – which makes . . . *fifty* kilometres, innit.'

'It makes *forty*,' said Anjel*eek!*, who was brilliant at adding points.

''S'what I said.'

'I have asthma,' said Egbert. 'For real.' He spoke so quickly that the words ran together – *Ihaveasthma* – so by the time you worked out what he'd said, someone could've told you the same thing three times over. 'So it wasn't fair. No way could I hold my breath for the last ten minutes.'

Egbert didn't really have asthma. He was in the habit of telling porky-pies (as his mother called them) as he usually got away with them. This is because the best way to tell a porky-pie is to speak really, really fast – so it can slip by the listener unnoticed or, by the time they work out what you've said, you're already on to the next porky-pie. (In case you're wondering, the 'Sugar Floyd' part of his

name had no significance whatsoever – Egbert had made it up quite
recently because he thought it sounded 'phat'.)

Basil Bakewell stepped onto a large lift-panel at the top of the room and it began to rise at an angle, remaining flush against the wall. It stopped about halfway up the twenty metre incline, whereupon Basil looked down silently on The Five. Without warning, a previously unseen door opened behind him, and Guttly Randolph stepped out, making the squeaky man look small in comparison.

'Everything ready?' boomed Guttly. 'You have the results?'

'The rocket is *ready* to leave, *on* time, in an hour and fifteen minutes . . . And I have *the* results here.' Bakewell reached for a floating monitor that seemed to have been attached to his back. He switched it on, letting it hover before Earth's baldest-ever President.

Guttly peered into the monitor. He looked pleased, then displeased. 'Based on an average score after *all* the tests this week, this is the following ranking that we will be communicating to the MilkyFed . . . Ranked first, Felkor Stagwitch.' Felkor leapt up and cheered – which Tommy felt sure was an unwise thing to do while Guttly remained speaking. 'Anjel*eek!*, ranked second . . . Egbert, third . . . ZsaZsa, fourth . . . And Tommy Storm . . . fifth.'

Felkor turned to look at Tommy and then came the familiar sound of a dog being kicked. In all the events of the last fifteen hours or so, Tommy had forgotten how annoying that laugh could be.

With that, Guttly turned and exited through the doorway. He probably didn't hear the chant that Felkor kept up until Basil Bakewell told him to get moving.

'Last. Last. Last. Tommy Last. Last. Last.' Over and over he chanted it.

8

GOOD RIDDANCE, EARTH

The Five were given ten minutes to return to their quarters, finalize the packing of their bags and assemble in the Great Cone Room next to the NUTS Rocket.

Tommy's bags had appeared in his room sometime during the night, but now he struggled to decide what to bring on the trip. There seemed no point in packing any of his Wilchester uniforms and surely he'd get in trouble if he brought any games or personal gadgets on the spaceship. Each of The Five had been given a cerise hold-all, no bigger than a microwave-oven, and this was supposed to hold everything they needed for the trip into space.

Once he changed into the official NUTS space outfit (a polka-dot skin-tight ski-suit with E for Earth imprinted on the back), Tommy realized how ten of these outfits could easily scrunch up into the size of a large sandwich. Somebody obviously thought it was pretty warm in spaceships and intergalactic space-stations.

At this stage, I should point out that most official uniforms (school, military, etc.) were based on archive footage of uniforms from the 20th century. Unfortunately, many of these archives were damaged during the Great Climate Enhancement, resulting in some odd colour and pattern choices.

They'd been given no official space underwear, but after

changing his mind twice, Tommy thought it best to wear a pair under his suit and take some spares for the journey. Do they have washing-machines in space? he wondered.

Along with the ski-suits, he packed a toothbrush, some soap and a pair of trainers – just in case he ever needed to change out of the suction boots. Then he said goodbye to all his old stuff and plodded heavily out of his room. (Suction boots can be a nightmare on carpeted floors.)

The blue rocket was known as BigLongThingy III and this was written in large yellow letters along one of its sides. Those in the know called it *BLT*.

In order of ranking – Felkor first, Tommy last – The Five stood to attention in the Great Cone Room, close to BLT, while Basil Bakewell inspected them. Basil was moving slowly down the line of children, ensuring their spacesuits were in place. Once satisfied that all was in order, Basil would take a helmet from a floating tray and place it upon the head of the nervous child before him. There was a bit of a commotion when Basil noticed that Egbert Fitchly had his suit on back-to-front and the proceedings were delayed while Egbert nipped off to the other side of the rocket to reverse it.

'If I smoke in the rain, my cigarette doesn't get wet'
(boasting big-nosed person)

Allegedly, the rocket engineers christened the rocket *BigLongThingy* as a joke on the chief designer, Byrano DeCergerac, who had a very large, prominent nose. (They almost called it *HumungousHooter*, but decided against it.) When Byrano found out that the rocket was named after him, he was very chuffed and never once suspected the reference to his nose.

47

'Dummy!' yelled Felkor.

'Don't you call me a dummy, dipstick,' said Egbert.

Not far from The Five, a pointy-faced man with yellow skin bowed sarcastically *(a good trick if you can do it)* to Guttly. Then he produced a sword, threw a ball of chocolate in the air and sliced it into neat segments that fell into his breast pocket. Because of the prominent forehead and bushy eyebrows, Tommy couldn't make out the eyes of the man. He was introduced to the party as Elsorr, but he was uninterested and hardly looked at the children. The only one he briefly considered was Tommy, who had no idea why this stranger (sporting a large ruby ring) should give him such a self-satisfied, yet eerie smile.

At last, Bakewell came to Tommy. He looked him up and down with a critical eye until his gaze rested somewhere above the young boy's eyes. A look of disgust settled upon his face. This is it, Tommy thought. They've found me out. They're going to leave me behind.

'Don't you ever *spike* your hair?' Bakewell asked.

What could Tommy say? Should he tell Bakewell about the melted marshmallows or the tube of *ITDDINEW*? Maybe he should shout and scream and finally admit how much he hated his hair. How sick of being different he was. Maybe this was the moment to finally burst into tears. Here was an adult actually asking him about almost the most important thing in his life.

If you'd been Bakewell and had been looking into Tommy's eyes at that moment, you'd hardly have seen a flicker of emotion cross his face. For Tommy kept his face resolute and decided that Bakewell didn't want to hear his woes. When he did respond, it was just to shake his head silently, in case he stuttered uncontrollably or in case something cracked inside him. Surely, they'd keep me behind if I burst into tears, he thought.

After an agonizing pause and seemingly against his better judgement, Bakewell placed the last helmet over Tommy's head. It was perhaps the best moment Tommy would ever experience on planet Earth.

If you're wondering why so few people would attend this important moment in Earth's history (as Tommy was), then you should know that over twenty-six billion people, most of whom were 'potty-trained' to international standards, were watching every second of the proceedings on their floating information screens at home. Dozens of miniature invisible floating cameras enabled ordinary folk to choose the angle from which to watch the event. Some chose the ChildCam option which showed the proceedings from a camera just above the head of the particular child chosen by the viewer – so you more or less got the view of that child as the camera panned up and down, left and right, in sync with the movement of the child's eyes. It was later reported that over six billion people had chosen FelkorCam, although most people chose EgbertCam as he was the tallest child and hence offered the best view. Nobody, not one person on Earth, chose TommyCam. The reason? There was no TommyCam.

In order to meet the condition of the Grand Council that Tommy's choosing should remain secret, it was decided to tell the world that only four children had been chosen (now, surprisingly, called *The Four*) and so the image of Tommy was digitally removed from all pictures beamed around Earth. Although none of The Five could see the miniature cameras, The Four had been warned about them during training. And so it was that Felkor kept flexing his muscles, feeling them exaggeratedly through his suit, then waving proudly at no one in particular.

Most peculiar – even for him, thought Tommy.

Nor could Tommy work out why Anjel*eek!* kept bowing, why ZsaZsa kept adjusting her hair and smiling coyly into the distance or why Egbert kept doing unprompted back-flips. Standing still and silent, Tommy wondered if everyone else had drunk a few litres of *Choke* while packing or whether itching powder had been inserted into every spacesuit but his.

What Tommy mistook for a tiresome few minutes of silence while Guttly and Elsorr exchanged pained smiles, was actually one of the most emotional telepathic speeches ever made by a President of Earth. Below images of the proceedings, poorer viewers saw a constant stream of moving words flowing across their screens during Guttly's speech. Richer viewers with *text-voice-converter screens* heard the speech in all its glory, as Guttly's voice, coloured with emotion, pitched high, then low, then high again, either side of a short bout of hiccups.

After a further thirty-second wait in silence (caused by a commercial break in the transmission), The Five plus Guttly marched to a large lift-panel and waved farewell to Basil and Elsorr.

'Goodbye, darlingk Earth,' cried ZsaZsa and she waved like a screen starlet.

'Good riddance, losers,' said Felkor. (This was meant as a jibe to his Wilchester classmates, but the networks received 1,001,795,850 complaints as a result.)

Tommy looked down on the shrinking figures of Elsorr and Basil Bakewell as the lift-panel rose some thirty metres in the air alongside BLT. It was strange, but the smug sword-wave that Elsorr was giving seemed directed at him alone. Feeling it would be rude not to, Tommy saluted back at the jaundiced figure – then wished he hadn't, as the shadowy-eyed man just laughed and reached into his pocket for a segment of chocolate.

The lift-panel stopped level with a big white letter *U* (*NUTS* was written on this side of BLT) and a small circular door opened once Guttly looked at it.

'Will there be any food in here?' said Anjel*eek!*. 'I could wolf down a grape – it's only twenty-three points.'

Anjeleek! attributed points to every type of food and tried to eat less than 450 a day. She'd always manage to keep this up for six weeks at a time – until she looked as skinny (and as attractive) as a broom handle. Then, unable to stand it a moment longer, she'd suddenly binge on all the food she'd foregone in the previous six weeks and balloon to the size of a small sofa. Depressed, she'd continue bingeing for a few months, before starting the diet and the cycle all over again.

'Yuh don't look like y'ever eaten food,' said Felkor.

'Nonsense, I had almost 200 points for breakfast.'

'Man, I once ate 375 potatoes in a single day,' said Egbert.

Guttly feigned deafness and ushered everyone forward. One by one, The Four clambered into the port-hole, then Tommy climbed in, with Guttly following behind, trying to ensure that none of the floating cameras got a look up his robes (he'd refused to wear a NUTS space outfit).

Thirty metres below, on the Purple Floor, Elsorr saw the heavy door close behind them. He was still laughing at the pathetic salute from that fool, Tommy Storm. 'Things are working out perfectly,' he chuckled. 'Just perfectly.'

The passenger capsule was a small, circular room, running the circumference of BLT. Everything was purple, except for a large window, a floating information screen and six yellow

51

beanbags. Five of the beanbags sported large purple printed names – Felkor, Anjel*eek!*, Egbert, ZsaZsa and Guttly. The last one just had *Latecomer* printed on it (because NUTS didn't have enough warning of Tommy's participation).

Felkor smirked. 'Nice beanbag, Darky.'

Egbert gave Felkor a push. 'You calling me "Darky"?'

'No, I was talkin' to him,' said Felkor, pointing to Tommy and shoving Egbert against the wall.

'No fighting!' said Guttly.

Everyone else had obviously had some training on what to do, so Tommy copied them as best he could. The beanbags were arranged in a semicircle against the capsule walls, facing out the large window. Above each was an oblong piece of material and Tommy watched Anjel*eek!* press her hold-all against one. 'Must be some super-velcro,' he reckoned. He did the same thing with his bag, but it insisted on maintaining a funny angle, like a painting you can't get to hang straight. 'Oh, well,' he thought and fell backwards into his beanbag as all the others had done.

Tommy reached down and pulled the edges of the beanbag over his tummy and legs – copying everyone else. The sides of the beanbag stuck together (more super-velcro) and then, immediately, he felt the beans inside his bag begin to hum and vibrate. Activated by body heat, they moved underneath, alongside and on top of him. His arms were trapped by his sides so he felt a bit like a hotdog sandwiched inside a bun – a bun resting on an activated electric razor. It wasn't an uncomfortable feeling, but he did wonder how he and his fellow travellers would free themselves later. What if he needed to go to the toilet?

At least I feel safe, he thought. Should they get thrown around the inside of the capsule during take-off, it would be like jolting marshmallows inside a paper bag. No one would get hurt – particularly with their helmets on.

ZsaZsa was lying next to Tommy, being jiggled in the same way, and she looked across with concern. 'Darlingk, does my hair look OK?'

'Em . . . Y–y–yeah. It's f–f–f–fine.'

'Everyone alright?' boomed Guttly as the engines began to rev. They were really going now.

Egbert mumbled something very, very fast – too fast for Tommy to understand, but it sounded suspiciously like, 'Mummy, Mummy, I want to go to bed.' ZsaZsa didn't reply to Guttly, except to close her eyes and chew on her manicured nails. Anjel*eek!* screamed loudly enough to make a deaf elephant fall over, which was evidently meant to signify that she was fine. From the other side of the capsule, the smell of rotten Brussels sprouts wafted over – Felkor's contribution to the proceedings.

'Wasn't me,' said the pale-faced boy.

'I'm f–f–f–f–fine,' said Tommy, looking over to Guttly and jerking his head backwards to remove a wedge of hair from his eyes. 'Never b–b–b–been b–b–b–better.'

He was actually telling the truth. He felt great. Guttly looked unconvinced, but there was no turning back now.

'OK,' said Guttly. 'Prepare yourselves.'

The information screen flashed on and showed an image of the interior roof of the Great Cone Room. In the top corner of the screen, split from the main image, was a green circle with the word *COMMAND* printed in red inside it. Beneath this, the words *Check surroundings* appeared in white. The rocket was under Guttly's telepathic control. On the screen, Tommy saw that the top of the Great Cone Room, the nose, had opened, so that the clouds and the darkness above were

53

visible. Then the image switched to the purple floor . . . Elsorr and Bakewell had gone.

The white words in the circle disappeared and were replaced with another command. *Prepare for take-off.* Tommy felt the rocket shuddering. Combined with the vibration of the beanbag, he was beginning to feel like a bottle of Choke tied to an out-of-control pogo stick. A thundering sound emerged from the engines – so loud even Anjel*eek!* couldn't be heard above it as she started to scream hysterically. Amidst the shuddering and the roaring noise, Tommy thought fleetingly of his classmates at Wilchester. They were probably doing maths or a telepathic essay on the merits of seaweed.

The words in white changed once more. *Take-off.* Tommy read the command and felt the same pang of butterflies he'd felt a week earlier. He just had time to think – *We're going. We're really going. I'm off to space.* – before the rocket started to move and an enormous force pressed down on his chest, his head, his legs and his tummy.

9

Hello, Space

At the end of the Mercy Mercy Art-o-pathy test, Basil Bakewell had made a silly remark to The Five. At least, Tommy thought it had been a silly remark. He'd said that when you're flying out of Earth's atmosphere, it feels like there's a giraffe sitting on your tummy. As BLT penetrated the lower clouds of Earth's atmosphere, Tommy felt like he must've just fainted. Everything had gone black and it felt as if a giraffe, an elephant *and* a rhinoceros were stacked on top of his beanbag like cocktail sausages on a stick. He was being crushed.

A moment later, and the window was visible again – the elephant and rhino had vanished. Only the weight of the giraffe stayed with him. He strained to move his head and when he looked around the capsule he realized where the elephant and rhino had gone. Somehow, Guttly's beanbag must've rolled on top of him because now Guttly was pressed sideways against the information screen. At various times before they finally emerged from Earth's atmosphere, Anjel*eek!* got squashed under Guttly, ZsaZsa and Egbert kept rolling back and forth across the capsule like peas on a boat in a typhoon, and Felkor ended up upside-down, blocking the view out of the window. Only Tommy somehow remained stationary. He knew it was through nothing very clever or deliberate on his part, but he just did. He stayed in the one place for the whole juddering experience.

FFHHWWOOOOOOOMMM . . . .

Earth's atmosphere suddenly freed them, and BLT whooshed noiselessly into space. Tommy's beanbag immediately released and he found himself beginning to float up off the floor of the capsule. 'The beanbags are weight-activated,' explained Guttly. 'As soon as gravity loses its grip on you, they open.'

Felkor was no longer blocking the window and the great curve of planet Earth cut across the blackness of space. The vision – a white woolly mass – astonished Tommy. He removed his helmet and stared for a while as the curve shrank and the full sphere of Earth became visible. 'Wow,' was all he could mumble. As the size went from tractor wheel to car wheel, he noticed the great space beyond. 'Wow,' he said again, completely mesmerized. Where were all the other planets squished against Earth? It wasn't cramped at all. Clearly there were vast distances between Earth and other planets. So vast it made you dizzy just to think of them. The Great Cone Room had seemed big, but it was like the tiniest speck of water vapour compared to the great ocean of space. This was amazing.

'Could you kindly remove your foot, young man?'

Tommy looked up – or was it down? – to see his suction boot placed firmly upon Guttly's bald head. He suddenly realized that he'd turned upside-down to get a better view of Earth and he'd floated over – or under – Guttly, who was walking upside-down with his suction boots stuck to the ceiling. And like all the children in his care, Guttly had removed his helmet.

'Eh, sorry, sir.'

Unfortunately, the suction on the boot was so strong that it needed Egbert and Anjel*eek!* to pull Tommy, and Felkor and ZsaZsa to pull Guttly, before the boot finally released from the shiny scalp with a *SSSSCCHLLOCCKKKKK!*

'I'm very sorry, sir. I didn't mean . . .' Tommy felt bad. A big welt was visible on Guttly's scalp.

'Just be careful,' said Guttly crossly. 'And that goes for all of you.'

'Yeah, be careful yuh moron,' said Felkor and he shoved Tommy, who didn't move because his suction boots were now firmly planted on the floor. Instead, it was Felkor who moved backwards, only stopping when his head hit the wall of the capsule.

'What kind of food will we get in this training school?' asked Anjel*eek!*. 'Will they have chocolate?'

By the window, ZsaZsa was eyeing her reflection, aghast. 'My hair! Weightlessness is horrid, horrid, horrid.'

'Yo, I been in space thirty-eight times before,' said Egbert. ''S'no big deal.'

As Earth continued shrinking to the size of a melon, Tommy set his suction boots firmly against the wall of the capsule and stood sideways to get the best view out the window. Guttly remained standing upside-down with his eyes shut and, from the images appearing on the information screen, it appeared that he was checking co-ordinates and arranging the docking procedure with the MilkyFed vessel. For the rest of the short journey to the Moon, Tommy was vaguely aware of Anjel*eek!* screaming very loudly now and again (whenever she turned upside-down) and of Egbert Fitchly mumbling something that sounded like a prayer (it was actually a David Bowie song).

Music *so* Bad, my Dad would Like It!

During training, The Four had been given the lyrics to over thirty songs from the 20th century that mentioned *space* or anything to do with it. Egbert was the only one who learned all the lyrics off by heart. He could recite all the songs in forty-eight seconds and his favourite, *Major Tom*, in under two seconds. 20th-century songs were used because songs at the end of the 21st century no longer had any lyrics. If there were any human sounds in a song, they were usually generated by recording human bodily functions with super-sensitive microphones and then repeating the resulting sound over and over again in *rap* music fashion. The main sounds recorded were breathing, scratching, digesting, nail-cutting and the resulting noises from an advanced yoga position assumed after eating a hot curry.

So enraptured was Tommy, that he didn't notice Felkor spitting large amounts of saliva out of his mouth and then patting the resultant floating blobs with his hand to make them move back and forward like slow-motion jellies. Nor did he notice that ZsaZsa had taken two of the 'jellies' from Felkor's juggling performance and had pressed them against the wall of the capsule so they formed a pattern of tiny droplets. With one hand holding her hair at all times, she was trying to shape the droplets into circles on the wall. By the time BLT docked with the MilkyFed spaceship 300 kilometres above the Moon's highest mountain, AWATTY, she'd created ever-decreasing rings of droplets, one within the other – and had unwittingly invented a new form of art (*no-gravity art-o-grossy*) that would become popular in many galaxies in the years to come.

Despite all the commotion around him, Tommy just stared out the window in dumbfounded amazement. He didn't even notice that his hair no longer lay so firmly upon his forehead.

The stars looked so twinkly. And so many of them! The blackness, the great ocean of space, it wasn't scary, it was exciting – just the empty distance between friendly lights. Waiting to be explored . . .

A Giant Step for Man. A Small Step for Mankind

AWATTY was christened in 2017 by the famous moon mountaineer, Chris Bovril. The official name of the mountain is, *Are We At The Top Yet?* The Royal Pedantic Society of Mountaineers derided Bovril's achievement because he didn't wear suction boots while scaling AWATTY. It was therefore six times easier to climb than a similar mountain on Earth.

The docking procedure was easier than Guttly or anyone at NUTS had expected. The MilkyFed spaceship was much smaller than BLT, and looked a bit like an old brown hat – a fedora to be exact, and a slightly crumpled one at that (actually, this spaceship was known affectionately as *Fedora* by her crew). Fedora turned sideways to let BLT fly into the part where someone might be expected to put their head and, instead of hitting the back of the hat, as Tommy expected, BLT kept going until it had been completely swallowed. It was as if BLT had shrunk to nothing (or else Fedora had become gargantuan). By the time BLT came to rest, it resembled a fly stuck to the side of an elephant (one turned inside-out).

It was quite dark outside the window, but as Tommy's eyes fought the blackness, he swore he could make out hundreds of windows dotted all over the inside of Fedora. The lights were off inside each window, but a slight movement of curtain was just perceptible behind some and he could feel the gaze of thousands of pairs and triplets of eyes upon his face.

'Where are we?'

'What's this dumb hat thing?'

'This is freaky, darlingk.'

'I been here before. Three or four times.'

'Quiet!' said Guttly. 'This is our transporter to the MilkyFed training school.'

'You mean we're not there yet?'

'But this is just a stupid old hat.'

'I'll get travel-sick if we go one mile further. And look – my hair's ruined!'

'I have to eat something – but nothing that's organic.'[3]

'Wh-where is the MilkyFed training school?'

'How long will we be there?'

'Stop!' Guttly raised his arms. 'That's better.' His beard kept floating up in front of his eyes as he surveyed the floating children. 'As you were told on the first day of training, we don't know where the training school is exactly because we thought it would be rude to ask – like being invited to dinner and asking what's on the menu.'

Tommy decided against reminding Guttly that he'd missed the first day of training.

'I wouldn't go to any dinner *without* asking what's on the menu,' said Anjel*eek!*.

'All we know is that the training will take no longer than six months – except for any of you chosen for the dangerou—' Guttly halted, hoping no one realized what he'd almost said. 'For the *mission*,' he corrected.

This generated a new barrage of questions, including how likely was it that a human could get eaten by an alien on the

3 By 2096 organic food was derided by the health-conscious. The lack of pesticides and fertilizers, they claimed, was making people smaller and less resistant to disease.

mission. Guttly refused to speculate. 'We asked about the mission, but were told that it's too confidential to divulge . . . All I can say is that if any of you are chosen, it would certainly look good on your CV.'

'What's the capital of the Milky Way?'

'NO MORE QUESTIONS!' Guttly's face was the colour of the capsule's walls. 'Now, I don't know what's in this hat – *spaceship*, I mean – but I do know that all of you are representing your planet. So you will all behave and act like true ambassadors of Earth!'

As Guttly said *Earth*, BLT's port-hole opened and everyone in the capsule fell to the floor, causing Anjel*eek!* to let out her loudest yell yet. Egbert Fitchly's foot was prodding the side of Tommy's ear and someone else's elbow was digging into his side.

'The open door has activated the damn gravity gravitator,' said Guttly. 'They must have normal gravity inside this hat. *Spaceship*, I mean. Spaceship.' He scrambled to his feet and plodded to the open door.

Thankfully, Egbert's suction boots hadn't taken hold of his ear, but Tommy still felt a little shaken as he climbed to his feet. He noticed Felkor had a load of spit all over his space-suit and there was more spit dripping down the wall above ZsaZsa's head.

'I'm not sure of the best way to get in here,' said Guttly, peering out the port-hole.

Tommy was about to join Guttly when Felkor pushed past. 'Outta my way, idiot.'

Because his suction boots were so firmly rooted to the floor, Tommy fell hard on his bum. There was a brief sound of a dog being kicked, then Felkor stopped laughing and joined Guttly at the door. Tommy rubbed his bum and tried to move his boots. From his position on the floor, he had a view between Felkor and Guttly. All he could see was a brightly lit cylindrical tunnel, exactly the same width as BLT's round door. This tunnel seemed to slope upwards and disappear around a bend, so you couldn't see more than six metres along. He supposed it was like a curly straw which had stretched out to greet them and, somehow, it was supposed to be their path to the inside of the MilkyFed ship.

'We hafta wait for a rope, innit,' said Felkor. 'When they drop one, I'll climb up first. I'm easily the best climber here.'

'I'm not so sure we're supposed to do that,' said Guttly, scratching his beard.

'Darlingk, I'm not going up there without a hair-band.'

'I been up there before. Twice.'

'But maybe these are for a purpose,' said Guttly.

Suspended just off the ceiling at the opening of the tunnel was what seemed like a mini stack of very thin table-mats. Guttly reached up and took them down. There were six of them and they were as thin as paper, yet strangely strong. The bearded man handed everyone a mat. 'Let's see what we can do with these,' he said.

Felkor began jumping on his mat, while Egbert started banging his off his head so that it made a sound like someone punching a jellyfish. ZsaZsa breathed heavily onto hers and started drawing shapes on the condensation. Anjel*eek!* licked the mat, pressed it to her lips and screamed – the scream came out like an underwater ambulance siren. Guttly just studied his mat intently and scratched his beard.

Tommy wasn't sure what to do with his mat, but he did know that his suction boots were beginning to irritate him. He could hardly move in them and he didn't want to be pushed over by Felkor again. If you've ever tried walking across a floor of treacle then you'll know how he felt. He placed his mat on the floor and sat on it to take his boots off. No sooner had he done so than – *SSSCCHHHLOCKKKK!* – his suction boots came unstuck from the floor as the mat rose. Before he knew what was happening, he started careering upwards into the tunnel.

What followed was one of the most memorable rides Tommy would ever experience in his long life. He must've been travelling as fast as an avalanche and yet he never felt that he was going to fall off the mat. At first he clung on for dear life, then he realized, as he sat up, that it wobbled and tilted automatically to adjust for shifts in his weight, ensuring perfect balance at all times. Even going around corners, it tilted at a steep angle so he was just pressed more firmly onto it, with his hair flying madly above and behind him. After the first bend, the tunnel did a kind of corkscrew, then rose swiftly to what seemed like a great height. Once it reached the arc at the top of this climb, the tunnel went pitch black and Tommy, going by his senses, realized he was falling – faster, faster.

As soon as the fall started to curve into a more horizontal plane, Tommy heard a welcome burst of sound and the lights came on again. The tunnel became transparent and he was travelling through a great, crowded room. (I say *room*, but this enclosed space was as big as a football stadium.) The glass tube twisted and turned, soared and dived, criss-crossing this great hall many, many times. Despite the speed he was travelling, Tommy snatched brief glances above, below, left and right, through the walls of the tunnel.

It seemed as though the floor of the great room was crowded with lots of creatures who could best be described as stripy koala bears, each with a unicorn-type horn jutting up from their forehead. Every one of these 'koalicorns' was blowing into a trumpet or one of a variety of enormous wind instruments. Above them, on large floating balconies, dotted about at various levels, were hundreds of other creatures, many of them also playing instruments. At least a dozen grandiose pianos (six times the size of grand pianos) were occupied on one balcony by strange creatures that looked like a cross between reptiles and other animals (including kangaroos, rhinos and ostriches). These reptilian creatures were hitting the large keys with different parts of their body and were creating a sensational sound. Some of them were even tap dancing on the keys!

In the rafters, there were too many drums to count and an enormous group of round furry creatures, the size of beachballs, were bouncing back and forth off the drums (almost like a pin-ball machine), generating a perfect drumbeat. There were too many other creatures to take in. Some that looked like big, fat, woolly three-armed bears standing on their hind legs, some that looked like very large humans with waggly tails where their noses should be and a few that looked like Danny DeVito (albeit covered in fur). Almost everyone was either playing an instrument or singing in a tightly packed group. Those that were doing neither, were spinning around in pairs and wiggling to the music.

Curse of the Bermuda Triangle

Unfortunately, almost all videos, CDs, movie-reels, photographs and computer images were destroyed by water-vapour during the Great Climate Enhancement – although, inexplicably, most audio-tapes survived (as did a few Barry Manilow posters). Hence Earthlings' patchy appreciation of music and other such things.

I should mention that Tommy had never actually seen dancing in real life. At the end of the 21st century, Earthlings couldn't believe that people used to jolt their bodies around in funny ways whenever they heard music. No wonder the savages of the 20th century hadn't practised art-o-pathy, they thought. They were obviously too uncivilized.

Round and round the tunnel Tommy fired – under balconies, over balconies, across pianos, just missing twirly horn instruments, through the pinball routine of drums and in between dancers. He must've heard almost two full musical pieces before the tunnel whooshed him up through the roof of the great room. It then did two complete circuits on the outside edge of Fedora, giving a dazzling, panoramic view of space. Earth was no longer visible, but among the many stars Tommy wondered at, one was surely Earth's sun. The Milky Way itself presented a glorious spectacle as it whisked nearer, looking like a waterfall of stars flowing towards him.

Then suddenly, the tunnel went dark and a moment later Tommy felt his mat stop abruptly while he continued to shoot forward. Everything went bright again as he was spat out of the tunnel and found himself falling through the air. He only just had time to realize that it was a large glass bubble of a room, half-filled with water, when – *SSSPLASSHHHH!* – he landed in the pool of water.

After splashing down quite deeply, Tommy popped up to the surface of the pool and wiped the water out of his eyes and pushed his hair up off his forehead. The water was very warm and smelled of fresh moonlight and spices. The moonlight smell was actually the famous scent of moonlight from the third moon of planet Gargle, which has a chocolatey-banana smell (rocks from its surface are alleged to contain *great healing properties*, although they're very slippery and have *great injury*

65

properties if you stand on them).

Because of the high level of salts and minerals, it was very easy to float and very difficult indeed to sink – even with his suction boots still on. Breathless and exhilarated from the ride, Tommy looked about and saw that once again he had a clear view of space. This glass bubble, maybe four metres across, was like a bead on the outside of Fedora. Even when he looked down through the water, he could see a vision of space through the glass below. It was only when he heard a faint scream that he looked away from the panoramic vista of space and saw that there were five other glass globes at a distance surrounding his. And Anjel*eek!*, of course, had just landed with a splash into hers. Moments later, one after another, the others were deposited into separate pools of water. Guttly was last and he made such a splash in his globe, that for a moment almost half the water in it seemed to hit the roof.

Tommy gazed out at the stars for a while until he noticed a glass jug and a glass plate, almost invisible, floating just above the water to the side of the pool. He swam over and saw that the jug was full of water with a straw sticking out of it and the plate was stacked with little transparent balls. The balls felt squidgy when he squeezed one of them. Surely this is space-food, he thought. Feeling quite hungry and hoping for something tasty, he popped one of the balls into his mouth and took a swig of the liquid. There was definitely something in his mouth and when he swallowed he felt his tummy get a little fuller, but as for taste – absolutely nothing! The liquid had less flavour than water – it didn't even taste wet. How strange, he thought, disappointed, and floated away from the tasteless fare.

Glass-balled floating pools (a.k.a. *floating globes*) are extremely popular with many space-people and after a while Tommy could understand why. Despite his yearning to stare at the ever-changing view of space outside, he soon closed his eyes, bobbing safely on the water's surface. After all the excitement, travel and poor sleep of the night before, he fell into a deep and restful slumber.

Fedora continued travelling silently at a few trillion kilometres a second. And the Milky Way grew larger as they hummed towards its cloudy centre.

~ 10 ~

A New Friend

Tommy was awakened half an hour into his nap by an enormous splash. Seconds later, a cheeky face appeared from below the surface and wiped the water from its eyes. The creature smiled broadly, swam to the edge of the globe and hauled itself out of the pool and onto an invisible ledge that Tommy hadn't noticed before. There he sat, his short legs dangling just above the water's surface.

'Can never stay long in these pools,' he said. 'Always send me straight to sleep.'

This comment was unsurprising as sleep in a floating globe is sixteen times more restful than ordinary sleep.

The little creature was like a very furry, short human. He was covered in thick, reddy-brown fur and his eyes were absolutely enormous. They were shiny green and twinkled brightly. His ears were large, yet his nose was quite small and his mouth revealed white teeth whenever he smiled – which was very often.

'You almost killed me there,' blurted Tommy.

'What? That little splash?'

Tommy nodded indignantly.

'Ah, I'd never've killed you. Bruised you a bit, maybe. But never killed you.'

'Well you should be more careful,' said Tommy, failing to sound angry in the face of those twinkling eyes.

'OK, sorry,' said the creature. 'You're Tommy Storm, aren't you?'

'Yes. How did you—?'

'Oh, I been briefed a little on you.'

'What do you mean you been . . . ?' Tommy was lost for words. How did this creature know all about him? Who was this little fellow?

Sensing his questions, the creature extended a furry hand. 'I'm a wibblewallian.'

'A what?'

'The name's Wibblewoodrow. Woozie Wibblewoodrow.'

Tommy lifted a wet arm out of the water and shook the warm, furry hand. 'Hello, Woozie.'

'*Woozie?*' The creature looked perturbed.

'Yes . . . Woozie?' That's what he'd said, wasn't it?

'Just *Woozie?*' said the creature. 'On its own?' Tommy nodded, unsure if he'd said something wrong. Finally Woozie smiled again. '*Woozie* . . . Yeah . . . I like it. On my planet everyone calls me Wibblewoodrow . . . But fine. Call me Woozie if you like.'

Tommy swam to the edge of the globe and tried to reach up to the shelf Woozie was sitting on. 'How did you . . . ?' It was impossible to climb up the sleek walls of the globe.

'Just feel for the ladder there,' said Woozie. 'Completely see-through, so it's hard to find . . . That's it . . . There you go.'

Tommy hauled himself up beside Woozie and sat with his feet dangling in the warm water below. He felt a little self-conscious because his skin-tight suit was almost see-through when wet.

'Like your suit,' said Woozie. 'Lucky they didn't give you a smaller size.' He stopped laughing when Tommy squirmed noticeably. 'If you're worried about being all wet, you'll find that floating pool water dries real fast.'

Sure enough, his suit was drying fast and there was no water dripping from his hair.

'You want a hand out of them boots?' Tommy looked quizzically at the little fellow, who continued: 'Just seem to weigh you down.'

'They're suction boots for non-gravity,' Tommy explained.

'Ah. Well, you won't be needing them here. Or in the Intergalactic Space-station. Suction boots were banned millennia ago by the MilkyFed. Very dangerous. 'Specially in bunk-beds or elquinine crystal shops.'

Tommy started on one boot and Woozie heaved the other, almost toppling himself into the pool when it came off.

'Poo-wee! Don't you humans ever clean your feet?'

Woozie looked as if he was going to be sick, then tossed the boot into the pool, where it sank despite all the salts and minerals. Tommy was about to say something indignant when he noticed Woozie's eyes smiling larger than ever. 'Only joking,' said the furry fellow. 'Don't smell too bad. Not as bad as a thunderbumble's armpit.'

Feeling more mobile already, Tommy threw his other boot into the pool and watched it sink.

Woozie flicked a switch at the end of the ledge and it began to turn so that they faced out to space. 'Much better view this way,' he said.

Tommy marvelled at the astonishing spectacle. The entire Milky Way in all its glory was there before them. A cascade of stars and suns and moons and planets and super-novas. Tommy and Woozie sat and stared silently for a time.

'Beautiful. I never tire of this view,' said Woozie finally.

'It's amazing,' said Tommy, unable to find the words that

70

would do justice to the incredible vision before them.

'Almost the same view you get from my planet.'

'*Your* planet?'

'Yeah,' said Woozie, pointing to a cluster of glinting pinpricks far below. 'There. Just to the left of that bright star . . . The planet Friggletenbygumpyjamas. Friggle, for short.' He looked very proud and beamed at Tommy.

The broad smile gave Tommy the courage to ask a question he'd been holding back for some time. 'Are you a MilkyFed policeman? Or politician?'

Woozie started laughing hard. So hard, he fell off the ledge into the pool and swallowed some water. He continued laughing and coughing for some minutes – even after Tommy helped pull him back onto the ledge. Eventually, he stopped and said, 'Sorry. Meant to explain – I'm going to the Intergalactic Space-station for the same reason as you. But I'm here now to ensure you're alright.'

'I don't understand.'

'I'm only eleven,' said Woozie. 'Just a kid – and I been chosen to represent Friggle. They collected two of us from Friggle and three others from neighbouring planets. Since then, this spaceship has been collecting kids from loads of other planets. You guys were the last we collected. From Earth, wasn't it?' Tommy nodded. 'They didn't give us quite the welcome they gave you Earthlings – cos they're well-used to Friggles and to all the other peoples.'

'Do you know exactly why they're gathering all of us children?'

The sparkly-eyed creature nodded. 'A training and selection process to do with a dangerous mission.'

'You don't know what the mission is, do you?'

Woozie shook his head. 'A secret, supposedly . . . But I

71

heard rumours it's not dangerous at all. They're just saying that so they won't get kids from all over the Milky Way complaining that they weren't chosen.'

'So if it's not dangerous, then what's the mission?'

'I heard the five kids they choose will be taken to a newly constructed planet and will be made rulers of the planet.'

'Why would they do that?'

'An experiment. They want to see what happens if they make kids the absolute rulers of a planet . . . The five kids – the rulers – will be given free sweets and ice-cream for life . . . It's just a rumour, though.'

'And how did you—?' Tommy wasn't sure what he wanted to ask. 'Why did they send *you* to talk to me?'

'Well, cos I speak English – plus another 3,823 languages. We're all great linguists on Friggle. Not much else we're good at, really . . . Here.' He pulled a silver box out of a pocket in his fur. 'I'm s'posed to give you a few things before we get to the space-station.'

Woozie did a lot of talking over the next hour or so. At one stage, he started a short movie that was projected out of the silver box and onto one half of the glass globe. The creature in the movie looked like a cross between a reptile and a kangaroo, with a very long beard. He seemed to be addressing himself straight at the camera because his mouth was moving, but the only sound Tommy could hear resembled sea-lions having a food fight.

When Woozie realized that Tommy couldn't understand a thing, he was very apologetic. 'Sorry. Of course. Totally forgot. Almost the most important thing.'

From the silver box he took a small, silver thingy that looked like a silver penny. It was called a talkie-max and Woozie pressed it onto Tommy's tongue. It hurt a little as it sank below the tongue's skin. Then it disappeared so he couldn't feel it any more. Woozie did the same thing with two smaller pennies called talkie-waxes, except that he pressed them into Tommy's earlobes. 'Now,' he explained, 'every bit of speech you hear from someone with a talkie-max embedded in their tongue will be converted by your ears into whatever language you're thinking in. And everything you say will be converted in the ears of the listener into whatever language they're thinking in – so long as they have talkie-waxes embedded in their ears.'

'No way!' said Tommy.

'Yes way.' Woozie stood up on the ledge and smiled. 'I've stopped speaking English, I'm speaking Nonsenseaplenty . . . Now I'm speaking Marriahkerrian . . . This is Obliquean . . . This, Waffleooglian.' He bent over, facing away from Tommy and it looked as if his mouth wasn't moving. 'Now I'm speaking Pollitishun.' It sounded remarkably as though the voice was coming out of Woozie's bottom! Then the furry fellow started tap dancing. 'Now I'm speaking Sammydavisjuniorism.' It was amazing. His mouth definitely wasn't moving and yet he was speaking. 'You see, some groups of people speak by contorting their body into shapes or by dancing.'

No matter what Woozie did, or how often he named a language, everything sounded like perfect English to Tommy. 'What's your name again?' asked Tommy, and he strained to think in French.

'Je m'appelle Woozie Wibblewoodrow.' It was said in a perfect French accent, with rolling *R*s and a Gallic indifference. Abruptly, Tommy stopped thinking in French and reverted to English in case he couldn't understand what was said and missed something important.

A Rude Word by any other Name . . .

In 2096, English was the first language of every one on Earth because the building of floating cities had required a level of global co-operation that required everyone to speak one language and English had come out the winner in the global vote on the issue – just pipping Hungarian. However, most school kids were taught a smattering of French as it was deemed the most elegant language in which to speak regarding all things made of plasticine. It should be noted that many school kids still tried to learn as many rude words as possible in as many different languages as possible. Incidentally, wibblewallians aside, *Marriahkerrian* is a language understood by only the very smartest creatures in the universe.

Woozie removed a tiny silver bottle from the box and without warning sprayed the contents into Tommy's eyes.

'Ahhh!' Tommy yelled. 'That stings.'

'Sorry. Best not to warn you before I did that. Otherwise, you'd only close your eyes too early like I did. Took me twenty goes before I got any in my eyes.'

'What is it?'

'Concentrated *Maykscents4usNow* . . . The good news is, you won't need to spray your eyes again for at least a thousand years.'

'That's great,' said Tommy sarcastically, 'but what's the point of it?'

'Ah, well, now if you look at any sign, any print or any writing that's coated in *Twaddle* – no matter what language it's printed in – you'll see the language you're thinking in. So it's a bit like a visual talkie-max.'

Tommy's eyes were beginning to stop stinging, but he continued blinking.

'And are many things covered in Twaddle?'

Woozie laughed. 'You don't know very much, do you?' Then he stopped laughing when he saw that Tommy looked a little hurt. 'Sorry . . . Almost everything in the Milky Way has been sprayed with Twaddle at some time or another. And for extra measure, all inks are infused with Twaddle . . . You can read anything in the Milky Way now.'

Once Tommy stopped blinking, Woozie started the movie again. The same bearded kangaroo-reptile appeared and spoke very clearly in English. 'The MilkyFed and I, Lord BeardedmoustachedWiseface-oh, we welcome you, visitor, on your journey to the InterGalactic Space-station. We hope that you will relax, sit back or lie down and enjoy the journey. Some light refreshments are available for your enjoyment and we hope that they are to your taste. May I wish you luck with the challenges that lie ahead and may I say that I look forward to greeting you in person when you arrive at the space-station. Fare thee well until then.'

The movie ended and the projection disappeared, whisking itself back into the tin box.

'Who was he?' asked Tommy.

'The head of the MilkyFed. Everyone calls him *Wisebeardyface*, but I'm told you shouldn't call him that in person – apparently, it was his nickname when he was a child at school and he's still annoyed about it. He's a kangasaurus . . . Wait here a moment.' Woozie leaned forward and belly-flopped into the water. He resurfaced at the far side of the globe and smiled back at Tommy. 'Only just noticed this food. I'm pretty hungry. You must be starving.'

Woozie swam back, holding a see-through tray that held the see-through jug and plate with the tasteless fare. He handed it up to Tommy, then climbed up beside him.

'I'm not really that hungry,' said Tommy who didn't want

to be rude. Woozie was so enthusiastic, after all.

'Oh, you must. This is the best *favo-fant* you can get. They laid it on 'specially.' Woozie put one of the transparent squidgy round things in his mouth. 'Mmmm. Delicious. Altrusian larvae eggs with a dash of homemade Friggle sauce.'

'I don't . . .'

'What?'

'I don't taste anything when I eat that stuff,' Tommy ventured. 'I don't really like it.'

'You tasted some earlier?'

Tommy nodded and Woozie threw his head back and laughed hard. He almost fell into the pool again, but Tommy caught him in time.

'What's your favourite food?' Woozie asked. 'What would you like to eat right now?'

Tommy thought about it for a moment. 'Hmm. Cheeseburger and fries.'

'Alright. Hold that thought and try some favo-fant.'

Woozie handed him a squidgy transparent ball and, reluctantly, Tommy put it in his mouth. He was unprepared for what followed. The ball felt warm and as he bit into it, he tasted toasted bun, melted cheese and a beefy burger cooked just the way he liked it. There was also a bit of lettuce, a hint of mustard and a dollop of ketchup within the mouthful. The next ball tasted of piping hot French fries, crisp and slightly salty. *Absolutely delicious!* He must've been hungry because he ate about seven of the squidgy balls – equivalent to two cheeseburgers and one and a half portions of French fries.

'Not eaten for a while, eh?' said Woozie.

'I was famished,' said Tommy. 'Completely famished. But I don't understand . . . The favo-fant tasted awful earlier.' He took a few sips of liquid out of the jug. While eating, the liquid tasted like Choke, now it tasted of a thick chocolate milk-shake.

'That's cos you didn't have a *yumm-yumm* in your mouth,' explained Woozie. 'One's incorporated in the talkie-max I put in your mouth. You got the latest model. I had an older model put in years ago and then had to have a favo-fant yumm-yumm put in separately. Look.' He stuck his tongue out and Tommy could see two slight bulges on the underside of his tongue.

'Carrots can be a bit dicey'
(Anti-Vomit Pills slogan – marketed by E-Zee-Singles tourist board)

If there are any health-nuts out there, you may have been surprised to see Tommy's first choice of food was a cheeseburger and fries . . . Well, towards the end of the 21st century, physicists, biologists, jugglers and taxidermists on Earth finally put their minds to the question: *How come food that tastes great is bad for you . . . while food that's healthy tastes yucky?* After some years, they discovered a way of converting very tasty food into very healthy food. This meant that cheeseburgers, chocolate and fizzy drinks no longer had high fat or sugar content. In fact, they were better for you than broccoli or carrots or British bovine spinal cord (which scientists proclaimed 'a healthy option' in 2029).

Tommy stuck his tongue out. 'Here, can you see mine?'

Woozie shook his head. 'The latest models are almost unnoticeable . . . So long as you've got a yumm–yumm in your mouth, you can eat and drink this stuff and you taste whatever food or drink you feel like at that moment.'

Tommy felt quite full and very content. 'That was delicious,' he said.

'Yeah, but a bit bland without favo-fant goggles . . . You

put them on and you see the food you want to eat while you're eating it.'

'This is some invention. It's fantastic.'

'Except when the yumm–yumm malfunctions.'

'Why? What happens then?'

'You don't want to know.'

Tommy thought for a moment. He now had one of these devices embedded in his tongue. 'I *do* want to know,' he insisted.

Woozie shrugged. 'Well, every five years or so, the yumm–yumms start to malfunction, so you start tasting the food you hate most.'

'Does it taste bad?'

'Bad? Bad?' Woozie's eyes bulged and he looked like he was going to faint for a moment. 'Two years ago, I started tasting a badgersaurus' bottom every time I had a favo–fant meal! Nightmare! 'Specially as it took three days before I could get it fixed and there was nothing but favo–fant food in the house.' Woozie looked a little green. 'I need some Fizzalicious Overhypt Moonbeam to take the thought away.' He took a few enormous gulps from the jug, then wiped the whiskers above his mouth. 'Oooohh,' he groaned, rubbing his tum. 'Too full now – all those bubbles!' And the poor fellow couldn't move until he'd belched.

Meatloaf covered in Marmalade?

Favo-fant stands for FAVOurite FANTasy food. The manufacturers stress that no matter what you think you're eating, their food is full of essential nutrients. Technically, vegetarians can eat favo-fant and think of steaks without violating their principles, although all favo-fant packaging discourages users from thinking cannibalistic thoughts.

⚡ 11 ⚡

WELCOME TO IGGY

From a distance, the Intergalactic Space-station looked like an enormous coatstand made out of thousands of lights. It wasn't really what Tommy was expecting – he'd envisioned something like a giant fexa-cetter or a large saucepan.

A little earlier, the water had drained out of the glass globe and he and Woozie sat on the clear ledge admiring the view. The IG Space-station was a tiny speck when another glass globe appeared not far away. It hovered, then flung itself towards them. Tommy dived for the floor, covering his head with his hands. But the expected crash never came.

'Nice dive!' said Woozie, laughing.

Tommy looked up and saw that the globe they were in and the newly arrived globe were attached like two sudsy bubbles – except there was no partition in-between. He stood up, slightly embarrassed, his knee a bit sore. 'I thought . . .'

'Less painful if you dive when there's water in the globe.'

'Ha ha.'

'This is my taxi . . . We'll be there soon, so I better go.' The furry creature walked along the ledge that now stretched into the other globe.

'But . . . Will I see you later?'

'Hope so,' replied the twinkling face.

As soon as Woozie stood still in the middle of the other

globe, it moved away, leaving Tommy's globe intact. Two seconds later, Woozie was gone from sight.

Tommy climbed up onto the ledge and looked out. It felt as though he'd been on Fedora for quite some time – what with the musical welcome, the restful sleep and the time with Woozie. But the whole journey had taken just under three Earth hours.

Fedora made for the top of the looming coatstand and docked on one of its 'hooks' at a rakish angle. As soon as Fedora came to a standstill, the lights on the coatstand went off and a million others came on, revealing a space-station of gigantic proportions.

This was a *Bright Welcome* – the MilkyFed's way of rolling out the red carpet for the new arrivals.

The MCU (or MilkyFed Curtain-makers' Union) has asked it to be pointed out that generally most windows in the IG Space-station have curtains drawn across them – to discourage Peeping-Tomaliens from hovering outside. By illuminating its interior and opening certain curtains, the Space-station can take on various shapes, such as coatstands, sandwich-toasters, combine-harvesters and chewed-up insoles.

Tommy couldn't see, but on one side of the space-station, the lights in the many rooms now made up a set of words that could be seen from up to twenty thousand kilometres away: '*Drink Fizzalicious Overhypt Moonbeam for a longer immortal life.*' On the other side it said, '*Lose Weight. Get a Gravity-Lite machine.*'

Shortly after Fedora docked, Tommy felt his globe start to move. It twisted this way and that, prising itself off Fedora, then started floating into space. By the time he looked round to see what had held them to Fedora, the stationary hat-like spaceship was already shrinking into the distance – so much so, that if he raised his hand, Tommy could blot it out of sight.

'Thyme Weights for No Man'
(Jabba LeHut – founder of Phoolyoreself Inc.)

Most spaceships in the MilkyFed had gravity machines calibrated to the level of gravity on the planet where the spaceship was registered. Anyone concerned about their weight and weighing themselves on a Sloberian spaceship, for example, would become very alarmed, since gravity on Sloberia is nineteen times that of Earth. In recent times, spaceships running health programmes tried to register on the planet Sooperfishall (where gravity is 1/36th that of Earth) and amongst owners of family spaceships, gravity machines with minute levels of gravity were beginning to sell heavily. (The *Phoolyoreself* TM range of luxury bathroom scales – recognizable by their fluorescent thyme emblem – famously claimed that no one need be 'as heavy as a handful of thyme' any more.)

Surrounding Tommy's globe, there were lots of other transparent globes gliding through space (twenty-five to be exact), each with a single occupant. They were travelling in the shape of an arrow and Felkor was just above him, Anjel*eek!* below. There was Guttly some way behind, standing, arms folded, looking very formal. And Woozie, two globes above. Many of the other individuals looked like the type of creatures that had been playing music earlier in Fedora's great hall. Reptilian, furry, round, tall, small, fat – so many funny-looking species.

Tommy would soon learn that in addition to Earth, four solar systems contributed children from lots of different planets. Earth was the only 'single-planet contributor' and the only contributor that sent five children of the same species (human).

81

The swarming arrow glided over lights and dells and valleys, and Tommy saw that the space-station was covered in places with black fur. They rounded a skewer-like extremity, dodged a gargantuan jutting thingy and headed straight for a small pore in the distance. As they plunged into the opening, Tommy guessed its width to be half a mile. The globes started bunching together into groups until there were four groups of five a little distance away, followed by the six Earthlings. Speeding to the heart of the space-station, Tommy noticed Egbert doing a back-flip. Anjel*eek!* had her mouth pressed to the wall of her globe and it looked like she was screaming.

A bright dome of glass glowered in the distance and, one at a time, each of the other groups of five passed through the dome, then re-emerged moments later, hurtling up the tunnel towards space – at which point the next group would go through the dome.

'It's three freckles past a hair'

Although time machines wouldn't be invented for many millennia to come, the MilkyFed had found ways to slow time. To ensure maximum efficiency, it was decided to slow time within the dome while the groups were being 'welcomed'. As a result, however long any group spent inside the dome, they would re-emerge into the tunnel fractions of a second later.

No more than seven seconds after the first group had gone before them, the six 'Earth' globes headed straight for the dome. One moment it was in front of them, the next, they seemed to have passed through it like a bubble through a bubble and the globes were wafting downwards, until they came to rest on an expansive wooden floor.

A large hole appeared in Tommy's globe and he stepped out onto a plush, orange rug. The others stepped out of their globes at the same time, so that they stood in a line of six, in order of rank, with Guttly at one end, then Felkor, Anjel*eek!*, Egbert, ZsaZsa and, lastly, Tommy. Before them, upon a stage, stood a reptilian creature (who Tommy recognized as Wisebeardyface, the kangasaurus), smoking a funny-looking cigarette.

Tommy looked behind and saw a cavernous room full of tables (each covered in checked tablecloths with flickering candles atop), fountains, palm-fronded trees and enormous vases. Assorted creatures were standing in the dancing shadows. Some seemed to be wearing light-coloured suits and ties (and a smattering of fedoras), while others wore colourful dresses. At the back of the room, a motley crew was playing jazz – better jazz than has ever been heard on Earth. The ceiling – the great dome – was high above and somehow dancing moonlight found its way through.

Wisebeardyface dropped the cigarette, stubbed it out with his foot and the music hushed.

'Earthlings, Earthlings, we bid you welcome to our small space-station. We call it IGGY, which stands for the InterGalactic Great Youth space-station – the *space-station* Ss are silent . . . And that is what we are gathering here. The great youth of our galaxy.'

'Greetings from Earth,' replied Guttly, putting his thumb in his nose (this gesture was voted Earth's official Sign of Peace in 2094). 'It is indeed an honour to be invited here – to IGGY – as guests of the MilkyFed.'

Some of The Five took this opportunity to speak.

'How many calories are there in favo–fant food?'

'Dude, my name is Egbert and I am the President of Earth.'

'Could I borrow a hairdryer, darlingk?'

Wisebeardyface waddled down from the stage and Tommy felt sure he was making a bee-line for him.

'The last shall be first,' said Wisebeardyface loudly, looking at no one in particular.

'So it should always be,' replied Guttly.

'That's stupid,' said Felkor.

As he moved closer, the lines on Wisebeardyface's orange, scaly skin became clear. He must've been very old. His long beard trailed down almost to the floor, so that he had to tread carefully lest he stood on it. He walked on two feet and was no less than three times as tall as Tommy. His long tail was festooned with grey triangular things, like slates, that grew larger as they continued up the middle of his back, then shrank to nothing as they approached his neck. His face looked a bit like that of a kindly dragon. Tommy noticed that Wisebeardyface's short arms were stuffed into a large pouch in his belly.

As soon as he was near enough, Wisebeardyface's arms shot out of his belly-pouch and he grabbed Tommy and flung him into the air. This was most alarming for Tommy. What had he done? Surely he hadn't travelled many millions of kilometres just to be killed as soon as he arrived?

Tommy flew high, spinning slightly, then plummeted towards the ground. Just as he tensed for impact, Wisebeardyface's strong arms caught him. 'Welcome, Tommy,' he said.

'Thank you,' said Tommy. And he wasn't quite sure what made him do it – maybe it was Wisebeardyface's enormous dragon-like smile or the relief from not hitting the ground – but he threw his arms around Wisebeardyface's neck and gave him a brief hug. It was such a quick hug you'd have missed it if you weren't watching carefully, but it was enough to make Wisebeardyface's face go a mild shade of scarlet. Future scholars of Tommy Storm's life would argue over many things, but one thing they did agree upon: the Wisebeardyface hug (as it became known) was Tommy Storm's first-ever hug – *excluding*, of course, any hugs he might've received as a baby, before he was old enough to remember, or any times he hugged himself (from the cold, perhaps).

Wisebeardyface stared into Tommy's face for the first time and looked a little startled.

'Are you—?'

'Yes?' said Tommy, unsure why Wisebeardyface was looking at him so strangely.

'No! It could not be! It must be a coincidence!'

'What?'

Wisebeardyface looked astonished. What had Tommy done now?

'What is it?' said Tommy again.

The kangasaurus snapped out of his trance quite suddenly and shook his head.

'Oh, nothing, sorry. Do not mind me. I must be going mad. I just thought– . . . Never mind. It is just that I have not seen a human in a long time.'

Still looking shaken, Wisebeardyface placed Tommy gently on the ground and looked towards a fountain for a few moments. Eventually, he turned to the gathered Earthlings, his composure regained.

'That, my friends,' he said, 'was a vee-eye-pee toss. The most respectful form of personal greeting known to the MilkyFed.'

In turn, he tossed the other five in the same way. Anjel*eek!* screamed of course (she went extremely high because she was so light) and, soon after his toss, Egbert threw up (having run behind his globe). ZsaZsa did a triple-salchow-loop in the air, while Felkor didn't go very high at all – mainly because he held firmly onto Wisebeardyface's beard. Guttly seemed a little embarrassed, but whether that was from the toss itself or because he feared that people could see up his robes while he spun in the air, was open to debate.

Wisebeardyface waddled back to the stage and managed to sit on the edge of it with his legs dangling down. He rubbed his chin, clearly still feeling pain from the unprompted yanking his beard had received. 'Do you recognize anything about this room?' he asked. 'We call it the *Ballroom.*'

'I used to live here,' said Egbert. 'Totally.' He looked embarrassed when nobody said anything.

The six humans, even Egbert, shrugged eventually.

Wisebeardyface sighed. 'You could say that it is modelled on the early 1950s on your planet. In the western world, that is. Or rather,' he laughed, 'I should say that your 1950s were modelled on us.' He saw the blank faces staring back at him. 'All will be revealed during training. You have a lot to learn . . . The five of you youngsters have each been allocated to separate dorms . . . Now I suggest that you all find your quarters and make yourself comfortable. Training starts tomorrow and you will need to have your wits about you – particularly as it might affect whether or not Earth is to be obliterated.'

Tommy wasn't sure if he'd heard correctly. 'Sorry?' he blurted.

Wisebeardyface looked at him and smiled. 'Yes?'

It was at this point that Guttly stepped forward. 'Em, I think what Mr Storm meant . . . That is to say, did you say, *whether or not Earth is to be obliterated*?'

'Why, yes of course, did you not—?' Wisebeardyface stopped and called over to one of the waiters standing near a particularly large vase. 'Duncan, we did mention planet obliteration on the welcoming movie? The one that was shown on Fedora.'

'No,' replied a voice. 'Remember, we said we'd leave it out and mention the refreshments instead.'

'Oh, yes. So we did.' Wisebeardyface looked towards the six Earthlings with a large dollop of humility and not a little embarrassment. 'I am awfully sorry,' he said. 'I totally forgot that we had not mentioned planet obliteration in the video. That was most remiss of me.' He clapped his hands and stood up smiling cheerfully. 'Well, not to worry. Perhaps you will join me for dinner this evening, Mr Randolph? There, I will tell you all.' Guttly nodded in a shocked, hypnotized fashion and pressed his hand to his chest. 'And then I can explain planet obliteration to everyone else tomorrow morning at assembly.'

No one quite knew what to say.

'Your globes will take you to your dorms where you will each meet your own particular dorm-mates.' Wisebeardyface swept his tail across the air – a gesture to indicate that the formalities were over. Tommy and the others stepped back into their globes. Before the openings closed, Wisebeardyface leapt from the stage, his eyes fiery. 'You must strive to get on with your dorm-mates, however strange they seem to your eyes. Your lives – everyone's life – could depend on it! . . . Do not fail us, Earthlings.'

The openings closed in the globes and they lifted off. As they floated upwards, Wisebeardyface blew a flame of fire high up between them. Seconds later, the six Earth globes morphed through the dome again, emerging at high speed, only a short distance from the other globes which were travelling fast towards the end of the tunnel, back into space.

12

A Mad Game

After another bubble journey in which his globe left the group of Earthlings to chase after four other globes and then conducted another landing procedure, the door to Tommy's globe opened and he stepped into a room in the side of IGGY. This room was to be his dormitory. It was roughly the length of one and a half lorries, and as wide as six cows standing in a straight line (head-to-tail, not side-by-side). One whole side of the room was made of glass and looked out into deep space.

'Hey-hey, Tommy!'

Something heavy jumped on his back and he fell forward, knocking over an array of red and yellow skittles. *Where had they come from?*

The only thing hurt was his pride, but he still looked around angrily until he saw Woozie standing over him, offering him a furry hand.

'Stop lazing about,' said Woozie. 'Plus, you're cheating. You're not supposed to knock the skittles over like that.'

'You've got a cheek, you have,' said Tommy. 'Jumping on my back like that, you made me—'

He stopped abruptly because a blue ball was heading for his midriff. Woozie had called, 'Here! Tommy!' just before he lobbed it. Tommy caught the solid sphere – just – buckling so it wouldn't wind him. Woozie was already picking up the skittles and putting them in a bag. They each had a little suction-pad at the bottom.

'You shouldn't throw a heavy ball like that. It's dangerous.'

'You sound like my mother,' said Woozie, slinging the bag of skittles over his shoulder. 'Kept telling me not to set my brother on fire . . . Come on. And bring that ball with you – we need it.'

Before anyone thinks of reporting Woozie to the police, please bear in mind that the skin under Woozie's brother's fur – as with all wibblewallians – was completely fireproof, so setting fire to his fur wouldn't be dangerous. It would be embarrassing for a while, until the fur grew back, much like a human having an eyebrow shaved off.

Woozie skipped up a spiral staircase towards an entrance of sorts. The entrance led into a long, rectangular, glass room that looked like a see-through container attached to the inside wall and ceiling of the dormitory. This oblong 'tube' was two metres wide and ran the length of the dorm.

'Where are you going?' asked Tommy.

'You'll see.'

Tommy wondered if there were any more dorm-mates, but no one else was in sight so he followed Woozie up the staircase. The entrance at the top was very strange. It looked like a very long, heavy, rubber sock was attached to a football-sized hole in the glass. The rubber sock became narrower and narrower, until it was only a couple of centimetres wide and hanging down from the hole like an elephant's trunk. Woozie unzipped the end of this trunk, prised a tiny part of it apart and started sticking his head into it. It seemed ludicrous to Tommy. Like trying to pull a tiny washing-up glove over your head.

Woozie spoke before his mouth was covered. 'Gimme a push when I'm half-in.'

He squirmed and twisted and soon, somehow, he was half-way in. Tommy grabbed his legs and pushed. After an exhausting minute, Woozie disappeared into the room. (Some professional floating-bowling players have assistants called Middwyves who help them in and out of anti-gravity courts.)

'WeeeHiiiiiiii!' yelled someone below.

Tommy looked down and saw three 'people' who'd suddenly appeared and were scrambling over a set of five bunk-beds (two sets of two bunk-beds side-by-side and then a fifth bunk suspended crossways over the other four). There were no ladders and the three wild creatures were making use of a springboard instead. Twice, Tommy saw a creature over-shoot the top bunk and slam himself or herself off the wall on the other side.

When they all eventually made it onto the top bunk, they leapt down and opened automatic sliding cupboards, taking out balls of various kinds and foam mallets and little space-ships the size of hamburgers (which flew across the room when you let them go). One of the three looked human and she was going completely bananas – much worse than the other two. But she suddenly became serious as soon as one of the toy spaceships hit the glass window looking out to space and broke in two.

'Now that was silly,' she said. 'We really should be more serious. And you two should be less childish. You'll get us all in trouble.'

She was wearing blue dungarees and had blonde hair, pulled into two pigtails. Her bossiness worked, because the other two – a reptile-like creature in red pyjamas and a huge hairy bear-like creature in mustard-coloured undies – started tidying the place up.

From his vaunted position, Tommy scanned the layout of the dorm. Just behind him, a large curtain, patterned with images of spacecraft, covered the entire wall. To his immediate right was the exit to space and then a wall of glass providing a glorious view. At the far end of the dorm, beyond the bunks and cupboards, was a door that led (he'd later find) to the bathroom.

People in Burdynumnum Houses Shouldn't Throw Stones
(cos they'll bounce off the ceiling and fall on top of them)

For simplicity, I'll use the word *glass* throughout this tale to refer to the toughened see-through material found throughout IGGY. The real name of the substance is *burdynumnum* and it's 7,717 times stronger than the substance Earthlings know as 'glass'. Of course, a flashscimitar can cut through burdynumnum like butter (I'll explain flashscimitars later).

Realizing he'd been distracted, Tommy pushed the ball ahead of him and dived head-first through the hole – into the wide end of the rubbery trunk that Woozie had left hanging inside the room. (This is the easier and correct way to enter a floating-bowling alley.)

The trunk got narrower, but after some pulling from Woozie – *POP!* – he was in. And instead of falling in a heap, he floated in the air and was moving fast behind Woozie to the end wall. Together they banged heavily against it.

'This is an anti-gravity court,' said Woozie. 'That's why it's so difficult to get in. They have to separate it from areas of gravity.'

'How did you know what this was?' Woozie seemed to know so much more than he.

'Oh, we have loads of anti-gravity courts on Friggle. Normally use them as floating-bowling alleys . . . Let me show you – it's great fun.' Woozie moved to the far end of the court and started to set up the red skittles, upside-down (stuck to the ceiling). Once finished, he closed the zip on the end of the trunk, pushed it back through the entrance hole and pulled a glass screen down over the hole. Then he moved the length of the alley and stuck the yellow skittles on the ceiling. 'Red or yellow?' he said.

'Sorry?'

'Sorry. You always say that . . . Want to be red or yellow?'

'Red,' said Tommy, not sure what he was getting into.

'OK, that's your end then . . . Down you go.'

Tommy glided down to the far end, grabbed the ball, which was floating near his skittles, and turned to face Woozie. 'What are the rules? I've never played this before.'

'Oh, it's easy,' said Woozie, moving towards the middle of the tubular court. 'Put this on.' He threw a piece of material towards Tommy and it floated slowly towards him. 'Over your eyes. Like this.' Woozie put the material over his eyes like a blindfold.

Tommy put the ball between his knees, then put on the blindfold. He couldn't see a thing.

'OK,' shouted Woozie. 'When I flick this switch, we wait five seconds, then the game lasts three minutes. Some buzzers will sound at the end – then we remove the blind-folds. Rules are simple. Soon as you catch or lift up the ball you have to throw it. No holding on and travelling. The aim is to stop the ball knocking over any of your red skittles, while trying to knock over as many of my yellow skittles as possible.

And if you remove your blindfold at any time during the game, you lose the contest . . . Got it?'

Tommy wasn't sure he got it. He'd just travelled halfway across the galaxy and then had the head of the MilkyFed mention something about obliterating his planet. Surely, Wisebeardyface had been mistaken when he mentioned obliterating Earth. Yes, thought Tommy, I must've misheard him or imagined it.

'Here goes,' shouted Woozie.

Humming and drumming sounds started. The roof opened over the dormitory and the rectangular glass tube floated into a wide-open space. Now the tube was free to rotate sideways or lengthways or at any angle it chose and it started twirling and spinning quickly. (This was designed to eliminate cheating by competitors. Since there's no gravity in the sealed tube, it makes no difference to those inside what way the tube is moving. It appears stationary to them. However, if you remove your blindfold and look through the tube's walls, you can quickly become very dizzy and disorientated indeed.)

'We're both supposed to do five somersaults,' yelled Woozie, 'before the humming stops.'

After a few somersaults, Tommy didn't know which way he was facing because there was no gravity to tell him which way was down. The humming stopped and he flung the ball towards where he thought Woozie's skittles stood.

BANG!

The ball hit his knee and then went who knows where. 'Ow!' he yelled.

'Forgot to mention,' said Woozie. 'The ball is extremely bouncy in anti-gravity conditions . . . Ow! Here it is.'

The next three minutes were something of a blur. By the end

of it, Tommy knew how the walls of a squash court must feel after a particularly aggressive game. The ball hit every part of his body half a dozen times and it was the knowledge of this pain and a self-preservation instinct that taught him to hear the ball moving through the air. He didn't get hit once in the last thirty seconds and even managed to catch the ball between his legs before the final buzzer went.

'Ahh!' he screamed when he peeled off his blindfold. The tube was still moving like a flipped coin in a hurricane, which was pretty disconcerting for Tommy, who was expecting a calm stillness. It made him feel like throwing up.

'Keep your blindfold on till the second buzzer goes,' said Woozie.

'*Now* you tell me!'

The tube slowed to a stop, floated back to its original position and the dorm ceiling closed. Then the second buzzer went. Through the glass, Tommy could see the three people below clapping heartily. He looked around and realized he was upside-down, facing the corner beyond his own skittles. How humiliating. He must've been facing that direction for the whole game. He'd probably knocked down more red skittles than yellow ones with his own throws.

'Not too bad.' Woozie's hand was on his shoulder. 'You did OK.'

'Very funny,' said Tommy, turning around.

'It *is* funny,' said Woozie. 'You did good.'

Tommy looked down the tube and saw four of the yellow skittles were no longer attached to the ceiling. A better outcome than he'd guessed. But sure enough, when he looked around, he saw *seven* red skittles floating aimlessly. Just as he'd expected . . . He'd lost.

But at least Woozie was pretending he'd done OK.

'Closest I ever came to losing,' added Woozie.

'The closest?' Was Woozie making fun of him now?

'That's why I was chosen to come here.'

'I don't . . . ?' Tommy was lost.

'Floating-bowling – I'm a national champion.'

It didn't sink in straight away – and he had no idea how he'd done it – but in his first-ever game of floating-bowling, Tommy had given the Friggle under-12s champion a run for his money.

Is *Squish* the same as *Squash*?

Anti-gravity courts are often used for a sport called *squish,* which is remarkably like the Earth-game *squash*, except that the two sports having absolutely nothing whatsoever in common, apart from the fact that their names sound the same if you try and pronounce them under-water. Squish is really a spectator sport (unless you're a 'bit different' or strangely itchy) as it involves seeing how many people you can get into an anti-gravity court in under six days, using nothing other than brute force and a lubricant owned by squish's main sponsor.

For those of you with pay-per-view, the popular programme *Xtreme Squish* is banned in TeCKsAss, which is a lone star-system, located far out on the 'right wing' of the Milky Way.

⟶ 13 ⟵
MORE NEW FRIENDS

'Not bad going,' said the girl in dungarees as Tommy and Woozie returned back down the spiral staircase to the dormitory floor. 'I suppose you're a national champion like Woozie?'

Before Tommy could respond, the enormous bear-like creature stepped forward, ruffled his unkempt hair without moving either of the two enormous arms by his side and gave him a hug that seemed to clamp him from all angles, burying him in a wall of fur. 'I'm Rumblethunderbumbles,' he said when he finally released Tommy with a grin. 'You're good at floating-bowling, you know . . . I always get stuckskeeys, climbing into glass courts.' (*Stuckskeeys* was his way of saying *stuck*.)

Rumbles, as Tommy came to call him, was well over two metres tall, with feet like loaves of bread and even though he had broad shoulders, he was pear-shaped. His fur was charcoal grey and his wide eyes were a deep orangey brown. The only thing he was wearing was a rather moth-eaten pair of mustard undies. Although he was a *thunderbumble*, he really did look like a big bear – except, Tommy noticed, that he had three arms. His third arm stemmed from the centre of his shoulder-blades. Sometimes he let this arm hang limply down his back, but most often it curled round his neck and hung loosely down his chest. (You may not be surprised to learn that thunderbumbles have produced many Milky Way boxing champions – the hidden third arm can come in very handy at crucial moments. They're also great masseurs.)

Rumbles stepped back, a little bashful after the hug, and knocked over a chair behind him. He caught the chair with his third arm before it hit the floor, but this caused him to overbalance and bang against the table close by, making a large bowl and jug slide off the edge. 'Ooops-a-dungly,' he exclaimed as he twisted his bulk, flung himself backwards and caught the jug and bowl – before anything spilt – with his first two arms. (A dungly is a flower said to be similar to a daisy, although no living creature has ever seen one.)

The big furry mass made a strange spectacle, lying on his back, with his third arm curling round his neck holding a chair aloft and his other two arms outstretched, balancing a bowl and a jug.

'I'm not clumsy, you know,' he said, looking up at Tommy. 'Who else could've caught all this stuff? I tell you, if there's one thingskeey I'm definitely *not*, it's *clumsy*.'

In case you're wondering, talkie-maxes and waxes are specially calibrated so that people's accents and quirky ways of speaking (in their own language) are reflected in the translation. Among thunderbumbles, using words like 'thingskeey' in place of 'thing' was considered a bad habit (like smoking is on Earth). That's probably the reason many kids continued to do it. Rumbles' father would throw prickly pears at his son whenever he heard him using such 'gibberish' – not realizing that Rumbles loved being bombarded with prickly pears.

'Yes, well, for the childish behaviour you've been forced to witness, a trillion apologies,' said a dragon-like creature addressing Tommy. He was kind of pink and yet sort of blue, though some might argue that he was greenish.

'I'm not childishskeeys,' said Rumbles, still prostrate on the floor.

'Yes, well . . .' repeated the dragon-like fellow, clearly unconvinced. Then he turned back towards Tommy. 'If I may introduce myself . . . My name is Sum-Wun-Saurus.'

He looked like a smaller, differently coloured version of Wisebeardyface, except that he had a small pair of wings folded neatly on his back (they looked far too small to ever carry a creature of his weight). He had purple eyes and, from the side, when he smiled, you could see about fifty gleaming teeth peeking out from half a foot of open mouth. Summy, as Tommy came to call him, lifted both arms out of his front pouch and shook Tommy's hand vigorously with both of his. 'To meet you, a pleasure. A pleasure most absolute. Quite unusual you look, I have to say – and most interesting.'

'Sorry we missed you arriving,' said Rumbles. 'We must've been in the bathroom looking for my undies.'

Tommy wasn't sure how he should respond to this so he said simply: 'My name's Tommy and I'm from Earth.' It was said to the group as a whole, a little breathlessly – since he was still recovering from the three-armed hug and somewhat relieved that Summy hadn't given him a *vee-eye-pee* toss.

'Super-nova! An Earthling you are!' said Summy.

'But you don't seem too unfriendly,' said Rumbles.

Woozie laughed. 'Hasn't bitten me once. Not yet anyway.'

'Billions of you on that planet, there is. So I have read,' said Summy, getting quite excited. 'Is that correct? A school project I did on it once. Fifty words long, it was, of data mainly consisting. Breed like rabbitaliahs apparently, do Earthlings. Is it true that only 40,077 kilometres is the equatorial circumference of your planet?'

Tommy never got to answer any of these questions as the girl in dungarees stepped forward.

'Tommy, this is Marielle,' said Woozie.

A pair of eyes, one bright blue, the other hazelnut brown, looked into Tommy's eyes. 'Hi,' said Marielle. She looked him up and down. 'What a funny suit you're wearing.'

'Hi,' said Tommy, wondering if he should explain that he'd been forced to wear the ski-suit by NUTS. He did feel quite silly – which was remarkable given that Rumbles, Summy and Woozie looked so strange to him. Marielle shook his hand and gave a small curtsy. Her hand was very small and smooth and it was only when she stood back that Tommy saw her hands clearly. They both had thumbs, but only three fingers.

She suddenly burst out laughing. 'Oh my goodness! Look! You've got *four* fingers plus a thumb on both hands. How incredible.'

The others all crowded round, grabbing his hands in turn.

'Yes, he does. Look.'

'Extraordinary.'

'What's this extra one for?'

Now that he looked closely, Tommy could see that everyone else had three fingers and a thumb on their hand and he wasn't able to give anyone a good reason for the exis-tence of the finger next to his little finger. It really didn't do much, he finally admitted. Maybe helped with extra grip or something. The attention on him was beginning to wane when Marielle burst out laughing again.

'I just thought of something,' she said.

'What?' said Rumbles.

'Oh nothing. I'm just being silly. I was just imagining if . . .'

'What?'

'No, it's really too silly, but imagine if he had an extra toe on each foot as well.'

'What, you mean *five* toeskeeys?'

'Don't be ridiculous,' said Woozie.

'Don't be so mean.'

The four of them were standing in a tight circle jabbering at each other.

'Yeah, you really go overboard sometimes, Marielle. Tommy's my friend – even if he did knock over three of my skittles.'

'*Four* skittles over he knocked.'

'You only know me an hour or so – how can you say I go overboard *sometimes*?'

'He's right. You were overboardskeeys. OOPS!'

'Ow! You stood on my foot!'

'It wasn't *my* faultskey. I was trying to balance on one leg.'

'Be more careful.'

'A creature who inhabits Hadrius Seven, there's supposed to be. Four and a half toes they're said to have.'

'Rubbish.'

'No wayskeey.'

'But *four* is the maximum possible. It's a universal constant.'

'Eh-hem.' Tommy cleared his throat loudly and still everyone kept arguing. Eventually, he peeled a sock off his foot and threw it into the middle of the group. It stuck to Rumbles' fur and the three-armed bear shrieked as though it were a creepy-crawly. In the same instant, he jumped backwards and started rolling on the ground, trying to shed it. He bumped into a cupboard door and it opened, spilling all its contents on top of him.

'I'm not clumsy,' cried the enormous creature. 'That wasn't my fault. I'm not clumskeey, I tell you.' Then he remembered the sock, brushed all the toys off his belly and started rolling frantically again.

'It's really very clean,' Tommy yelled. 'It's been soaked in a floating globe for quite some time.'

There was a sudden gasp from Summy who stood paralysed, staring at Tommy's foot. One after another, everyone else did the same.

'It's perfectly alright,' said Tommy, wiggling his toes. 'All Earthlings have five toes.'

'Really?' said Summy, who seemed particularly astonished. *'Everyone?'*

Tommy nodded. It was true – as far as he was aware, anyway. He looked, and yes, all the others had four toes on their feet, although he couldn't tell with Marielle because she was wearing silver rubbery trainers.

After everyone got over the shock of eight fingers, two thumbs and ten toes, they all sat down in a semicircle at a table by the large window looking out to space and had a favo-fant supper. This time, favo-fant goggles were supplied, so Tommy could actually see his chosen sweet-n-sour chicken with rice, followed by hot apple tart and cream. It was quite delicious.

In the chat and banter that went on, he learned that Summy was actually a kind of dinosaurus and that dinosauri of many varieties were common on many of the MilkyFed planets and their moons. It was Summy's history and geography knowledge, together with his unique ability to chant the seven times tables using binary numbers, that had lead to his selection from the planet Uh-oh-Ithinktheysaurus.

If you're not sure what binary numbers are, ask someone nerdy. They're very boring actually – the numbers that is, not the nerds . . . OK, so they both are.

Summy was only a toddler – five years old in Ithinktheysaurus terms, but each of those years was worth

101

twelve Earth years, so he could've almost applied for a bus pass on Earth if he didn't have such a fear of double-decker things. (He was horrified when Tommy once told him about double and even triple cheeseburgers.)

I say *he* because Tommy thought that Summy was possibly a male at first (which Summy was disgusted to hear some years later), but Summy was in fact a female. The youngest daughter in a family of twenty-three to be precise. It was the make-up box and the high-heeled roller-blades under Summy's bottom bunk (she flatly refused to sleep over anyone else) that clarified matters for Tommy.

If there are any non-Earth readers amongst you, you'll know that male dinosauri have been known to wear high-heels and make-up, although most of these present game shows on TV TV – a sort of intergalactic television station.

It turned out that Rumbles was neither male nor female exactly and yet he – or should I say *she* – was both male *and* female. Confused? Well Rumbles was a species of thunder-bumble from the planet Shaggyfurmop, and all thunderbumbles are both male and female. When a thunderbumble is in a good mood (most of the time) they exhibit all the best male and female characteristics. But when they're annoyed, drunk or itchy, they exhibit all the worst male and female characteristics. (Throughout this tale I'll use *he* or *she* depending on which is most appropriate for Rumbles' state of mind at the time, which may even vary during sentences.) Although thunderbumbles can give birth to baby thunderbumbles after eating a peculiar type of strawberry jam, most young thunderbumbles have two parents, and the parents swap around being mummy and daddy once a year on the youngster's birthday. This causes some diffi-culties when a couple has two or more kids who have different birthdays, as a parent may have to play daddy to one child and mummy to another child for a few months at a time. The fact that there are nine Shaggyfurmop years to every Earth year means that birthdays come around quite often in a thunder-bumble household. It also meant that Rumbles, who was thirteen, would be under one and a half in Earth terms.

Because Rumbles and Summy did most of the talking (and because Rumbles kept knocking plates and glasses off the table with one of her three elbows – but then catching them before they hit the floor), Tommy learned little about Marielle, except that *Marielle* was short for her full title: *Most-Awsomely-Radiant-ickle-Elegant-Lusciously-Laughterful-Empress* and that she was an *elquinine* rather than a human. From what he could gather, the main differences between an elquinine and a human were the number of fingers and toes (Marielle did have eight toes in total), the fact that elquinines can breathe underwater without artificial breathing apparatus, that they never get hiccups and, most importantly, that they're genetically incapable of trimming hedges into neat shapes. (On the planet Wild-Elqui-9, hedges are generally allowed to grow very wild indeed.)

Rumbles became a focal point of laughter when she kept thinking of dessert during her main course, so that she'd get a type of Shaggyfurmop vegetable and a type of Shaggyfurmop ice-cream in the same mouthful. During dinner, Tommy couldn't help noticing that the walls in the dormitory changed colour. They turned a soft yellow from a deep orange and surely they'd been bright red when he first arrived. The view out to space was enchanting and he stared out, finding it harder to concentrate on the chatter once people stopped giving personal information and started speculating on the size of IGGY and such things. At one stage, while they were eating, a glass globe flew past the window, stopped outside the dorm and a door opened from the dorm into the globe. The globe vomited a pile of bags and cases onto the floor, the door closed again and the globe whisked off into space.

'My bags!' cried Marielle and everyone stopped eating for a while to bring the bags over beside the bunks. Tommy found his small cerise hold-all and then made three trips to carry over all Marielle's bags. Everyone except Marielle had a single bag in which they'd compressed their vital belongings. 'How could I know if it would be hot or cold here?' she explained.

After dinner, the walls turned a darkish blue and then, quite suddenly, Wisebeardyface appeared in the middle of the table. Only Tommy jumped back at the suddenness of the apparition.

'Greetings, children of the galaxy,' he said, his eyes staring past them towards the bunk-beds. 'Your dorm shall be known as the *Dream5s*. Each of you has been ranked number *five* by your people and so the odds are more greatly stacked against you. Tomorrow sees the start of your challenges and your training. You are honoured to represent your peoples and your planets and I hope you do them justice . . . There will be an assembly in the morning for all the dorms – from the Brillo1s to the Dream5s – in the AlphatronRoom at thirty-eight tempusfugits. Classes will commence after that. Good luck.'

'That's in six tempusfugits from now,' said Woozie.

And you think *you*'ve been jet-lagged!?

The MilkyFed uses a 53 tempusfugit clock (a tempusfugit is about 1½ Earth hours) and each set of 53 tempusfugits represents almost 3.3125 MilkyFed days. This means that bedtime is at a completely different time every day. As an Earthling, until you get used to it, you can feel very jet-lagged while on MilkyFed time. Wherever practical, I'll endeavour to convert all MilkyFed time references into Earth seconds, minutes, hours, days, weeks and so on.

'Fantastic project-o-beam technology,' said Summy. 'Like Wisebeardyface was standing here actually, it looked.'

'What? That was just a projection of Wisebeardyface? Like a 3-D movie?' Tommy couldn't believe it. He thought Wisebeardyface had somehow transported himself into the dormitory.

'An assembly in the AlphatronRoom,' said Woozie. 'Where's that?'

'How to get there – I think I know,' said Summy.

'I like the name Dream5s,' chirped Rumbles. 'Anyone else want the last piecekeeys of favo-fant?' She just caught another glass with her third arm before it hit the floor.

Marielle stood up and looked very serious. 'Excuse me,' she broke in. There was still some chatter because Woozie was offering to share the last piece of favo-fant and Rumbles was muttering something about not being clumsy. 'Excuse me!' shouted Marielle. Everyone shut up and stared at her.

'I'd just like to say,' she said, 'for the record – that they've made some mistake. I should really be in the top dorm. The *Number Ones* or whatever they're called. They'll probably move me tomorrow. I'm an empress after all.'

'Eh, also me,' said Summy. '*Not an empress*, but in the first ranked dorm I should be. With us dinosauri, a sack-race and a toe-nail-biting competition the final ranking exam consisted of. If they'd stuck to history and geography, number one I'd most certainly have been ranked.'

Rumbles said she was ranked last because she'd slept in and missed the ranking tests.

According to Woozie, the only reason he was ranked fifth was because his group of five (including one other wibble-wallian) had been allowed to do their written test as homework and, overnight, Woozie's pet alsayshun had eaten all his work. (An alsayshun is a species best described as a cross between a Yorkshire terrier, a piranha and a postman.) Next morning, the examiners refused to believe Woozie's excuse and awarded him last place.

While Woozie was telling his story, everyone started getting ready for bed. After it was agreed to give Summy one of the bottom bunk-beds, they drew lots and Rumbles was given the very top bunk, Woozie and Tommy the two underneath. Much to her disgust, Marielle drew the remaining bottom bunk. Then, in turn, each of the Dream5s used the bathroom – which was really a floating globe located through the door at the end of the dormitory.

When Tommy went through the door with his toothbrush and toothpaste, he jumped into the pool below and swam around for a bit. He wondered if any inhabitants of the space-station could look out their bedroom windows and see him (luckily, he hadn't yet heard about *peeping-tomaliens*). Looking up, he noticed there was an empty globe, much smaller in size, attached to the outside of the floating globe. It was attached a metre or so above the water-level and there was a big pipe coming out the top of it that wound back into IGGY. Tommy brushed his teeth over a little basin on the far side of the pool and then realized that he needed to go to the toilet. Badly.

What should he do? Surely he wasn't supposed to go here, in the water. Imagine the embarrassment if all the inhabitants of IGGY were called in to see what he'd done. Eventually, as he crossed and uncrossed his legs, he saw a faint square on one wall of the globe – and written in the middle of it, in ridiculously transparent print, were the words:

EXTERNALIZATION OF INTERNAL WASTE

Tentatively, he pressed the square and immediately the glass barrier between the two globes melted away. He grabbed the handles of a glass ladder and climbed into the smaller globe. As soon as he was in, the glass barrier returned between the globes and a voice spoke: 'Are you here for a number one, a number two, a number three, a number four or a combination of these?'

He wasn't sure what a number three or a number four were, so he thought he'd just chance a number one to begin with.

'One,' he said solemnly.

'Curtains or no curtains?' the voice said.

'Curtains.'

Some paisley curtains fell from nowhere, pressing themselves tightly around the walls of the globe, but leaving a gap for the pipe entrance above.

'Remove undergarments and prepare for procedure.'

Tommy had difficulty removing his ski-suit and he hadn't touched his undies when a buzzer sounded and all gravity was suddenly removed from the curtained globe. He started floating aimlessly until a roar, like a powerful vacuum-cleaner, started coming from the pipe above. Tommy spun in the air until he was upside-down, did the necessary arrangement of undies and allowed the suction to pull him up towards the hole at the top. Eventually, he was sitting upside-down over the pipe-hole and the suction felt like a pleasant breeze across his skin.

After a few seconds the voice repeatedly said: '*Finished? Finished? Finished?*'

When he was done, he said 'Yes' quite firmly and the suction stopped suddenly, gravity was reactivated and he fell in a heap at the bottom of the globe.

'You bruised your shoulder?' said Woozie from his bunk-bed when Tommy explained what had happened. 'What were you doing? A number *six*? . . . I only do them once a year.'

Woozie explained that you're only supposed to say *Yes* (meaning you're done) when you've twirled yourself round and your legs are dangling downwards. For Tommy that would leave a six-centimetre drop, for Woozie a sixty-centimetre drop. But poor Rumbles . . . Going to the loo was always an exercise in yoga for him.

Funnily, Rumbles was beginning to get cranky for another reason (although it wasn't so funny for him because she was now even more bruised than Tommy). Whereas both Woozie and Tommy bounced onto the springboard in front of the bunk-beds and landed on their bunks first go, Rumbles wasn't so accurate. The first time, she took a run-up from the bathroom door, bounced heavily on the springboard, flew over all the bunks and hit the back wall in an upside-down position. Twice she landed on top of Woozie, who was so annoyed that he knocked Rumbles back onto the floor with a fierce barrage of pillow blows.

Eventually, Rumbles made it – her third arm just catching the top headboard as it looked like she was over-shooting once again. Moments later, the walls in the dormitory went charcoal grey and the lights started to dim. Everyone was in bed and Tommy changed into his pyjamas under his dormi-cover.

Those of you reading in bed may be interested to know that dormi-covers are as thin as a sheet, but they can be very warm or very cool depending on your requirements. They're made of a material that calculates your body temperature and then applies enough heat or coolness to keep your body at that constant temperature during the night. They're particularly good for storing snowballs during the day.

Candy-striped pyjamas had been laid out for everyone on top of five large silver chests, each bearing the name of one of the Dream5s. The chests were for storing bags, clothes and belongings. As well as pyjamas, a few sets of new MilkyFed clothes were also neatly folded in piles atop the chests. These clothes fitted the Dream5s perfectly, since, unbeknownst to Tommy or anyone else, everyone's exact body measurements had been taken automatically while they travelled to IGGY in the floating globes.

It felt a long time to Tommy since he'd last been in bed. He twisted and turned, trying to get comfortable, finally settling on his side – which afforded a perfect view out of the window, at the swirl of stars and planets and moons outside.

'Did you know,' said Summy to no one in particular, 'that further and further away from each other, all the stars in the Milky Way are actually moving? And that the Milky Way itself, from all the other galaxies is moving further away.'

'I'd very much like it if your bed could move further and further away from mine,' said Marielle, who was being kept awake by the constant rustling of Summy's wings.

'Anyone seen my undieskeeys?' asked Rumbles.

The walls gradually lost all colour and Tommy started to snuggle into his bunk. There was something about this place. Strange, yet nice. He felt as though he was being watched at all times. Not in a bad, scary way – more like being *watched over*. Yes, that was it.

Woozie reached across and prodded him, disturbing his thoughts. 'You awake?' he whispered.

'I am *now*.'

'So why are *you* ranked fifth?'

From the sound of the breathing below and the snoring above, it seemed that everyone else was asleep.

'It's a long story,' said Tommy.

'Can't be that long.'

'Well, it's . . . How can I put this?' Tommy thought for a second. It was incredible how excitement made you forget about some things. 'It's mostly down to my stutter. And my hair.'

'Your hair?'

'Yes. The way it always flops around my face.'

'But your hair doesn't flop,' said Woozie. 'I'd say you've the wildest, spikiest hair I ever seen.'

'Stop teasing me. That's not funny.' You'd think you could get away from teasing once you climbed into a rocket and it flew you halfway across the galaxy.

'I'm not teasing,' insisted Woozie. 'Feel for yourself.'

Woozie was annoying him now, so Tommy pulled the covers over the back of his head so that Woozie couldn't see him and concentrated on watching a series of shooting stars in the distance.

'And what's this about a stutter?' asked Woozie. 'I never heard you stutter once.'

What!? Tommy watched the shooting stars disappear out of sight and let Woozie's words sink in. He hadn't . . . *Had he . . . ?* No, it was impossible . . . And yet . . . *Maybe* . . . He thought about it for a moment, reliving all the conversations of the day.

'You're . . . By Jiminee!' He whipped around, facing the wibblewallion. 'Woozie, you're right. I haven't stuttered once since . . . since . . . well, since I left Earth.'

'Ssshhh!' said a cross voice below.

Woozie lowered his voice to a whisper. 'And feel your hair.'

Tommy ran his fingers through his hair and, sure enough . . . *No . . . It couldn't be . . . No way!*

110

It was all sticking out at wild angles! *Spiky!* Of its own accord . . . *Unbelievable* . . . What had happened to him?

'Told you,' said Woozie, sensing Tommy's delight. 'Night-night.' And then, as an afterthought: 'Shame about the upcoming planet obliteration, isn't it?'

What?

A few seconds later Woozie fell asleep. In fact, everyone but Tommy slept soundly that night. Evidently, Wisebeardyface had said it clearly to every last one of them. Tommy hadn't imagined it, after all. He tossed and turned feeling guilty at being so happy about his hair and his lack of stutter when clearly, now, his planet really was going to be destroyed.

━ 14 ━
A CONFRONTATION

IGGY was so large that most people negotiated travel within her by making use of *wigholes*. Wigholes are large pizza-sized holes that look pitch black inside, no matter what angle you peer into them from. They're generally located on a wall, though they can theoretically be found on any flat surface or even suspended in air, so long as there's a force to hold them in position.

When you jump through a wighole (generally, head-first), any part of your body entering the hole shrinks to an alarming degree. For this reason, no matter how large an object, it will almost certainly fit through a regular-sized wighole. Wigholes work in pairs and so if you jump through one wighole, you emerge out of another located somewhere else.

Most engineers agree that wigholes are made from specks of dust from the powdered remains of an extinct black hole, but no one is sure as the manufacturers of wigholes keep the secret ingredient very secret indeed.

━━━━━

Next morning, once the Dream5s were dressed and ready to go to assembly, they noticed that the large spacecraft-patterned curtain at the back of the dormitory (at the opposite end to the bathroom) was no longer draped across the back wall. The wall was now exposed and there were twenty-three pizza-sized holes dotted across it, at varying heights. Over every hole was a plaque, and each plaque was encased in glass and engraved with a single word. Tommy scanned some of the words: *FutilityRoom, StableRoom, GarageZone, WindyRavine, Le-Luuhhvv-Boo-Dwar, Atticus, UnstableRoom, BizzR, KangasaurusCourtGallery, TrepidationRoom*. The only name he recognized was *AlphatronRoom*.

'Where we're going that is,' said Summy, noticing Tommy's eyes fixed on a particularly high plaque.

Woozie moved the springboard away from the bunk-beds and in front of the wall. Then each of the Dream5s lined up behind each other at the far end of the room to get a good run at it. There was no real discussion as everyone except Summy seemed a bit tired. They were lined up in the order in which they'd clambered out of bed that morning – Summy first, followed by Marielle, Tommy, Woozie and, lastly, Rumbles.

Once Summy bounced off the springboard and disappeared through the Alphatron wighole (which was over two metres off the ground), Tommy started running after Marielle. She disappeared through the wighole and a few seconds later Tommy launched himself into the air in the same way as the other two. The hole grew enormously large once he entered it – it seemed as vast as a starless universe and twice as dark. As his head travelled further inside, he looked back but couldn't see any light. The dormitory had disappeared and for an eerie moment there was a nothingness and a silence that was so absolute, it made him realize that he'd never seen real darkness or heard real silence until this moment. Before he had a chance to feel frightened, the dark universe seemed to turn itself inside-out and spit him into a screaming light.

A casual observer in the AlphatronRoom would've seen Tommy Storm fly out of a hole in the wall and land on a large crash-mat below. He just missed hitting Marielle, who rolled away in time and clambered to her feet beside Summy. Tommy felt a little winded and still dazzled by the sudden light of the AlphatronRoom – and his efforts to reorientate himself were not helped by Woozie flying out of the wighole and landing squarely on top him.

'What're you—?' said Woozie, disentangling a leg from Tommy's arm. The furry fellow rolled away in alarm. 'Move it! Rumbles is coming next.'

Realizing the danger of his position, Tommy scrambled off the mat.

'Welcome,' said a voice that echoed around the room. It sounded like Wisebeardyface.

Tommy saw that there were about twenty people already in the round room and they were all lying down on their tummies. Then he noticed the floor. It was made of glass and when you looked through it, you saw the most enormous drop. This drop went on for thousands of metres, and either side of it were lots of bright windows, some curtained, some not.

Tommy and the others lay down on the floor like everyone else. It was definitely the best way to be because when you were standing and looked down, the drop was so great it made you feel as if you were going to fall over.

'IGGY Cadets! Glad you could all make it,' said Wisebeardyface's voice.

A tiny round speck in the distance started to grow larger and then it became apparent that it was a smoked-glass half-globe, travelling fast towards them. (It had a transparent flat side which wasn't visible from where they lay.) The half-globe headed straight for them until it hit one side of the glass floor and jolted everyone. Next thing Tommy knew, the enormous drop had disappeared and Wisebeardyface was floating in the air in front of them with a curved smoky-white floor beneath him. Tommy wasn't sure if it was due to the trip in the wighole, but all his weight started pushing backwards onto himself and his blood started pressurizing in his veins.

'Take a look behind you,' said Wisebeardyface to all the children pressed against the glass floor.

Tommy turned and saw that the enormous drop was now behind him and there was nothing between him and the chasm below. Somehow, Wisebeardyface's half-globe had flipped the floor in the room, so that they were all upside-down looking up at Wisebeardyface. Even the crash-mat was still there, close by, stuck to the floor.

'Don't worry, you're perfectly safe,' said Wisebeardyface. 'Expect the unexpected. That's what you'll learn here.'

'We're not going to fall, are we?' said one of the children next to Tommy. He was a wibblewallian like Woozie, except that his fur was quite pink.

'No, no, the glass is very sticky and I can increase the stickiness if you like.' Wisebeardyface pressed a lever beside him, moving it from a notch that said *Very Sticky* to the next notch that said *Ridiculously Sticky*. Tommy noticed that he could no longer lift his arms off the glass. He also guessed that Wisebeardyface's half-globe was an anti-gravity room of some sort because Wisebeardyface was now suspended at a quirky angle.

'My hair!' cried a young female voice. 'Darlingk! It hates sticky things.'

'Well, then,' said Wisebeardyface, 'I do not want to delay

your classes, so let me explain everything very quickly . . . And by the way, please forgive my angle of address. I am really not used to anti-gravity conditions.' Wisebeardyface put his hands in his pouch and continued. Somehow this made him start to spin very slowly. 'The first thing I must emphasize is that my name is Lord Beardedmoustached-Wiseface-oh and if I hear any use of nicknames where I am concerned, there will be big trouble.'

There were a few giggles from the group as everyone fought the mad urge to yell out 'Wisebeardyface!'

'Cease your laughter!' boomed Wisebeardyface and something in his voice banished all mirth. 'You are now known as IGGY Cadets and over the next few weeks you will receive a vigorous training which should prepare you for the trip that five of you will take to distant galaxies. Quite simply, we will choose one of the dorms you have been divided into – most probably the Brillo1s or the Great2s. However, it is up to all of you to learn as much as you can and to prove yourselves. No dorm is guaranteed to make the trip and so you must all work together if your dorm is to be chosen. A group of judges, including me, will make the final decision . . . Any questions?'

'Yes,' said a prim voice next to Tommy. 'Might I ask, how big is IGGY?'

'Ah! Madam Sum-Wun-Saurus, if I am not mistaken . . . It is very big, really. *Large*, you might call it . . . The space-craft that five of you will take to distant galaxies is known as *SWIGS*. Over fifteen thousand people live on IGGY – most of them involved in the manufacture of SWIGS or items to be taken on the mission – although sometimes we let them off for band practice.'

Various voices piped up.

116

'What's this dangerous mission that five are to be chosen for?'

'Did you know that on Earth I was a super-hero?'

'Will the mission involve the dark and if so will we be given torches?'

'You will find out about the mission in due course,' said Wisebeardyface.

'If it's so dangerous, why are there only twenty-five of us kids here to choose from?'

'Because this way we can really see how you perform and pick the best five.'

'Why only five on the mission?'

'Due to a union dispute, we could only get five bunks on SWIGS. In any case, if five cannot achieve the mission, there is no reason why ten or twenty could.'

'What time is lunch? And can we get diet favo-fant food?'

'What kind of shampoo do you provide here, darlingk?'

'SWIGS nearly rhymes with IGGY. Is there a reason for this?'

'There is not,' said Wisebeardyface, ignoring the two previous speakers. 'No more questions? Excellent . . . As I said before, good luck.'

'Em . . .' Tommy had to say something. Clearly, Wisebeardyface was forgetting the most important thing.

'Yes . . . ? Mr Storm, isn't it?'

'Yes. Sorry, sir, I was just wondering . . . Yesterday, you mentioned something about possibly obliterating Earth. You said you'd explain it today.'

'Did I . . . ? Oh, yes, so I did. Sorry.' He pulled a coin, a small pencil, a bit of fluff and a sweet wrapper out of his pouch and examined them all as if he'd never seen them before. Then he realized there were ninety-six eyes watching him and he quickly stuffed the items back in his pouch.

The mathematicians amongst you may be interested to know that apart from those with two eyes, two of the creatures present had one eye, two had three eyes, one had four eyes and one poor (or lucky) fellow had forty-six eyes.

'I . . . I told you all about the SWIGS Craft travelling along the SickoWarpo Speed Runway, didn't I?' said Wisebeardyface falteringly as he floated before the ninety-six eyes, two of which were crossed (ZsaZsa was trying to make out the tip of her nose).

Those whose heads weren't stuck to the floor, shook them from side to side.

'Oh, dear,' said the long-bearded figure, who could see the shaking heads from his upside-down position. 'Well, let me put it simply, like this, then. In order to travel to distant galaxies, you need to travel at many times the speed of light. Otherwise, it would take far too long to get anywhere and you would all be using walking sticks or ZimmerDimmer frames by the time you reached another galaxy.' (ZimmerDimmer frames are jet-propelled walking frames for the elderly, best used in anti-gravity conditions.)

The old dinosaurus continued. 'The SWIGS Craft can travel incredibly fast, but in order to take off it needs a straight runway many, many trillions of kilometres long with as few obstacles as possible. It is very difficult to find a suitable straight runway leading from IGGY. Most straight routes from here, going in the right general direction, pass through hundreds of planets. And every time the SWIGS Craft hits a planet, it slows marginally. If this happens too many times, the SWIGS Craft cannot reach SickoWarpo speed.'

Wisebeardyface paused to chew something, then he blew a large bubble which burst around his nose. When he removed the chewing gum from his face and replaced it in his mouth,

118

he continued: 'Luckily, we have identified three possible routes for the SWIGS mission. The only trouble being, in each case there is one planet blocking the middle of the route.'

'So what?' said a recognizable voice across the floor. 'Just fly the SWIGS Craft through the middle of it and destroy the planet. It's just one planet, innit. It can't slow you too much.'

'Very good, Mr Stagwitch. That is precisely the plan.'

'But what about all the people who'd get killed in the process?' said Tommy, shocked at Wisebeardyface's flippant attitude.

'The three planets we have identified have been chosen carefully to minimize the negative impact to the Milky Way,' replied Wisebeardyface.

'I thought you said that Earth might be one of the planets.'

'Exactly . . . I did, Mr Storm. If Earth had the honour of being chosen, it would be a chance for Earth to achieve a level of glory it can never hope to attain while existing as it is. It could help in saving the Milky Way.' He noticed that Tommy looked unconvinced. 'Look, the average Earthling lives for under a hundred years, compared to most species in the Milky Way who live for many thousands of years. So, if we obliterate Earth, we will only be cutting short a few billion lives that are extremely short in any case . . . It would be much like killing a wasp on Earth at the end of the summer. Oh, sorry, I forgot! You do not have summers there any more.'

Tommy was still scowling, so Wisebeardyface continued: 'Apologies, but an Information Pack has been prepared for all of you and it will be on your bunks when you return to your dorms for lunch. It will explain about the SWIGS Mission and everything else. You should have received it yesterday, but there was a delay when Miss LeWren discovered some

119

spelling mistakes.'

It was at this point that Rumbles came flying through the wighole and smacked into Wisebeardyface. This was possible because the half-globe was touching the edge of the wighole in the AlphatronRoom, enabling Rumbles to morph through its glass. The pair then flew towards the side of the half-globe and pounded into it, leaving Wisebeardyface sandwiched between the smoked-glass wall and the three-armed thunder-bumble.

'Oh, sorry. Sorry, sir. I'm not clumsy.'

'What are you—?' How did you—?' Wisebeardyface was lost for words.

'I jumped through the wrong wighole by accident. Took for ever to get back to the dormskeey and make it through the right wighole . . . Sorry, Wisebeardyface, I—'

'*Wisebeardyface*!?' Wisebeardyface's face went red with anger and he seemed to swell in size.

'Oh, sorry – I meant Lord MoustacheLipsCleverclogs-Oh, or was it—?'

Wisebeardyface leaned back and shot a blast of fire from his mouth. The flames licked the top of the ceiling and fanned outwards, around the walls of the half-dome. For a moment, Tommy could see neither Wisebeardyface nor Rumbles. When the flames disappeared, Rumbles was patting her undies frantically.

'Fire! They're on fireskeeys!'

Wisebeardyface put out the flames with a violent sneeze and then he pushed the slightly smoking thunderbumble back through the wighole and told her not to return for at least three minutes. Before he disappeared, Rumbles gave Tommy a shrug.

'Yes, well . . .' said Wisebeardyface, his anger disappearing.

He looked down at the Cadets. 'I had better go . . . I am already late for a runway construction meeting.' He saw Tommy's concerned look. 'We will choose which planet to destroy before we choose which dorm shall be made IGGY Knights. Do not worry – we will make our decision based on the best interests of the Milky Way. Whichever planet is least deserving will be the one to go.'

'And who will make the choice?' asked Tommy, seeing Wisebeardyface blow another bubble. He was surprised how strongly he felt about his planet being proposed for destruction.

Wisebeardyface let the bubble deflate before he spoke. 'Your four tutors and I – together we will make the choice. All your tutors, like me, are Masters of the Way. You will meet those tutors presently. There is a class timetable at the back of the room.'

No one saw Wisebeardyface do anything sudden, but the next moment the floor had spun around, they were all facing downwards, looking into the enormous abyss and Wisebeardyface's half-dome was hurtling out of sight. Everyone staggered off the floor, which was no longer sticky.

Tommy saw that there were lots of species in the room besides those represented by the Dream5s. There was someone who looked like an ordinary girl, except she had two different faces on either side of her head – she spoke out of the pretty face whenever she spoke ill of people and out of the ugly face whenever she was being sweet (such creatures are called *kissentells* because if they ever kiss someone they talk about it using the mouth that wasn't involved in the kissing). Someone else looked like a human with no head. Only when this creature turned round did Tommy see that it had a third arm and its head was attached to this arm's hand (the way a large hand holds a football).

Felkor wandered over towards Tommy, flanked by the kind of round, furry creature that had played the drums in Fedora (a furballia – this one was red) and a dark brown creature who resembled a wolf standing on three legs (a toothwolf). The toothwolf, Trevor, had a dark look on his face – whether by design or due to indigestion, it was hard to tell. Brendan the furballia growled and bared a set of viciously sharp teeth.

'If yuh're gonna go soft and start stickin' up for Earth,' said Felkor, once he was close, 'yer group hasna chance o' bein' chosen to go on the expedition . . . But, hey, you havna hope anyways.'

'We'll see,' said Tommy, refusing to shrink before the larger boy. 'I think standing up for your own planet is much more important than being chosen for some expedition – no matter how prestigious it is.'

Felkor smirked and went to shove him, but Tommy stepped back and Felkor missed, falling towards the crash-mat. Felkor turned in mid-air and landed on the mat in a sitting position. He kept his composure and tried to look cool.

'I was just tryin' to sit down here. My legs get very tired, don't yuh know . . . Say, what've yuh done to your hair, Storm? Hey fellas, looks like he's been dragged through a bush backwards, innit.'

Several people looked over at this comment – particularly Marielle and another elquinine who both thought of plants the size of Iceland whenever they pictured a bush. Tommy's hair did indeed look madly spiky – especially as Egbert's and Felkor's hair had started to wilt since they entered space. There was something about the air and the gravity conditions that made *their* hair start to flop and lose all spikiness.

Everyone looked over once they heard the sound of a dog

being kicked. Repeatedly. Felkor was laughing because Woozie and Summy had moved over to stand beside Tommy.

'Who're yer friends, Storm? They look nearly as ridiculous as you . . . Me, Trevor and Brendan might just hafta teach you weaklin's a lesson.'

'Leave them alone or you'll be sorry,' said a firm voice. Everyone turned to see Marielle standing, hands on hips, looking very stern.

Again the sound of a dog being kicked. Repeatedly. 'An' just why will I be sorry, little girl?' asked Felkor, sarcastically.

Tommy was about to advise Marielle to keep out of things when a huge charcoal blur appeared from nowhere.

KERRSCHLUMMMMMPP!

Felkor had completely disappeared and Rumbles was sprawled across the crash-mat.

'I'm not lateskeeys, am I?' she asked.

There was a muffled yell from underneath him.

'Oops-a-dungly,' said Rumbles, rolling off the crumpled figure beneath her. 'I didn't mean– I'm not clumsy, you know.'

Felkor was too dazed and bleary-eyed to respond.

⚡ 15 ⚡

SPACE CLASSES

> If you are chosen to save the Milky Way (quite a dangerous mission!), you should have some idea what you are saving and why you want to save it.

This sentence was scrawled across the blackboard in the FutilityRoom where Mr Crabble would take the Dream5s for a class known as *Philosophy and Custard*.

The FutilityRoom was really an old fusty science laboratory. The floor was wooden, the old work-benches dilapidated and the cream walls stained from years of something – experiments hopefully. Tommy and the others took their seats around a large work-bench, while Crabble stood before the class on a raised platform behind a rickety desk.

'Hmm, yes, who can tell me something intelligible about the computer program, *HappinessIzzzAh 98.9*?' cried the tutor as soon as they were seated.

I inserted the word 'computer' into Crabble's speech to make his meaning clear. You see, to a MilkyFederan, a 21st-century Earth computer would be as sophisticated as an abacus is to you. MilkyFed computer programs didn't need computers. They could run on their own and when doing so often took on a form that could be touched or prodded.

Crabble, a middle-aged fellow, had tiny arms and legs, but the most enormous head, crowned with mad blue hair. The hair was quite long and stood on end as though he'd stuck his finger in an electric socket. Proportionally, he looked like a large, wild-haired potato with matches for arms and legs.

Woozie stuck up his hand. 'Is it an updated version of *HappinessIzzzAh, version 98.8*?'

The round tutor's face was actually quite human-like. It was very pudgy and one of his eyes boggled through an enormous monocle as big as a dinner plate. There was a nervous, fidgety energy about him, which was accentuated by his breathless, excited way of speaking. A pipe, the size of a guitar, protruded from the side of his mouth and he puffed on it vigorously at intervals, sending a thick pungent odour around the room.

'Splendid! Correct, wibblewallian. Hmm, spiffing, and the next update should be out in a few weeks' time, which promises to be most exciting, yes?'

'With inter-stellar efficiency has the program something to do?' said Summy eagerly.

'Yes, yes, precisely, kangasaurus! Hmm, now let me explain more fully for the benefit of your feeble minds.'

Crabble opened a drawer and removed something which he placed in his mouth. Then he blew into his pipe and an enormous bubble rose up from the end of it. The bubble looked like an ordinary soap-and-water bubble, except that it was shaped like a pyramid and was full of little numbers that were jostling forcefully with one another. Gangs of 2s were jumping on top of lone 37s and beating them up. All of the figures were arguing loudly and fights kept breaking out. Tommy noticed that the even numbers seemed more violent than the odd ones – which surprised him, but he wasn't sure why. There were a few Xs and Ys, definitely some As and Bs and a smattering of equals, addition, subtraction and division signs.

Then the pyramid-shaped bubble started to spin and a few mathematical signs that Tommy didn't recognize started to make loud noises, like an orchestra tuning up.

'Hey-ho, what you are about to see and hear has never, ever been shared with children of the Milky Way – good Lordus, no! Oh, no, no, no.'

Due to liability concerns, the manufacturer of HappinessIzzzAh stipulated that 'in the absence of exceptional circumstances, only those who have reached adulthood' could be told about the program. (You could graduate to adulthood at any time by wearing dowdy clothes and lying – supervised – on a giant marshmallow for forty-eight hours without eating any of it.)

Crabble took something silver from his pocket.

'Behold the HappinessIzzzAh program in action, yes . . .? Now, hmm, the final ingredient . . . *Infinity*.'

The pyramid had begun to look milky when Crabble tossed the silver infinity sign towards it. The small sign passed through the bubble and almost immediately the bubble went berserk.

For two minutes the angry pyramid spun faster and faster, whisking round the class at breakneck speed. This spinning whipped up a minor hurricane in the classroom so that empty stools were lifted into the air and sheaves of papers blew out of a drawer in Crabble's desk. The Dream5s cowered under the work-bench to avoid being hit by flying debris.

When the bubble came to a standstill, the hurricane disappeared and the room was full of papers gently floating to the ground. Tommy and the others climbed out from under the work-bench and peered over at the bubble. It looked very serene and was full of hundreds of tiny pyramids that each had moving pictures on their four sides.

'My, oh my! Looky-look-look!' cried Crabble, pointing to one pyramid with images of dozens of different MilkyFed species building a huge tower together. They all seemed to be helping each other and getting along very well. The moving pictures on the other pyramids showed similar scenes.

'Oh-ho, the *HappinessIzzzAh* program works out the solutions for how we can be happy,' explained Crabble. 'It does a squillion calculations a nanosecond – splendiferous! – and works out what would happen in the Milky Way under gazillions of scenarios, yes? It finds the scenario that produces the best outcome for all and tells us how we should act to achieve that outcome. Hey-ho!'

Crabble took a few puffs of his pipe and then coughed hard because some of the bubble mixture must've still been in there. When he regained his breath, he threw the pipe on the floor and continued with the lecture.

'Indeed, different versions of the program have been employed in the Milky Way for thousands of years, hmm, and it's instructed us not to have wars, not to fight, to share as much as possible and not to get involved with Morrrissshh Dancing, yes?'

Morrrissshh Dancing is a strange form of dancing that used to be practised by unfit male beings in some outlying planets of the Milky Way. To become proficient, it helps to be mad and clinically unco-ordinated.

'Why does he keep saying "*yes?*"' whispered Woozie.

Tommy didn't know and Crabble continued: 'With the help of this program, we have learnt not to steal, not to kill others for selfish gain and not to snore. Oh my! That's why all species in the MilkyFed co-operate fully with each other . . . We can

127

create more if we work together and become more efficient, yes? Efficiency equals happiness. Hey-ho!'

Crabble pressed his finger into the bubble and a nasally voice spoke that sounded not unlike the Queen of England sitting on a gerbil.

'The secret of happiness is not to try and grab things for oneself. Selfish grabbing leads to inefficiency in society. One must try to give things to others without expecting anything in return. Statistically, this results in the most efficient and harmonious society.'

'Is that *it*?' said Tommy, when the voice went silent. It seemed a bit too simple and not something that would work on Earth.

'Golly-whizz, an Earthling I supp—' The tutor's words cut off when he looked into Tommy's face.

'Yes . . . Yes, sir.'

Crabble said nothing and just stared at him – seemingly in shock – which was most disconcerting.

'What is it, sir?'

'Good Lordus, are you—?'

'Yes?'

'Heavens, have you—?'

'What, sir?'

'No, yes, no! Hmm. Must be a coincidence, yes?'

'What, sir?' This was perplexing and a little embarrassing.

'Oh, eh, nothing,' said Crabble suddenly, looking flustered. 'I must have mixed you up with . . . Hmm, never mind, yes?'

The round tutor turned and jumped into the bubble – it disappeared with a wet wink. Then he waddled up to his desk, regaining his composure.

'Lordy-lordy, I've only actually met two Earthlings before in person – and they were quite . . . hmm, well, not as bad as the ones I've read about. Splendid, spiffing, most fascinating to have an Earthling here, yes? A most fascinating planet that is. Hey-ho. Most fascinating.'

Crabble must not have met those Earthlings in a long time because he launched into the subject of Earth with the enthusiasm of an obsessed football supporter explaining the off-side rule to his (bored) girlfriend.

He said that the MilkyFed had watched Earth with interest for some considerable time. Earthlings had lived like savages in caves for many thousands of years until day-trippers from the MilkyFed started sneaking onto Earth and 'helping' Earthlings with inventions. Whenever MilkyFederans left some new technology, they'd fly off and watch the consequences from afar.

Tommy was amazed to hear that the MilkyFed was responsible for almost all the inventions that had occurred on Earth over the last few thousand years.

Crabble's full explanation is outlined in *Extra Bits no. 3*, page 421.

'So, yes, ho!' said Crabble, wrapping up. 'Many think it would be for the best if we choose Earth to be the planet that's, hmmm, destroyed by the SWIGS Craft travelling at *SickoWarpo* Speed . . . Oh my! SickoWarpo Speed is jolly fast, yes?'

What about the other two planets that are being considered for obliteration? Are they large? Do lots of people live on them? Surely there's a way to avoid destroying a planet just to travel at SickoWarpo Speed? These were some of the questions on the tip of Tommy's tongue, but before he could ask any of them, Crabble ran over to the wighole on the classroom wall.

'Gosh! Sorry. Just realized – am frightfully late. Indeed, hmm, must dash.'

He lifted the wighole deftly off the wall as if it were a black hole painted on a thin sheet of see-through plastic.

'My Lordus! Jolly late! A thousand apologies, yes?'

Then he threw the wighole in the air like a pancake and stepped under it. The wighole fell, encircling him – his head, shoulders, chest disappearing as it did so. In a fraction of a second, the wighole hit the floor and the round tutor was gone.

Anyone Feeling Car-Sick?

Certain MilkyFed craft could already travel at *BluddyFasht Velocity* (48 million times the speed of light), but no craft had yet achieved *SickoWarpo Speed*, which is 4.3 billion times the speed of light. SickoWarpo Speed is so called because, according to *Ferment's Lost Theorem*, it's the exact speed at which living beings are travelling so fast that it becomes impossible to suffer from travel sickness – unless you've just eaten cooked carrots. This can of course be simply stated using the formula:

$$[\breve{e} + (\psi x (\male + \female)/\Theta . \{ \copyright^2 . \xi \} - \sqrt{\infty} \neq 2 + (\musnote /\$)^3)].$$

It's called the *Lost* Theorem because mathematicians have lost the key to what each of the symbols in the formula stand for and therefore have no idea how to apply it.

⚡ 16 ⚡
A BRIEF WORD ABOUT
CLOTHES

As Crabble explained, all of the fashion trends that've been on Earth were planted there by MilkyFederans and reflect fashions worn by MilkyFederans themselves (see *Extra Bits no. 3*, page 421). This may explain why the silver chests that arrived in each of the IGGY Cadets' dorms on the evening of Tommy's arrival contained a variety of outfits that would be recognizable from Earth's history.

Each of the Cadets had to select a uniform for their training in IGGY. In practice, this meant that everyone had to press a combination of buttons on the inside of their clothes chest to confirm their choice of uniform, whereupon all the other clothes disappeared. From then on, Cadets only had to place their used uniform in their chest before going to bed at night and it would be there – clean and ironed – in the morning.

Despite the protests of her friends, Rumbles insisted on sticking with her mustard undies. 'I feel comfortable in them,' she explained.

Summy chose a plain yellow *ZanyFowl* T-shirt with $\sqrt{-1}$ printed in large font on the front and *It's Irrational !!* printed on the back. (ZanyFowl is a very popular MilkyFed game and $\sqrt{-1}$ is the number of the shirt worn by ZinnyDeenZinnyDann, a famous female ZanyFowl striker.)

Much to everyone's surprise, Summy dispensed with the idea of trousers, skirts or shoes.

For some classes, Woozie wore a pair of thigh-high boots and a sparkly waistcoat. Often, he wore nothing because he maintained that he was warm enough with his fur alone.

Marielle wore dungarees – a different colour every day – with a simple, thin sweatshirt underneath. Sometimes the sweatshirt was stripy, but mainly it was plain – again, a different colour every day. Marielle was the only IGGY Cadet to wear different colours every day.

The people in the other dorms wore a variety of clothes – from 1970s flares and platforms to Arabian garb. The two furballias both chose a punk style and set their fur in a *mohican* along the seam of their head (which was at an angle off-centre) as well as safety-pins through their noses. Trevor the toothwolf wore a ska suit – light grey, drain-pipe legs, with a white shirt and skinny leather tie.

Egbert Fitchly wore something resembling a cowboy outfit (with hat, without guns) topped off with a navy cape. ZsaZsa Vavannus chose a mauve, drop-waist 1920s dress – wearing it with either a mink stole or a one-feather headband, depending on her mood. (The tall, grey and white feather stuck up from the narrow headband on the left side of her head. The 'mink' was actually artificial fur.) Anjel*eek!* Jalfrezi went for roller-skates, leg-warmers and a lime-green jump-suit.

Felkor wore a burgundy velvet suit – the jacket came down to his thighs and the trousers tucked into cream stockings at the top of his calf. He had a cream shirt, ruffled at the neck and cuffs, and his black shoes sported an over-sized buckle. It was all topped with a black hat that was triangular if you looked at it from above. (Rumbles crumpled this badly when she arrived late in the AlphatronRoom and landed on top of Felkor.) Historians disagree on whether Felkor looked like Captain Hook from *Peter Pan* or King Louis IV of France. They concur that he was aiming for a regal look.

Tommy was delighted with his chest of clothes. Anything would be better than the NUTS space outfit. He finally decided on a black outfit – black trousers, black trainers and black shirt. On the night of his arrival at IGGY, he looked at himself in the reflection of the dorm's window and wondered if he looked a bit silly.

Marielle watched the boy with the spiky hair and the twinkling eyes look uncertainly at his own reflection. He stuck his thumbs into the pockets of his trousers and then removed them in case it looked silly. She didn't think he looked silly. He was really rather dashing.

So you want to know about Undies?

As with all thunderbumbles, Rumbles appeared to have an inexhaustible supply of undies. Whenever she went through the ordeal of unwrapping a new pair and promoting them to the rank of *my undies*, he'd show intense, monogamous loyalty to that specific pair (for years if necessary), refusing to wear any others. A new pair would only be opened and duly promoted when the 'old' favourite pair ended up irretrievably lost or irredeemably damaged.

A number is included on the gravestone of all dead thunderbumbles – representing exactly how many pairs of undies they wore in their lifetime. If the number is very low (below thirteen), then the thunderbumble is assured of a big funeral and a place in thunderbumble history. If the number is above 1,213 the dead thunderbumble has his name officially incorporated into *The Chunderbumble Joke Compendium*.

134

17

WORRISOME HAPPENINGS

Elsorr Maudlin raised his eyebrow and, simultaneously, the platform he was standing on lifted higher into the air. He chuckled to himself. He was feeling very pleased about being the ultimate ruler of Earth and he also enjoyed pretending that it was his eyebrow and not years of telepathy training that caused the platform to move.

He looked down on the Councillors seated around the Majestic Table and moved the platform a bit higher so they'd all have to crane their necks upwards to see him. He could get used to this presidency lark. People bowing and scraping. Everyone doing exactly what you told them. It was truly marvellous. And, he thought, Earth's citizens have it very lucky too. They now had a ruler who was superior to them in intelligence and who could make decisions for them. It wasn't their fault if they were too stupid to realize how brilliant Elsorr Maudlin really was. They couldn't be blamed for voting in Guttly Randolph as President all those years ago. But now they'd understand and grovel to the Great Elsorr. And they'd never allow Guttly to return as President.

He took out his sword and admired his reflection in its shiny steel. Maybe one of his eyebrows was getting a bit long. He tilted the sword and started trying to cut a few stray hairs.

'What was that you were saying?' he said, chopping the

first hair. He hadn't been listening to a word the boring idiots below had been chattering on about.

A number of voices spoke up.

'Well, we've agreed to enact a law which would make it illegal to sell underwater toasters. They can really be very dangerous.'

'Plus the city of Goats is considering wrapping itself in clingfilm to reduce heating costs.'

'And I have a plan to reduce poverty in the city of E-Zee-Singles. If we allow fexa-cetters to drop food parcels—'

'Yes. Yes,' said Elsorr impatiently. That Helena Jadely really bugged him. Food parcels? What was she on about? 'The first two points are fine, I agree to sign them into law, but scrap the poverty idea. I don't like poverty very much.'

Helena jumped up in a rage. Her cheeks flushing, her eyes flashing. 'How can you–? This is outrageous, Elsorr. I'm talking about kids who don't get proper meals—'

'Guards!' shouted Elsorr, brushing his eyebrow and admiring its reflection. That Helena really irritated him. Never mind the annoying things she said – the very sight of her auburn hair always made him angry. Those stupid plaits formed into circular shapes on either side of her head. Why couldn't she just backcomb her hair like most women over thirty?

From nowhere, six men in dalmatian-spotted uniforms, wearing visored helmets, appeared in the room.

'Seize Miss Jadely,' ordered Elsorr. 'She's being disrespectful to the President.'

'You can't do this, Elsorr!'

Elsorr nodded and a guard put his hand over Helena's mouth.

'Take her away. Put her in maximum-security *Domesticity*.'

A Sentence too Cruel for Words

Domesticity was the most barbaric form of imprisonment on Earth. It was designed for the very worst criminals who never seemed to mend their ways after being sent to ordinary prisons where inmates watched videos all day and received a foot massage twice a week. In *Domesticity*, the inmate was required to perform vacuuming, dusting and ironing duties all day to the sound of a high-pitched screaming noise (such activities were extinct in ordinary Earth homes, long since performed by a tiny robot that looked like a hamster wearing a large sombrero – known colloquially as *hambreros*). The high-pitched screaming noise was also activated in the middle of the night to deprive inmates of a sound night's sleep.

The guards left the room, carrying Helena as though she were a second-hand carpet. The ten Councillors around the Table started murmuring amongst themselves and for a moment it looked like some of them might stand up to Elsorr. But none of them did because the thought of *Domesticity* was too frightening.

'Silence!' yelled Elsorr. 'That's the problem with this place. For too long there's been a complete lack of discipline amongst Councillors in this room. From now on, you shall only speak when spoken to. It's time you started showing respect to the leader of the planet – *Me*!'

A number of Councillors exchanged worried glances. Maybe they should get together after the Grand Council meeting and decide to have Elsorr removed as President. Since he was only *Acting* President and not the actual *Permanent* President, there should be a way to have him ousted.

'I have grave news,' said Elsorr to the gathering as he tried to catch the reflection of his nostrils in the sword. Nasal hairs could be such a damn nuisance.

He'd been wondering for some days how he should lie to

137

the Councillors. He'd thought of secretly sending a manned rocket outside Earth's atmosphere to fire some missiles at a few of Earth's poorer cities. That way, Elsorr could blame the missiles on the MilkyFed and then the Councillors would certainly vote him, Elsorr Maudlin, in as Permanent President. They'd need a Permanent President to fight a war. If he placed a bomb on the rocket, he could detonate it after the astronauts shot the missiles and then no one on Earth would ever know what had really happened.

It was a good plan, he thought, but he hadn't had enough time to put it into action yet. And the Councillors were already becoming restless. It might be best to tell them a whopper of a lie first and then think about how to back it up later. If the lie was big enough, if it was suitably outrageous, the Councillors might give him the benefit of the doubt for a few weeks at least. That would give him time to secretly order a manned rocket into space.

'I've heard on very good authority,' he said gravely, 'that the Milky Way Confederation is planning to take over our planet. That is the only reason that Guttly chose to leave us.'

A number of people seated at the Majestic Table jumped to their feet. The second-eldest Councillor, Hugo Ignominious, was shouting the loudest: 'This is a cheap ploy, Elsorr. A cheap ploy to try and claim the full Presidency for yourself.'

For many years Elsorr had worked to perfect his powers of telepathy and mind power. Since the age of twelve he could bend bananas back to being straight just by staring at them and, in recent years, his favourite (secret) party trick was to move people's chairs away from them just as they started to sit down. It was especially hilarious if the poor person was holding a drink or – even better – a tray of food. No one ever suspected that Elsorr had moved the chair just by looking at it – mainly because they were usually too busy accusing the person who'd fallen of being drunk.

As Hugo waved his finger up at Elsorr in an admonishing fashion, Elsorr lowered his sword, closed his eyes and thought of Hugo's chest. This could never work on someone who was young and fit, but Hugo was getting very frail indeed. Even to stand up and shout angrily at Elsorr put an undue strain on the old man. Elsorr felt a power surge through his mind and he almost felt that he was squeezing Hugo's heart with his bare hands. He squeezed and squeezed with his mind – so hard he could've straightened a whole field of bananas.

Elsorr had done this many times before to Guttly and the bearded fool had never suspected a thing. Maddeningly, he'd never died either, but Elsorr felt confident it was taking years off the old git's life. Guttly must've had a very strong heart indeed.

Suddenly, a chair keeled over beside Hugo – apparently of its own accord – and then the old man fell to his knees, clutching his chest. Everyone stopped thinking about Elsorr and rushed to the old man's aid. Medics were called and an ambulampoon was sent for. (This was a type of ambulance that could fly between cities. To warn other craft or people of its approach, it made a continuous noise like a fat bottom being smacked with a wet kipper.)

Try as they might, the medics could do nothing to save the situation.

Sadly, Hugo Ignominious, the second-eldest Grand Councillor, died on the floor by the Majestic Table.

Later, people would say that Hugo's heart gave out when he lost his temper. But some people came to believe Elsorr's opinion. Elsorr maintained that the old man's heart stopped out of fear. The fear that the MilkyFed wanted to invade planet Earth.

⚡ 18 ⚡

NOTICE TO ALL IGGY
CADETS

When the Dream5s returned to the dorm for lunch, there was a folder for each of them, marked, *Information for IGGY Cadets.* If you ran your finger along some of the documents inside, they'd speak the printed words beneath your finger – which was very handy for anyone wanting to read with their eyes closed (so long as they could move their finger blindly in a straight line – otherwise they'd keep careering into unrelated sentences). Other 'documents' were 3-D holograms that floated in the air when released from the folder and you had to walk right around them to read every bit.

Many of the documents were about boring things like timetables, the appropriate dress-code for certain events, locations of classes, biographies of the tutors, laundry procedures and the etiquette for pointing at funny-looking creatures.

The documents that Tommy found most interesting are set out on the following pages.

SO YOU WANT TO BE AN IGGY KNIGHT?

As one of the twenty-five children who have arrived for training at IGGY, you are now officially an *IGGY Cadet*.

All IGGY Cadets will receive training from tutors who are each *Masters of the Way*. During the training period, you will be assessed by the Milki Masters' Council and Bright Stars or Black Holes will be awarded to your dorm as appropriate. These will eventually be converted into points. For your information, the Milki Masters' Council is comprised of IGGY's five Masters of the Way. Lord BeardedmoustachedWiseface-Oh is head of the Council.

You will be set tests at the end of the training period. More points will be awarded to your dorm depending on the outcome of these tests.

At the end of the tests, the Milki Masters' Council will decide which dorm is to be chosen. The five people in the chosen dorm shall be made *Milki Knights* (also called *Knights of the Way*) and their full title shall be *IGGY Milki Knights of the Way* (or *IGGY Knights* for short). There will be a formal investiture procedure for the IGGY Knights, after which, all the children in the other dorms will return to their respective planets*.

The five IGGY Knights shall be the children to travel in the SickoWarpo InterGalactic Spacecraft (SWIGS Craft) in the name of the Milky Way. The IGGY Knights' journey to distant galaxies shall be known as the *SWIGS Mission*.

All IGGY Cadets have been allocated a dorm. Your dorm is called the Dream5s because you are ranked last of the five dorms and while other dorms *expect* or *hope* to be chosen as the IGGY Knights, you are the rank outsiders and so you can only dream about it.

The dorms you are up against are:

p.t.o

Name	Remarks
Brillo1s	Ranked 1st. Everyone is brilliant.
Great2s	Ranked 2nd. Everyone is great.
VGood3s	Ranked 3rd. Everyone is very good.
Alright4s	Ranked 4th. Everyone is alright.

* Note: If Earth is to be destroyed, the Earthlings who are not made IGGY Knights will be permitted to stay in IGGY (working in the catering section) rather than returning to their planet (see document entitled: So My Planet May Be ~~Obliterated~~ Honoured).

NOTICE TO EARTHLINGS

We apologize to those Earthlings who were led to believe that the training would take six months. It will actually take five Earth weeks. The mistake was due to a calculation error because we forgot to factor in the fact that time will be slowed down in IGGY on numerous occasions. This allows much more training time to be fitted into five Earth weeks.

Please note that the IGGY Knights will receive many, many years' worth of training while on board the SWIGS Craft.

THE SWIGS MISSION – WHY, OH WHY?

If nothing is done, our galaxy and, indeed, the whole universe will be completely destroyed in 117,067 tempusfugits (about twenty-one years) – or thereabouts. All scientific data and Horrorscopes™ confirm this, although it is unclear how or why the universe will be annihilated.[4]

Please note that this information is HIGHLY CONFIDENTIAL. It has not been communicated to ordinary MilkyFederans as it could engender an outbreak of Morrrissshh Dancing.

In order to lower anxiety levels among those who know, and to keep everything secret from those who don't, the pending obliteration of the universe shall be known only as The TFC – which stands for, The Terrible Future Calamity. The TFC. Remember it. It is forbidden for anyone (except Milki Masters) to use any other words to describe it. IGGY Cadets are prohibited from discussing The TFC amongst themselves. Any transgressions will result in immediate expulsion.

The objective of the SWIGS Mission will be to stop The TFC by any means possible.

(PLEASE SIGN YOUR NAME AT THE BOTTOM OF THIS DOCUMENT, GIVING PERMISSION FOR A MILKI MASTER TO ERASE ALL KNOWLEDGE OF THE TFC FROM YOUR MEMORIES SHOULD YOU NOT BE CHOSEN AS ONE OF OUR IGGY KNIGHTS)

_ _ _ _ _ _ _ _ _ _ _ _ _ _ _

Praise be the SWIGS Mission. May the luck of the Nduljdrock Star[5] be with the chosen IGGY Knights.

---

4 Some of the suggested Hows & Whys of the destruction of the universe are detailed in *Extra Bits no. 4* on page 425.
5 Often wished upon by MilkyFederans.

WHY KIDS?

Some have asked why we don't send five Milki Masters on the SWIGS Mission. Others have suggested four Milki Masters and a plumber. It is important to note that we have no idea where the IGGY Knights will need to travel or what will be required to stop The TFC. Therefore, we are sending kids rather than adults for a number of reasons:

- There are some places that kids can go that adults can't (e.g. The *Ancient Script of Babble-On* reads: 'Except ye become as little children, ye shall not enter The Place of Fun').
- Stopping The TFC will require ways of doing things and ways of thinking that no one has ever contemplated. Kids are better than adults at learning new things.
- Sending one adult with four kids was an option, but then the kids would defer to the adult and not find their own way.

Well-trained, thoughtful kids can achieve anything when they are given the chance (at least that's what we hope).

You might be interested to learn that when the 'kids' subject was being debated by all 1,297 Milki Masters of the Milky Way, those who had come to believe that kids provided their best hope, created a song with a line that repeats over and over. ('All we are saying . . . is give kids a chance.') Some say that this song won over many sceptics.

WHY KIDS FROM EARTH? [6]

Because Earthlings know so little, we think that their kids are likely to be more of a 'blank slate' than other kids – so they may be even more open to learning new things.

Also, we will need a lot of luck to stop The TFC, so we thought we'd take a chance on humans – we have nothing to lose (except our lives plus everything and everyone we know).

6 Only Earthlings received this document.

THE ROUTE OF THE SICKOWARPO RUNWAY

One of three planets must be destroyed to allow the SWIGS Craft to make its journey along The SickoWarpo Speed Runway.

In actual fact, the planet will be destroyed by the SWIGS Craft itself. The SWIGS Craft is made from the same substance as a *flashscimitar*, which is the second-hardest known substance in the galaxy. The SWIGS Craft will fly directly at the planet in question and will pass through it like a bullet through an egg. The SWIGS Craft will be moving so fast that it will be well beyond the planet by the time the planet explodes as a result of the impact.

This will be a very small sacrifice for one planet to make in order to preserve the future survival of the Milky Way.

If the SWIGS Mission were not to take place and if none of the three planets were destroyed by the SWIGS Craft, then these planets would be destroyed anyway by The TFC.

Whichever planet is destroyed will be very honoured and a commemorative plaque will be commissioned in its memory.

FAQs (AN EXCERPT OF THE FAQs DOCUMENT)

(Q) Why doesn't the SWIGS Craft journey to the edge of the Milky Way, avoiding all planets, and then try to reach SickoWarpo speed?

(A) There are two reasons for this:
  (i) It is important that the SWIGS Craft reaches SickoWarpo speed *before* leaving the Milky Way so that MilkyFed scientists can be sure that there is no problem with the mission.
  (ii) The SWIGS Union has refused to map a SickoWarpo speed runway outside the Milky Way.

(Q) What's for dinner?
(A) Mind your own business.

SOMETHING NEW

You will find that you have some free time between classes and before you go to sleep in the evening. In order to take your mind off your studies and any fears of The TFC, we would ask you to take up an activity of your choice – an activity that you have never tried before (choose from the activities below). We will make the necessary items, facilities and training holograms available to you to pursue your chosen activity.

This is an opportunity not to be missed!

Note: To save space, I have not included the list of suggested activities as they number 281.

Now that they knew what it meant, Summy and Woozie were a bit annoyed about the dorm name, *Dream5s*.

'A *dream-team*, that's what it meant, I thought.'

'Me too.'

146

'Oh, well . . . We know, now, at least, why we're here.'

'You mean . . .' Woozie looked around, before continuing. 'The T-F . . . ?'

'Ssshhh! Expelled, you'll get us all.'

'Didn't say anything!'

'You did!'

'All I said was, *T-F* – which stands for *Toe Fungus* . . . I'm always saying *T-F*. You've heard me say it before . . . haven't you?'

Woozie and Summy fell into a nervous silence.

Tommy sat alone and tried to banish thoughts of The TFC from his mind. Of more immediate concern was the document about planet obliteration. On the one hand, it seemed to be suggesting that Earth should be honoured if it were chosen. On the other, it compared the chosen planet to a poisonous weed.

He tried to be positive. There were another two planets that might be selected. Earth wasn't the definite choice. And maybe he, Tommy Storm, might be able to influence events in Earth's favour.

'Don't worry,' said Marielle, brushing her hand across his shoulder. 'I'm sure they won't choose Earth.' Then she disappeared to change into another pair of dungarees.

Tommy's thoughts were disturbed when Rumbles careered backwards into the 3-D Hologram he was reading.

'Oops-a-dungly!' cried the bear-like creature, knocking over a pile of clothes that Summy had folded neatly on a chest. 'I'm not clumsy, you know . . . I just can't get the hang of these high-heeled rollerbladeskeeys.'

147

19

BANG! BANG! YOU'RE DEAD

A crescent moon appeared on the horizon of the windscreen. It grew larger and larger, then passed underneath Tommy at several thousand kilometres an hour. Marielle and Woozie waved across from two other JeggMaBelchers as they flew alongside, then peeled away. Sitting alone in the cockpit of his JeggMaBelcher (known by most pilots as a *jegg*), Tommy closed his eyes and wondered if he should try a loop-the-loop that would take him on an upside-down circuit of the Blue Moon.

The cockpit was much like that of a racing car or a fighter plane. It was very cramped and you sat with your feet stretched out straight before you. Tommy pressed his foot on one of the pedals and immediately the cabin filled with loud 1970s style music. (Historians agree that the song was probably *Black Betty Bam-a-lam*, which is all about a characterful black hole who spawned a somewhat wilder black hole.) Tommy tried another pedal and got some classical music (you'd probably know it as *Beethoven's 4th Symphony*, but it isn't really Beethoven's at all – as explained in *Extra Bits no. 3*, page 421). Then the little pedal on the left heated his seat and started a massaging motion in the headrest. He tried to remember everything that Miss Zohfria LeWren, the beautiful tutor, had told them.

'You must uze *ze Surge*,' she'd said in an accent that

148

sounded vaguely French. 'Uze your mind to feel what you need to do. Cloze your eyez and feel ze inner power surge sroo your body. Zat, my children, is ze Surge.'

Try imagining an ostrich with only one leg and a very beautiful face, and you've come some way to picturing Miss LeWren. She had thick blonde hair which stood in a high semicircle around her head. Her multi-coloured feathers were almost completely covered by a black leather top that clung tightly to her body and opened in a V-shape around her neck. She stood on a very tall high-heeled shoe and a fishnet stocking rose up her leg, coming to an end a little way from the top. A strap that was hooked onto a buckle in her leather top seemed to hold the stocking up. She had more, even longer, blonde hair fanning upwards from where you might expect a tail to sit. It made you think of a giant peacock.

How do you spell DNA?

Miss LeWren was in fact a Gallicvamp. Future scientists would find a 29% correlation between the DNA of the Gallicvamp species and that of the common wren found on Earth before the Great Climate Enhancement. Incidentally, those same scientists found a correlation of 83.6% between the DNA of hyenas and that of humans who sell insurance.

Miss LeWren blinked her single dark eye with its long curly lashes. 'You must learn how to fly a jegg,' she said, 'if you are to become true eggsplorers of ze galaxy.'

She gestured to a silver jegg suspended in air behind her. The jegg's body wasn't much bigger than a family car with a fin arcing down two metres from its underbelly. The wings were a bit longer and arced back in a similar style.

149

'You will see zat ze dashboard haz all ze information panelz to tell you where you are and what speed you are going . . . Eventually, you will learn to fly with no controlz. Purely by uzing your mind. By uzing ze Surge.'

An almost invisible bubble lifted the Dream5s until they were hovering over the cockpit. Miss LeWren rose also, then lay across the front of the jegg where she could point inside it.

The cockpit was a smorgasbord of dials and screens and, protruding from its centre, beside a little rubber ball thingy (the claxon), was a funky-shaped steering wheel. Marielle leaned over and peered closer.

'Go on. Get in,' said Miss LeWren. 'Try eet out.'

Marielle climbed confidently into the cockpit. 'This is a bit like the *GoGoGoCart* I used to drive at home in the palace,' she said proudly. 'I came second in a competition only last month.'

'How many in the race?' said Woozie. 'Two?'

'Ha. Ha. Very funny. I'd beat you any day.'

'Super-nova!' said Summy, caressing the side of the jegg with admiration. 'In a different league to a GoGoGoCart is this piece of exquisite machinery.'

'Anyone seen my undies?' said Rumbles.

Miss LeWren pulled the glass roof over the cockpit and Marielle rolled down the side windows. There was a strange contraption attached to the inside of the roof and Miss LeWren pulled it down in front of Marielle's face. It was a dark visor with a curved wire extending from its base to a strange-looking pair of pink false teeth. Once the visor was in front of Marielle's eyes, the false teeth dangled in front of her mouth.

'Zat eez your triggertron,' said Miss LeWren, referring to the false teeth. 'You chooze your target uzing your eyez. Ze vizor will work out what you are looking at. When you want to fire, juzt chew on ze triggertron.'

Marielle opened her mouth and let the triggertron settle around her teeth like a couple of gum-shields. Then she bit on it fiercely.

'Zis jegg eez not loaded,' said Miss LeWren. 'We will not give you loaded jeggz during your training. Eet eez far too dangerouz when you are so new to flying.'

She pushed away the visor and triggertron, then reached into the cockpit and pulled a lever by Marielle's elbow. Immediately, the steering wheel came off in the elquinine's hands and the dashboard revolved inwards so that all the dials and screens disappeared. Now it looked like a flat empty counter and there were no controls whatsoever.

'When you become a fully-fledged IGGY Knight, you will fly a jegg with no manual controlz whatzoever. You will cloze your eyez and uze ze Surge . . .' Miss LeWren seemed to go into a trance, but she suddenly awoke and became animated. 'If ever you become good enough to release ze controls and rely on ze Surge, remember what I said . . . Be careful not to be seduced by ze silly side of ze Surge – *ze Farce*. Ze Farce will do eetz best to take over ze controlz whenever you start relying on your mind alone. Ze Farce will try and play on your fearz and insecuriteez, so beware.'

Completely Irrelevant Heading

An IGGY Knight is a particular brand of Milki Knight, in the way that Commandos or Gurkhas are all soldiers. A Milki Knight (or *Knight of the Way*) is, literally, a knight of the Milky Way. All Milki Knights take an oath to protect the Milky Way from attack and preserve many of its oldest secrets, including the origin of support-tights. Other 'families' of Milki Knights include Delphinus Knights, CastorPollux Knights and DrunnKenn Knights.

Before she introduced the jegg, the first half of Miss LeWren's class was devoted to talking about telepathy, mind control and the Surge. It transpired that MilkyFed people used to use a very crude form of telepathy, in the same way as Earthlings did in late-21st-century Earth for controlling lots of devices like doors and lifts and lights.[7] However, MilkyFederans began to get better and better at the art (lifting it far from the mediocrity enjoyed on Earth), and then things started getting out of hand. Vandals would open doors in people's homes from a few kilometres away and make the lights go on and off all the time. Nosey people started reading other people's minds when these people were thinking things that should be very private. Also, after a while, people got very bored with never actually doing anything physical themselves (DoalSkrownjers, for instance, were a species that learnt to do a whole day's work just by closing their eyes and sitting on the sofa).

In the end, telepathy was removed from the school curriculum of all MilkyFed schools, mind reading was banned in public places and the use of all forms of telepathy gradually dwindled to almost nothing amongst ordinary folk. Excluding the very crude forms as practised by Earthlings and games of PlanetChessy apart (I'll explain later), only the Milki Knights and the Masters of the Way continued to use a form of telepathy – and even then it was used exclusively within the many martial art disciplines they practised (known collectively as Milki Foo).

When Miss LeWren talked about the Surge, she seemed to grow larger. 'Ze Surge is everything you want it to be. Eet eez ze life-force, ze positive energy within yourself. By success-

7 Note: Earthlings' level of 'telepathy' stretched nowhere near the ability to read minds.

fully channelling eet, you can do anysing you want.' And with that, she disappeared.

'Potty she has gone,' said Summy. 'Fancy thinking whatever you want you can do just by using your mind.' Suddenly, Summy started rising into the air. 'Hey! Put me down. Say I, put me down.'

Summy stopped rising abruptly and a big pink tree appeared beneath her. She leapt off the tree and Tommy was relieved to see that her wings did, indeed, work. They enabled her to float safely back down to floor-level.

Then the tree turned into a pair of mustard undies that fell to the floor.

'Hey, there they are,' said Rumbles, wandering over to pick them up. Just before he did, the undies started growing and changed colour until Miss LeWren was back to normal.

'With ze Surge, I can be invisible and I can turn into any shape I want,' she explained.

153

'That's brilliant!' said Marielle. 'How long does it take to get that good at using the Surge?'

'A few souzand yearz maybe,' said Miss LeWren modestly. 'I am actually a Transparent Belt in Milki Foo.' (This is 7,919 levels higher than a Black Belt.)

She warned them about the dangers of the Surge, explaining that the *Urge* is the dark side of the Surge, while the Farce is the silly side. She gave an example from the Milky Star (a local news–hologram) of a furballia who used the Surge to become invisible in a middle-handed shop. Shortly after, he gave in to the Urge by deciding to steal a triplet of gloves. Then he gave in to the Farce – as he tried to leave, someone burst through the revolving door and knocked him halfway across the shop where he landed, unconscious, immediately becoming visible.

Marvellous Traffic Cops

Middle-handed shops became very popular in Altrusia after it was agreed that people who were middle-handed shouldn't be forced to do things with their left hand as had been the custom for some centuries. Whether or not middle-handed Altrusians are better at playing the triangle than right-handed Altrusians is still a hotly debated issue in the MilkyFed.

Once the Dream5s had finished examining the silver jegg, Miss LeWren announced: 'OK, neggst stop . . . ze GarageZone.'

There was no wighole to the GarageZone from where they were, but there was a pole, three kilometres long (like a lanky fireman's pole), that dropped from the floor of Miss LeWren's office to the floor of the GarageZone. It ran through a dark shaft about two metres wide and when

Tommy first peered down, he could see no light at all.

Miss LeWren went first and whatever way she wound her leg and neck round the pole, she could travel at a very fast speed indeed. Summy went next and opted to tie her tail around the pole. When she stepped over the edge of the shaft, she disappeared like a stone. Marielle then stood with her back to the pole and asked Tommy to tie her pigtails around it. When he'd tied them, Marielle hooked her arms around the pole behind her back, then jumped up and hooked her feet behind the pole. Once Tommy and Rumbles released her, she plummeted downwards.

Tommy went next and initially he found himself falling very slowly. His hands kept sticking to the pole and when he started going too fast, his hands would start to burn, so he'd squeeze his legs around the pole, come to a stop and blow on his hands. It was the sound of Woozie yelling 'Weeeeeeeee!' some distance above that made Tommy realize that he'd better get moving. He released the pressure on his legs, let go of the pole with his hands and wrapped his arms around it instead. The material on his shirt slid easily, so, in no time, he was travelling at the speed of a parachutist (one whose parachute has yet to open). The pole twisted and turned, bending this way and that – always at a very steep angle downwards. The shaft was made of glass and Tommy kept getting glimpses of funny rooms in the many floors within IGGY. Some rooms were like airplane hangars and took a few seconds for him to pass, others were full of strange liquids, while yet others were full of exploding substances that generated colours he'd never seen and blinded him momentarily.

The next thing he knew, the light below began to get stronger, so he started squeezing his legs tightly against the pole. Immediately, he slowed down. Then he hugged his arms and slowed again. When he emerged through the shaft into a vast, hangar-like room, he was travelling no faster than a parachutist (whose parachute is open). The GarageZone was eighty-seven metres from floor to ceiling, so, as he descended, Tommy had time to see that it opened out into space. On one whole side, there was no wall and no window. It looked as if you could walk to the edge of the GarageZone and leap into space itself.

Miss LeWren, Summy and Marielle were standing on the shiny metal ground below, yelling something up to him. Tommy noticed six gleaming jeggs before his feet hit the ground and the wind was taken out of him. His legs buckled, he let go of the pole and rolled forwards across the floor.

Half-expecting Miss LeWren to laugh at his pathetic efforts, he was surprised when she started clucking loudly (her form of clapping). 'Perfect landing, Meester Storm. Perfect.'

Then she stopped clucking abruptly and looked very serious. 'Fleeckerring constellations! You look just like—'

Miss LeWren was dumbfounded.

'Who, Miss?'

'Are you—'

'Yes, Miss?'

The look of surprise only lasted a moment, before Miss LeWren shook her head and gestured to Tommy. 'Watch out! Up you get.'

As soon as he stood up, Tommy saw Woozie come flying through the gap in the roof.

'Bend your knees and rroll,' Miss LeWren yelled. 'Bend your knees and rroll, Meester Wibblewoodrow.'

Woozie landed quite well, except that he rolled backwards, but he smiled at the others when he was back on his feet.

'My fur is made for pole travel,' he said. 'That was fantabulous.'

'Yes, Miss LeWren,' said Marielle. 'That was super. I'm going to get an even bigger, steeper pole erected in my palace when I go home.'

'Most dizzy am I,' said Summy. 'Most dizzy. What a way most foolish to travel.'

Apparently, poor Summy had spun uncontrollably round the pole during her descent. With her tail tied in a knot and her back to the pole, she'd been like a tennis ball on the end of a swingball.

A pair of mustard undies suddenly fell through the gap in the roof and landed on the floor near Tommy. 'Oooooopssssss-aahhh-dunglyyyyyyyyyyy!' Everyone heard the yell. A moment later, Rumbles plummeted through the roof at maximum speed. When he hit the ground he was just a blur of charcoal.

CRASHKERCRUMPLE!

Rumbles was nowhere to be seen. At the bottom of the pole, there was now a large hole through the floor. Everyone stepped forward. When Tommy looked through the hole, all he saw was space below – a few planets and a scattering of stars.

Summy was just about to start crying when someone noticed that they were standing on a furry hand.

'Get me up from here,' said a voice that was unarguably that of Rumbles. She was obviously dangling just below them. Tommy, Marielle and Woozie each grabbed a finger and they soon hauled Rumbles onto the floor where she lay like a beached whale while she caught her breath.

'Zat haz never happened before,' said Miss LeWren, a little taken aback.

'I'm not clumskeey, if that's what you're thinking,' said Rumbles.

The Gravity of the Situation

If you're wondering why Rumbles wasn't floating in space when she was dangling below the floor and how everyone could breathe, you should know that there was a huge invisible bubble surrounding the GarageZone. This allowed the GarageZone to be open, while maintaining gravity and oxygen supply. IGGY spacecraft could fly in and out through the walls of the bubble as though passing through a cloud.

Tommy thought about asking Miss LeWren why she'd looked at him with such surprise. *Who did she think he looked like?* But it didn't seem like an appropriate time to bother her with such questions.

He soon forgot his concerns when Miss LeWren announced that there was a brand-new jegg for everyone. Each was tailored specifically for its owner, with their name printed in black letters along the side. Tommy eyed his jegg with admiration: the word *STORM* stood out in large letters. Rumbles' one had a particularly large cockpit and Summy's had a gap in the back of the seat for her tail. Apparently, the jeggs were tailored to individual thought patterns, so that each could be telepathically controlled when (or if) the Dream5s eventually learned to make use of the Surge.

They were really very easy to fly. There was a throttle for controlling speed and the steering wheel controlled the rest – you could turn it left and right or pull it into your tummy to go up and push it away from you to go down.

All the jeggs were metallic grey, except for Miss LeWren's, which was metallic *Whooliguns Moon* (a pastel cherry colour, very popular in MilkyFed wallpaper). She told everyone to enjoy themselves and get the feel of the jegg by flying close to IGGY. 'Stay away from ze Blue Moon,' she warned. All the new jeggs were fitted with buffer-fields, which meant they could bump lightly into things without hurting the occupant or damaging the craft.

Once out in space and flying around in his own jegg, Tommy forgot about everything else. He concentrated on twisting and turning, pushing the throttle to maximum speed, then pulling back on the steering wheel and climbing steeply. Every now and again, he'd spot one of the others, flying about quite slowly. Rumbles appeared to keep stalling her jegg and when she did get it going, he just chased Summy around and kept bumping into her. He was having great fun and treating the jegg like a giant dodgem. Obviously, he thought the buffer-field was designed just for this purpose. Summy looked as if she was yelling angrily at Rumbles, but it made no difference, she kept getting bumped. Marielle was gradually travelling faster. Tommy was very impressed by a corkscrew spin she performed as he shot above her twisting fin.

For a while, Miss LeWren continued making comments and suggestions to everyone through the radio system. Then she announced quite suddenly that she had to return to the GarageZone to do something.

'Stay cloze to IGGY,' she said in a stern voice. 'Whatever you do, do not stray towardz ze Blue Moon. You haff no traffic clearance in zat area – eetz very dangerouz.'

After Miss LeWren had gone, Woozie flew past Tommy at high speed, spinning like a mad windmill. Tommy gave him the thumbs-up, then saw Woozie's face and realized that something was wrong. In fact, Woozie had grown quite confident and thought he'd try controlling the jegg using the Surge. He pushed the lever by his elbow and the dashboard swivelled inwards, taking all the dials with it. At the same time, the steering wheel came free in his hand. It was attached to nothing. Instead of closing his eyes and concentrating, Woozie panicked and his eyes boggled wide. He hadn't banked on this. He couldn't feel the Surge, but the Farce was swelling within him. His jegg started picking up speed and then it started spinning.

Woozie shot past Tommy, away from IGGY and towards the Blue Moon. Tommy turned and chased after his furry friend. He pushed the jegg to maximum speed, then throttled down once he was alongside Woozie.

Woozie looked pale, which was quite something for a reddy-brown-furred wibblewallian. Tommy pushed his jegg into a violent corkscrew so that he flew forwards in a circle around Woozie's jegg. As the Blue Moon loomed larger, Tommy's corkscrew became so fast that he was circling Woozie at the same speed as Woozie's jegg was spinning.

Tommy tightened the corkscrew twist around Woozie, moving in closer, until the fin on his jegg was just a few centimetres from Woozie's spinning fin. As he looked through the cockpit, the moon kept getting larger and appeared to be whirling madly. Tommy slowed the spin slightly and felt Woozie's fin bump against his. It pressed hard, threatening to throw his jegg into a faster corkscrew, but Tommy held the steering wheel tightly and twisted against the force. Gradually, their rotations started to slow.

The moon was now the only thing that Tommy could see when he looked ahead out of the cockpit. Both he and Woozie had stopped spinning and Tommy was now flying upside-down, over Woozie – their cockpits almost touching.

Woozie still looked pale. Tommy shouted at him to wake up and pointed to the lever beside his elbow. The moon was now so close that Tommy could make out the shape of mountains upon it. As a last-gasp effort he squeezed the rubber claxon by the steering wheel.

DIDDLE-EH-DEH-DEH-DEH-DEH-DEH-DEH-DEH-DEH-DEH!

The extremely loud and annoying noise seemed to rouse Woozie because he suddenly lost the glaze in his eyes. Tommy pointed frantically to the lever by his elbow and Woozie registered what he meant. A furry paw pressed the lever, the dial-filled dashboard swivelled back into place and the end of the steering wheel threw itself into the centre of the dashboard.

Not far behind, Marielle saw the two jeggs hurtling towards the surface of the moon. She pulled out of her dive to avoid any danger of crashing and, just then, the two jeggs swerved away from each other and pulled into a flat flight path not ten metres above the moon's surface. The jeggs flew like this for a few seconds, then rose up steeply, away from the surface. Marielle chased after them, only catching up when they slowed, having over-passed a small crescent moon.

Everyone was very relieved and they gave each other the thumbs-up before indicating that they should turn for home.

And so the crescent moon loomed once again, then passed underneath at several thousand kilometres an hour. Marielle and Woozie waved, and peeled off in diverging arcs so they could round the Blue Moon from different directions. Tommy couldn't see IGGY any more as it was blocked from view by the Blue Moon. This was when he kicked his foot on the pedals and heard *Black Betty Bam-a-lam*, followed by '*Beethoven's 4th Symphony*'.

He was starting to slow his jegg in preparation for a celebratory loop-the-loop attempt, when his jegg was jolted violently. It was a bit of a shock, but maybe he was entering a magnetic field or something similar.

KABOOOM!

It happened again, but this time all the controls went dead for a second. As soon as the controls returned, Tommy slowed the jegg so he could check in his wing-mirrors for damage and ensure he wasn't flying into something hazardous. He'd heard rumours of invisible magnetic storms in space.

As soon as he slowed, a fiery streak of orange flashed in front of his nose. He looked back in the direction from where the missile had come and there was a brown jegg roaring straight at him. Tommy pitched his jegg sideways and the brown jegg shot overhead. The attacker wasn't travelling at full speed, so Tommy got a quick view through the cockpit window and saw someone in velvet burgundy, their face obscured by a large black hat. *Felkor!*

Felkor turned and started coming back towards him. The throttle failed to respond immediately to Tommy's hand, which was most worrying since a fiery streak had just left the gun at the front of Felkor's jegg. Tommy could see it in the rear-view mirror – heading for his left wing. The throttle was still failing to respond and the missile was travelling much faster than Tommy. He wrenched the steering wheel and the wing raised itself upwards just before the missile flew past, passing through the point where the wing had been. Even though he'd twisted the steering wheel with all of his might, the jegg had only twisted a little – just enough to avoid the missile. The two previous hits had evidently damaged the controls. Felkor pulled up alongside and made a face. Tommy kicked a few of the pedals by his feet. The cockpit filled with Country and Western music, then a rousing folk ditty, then a voice that was filled with menace.

'Yuh little fool,' it said. 'I dunno what yuh've done to yer

162

stutter or yer hair, but yuh're still a disgrace to Earthlin's.' If you'd ever heard Felkor's voice, you couldn't mistake it. 'When a Dream5-er strays into Brillo1s' territ'ry, they find out why we're ranked higher than them. Innit, fellas?'

Felkor shook his fist at Tommy, then whizzed away. Tommy kicked the pedal a few times until he heard Marielle singing a catchy tune.

'Hey, it's me,' he said.

'Tommy?' said four voices.

'How did you . . . ?' said Woozie.

'That you, Summy?' said Rumbles.

'Where are you?' said Marielle.

'Each other we can hear,' said Summy.

'Yeah,' said Woozie. 'Maybe if one of us patches into the right frequency, it links everyone in.'

'Most interesting that is, because—'

'Sorry, Summy,' interjected Tommy, 'but I can't chat. Marielle and Woozie, you're closest. I'm in a spot of bother. The Brillo1s are attacking me.'

In the distance, Tommy saw Felkor bank towards him and another missile left his jegg. As he pulled vainly at the controls he was only vaguely aware of the questions and chatter of his friends.

Perhaps a second before the missile was due to strike the flailing jegg, Tommy closed his eyes with strain, gave an extra-hard tug on the steering wheel and his arm hit the lever by his elbow. The dashboard revolved inwards, the steering wheel came free in his hands and the jegg shot forward at top speed. He opened his eyes and noted the flash of orange streak past in his rear-view mirror. Immediately, the jegg started to slow and wobble.

I have to shut my eyes, he remembered. Use the Surge –

that's what she said.

He quickly surveyed all around him, committing it to memory, then shut his eyes tightly and willed the jegg forward. In his mind's eye, he saw Felkor steering towards him and unleashing another missile. A sudden power filled him from a vault deep within his centre and with that, the jegg shot forwards. It was astonishing. Like adrenaline but far more powerful. It seemed to fill all his senses until they were magnified to an extraordinary degree. The jegg felt as though it had become part of his body. It was as easy to move the wings up and down as to close your eyes and move your arms up and down. Inexplicable, yet simple.

He easily avoided the missile and zoomed away from Felkor. Then he did a backwards somersault at maximum speed and appeared on Felkor's tail. He immediately slowed until he was just a few metres away from the back of Felkor's jegg. His foot kicked a pedal and Felkor's voice was audible.

'That was some lucky move yuh pulled there, Storm. Now get off my back 'fore I destroy yuh with another missile.'

Tommy shunted the front of his jegg into the back of Felkor. Thanks to the buffer-field, he could give Felkor a good knock without damaging his craft (the buffer-field had also saved him from injury when the first two missiles glanced against him). It was time Felkor was taught a lesson. Maybe he'd be slower to bully Tommy in the future (and hopefully anyone else as well) if he was shunted a few times.

'OK, right, stop,' said Felkor nervously as his hat fell forwards over his eyes. If you'd been inside the cockpit of Felkor's jegg at this moment, you'd have caught a waft of rotten Brussels sprouts. ''S'not funny anymore,' he exclaimed.

Just then, Tommy felt the most enormous jolt he'd ever

experienced in his life. He opened his eyes and saw Brendan the furballia's jegg pointing his way. A missile had obviously made a direct hit. His jegg lost all power and started to dive towards the Blue Moon.

'Close your eyes,' he told himself. 'Use the Surge.'

He was just about to, when he felt another enormous jolt. A missile from Trevor the toothwolf's jegg had hit his tail. His jegg started to spin out of control and the surface of the moon hurtled towards him.

As the mountains and valleys screamed towards Tommy's cockpit, Marielle and Woozie rounded the moon and saw the scene. They'd later describe how they saw Tommy's jegg pick up speed as it plummeted towards the surface. There was nothing he could do to avoid it.

— 20 —

AN INFERNAL RACKET

As you may remember, the *Information for IGGY Cadets* contained a suggestion that all IGGY Cadets should take up a new activity in their spare time. The Cadets were provided with special training holograms (including some that employed a form of hypnosis) to promote extra-fast learning. (Such training holograms, for example, could enable a human child to learn a new language, or an adult human to remember a new PIN number, in less than a day and a half.)

Summy, who'd never done much sport, decided to learn a game called Sinnet, which is quite like tennis, except that each competitor holds a ball and hits a racket back and forth over the net.

Seal-clubberClubbing was chosen by Rumbles. Seals are common throughout the Milky Way and *seal-clubber* is the name given to those who attack seals because they'd like a pair of slippers made from seal fur. Over time, Rumbles learnt how to convince seal-clubbers to mend their ways – using nothing more than logic and a rubber mallet.

Woozie researched how to play computer games that had once been popular on Earth – such as *Space Invaders*, *Doom* and *Donkey Kong* – while Marielle mastered (or *mistressed*) yoga.

Funnily, without any consultation, all of the human IGGY

Cadets chose an activity related to music. Historians put this down to the fact that none of them had seen dancing or heard good music until they reached IGGY.

ZsaZsa took ballet *and* drum lessons. Anjel*eek!* decided to learn how to sing. Tap-dancing lessons were chosen by Egbert, while Felkor wanted to learn the guitar. Tommy opted for the electric violin. He made the choice having seen the hologram of Maximus Ven*Geroff!* playing with the Ursa Minor Concert Orchestra.

On the first few nights, Tommy stood before the great window in the dorm and sought to feel each note, each change in key, as he plucked the strings and strummed the chords. He'd end each session by selecting a sad, soothing adagio that was one of a number of pieces which his violin could play automatically. As it played, the strings would light up, so that Tommy could try and follow, even though his actions no longer made a sound.

This is the image that Marielle thought of when she saw Tommy's jegg diving into the Blue Moon. She saw Tommy, all in black, standing out against the stars, his hair on end, his arm ghosting to the sad adagio, as though a lament for his planet, Earth.

And from that moment forward, whenever she felt sad, Marielle would hear that same music. The sad adagio as played by Tommy Storm.

21

THAT STINKS

Lady MuckBeff WiLLyoofytus was the jegg tutor for the Brillo1s. Like Miss LeWren, she was a Milki Knight and a Master of the Way. It was rumoured that she was an EssenEmm Belt in the Arts of the Evil Way, but no proof had ever been furnished to substantiate this claim. When she walked, she resembled a black polar bear with six legs rather than four – when she was sitting or standing upright it looked as if she had four arms and two legs. Her fur looked dull and dirty and was almost completely covered by a dark green coat that extended down her legs and up to her neck and was tied in the middle with a brown belt. Looking oddly out of context, a delicate blue flower peeked out from the lapel collar. Finally, there was the coat's hood – always pulled over her head, so it was difficult to see what lay inside.

While many IGGY inhabitants poured scorn on Lady M's fashion sense, the real issue was the smelliness of the coat when you got up close. If you're imagining the smell of a dead rat stuffed into a mountaineer's sock, then you're on the wrong track – it smelt nothing like that. It was more like how a fish stuffed with chopped onion might smell if you left it for a month in a cowshed (assuming it wasn't eaten).

Lady MuckBeff didn't like Miss LeWren. It's unclear whether this was because the young Zohfria got so many boyfriends when they were trainees together or because Miss LeWren was two belts higher in the Arts of the Way (Miss LeWren was a Transparent Belt, Lady M, a Brown Dangleberry Belt).

Some time before Felkor attacked Tommy, Lady M had taken the Brillo1s out beyond the Blue Moon to practise flying their jeggs. She ensured that the missiles on the jeggs were loaded and encouraged the Brillo1s to shoot at moons and meteorites. When she saw Miss LeWren and the Dream5s embarking on jegg practice between IGGY and the Blue Moon, she was furious and flew back to IGGY to launch a formal complaint (' . . . a menace to the safety of my pupils'). Miss LeWren guessed what she was up to and followed her so that she could block the complaint before it was lodged and entered an irreversible 'space-violation' process involving no less than $113^{3}/_{4}$ committee investigations over the next 131 years.

Now Miss LeWren was standing in the middle of the

GarageZone, in front of the Dream5s. Lady M was standing close by, surrounded by the Brillo1s.

'This be all thy fault, Miss LeWren,' said Lady M. 'Thou shouldst never have let thy group of fools loose in space. They art too incompetent to fly a jegg.' (She always said *art* instead of *are*.)

'Eggscuze me,' snapped Miss LeWren. 'Zey had az much rright to fly zeir jeggz in space az anyone else. And – I will haff you know – zey are not foolz.'

'They dost be called *Dream5s* for a reason, Miss LeWren. They art the dregs. The worst of the knaves.'

'Your ignoranze knowz no boundz, Lady MuckBeff.'

'This Master Storm character, little wonder he lost control of his jegg. Flying like a lunatic. Overshot the Blue Moon and didst come into my pupils' airspace at breakneck speed.'

'Apparently, he waz shot at by some of your pupilz.'

'Poppycock . . . ! I'm afear'd I shallst be filing *another* complaint.' (Poppycock is the slang for MilkyFed garbage – it literally means 'soft dung'.)

Tommy stepped out from behind Miss LeWren and looked up at the angry tutor in the smelly coat. Immediately, Lady M started shouting at him.

'Dost thou realize what thou hast—?'

Everyone looked at Lady M, who'd frozen mid-sentence and continued to stare in amazement at Tommy. Tommy didn't like the feeling of Lady M's eyes gazing upon him and he shuffled his feet uncomfortably. Eventually, someone coughed and Lady M lifted her gaze to Miss LeWren. Visibly flustered, she continued more calmly.

'And I shallst tell Wisebeardyface that this strange Earthling, Master Storm, shouldst be remov'd from the training programme. They shouldst send him back to Earth

170

before they obliterate the curs'd planet.'

With a cry of 'Hie thee hither,' she turned and jumped through a wighole. The Brillols followed her, but not before Felkor pushed his hat up with one finger and threw a self-satisfied smirk at Tommy.

When they'd all gone, Miss LeWren turned on Tommy.

'What were you doing? If you cannot be rrezponzible enough to fly a jegg, zen zere eez no way you can go on a MilkyFed mission.' She was furious.

'I'm sorry,' said Tommy. 'It was an accident.'

'An accident? Zootallore!'

Zootallore is reputed to be the name of Miss LeWren's first boyfriend. He was an infuriating fellow – never calling when he said he would and often melting the toilet seat. She still uttered his name out of habit when she was particularly annoyed.

'Did I not tell you to stay near IGGY?' continued Miss LeWren. 'Well, did I not?'

'Yes, Miss.'

'And where did I tell you not to go?'

'To the Blue Moon, Miss.'

'Eggzactly.'

'Sorry, Miss,' said Woozie. 'It was really my fault.'

'Quiet!'

'What Woozie means, Miss,' said Marielle, 'is that it absolutely positively wasn't Tommy's fault.'

'I said, *Quiet!*' Miss LeWren glared at Woozie and Marielle. 'When I want a contribution from eizer of you, I will ask for eet. At present, I am talking to Meester Storm who haz cauzed many *barterz* worzth of damage.'

It turned out that the Blue Moon was actually an extremely expensive projection that had been created for the purpose of training Milki Knights. There was no physical substance to

171

it, but when Tommy's jegg plunged through it, all the calculations in the projections went into an even more violent tailspin than the one he was experiencing. The upshot was that the program used to project the moon was now destroyed and no copies had been made (for copyright reasons). This program had taken 241 years to develop so, naturally, Miss LeWren was a little annoyed.

There'd also been a minor drama when Marielle's jegg went into an uncontrollable spin shortly after Tommy's 'crash'. Miss LeWren had to chase after her and tow her into the GarageZone. Maybe that was why Marielle had such an embarrassed look on her face.

'Sankfully, your jegg only incurred minor damage,' said Miss LeWren to Tommy. 'I believe eet can be rrepaired in a matter of dayz.'

Miss LeWren disappeared to the far end of the room and, using a type of phone embedded at the back of her second knee (her only leg actually had two knees), she tried in vain to contact Wisebeardyface. When she returned, she announced that classes for the Dream5s were to be suspended for the rest of the day on account of the damage done by Tommy *and* the reckless disobeying of an order by Woozie and Marielle. As additional punishment, an educational movie would be sent to their dormitory to be watched as homework – and they'd be questioned on it the next day.

Before dismissing them, Miss LeWren spoke gravely. 'I should warn you zat I haff not yet spoken to Lord BeardedmouztachedWizeface-oh. Pleaze be aware zat he will surely want to take zings furzer.'

172

> 'If you ain't broke, don't fix it'
> (motto of the Royal Society of Scottish TV Repairmen)

The MilkyFed ceased having currency many thousands of years ago because they found that money made people too greedy and selfish – it led to hoarding and made stealing easy. Instead, a formalized bartering system was introduced. That way, communities found it best to work closely together to produce items of value for other communities that could be 'swapped'. Hence, Miss LeWren's phrase, 'many barterz (worth) of damage'.

~~ 22 ~~

A BEAUTIFUL MOTHER

'Sorry. All my fault,' said Woozie once they made it back to the dormitory. 'If I hadn't tried to use the Splurge or what-yuh-muh-callit, you wouldn't have had to chase after me.'

Tommy assured Woozie that it wasn't his fault, but he still couldn't bring himself to play a game of floating-bowling with the little fellow. He just didn't feel like any fun at the moment.

'Super-nova! Magnificent I thought you were,' said Summy as Tommy lay on his bunk and gazed up at the open ceiling above them where Woozie was playing Rumbles in a game of floating-bowling. 'Obviously, significant jegg training you've had on Earth.'

'No,' murmured Tommy.

'The way Woozie's spin you halted. Never anything like it have I seen. Not since the theory of *The Big Bang* my uncle disproved.'

Tommy and Summy gazed up at the swirling glass court in silence. Rumbles seemed to be mistaking Woozie for the ball, because twice he'd lifted the little fellow and flung him down the bowling alley. After the game, Rumbles became stuck in the rubbery trunk as she tried to exit the court. It took three of them to pull him out – a bit like pulling a mattress through the slit of a letter box.

'How was I supposed to know you weren't the ball?' said Rumbles, once they were all back down in the dormitory.

'Cos, unlike the ball, I'm furry and not very round,' replied Woozie angrily.

'Well, with my pawskeeys everything feels furry.'

'Let us watch the movie,' said Summy, trying to change the subject. 'Here I have it. Through the wighole a little while ago it came.' She opened her hand to reveal a multi-coloured ball of jelly.

'Where the squell is Marielle?' said Woozie. (For a MilkyFederan, *where the squell* is like saying, *where on Earth*.)

'I haven't seen her since we got here,' said Tommy.

'In the floating globe she is,' said Summy. 'A bath still having.'

'Still?' said Rumbles. 'She's been in there since I was in the looskeey. That was ages ago and I should knowskeey – I only do a number six twice a day.'

Tommy went and knocked on the door. 'You alright in there . . . ? We're going to watch the educational movie.'

There was a long pause before a muffled voice said: 'Eh . . . yeah, I mean *yes*. Just give me a moment and I'll be out.'

'Alright she is?' asked Summy.

'I think so,' said Tommy. 'But she doesn't quite sound herself.'

'Maybe she found my undies in the water,' said Rumbles. 'Girlies can get very uppity about that kind of thing.' He looked down at his midriff. 'They've gone walkies on me again.'

As soon as Marielle came out of the pool, Woozie suggested that they turn off the gravity generator so they could all float while watching the movie. Everyone agreed and Woozie eventually managed to flick the red switch above the wigholes with his foot (it took three painful attempts using the springboard). Then Summy floated in front of the large window and flung the purple ball of jelly at its centre.

SPPLATTTT!

The multi-coloured goo started to spread outwards until the whole window was covered and the view to space was gone from sight. Then, without warning, the various colours in the goo started jumping backwards and forwards across the window. A few seconds later, they'd formed a perfect image of a rocky-looking planet.

'Begin,' yelled Rumbles, Woozie and Summy in a chorus of laughter, well used to operating Grow-sss-Goo.

Gah-Gah About Goo

In much the same way that humans store DVDs today, MilkyFed households had cupboards full of labelled lumps of Grow-sss-Goo. Grow-sss-Goo has the advantage that it can be transported easily and then be watched on any flat object, producing a crystal-clear picture. Some GsGs (the equivalent of Earth DJs) made a lucrative living by mixing various Grow-sss-Goos to produce 'new' movies with actors from movie A reacting to plot points from movie B in scenes from movie C, and so on.

After a very brief drum roll, the film began.

The rocky-looking planet grew larger. It wasn't very pretty and there was nothing very memorable about its scenery. A dry olive-green-coloured powder covered everything.

'Welcome to the planet Dust2Dust, not to be confused with Dusty-too-Dusty or DustESpringfeeld,' said the voice-over. 'This is the first of the three planets that is being considered for obliteration as we map the route of the new SickoWarpo Speed Runway . . .'

The narrator gave various facts about the planet. It was about one tenth the size of Earth, no one had ever lived on it and it was thought to consist of tightly packed dust right to its very core. The problem with exploding this planet was that it would be like firing a bullet into a balloon full of dust. This would've been fine, except for two things. One, Dust2Dust was relatively close to many MilkyFed planets and would necessitate a significant increase in vacuuming by *hambreros*. Two, it had been scientifically verified that the dust particles which form Dust2Dust are the secret ingredient in the strongest itching powder in the Milky Way. An explosion of Dust2Dust would therefore be a nightmare scenario for all MilkyFed species, except, possibly, for twenty-three-armed Pickpocketonians who can scratch many crevices simultaneously.

'Hambreros?' I hear you say . . . These little fellows are explained in the box on page 137 and were, in fact, prevalent all over the Milky Way. The only reason they were on Earth was that a lost MilkyFed traveller accidentally dropped one while over-flying the planet in 2065. (And hambreros – which understand all known languages – have the ability to build new hambreros when asked to do so.)

The 'movie' moved on to a second planet which was no bigger than a football and looked like a giant diamond. It sparkled and gleamed as the light from distant stars reflected through it.

'And this is the planet Panthurpink,' continued the voice-over. 'Despite its small size, this is the heaviest planet in the Milky Way.'

At this point in time, Panthurpink had no inhabitants, although a colony of thunderbumbles had lived there several thousand years ago. (Check out the next box if you're confused!) This planet would've been the obvious choice for destruction, except that it was a very popular attraction for courting MilkyFed couples. These couples would fly their spacecraft out to Panthurpink, then turn off all their lights and invariably slip into orbit for fifteen to twenty minutes at a time.

'The Long and the Short of it'
(by-line for *Giant Dwarves* – a 'movie' that always makes it into The-Top-3-Million-'Movies'-Of-All-Time as voted by *ordinary MilkyFederans*)

Although Rumbles looks big on IGGY, thunderbumbles are actually one of the tiniest species in the Milky Way. Special unseen, built-in devices called *Dimension Levellers* keep all MilkyFed creatures at the same relative size when on or near MilkyFed space-stations and spacecraft. Wibblewallians, for example, are hundreds of times the size of humans.

Already a petition had been organized to protest against the very suggestion that Panthurpink would be destroyed and this had to be taken seriously since the MilkyFed elections were due to be held relatively soon.

If you don't swoon at the sight of a baby being kissed then you won't care that the elections were to be held in 114 years and that the Governor of TeCKsAss (see box on page 95) had already begun campaigning in earnest, demanding that creatures who don't believe that all goddesses have three tails and a certificate in metalwork should be precluded from joining the MilkyFed civil service.

The next planet on the movie was one that Tommy didn't recognize. It was white and blue from a distance, but up close it had valleys, mountain ranges, towns, cities and forests.

It should be noted that the MilkyFed's Earth records were almost 100 years out of date. The pictures and facts were from

2002. This, of course, is due to the fact that a hundred years is no time to MilkyFed people – some species take that long just to get round to cleaning their bedroom. (This also explains the MilkyFed's consternation about The TFC – due to befall the universe in twenty-one years.)

When the voice-over next spoke, it came as a shock to Tommy.

'Welcome to planet Earth. Home to over six billion people.'

Tommy couldn't believe it, but he stifled the urge to speak and concentrated even harder on the pictures before him.

The film gave lots of facts that were new to Tommy. He'd never seen a mountain or a tree or a pair of clogs before. He became mesmerized by the beauty of the place – the variety of scenery, the diversity of wildlife, the way that changing weather could create a thousand different scenes from just one place. It was like seeing an old picture of your elderly mother and suddenly realizing how beautiful she'd once been.

That was the moment that Tommy fell in love with Earth. In fact, it was the first time he'd ever felt a deep connection to his own planet. What an extraordinary feeling. He felt as if he was floating on air (which he was).

'If we destroy this planet, we will only be doing a job that humans believe to be their birthright. They don't like the planet. They pillage it for resources, which they either burn or war over. They don't like each other . . . They are happy to kill for material possessions or to claim chunks of land as their own. Humans are never satisfied. They always want what they don't have and whatever they *do* have, they take for granted . . . although they still want more of it . . .'

The film continued with the depressing commentary. By the end of it, Tommy was still in love with the planet, but ashamed of his fellow humans. The screen went blank for a

179

second, then the colours started bubbling and fizzing as the goo started crawling into the centre of the window. Eventually, there was just a small ball of multi-coloured goo stuck to the middle of the window and the vista of space was visible once more.

'Super-nova,' said Summy, 'quite mad you humans are.'

'Not all of them,' said Woozie.

'Did you see how a typical day adults spend?' Summy was becoming very animated. '*Two* to *three hours* commuting – a distance to cover that should take twenty seconds. *Ten hours* a desk sitting behind – doing what, to know I'd like. *Two hours* – feeding and various chores doing. *Four hours* at a twenty-six-inch screen staring, foolish *fictional* characters watching. And *six hours* sleep . . . . OK, that adds up to . . .' Summy started doing calculations on her fingers. 'Twenty-five hours.' She called over to Tommy. 'May I ask in an Earth day how many hours there are?'

'Twenty-four,' said Tommy defensively. He mightn't agree with everything humans did, but he was one of them. He should defend them against this barrage.

'Wow! So squished into an Earth day all those activities get? Super-nova! Like mad Hambreros you must run around.'

'It's a bit different for kids – we have time to have fun.'

'But why would anyone wish to be an *adult*?' said Marielle.

'Because then you have the freedom to do what you like,' explained Tommy.

'Freedom!?' exclaimed Summy. 'That twenty-five hour adult day I would hate.'

Tommy thought about Earth in 2002 and realized it had similarities to Earth in 2096. He tried to explain what Earthlings were thinking in 2002. 'If you work hard, you get rewarded because you can buy bigger TVs and bigger houses and bigger cars.'

'And when in the bigger house do adults get time to spend?' said Summy.

'When they're asleep.'

'I see . . .' She didn't really. 'At one time how many TVs can you watch?'

'Generally, just one.'

'OK . . .' This was very perplexing to Summy. 'The TVs forgetting . . . If a faster car you buy, faster in the traffic can you go?'

'No.'

'Then why a faster car have?'

'So you can *show* other people that you can *afford* a faster car.'

'And you would do that *why?*'

'To show them that you've lots of money.'

'What's *money?*' said Marielle.

Hmmm, how would he explain that one?

'When do parents get to play with their kids?' said Woozie suddenly. He'd forgotten about defending Tommy.

'They don't,' said Tommy. 'But if they work hard enough they can afford to pay *someone else* to play with their kids.'

'Someone *else?*' said Summy, shocked.

'Yes,' said Tommy hesitantly. Why was everyone so surprised? 'They're called *baby-sitters* . . . Or *nannies*, if they're there every day.'

Tommy was sure he'd got it right. He'd often heard kids at school complaining that they never saw their parents. It made him feel a bit better about not having any himself.

He was saved from more awkward questions by the big charcoal lump floating above him.

'Hey, look! My undies!!'

'Where?' said Woozie.

'Up there! Look!' Rumbles was pointing into the floating-bowling court. Sure enough, there was a bundle of mustard material floating aimlessly.

'Must've happened when you were climbing out.'

'Will you go in and get them? . . . Please! Pretty pleas-keeys.'

'I'm not touching them!'

'Ah, Woozkeeys.'

Eventually, in return for half Rumbles' share of dinner, Woozie agreed to a retrieval expedition.

Same old, same old . . .

A typical adult's day in 2096 was quite similar, from a *rushing around* perspective, to an adult in 2002. The main differences were: the traffic jams were in the air rather than on the ground; the time saved from no longer doing domestic chores was spent arguing with Hambreros; and TVs were replaced by larger trance-screens that filled an entire wall.

Note: Trance-screens were not the same as information screens. Yes, it would've been simpler to merge them into one screen, but manufacturers kept arguing over standards (should they be beige or cream?) and realized they'd make more money if they sold two screens rather than one.

23

A Fish in Water

That evening, Guttly Randolph appeared in the Dream5s' dorm, looking very cross indeed.

'You're a *disgrace* to Earth, Tommy Storm!' he roared, stamping his foot in fury. 'I can't believe you destroyed the Blue Moon! What were you thinking? Well? I feared something like this might happen . . . You're supposed to be an ambassador for our planet! The shame! The—'

Guttly had gone very red in the face and seemed suddenly out of breath. This was the chance for the other Dream5s to start talking at once – in defence of Tommy.

'Quiet!' roared Guttly eventually, and his face went even redder.

Then, for some reason, once silence was restored, the crimson-faced President of Earth started rubbing his chest and, through wheezes, suggested that they change the subject for a while.

After they led the old man to the dinner table and the introductions were made, Woozie turned the gravity generator back on (poor Summy landed head-first on the table because nobody warned her) and they all sat down for a favofant dinner which the Dream5s hoped would continue to distract Guttly from the topic of the Blue Moon. When the old man's breath returned and he finally got his goggles on, he enjoyed duck à l'orange with alphabet soup, followed by a peppermint sundae. He didn't seem to notice Rumbles looking longingly at Woozie's extra-full plate or that Marielle didn't eat a thing and eventually passed her plate to Rumbles.

Guttly explained that he was spending time with all the dorms during their training, playing the role of an official observer. He hoped to be involved – in an advisory capacity – in choosing the dorm to be made IGGY Knights for the expedition beyond the Milky Way.

What Guttly didn't mention was that the MilkyFed thought a 'baby-sitting' human dignitary was required since Earthlings were new to the MilkyFed. This wasn't deemed necessary for MilkyFed children.

By the end of the meal, Guttly no longer looked red-faced and he'd stopped massaging his chest. That was when he returned to the dreaded topic.

'Unfortunately, today's events have made it very unlikely that this group will be chosen as IGGY Knights,' he said, forcing a strained calmness into his words. 'I spoke to Lady MuckBeff. She told me all about the Blue Moon.'

Once again, they all tried to explain that it hadn't been Tommy's fault and this time the bearded man managed to restrain himself and listen silently until they were finished (mainly because everyone didn't speak at once).

'I'm afraid that Lady MuckBeff is a very important person,' responded Earth's President, 'and the Milki Masters' Council will surely believe her word above the word of children . . . And I'd tend to agree with them.'

Tommy was already feeling pretty bad, but this only made him feel worse. All his fellow Dream5s wanted to be chosen as the IGGY Knights – and now he'd ruined things for them.

After dinner, Guttly looked at a small pyramid stuck to his

wrist. He pressed a finger to it and two of the sides turned blue. The others stayed transparent. There was a noise like a penguin gargling hot tea.

'It's a MilkyFed watch,' he explained. 'Lord BeardedmoustachedWiseface-oh gave it to me. The time is . . . almost fifty-two tempusfugits – I think. Now, come on. They should be nearly ready for us.'

'For *us* ready?' said Summy, a little flustered. 'For us, *who* is ready?'

'The Milki Masters' Council is meeting now to discuss Tommy's behaviour. I'm to ensure you five are there on time. We should all hurry or we'll be late . . . Now where is the wighole for the GrandKangasaurusCourt?'

Guttly ushered the bewildered children towards the wigholes on the wall. Woozie spotted the right one and Guttly told Tommy to stand back while he helped everyone else through it (they pushed Rumbles through first as it took all five of them to lift him).

'Now, young man, we have to go through a different wighole,' said Guttly, once he was left alone with Tommy.

'Different? Why?'

'Because you must answer for your crimes today. And as I'm responsible for all humans on this trip, I'll have to go with you.'

'So are you in trouble, too?'

Guttly ignored the question. 'Where's the Room of Trepidation?' he asked. When they found the wighole, Guttly peeled it off the wall and placed it on the floor. 'I can't stand jumping through walls,' he said.

Tommy jumped through the wighole and, moments later, was spat feet-first from a wall – which made landing on the floor much easier than usual. Guttly followed seconds later.

They were in a dark, tiled room about the size of a bathroom. The only light came from a skylight some ten metres overhead.

'They should be nearly ready for us,' said Guttly once he steadied himself.

'Who?'

'I told you already . . . The Milki Masters' Council, that's who.' Guttly pointed towards the skylight. 'They're up there in the GrandKangasaurusCourt waiting to devour us.'

'I've ruined things for the other Dream5s, haven't I?' said Tommy, a wave of despondency overcoming him. 'They'll never travel beyond the Milky Way because of me. And now they're going to send me back to Earth. I don't want to go back to Earth. I don't want to go back to Wilchester.'

'Yes, you probably have ruined things, young man. You've been very foolish and irresponsible indeed.'

And then he saw how upset Tommy looked and softened slightly. 'Mr Storm . . . If you are sent back, it won't be the end of the world – well, hopefully not anyway. You've learned a lot here already. You've bloomed.'

'What do you mean?'

'Don't think I haven't noticed the loss of your stammer, the spikiness of your hair, the zip of life about you.'

'I still don't know what you mean.'

Guttly paused and seemed unsure if he should explain himself. Finally, he sighed and gave in.

'In Earth you were a fish out of water. So it seemed. Somehow, space is your ocean. It suits you and you've found unknown talents within yourself . . . If you go back to Earth, you can take those talents and that confidence with you. You'll return a better person.'

Tommy thought about this. True, he'd a new-found love

for Earth, but he still didn't want to be sent back.

'Please don't let them send me back.'

'I don't think there's much I can do. You recklessly destroyed their Blue Moon, after all.'

They sat in silence for some time, the sound of muffled shouting just audible above. Then Tommy thought of something that was almost too awful to contemplate.

'I hope they don't decide to destroy Earth because of my actions.'

Imagine being the person responsible for the destruction of your planet. Now that Tommy saw how beautiful the planet had been (and might be again one day), he was more certain than ever that he didn't want it obliterated.

'I think that's very unlikely,' said Guttly sternly. 'These are very clever people.'

Tommy felt like bursting into tears. 'If they do, it'll be my fault. If they kill everyone and destroy the planet, the fault will be squarely on my shoulders.'

'You should know, young man, that I won't blame you if they obliterate our planet.' Tommy was unconvinced. 'I'm not the President of Earth for nothing . . . Over the coming weeks, I'll persuade the Milki Masters' Council that we – our planet – is worthy of existence. I'll persuade them or my name's not Guttly Bernard Mary Randolph.'

The two humans stood in silence for a time. Tommy tried to pull himself together, he tried to believe Guttly, but both tasks were proving difficult. He kept telling himself how lucky he was to have been chosen as one of Earth's representatives on IGGY.

Yes, but Earth might be obliterated because I was chosen!

Then he remembered the six days of solitary confinement in Wilchester and the oath he'd made to himself before Mr

Withers told him to pack his bags.

'*I'll never give up.*' Wasn't that part of the oath? Surely it was the main bit? Then, like a mantra, he repeated a new phrase over and over. '*I won't let Earth be destroyed. I'll never give up. I won't let it be destroyed. I'll never, never, never give up!*'

24

THE PUNISHMENT

The skylight opened and the ceiling started to descend. Tommy and Guttly stood still as the GrandKangasaurus-Court devoured the Room of Trepidation. Eventually, the ceiling fused with the floor and Tommy and Guttly were left standing in a large room, surrounded by a silver square that had formed the sides of the skylight.

The room was dark, except for a spotlight aimed into the eyes of Tommy and Guttly.

'Behold – the boy who destroyed the Blue Moon.'

Tommy recognized the voice of Wisebeardyface. As his eyes fought the light shining in his face, he glimpsed Wisebeardyface and four others suspended in the air in front of him. They were maybe four metres up and all wearing sombreros and sunglasses, which are part of the strict uniform worn by judges in all MilkyFed courts. Tommy squinted and could make out Miss LeWren, Lady MuckBeff, Mr Crabble and a small person in a weird wheelchair. As his eyes became accustomed to the light, he could see that they were all in fact balancing on stilts, except for Miss LeWren who was on a single stilt. (Stilts are the most important part of MilkyFed judges' uniforms – *The Law Above All*, being their motto.)

'Fie! This be he,' said Lady M. 'Banish him hence to his planet. Fie! Banish *all* the Dream5s hence.' Then she sniffed

189

the small flower on her lapel.

This was greeted by a cheer from some voices overhead. Tommy looked back and saw twenty-four faces lying on a panel of glass above him. They were in the viewing gallery, listening to everything. He recognized the sound of a dog being kicked and all the Brillo1s seemed to be laughing. Some others joined in. Woozie was there (elbowing Felkor), as was Rumbles, who threw something mustard-coloured onto Felkor's head – which made him very angry. Marielle gave Tommy the thumbs-up and Summy flapped her wings nervously. Egbert Fitchly was there, saying something very fast that Tommy couldn't hear. And ZsaZsa Vavannus was blowing condensation onto the glass and drawing perfect circles with the end of her stole. One of Summy's wings must've touched Anjel*eek!* Jalfrezi because she screamed very loudly (despite her mouth being full of food).

'Quiet!' said Wisebeardyface forcefully. Almost everyone froze and stayed that way for some time. The silence rested heavily on Tommy. All he could hear was the slight flapping of Summy's wings and when he glanced up, he saw that annoying smirk on Felkor's face. 'I am very disappointed in what I have heard, Mr Storm. We have very strict rules here at IGGY and they must be obeyed. How can we send people to other galaxies if they are going to disgrace themselves and the people of the MilkyFed?' Tommy bowed his head and said nothing. 'What have you to say, Mr Randolph?'

Guttly cleared his throat and stepped in front of Tommy. 'Please, Lord BeardedmoustachedWiseface-oh . . . Mr Storm is very sorry. He pleads that you do not send him back to Earth . . . *I* plead too . . . Please give him another chance. I believe he will not disappoint you.'

'Poppycock!' cried Lady M.

'Quiet, Lady MuckBeff,' said Wisebeardyface angrily.

'You have had your say.' He turned to Tommy. 'Mr Storm, what have you to say for yourself?'

Guttly stepped back and Tommy stepped forward. He wasn't sure quite what he should say. These proceedings seemed very formal and everyone had obviously been discussing his behaviour for some time. Lady M glared at him furiously through her yellow sunglasses.

'Ophiuchus!' cried a voice, suddenly.

Tommy was startled, not least because he didn't know that Ophiuchus is a constellation in the Milky Way. The way the word was cried made it sound like a magic spell and he had no wish to be on the receiving end of any such thing. He soon realized that the yeller was the fellow in the wheelchair contraption.

'You must be—'

'Silence, MonSenior!' roared Lady M.

'Jinx, Double-Jinx, Lady MuckBeff,' said Wisebeardyface. 'It is for me to say *silence* round here. Now everyone . . . Please, let Mr Storm speak.'

'I knew you were going to say that!'

MilkyFederans say 'Jinx, Double-Jinx' to people who've just said something that they were going to say. In disputed cases, telepathy is used to prove the truthfulness of the claim. If a MilkyFederan says 'Jinx, Double-Jinx' to you, you're not permitted to speak again until someone says 'SchnozzConkRelivio' to you, while squeezing your nose. The penalty for breaching this strictly enforced law is so frightening that I've been prohibited from describing it.

A solar-urban legend involves a thunderbumble who was jinx-double-jinxed at the age of four. Supposedly, he never spoke again until his death (at 7,225 years of age) because he'd been unable to explain his predicament and get anyone to squeeze his nose. Everyone presumed he was just shy.

The interruption hadn't helped Tommy get his thoughts in order. If anything, they'd thrown him off his train of thought.

'I'd like to apologize for my behaviour,' he said finally, looking straight at Wisebeardyface. 'I apologize to you, to the Milki Masters' Council and to my fellow IGGY Cadets . . . I understand that you may feel the need to send me back to Earth, but I beg two things of you and the Council.'

Wisebeardyface seemed surprised. 'And what are they, Earth child?'

'Please don't obliterate Earth and please don't send the other Dream5s home.'

Tommy stepped back and returned Wisebeardyface's silent gaze until the old kangasaurus eventually spoke.

'Well spoken, Earthling . . .' The old master closed his eyes and chanted something to himself. Tommy could only make out the last two words – '*Gibbledibble blast*' – which were said almost like a sneeze with a wheeze of fire bursting forth from Wisebeardyface's nostrils.

A half-giggle from someone in the gallery brought Wisebeardyface back from his thoughts and he opened his eyes, seeing Tommy's quizzical look.

'I am sorry,' said the orange dinosaurus, 'that is an ancient poem I like to recite at times like this.' Tommy said nothing and felt the silence rest upon his shoulders. Eventually, Wisebeardyface continued.

'Some of my colleagues want to send you home. Some say you should stay.' He seemed to weigh the decision in his head before he spoke again. 'If you do anything else that brings disgrace to your species, you will be sent home immediately. Is that clear?'

'Yes, sir. Perfectly clear.'

'Because you have not sought to save your own position,

we will allow you to stay here on IGGY with the other Dream5s. You can continue the IGGY Cadet training.'

A cheer went up from a few in the gallery above.

'Silence!' roared Wisebeardyface. 'But since every one of you IGGY Cadets must learn to share the responsibility for the actions of others, you will *all* be punished . . . Now there will be no Grow-sss-Goo entertainment movies permitted for the duration of your stay in IGGY.' There was a murmur of disapproval from the gallery above, which hushed as soon as Wisebeardyface's expression grew thunderous. 'And there will be extra homework every day for the duration of your stay.'

Although everyone remained silent, Tommy could feel nineteen angry faces staring at the back of his neck.[8] Their eyes searing into his skin.

'And what about Earth?' said Tommy eventually, since Wisebeardyface seemed quite prepared to savour the silence.

'Alas, there is nothing I can do regarding Earth . . . Before today, Earth was the second most probable planet for destruction. Ever since we found a cure for itching powder, Dust2Dust became the favourite. But the cure is expensive and your actions today naturally lead to the position where Earth must be the front-runner . . . However, the final decision on which planet will be obliterated will not be made until the first DeeDay after the eight Altrusian full moons.'

DeeDay is one of the MilkyFed's twelve days of the week. The date Wisebeardyface refers to here is some time away for those in IGGY. I won't try to explain the lunar intricacies of Altrusia, except to say that the blood-pressure of some Altrusians is dangerously high

8 It was nineteen rather than twenty angry faces because one of the Brillo1s was joyous. This will make more sense later – when the rest of the Brillo1s are introduced.

when all eight moons are full and also that Altrusia has enormous tidal fluctuations which make sandcastle-building a most precarious pastime.

Tommy lay awake in his bunk again that night. He still felt like he was being watched over at all times. It was something he'd become used to and hardly thought of any more, although – strangely – the feeling had left him on the far side of the Blue Moon.

Everyone else seemed to have fallen asleep quite quickly once Rumbles made it into bed. (On the fourth occasion that Rumbles bounced on the springboard and overshot his bed, his undies somehow snagged on the bedpost. She was left suspended, dangling helplessly – if noisily – for some time until Tommy and Woozie climbed onto her bunk and managed to drag her up.)

All of a sudden, lying in his bed, Tommy felt quite miserable.

It's not every day you ruin the chances of your dorm being chosen to make an expedition beyond the Milky Way and, at the same time, consign your planet to almost certain obliteration. Tommy was staring listlessly at a comet streaking across the bottom corner of the window when he heard a faint whimpering below. It was Marielle.

'You OK?' he whispered.

She paused, then whispered, 'Yes.' Another pause and she added, 'No.'

She climbed out of bed and sat by the table. Tommy could see her silhouette blocking out a patch of stars. He climbed out of bed carefully, taking care not to put his foot on Summy's nose.

'What's wrong?' he asked quietly. From where he was sitting, Marielle's pyjamas looked a very dark shade of red and her eyes, reflecting the stars, stood out from her shadowed face.

She said nothing for a while, but then plucked up the courage. 'I'm an empress,' she said. 'Most of my life I've never had cause to be unhappy or to be afraid of losing anything . . . because everything I had could easily be replaced . . . But I felt a terrible loss a few years ago.'

Tommy was a bit confused.

'I don't . . .' He didn't want to admit that he didn't know what she meant. Girls could be funny about that sort of thing. It was best not to try and fill the silence. When she snuffled again, he stretched out his hand and held hers lightly. It was better than saying anything.

'When I thought you'd died today,' she continued eventually, 'well, it made me feel very . . .' She searched for the right word. 'Very *bad*.' Bad wasn't the perfect word, but it was the only one that came to her. 'It made me feel something I never thought I'd feel again.'

It had made Tommy feel bad too. He didn't like nearly dying and he didn't like all the trouble he'd caused. Because he felt so bad about ruining everything and because a girl had never talked so tenderly to him, he guessed that Marielle was upset because his 'crash' might've cost the Dream5s the chance of being chosen to journey beyond the Milky Way as IGGY Knights. But at least she was telling him nicely. He was thankful for that. She wasn't blaming him in a nasty way. He knew he should let go of her hand, but he didn't want to. It was the kind of night when you could do with your hand being held.

They sat in silence for an hour, perhaps . . . Saying

195

nothing. Looking out at the beautiful view of space with their hands lightly intertwined. Then Marielle slipped off to bed and, once she seemed asleep, Tommy snuck up to the floating-bowling alley to play his electric violin and to be alone with his thoughts. Some time later, he crept down to the dorm, managing to stay super-quiet – except that it was so dark, he bounced into the wrong bunk and landed on top of Woozie.

'Gerroff!' said a sleepy voice.

When he did climb into his own bunk, he fell into a deep, deep sleep.

25

THE OTHER SIDE OF PAIN

A flashscimitar can cut through any rock on Earth like a knife through jelly. Often called a *scimmy*, a flashscimitar is a type of sword which is very slightly curved and made from the strongest metal found in the Milky Way. Each is handmade over a period of 503 years (approximately). Their extraordinary sharpness is said to be due, in part, to the fact that every one passes through the centre of a dying sun during the crafting process.

Keep it in the Family

Technically, scimmies are *gulligle-made*, not *handmade*, since they're crafted by Altrusians. It takes 4,316 years to train to be a flashscimitar crafter (known as *flashscimitarerers*) and, as an Altrusian's average life span is 4,831 years and since a crafter can only work on one flashscimitar at a time (a principle known as whymonogomy), a crafter will usually produce only one flashscimitar in his life. Crafters are forbidden from starting training before the age of $11\frac{3}{4}$, although scimmy unions frequently call for this age to be reduced since so many scimmies are never finished due to some heavy-smoking crafters dying at the age of 4,830. The mysterious craft of the flashscimitar has been passed from father to daughter for generations.

As a sideline business, Altrusians make cheese-cutters using flashscimitar materials and techniques. These are something of a status symbol amongst wealthy MilkyFed families.

Marielle lifted a flashscimitar straight into the air until its handle touched her chin. Tommy did likewise. As soon as the handle touched his chin, Marielle lashed her scimmy towards his shoulder. He leapt backwards and lowered his scimmy in a half-hearted attempt at a block. Blue bolts of electricity escaped from the scimmies when they touched and the sound was a shattering, hissing, shriek. Tommy felt the reverberations travel all the way up his arm and across his chest. As he staggered backwards, Marielle raised her scimmy way above her head and brought it firing down towards his head. Tommy tripped in his efforts to avoid the blow, but just managed to sweep his scimmy in front of his face in time. It took the full force of the downward blow and he felt an even stronger shock through his system as the sparks flew higher and the metallic smack and hiss shrieked louder than before.

Rumbles, Summy and Woozie were standing on the periphery of the Uh-Oh-Doh-Joh Chamber, on the viewing level, cheering them on. MonSenior FuKung Leebruce, the oldest Milki Master in the Milky Way, sat in silence, watching intently from his hoverchair (a very advanced wheelchair). Marielle and Tommy were moving across a large circle, upside-down, high above their heads. Both of them were wearing skimming-field hover-boots which stopped them from falling into the abyss that dropped far, far below the viewing level (called *the Abyss of Visions* or, less surprisingly, *the Abyss*). The hover-boots looked like ice skates and they allowed the wearer to skim, like a skater, about ten centimetres off the surface of the BattleCircle.

MonSenior Leebruce had earlier explained the importance of mastering the flashscimitar.

'The flashscimitar has always been the weapon of the Milki Knight. If you are chosen for the SWIGS Mission, you will meet many obstacles on your way to averting The TFC. The flashscimitar may be your only friend in some of these situations. Without it you could die, the mission would fail and all inhabitants of the Milky Way and the universe would face certain doom.'

Rumbles grinned. It was a nervous reaction. She wanted to shout, '*The Terrible Future Calamity!* . . . We all know what The *TFC* means.' Also, *TFC* reminded her of the name of a fast-food chain on her home planet (*fast-food* in this case referred to food you eat when you're fasting).

'You've been told that it's forbidden to discuss The TFC, haven't you?' The Dream5s nodded. MonSenior stared at them for some moments, then explained the rules of flash-scimitar duelling. He said that one of the most important principles when training to become a Knight of the Way was to strengthen your weaknesses. It was for this reason that all pupils should wield the flashscimitar with their weaker hand.[9] (For Tommy, this would be his right hand.) The time-worn tutor also explained that they would have to train in strange and dangerous environments. In this way, they'd learn to overcome disorientation and to block out fear and other distractions.

MonSenior first demonstrated the art of the flashscimitar with Rumbles (probably because she'd grinned at the wrong moment). Rumbles put on her hover-boots and at this point the Uh-Oh-Doh-Joh Chamber looked like any other large empty room, except that it was diamond-shaped, it had a very high roof and it had a bright circle about twelve metres across in the middle of the floor, called the BattleCircle. There was one other strange thing: a set of stone steps (called, amazingly, the *Stone Steps*) stood at the edge of the

9 Or *weakest* hand, if they had more than two hands.

199

BattleCircle going nowhere. Apart from being made of stone, they looked like a set of steps you might use to climb into a jumbo jet.

MonSenior's hoverchair whisked into the bright circle and Rumbles hover-skimmed gingerly after him. MonSenior shouted, 'Key-eye!' and, much to Rumbles' consternation, the BattleCircle started to rise and then it started to revolve until it was upside-down and much darker in colour. The others peered into the hole where the BattleCircle had been and saw a darkness that seemed to plunge for ever. Tommy noticed that a platform had extended from the set of steps, so that it looked like a diving-board jutting out over the Abyss.

Who would want to dive into that infinite darkness?

The dark circle remained upside-down and stopped rising when it was about twenty-five metres above the diving-board. MonSenior demonstrated some extraordinary moves, somersaulting backwards and forwards in his hoverchair and pirouetting around the bewildered mass of charcoal fur. He never touched Rumbles – each time halting his scimmy half a centimetre from her fur.

'See the way that rug never falls off his knees?' said Tommy, looking up.

Marielle nodded. 'Amazing what 600 million years of training can do.'

Rumbles slashed her scimmy this way and that, but she was always two steps behind the dodging, chair-bound shadow. She was duelling with her left hand since she was generally middle-handed (except when it came to scratching or throwing wet things, in which case he was right-handed). MonSenior finished with a flourish and leaned back in his chair, with his scimmy almost touching Rumbles' nose. 'Sooper-dooper kee-eye!' he screamed. The BattleCircle started becoming bright again. He looked down upon the onlookers and it was at this point that Rumbles' third arm flashed over her head and grabbed MonSenior's scimmy.

'Gotcha!' she said proudly.

In a flash – and with a cry of 'Ophiuchus!' – MonSenior did a double-somersault over her head, twisting Rumbles' free arm as he did so. Somehow, this sent the furry mass into a blur of somersaults and then she landed on her bum. MonSenior grabbed both scimmies from her and when she stood up, he did an elaborate series of slashing movements and Rumbles' undies fell down (over her head).

After MonSenior screamed something that sounded like '*V-v-virtygoe!*' the BattleCircle returned slowly to its original position and the Abyss was once more hidden.

'My undies! They're ruined!' said Rumbles.

'That will teach you to attack someone when the spar is over,' said MonSenior, carefully tucking his tartan rug into position. 'An IGGY Knight never attacks when the BattleCircle is bright.'

Summy and Woozie had a spar next, which Woozie won, mainly because he kept standing on Summy's tail and attacking her from behind. They never touched scimmies and kept the blades at least half a metre from each other at all times. It was still possible to see who won because MonSenior would shout, '*point to Woozie*' whenever it was obvious that Summy's defences could've been breached by the little fellow.

Tommy expected a spar equally as tame once he skimmed into the BattleCircle with Marielle. The Circle raised high into the air and swivelled until it was upside-down. Under the strict rules of flashscimitaring, a fight only begins once both contestants have touched their chin with the handle of their scimmy and Marielle did so with hers, frozen like a coiled cat awaiting her opponent's signal. Tommy raised his scimmy before his face with his right hand and halted the handle before his chin. He took a deep breath and craned his neck to look into the blackness below. He'd seen many drops in the past few days, but none had the awful, forbidding intensity of this abyss. It smelled of death and horror.

And so the duel began. Marielle came at Tommy with a ferocious intensity and almost chopped his head off on numerous occasions. *What was she doing? Had she gone mad?* Tommy rolled to the edge of the Circle, just missing another slashing blow. You could travel fast on hover-boots, so he swivelled swiftly in a semicircle, like an ice-hockey player rounding the goal. It gave him a moment to see Marielle twist and come towards him again. The scimmy swept towards him and though he ducked, it caught a lock of protruding hair and sliced it clean off. *She was trying to kill him!* She twirled round him as he patted his head to feel the damage. Without looking, he sensed the scimmy slicing towards his back and he flung his right hand over his head, throwing the scimmy down the length of his back.

SSSCCHHHLASSSSTUWIZZZZZZZ!

His whole body shuddered in time to the leaping sparks and the metallic screech.

Down below, few noticed Guttly silently entering the room. He bowed to MonSenior Leebruce and then they raised their eyes to the duel above. The duel became even more ferocious and with it the cheering and suggestions from the spectators grew louder.

'Behind you.'

'She's trying to kill him!'

'Duck, Tommy!'

'Nice undies.'

202

Even Guttly joined in at one point. 'Watch out!' he yelled, and in an involuntary movement he dodged his body to the left and brought his elbow up in front of his face. When he saw that Tommy was OK, he hoped that no one had heard his yell or seen his frightened movement.

Finally, MonSenior clapped his hands and shouted, 'Sooper-dooper key-eye!' Marielle and Tommy turned to face each other and they lifted the handles of their scimmies until they were in front of their lips, then kissed them once. 'V-v-virtygoe!!' was yelled from below and the BattleCircle started to swivel and lower.

MonSenior called the spar a draw, since no one had scored a point.

'What were you thinking?' said Tommy once they were back on the ground. He rubbed the patch of neatly chopped hair at the back of his head. 'You almost killed me.'

'I'm an empress. I've been supremely tutored in the art of lances, sabres and swords.'

'All the more reason not to kill me on my first outing.' *Was that too much to ask?*

'I had complete control at all times,' said Marielle. 'Look.'

Marielle lifted her scimmy and swept it violently towards Summy, whose mouth was half-open. Summy had no time to react as the side of the scimmy swept full speed under her nose and into her mouth. Then, as if the blade had hit an invisible wall, it stopped, a finger's width from where Summy's back teeth began to meet each other. Marielle withdrew the sword and smiled at Tommy.

'Killed me you could have!' cried Summy who was quite pale and she swept her tail across the floor so that it took Marielle's feet from under her and she fell on her bum. 'Teach you that will.'

'Quiet!' said MonSenior, who'd just climbed to the top of the Stone Steps. 'That was a good duel, Miss Pigtails and Master Spiky.' (MonSenior could never remember anyone's name so he always made up his own names – he himself was known as *The Fossil* by many adoring MilkyFederans. That said, his mind remained sharp concerning most other things – except renewing his 46A Vulpecula Pass,[10] which he always forgot.) 'You've both been trained in the art of sabre fighting, I see.' He didn't seem to notice Tommy shaking his head. 'You use the ParrrKing Offence very well, Miss Dungarees. And you, Master Blackgear, rarely have I seen the Inn-San-Itty Defence so well deployed. I trust you had a few counter-moves ready up your sleeve?'

Rumbles patted Tommy so hard on the back that MonSenior thought Tommy was nodding.

'Well dunskeey,' said Rumbles quietly. 'I tried using the Igg-Norr-Ants Defence, but it got me nowhere. Look at my undies.'

Fore!

The ParrrKing Offence was popularized by the famous king of the Parrrs, TiGrrr Forest. The Parrrs were a curious tribe of people who wore check trousers, V-neck jumpers and used to whack balls around their planet into small holes with sticks ill-designed for the purpose (when not scimmy duelling). After the Parrrs were ravaged by a disease called CaddyRash, a certain Parrr visited Earth with the idea of cheering up his fellow-species. He succeeded. Parrrs now have many comedy 'videos' featuring humans trying to play 'golf' and any shot that is *not* a hole-in-one they find quite hilarious.

---

10 A type of bus pass free to over 64,000-year-olds.

Guttly put his hand on Tommy's shoulder. 'Quite impressive, young man,' he said.

MonSenior didn't look impressed. 'You should know that this was an *easy* lesson,' he said to the gathering. 'With hover-boots on, it was impossible to leap more than three metres from the BattleCircle – no one could possibly have fallen into the Abyss.'

'Still mighty scary,' said Woozie.

'What . . . ? What was that?' MonSenior took a small white thingy out of his ear and gave it a pat. Then he took a tiny something from his pocket and seemed to feed it to the white thingy. 'There, you go,' he said, putting the thingy back in his ear. 'Sorry, what did you say? My cochlea-roach wasn't working.'

Cochlea-roaches are tiny insects that are specially bred to act as hearing aids. Technically, whatever sounds they hear, they repeat to their owner (by banging on the ear-drum in Morse code fashion). However, if they aren't well-fed or given enough TLC (not to be confused with The TFC!) they stop working.

Once everyone removed their hover-boots, the lesson resumed.

'When you become a fully-fledged Master of the Way, you will close your eyes when flashscimitar duelling. You will use the Surge to guide you.' MonSenior closed his eyes and flung his scimmy high, high into the air. Still with his eyes closed, MonSenior Leebruce leaned back in his chair with his arms outstretched. The scimmy plunged towards his head.

Summy screamed then gasped as MonSenior turned his head a whisker at the last moment. The blade sliced past his ancient face and its point lodged in the hoverchair (in a mangle of rug). The oldest Milki Knight of them all opened his eyes. 'Now you know how I shave every morning,' he said.

And when they looked closely, the Dream5s saw that now, down the elder's face, cutting through the grey stubble, was a line of smooth skin as wide as a scimmy blade.

MonSenior's hoverchair turned and whisked up the Steps. 'It is my job to teach you the art of the Milki Knights . . . To save our galaxy, you will need all the skills that the Milki Knights have gathered over the generations. You will need to find all the qualities and strengths that are buried deep within your person. And to do that you will need to test yourself to the limit.' Then he made the Circle rise again by shouting, 'Key-eye!'

The diving-board (the 'Plank') extended before him above the Abyss. Guttly stood back from the group of onlookers and watched silently from the shadows.

'This chamber, the Uh-Oh-Doh-Joh Chamber, is millions of years old,' said MonSenior. 'We're very lucky that the MilkyFed has allowed the Chamber to be housed inside IGGY for a brief time. Although it is contained within IGGY, the Abyss has no bottom. It is a fall into infinity. This is where the kings, rulers and greatest heroes of the MilkyFed are "buried". When they die, their bodies are cast into the Abyss.'

'Don't tell me Captain Red Undies was buried here,' said Rumbles excitedly.

MonSenior Leebruce nodded. 'Why, yes. This is exactly where Captain WhatsitUndies was buried.' *(Captain Red Undies was a thunderbumble who had the number 3 on his grave-stone.)*

After a moment of silence, in honour of the dead hunch-backed hero, MonSenior continued. 'It is said that the Chamber was made by the gods and there are no MilkyFed records that refer to a time before the existence of the

206

Chamber. The Plank can see your fears and your inner—' He hesitated. 'Your *inner-lath* . . .'

'No one ever broke a leg falling into an infinite drop'
(Abyss construction worker)

The Uh-Oh-Doh-Joh Chamber was transported in a protective bubble to different planets from time to time, rather like a price-less work of art being passed from museum to museum. And yes, the Abyss really is an infinite abyss.

Confused about infinity being enclosed in a contained space like IGGY or a bubble? It's best to think of it as being like the infinite number of divisions that can be made between the numbers 2 and 3. If you're still confused, ask a know-all or just have a bowl of ice-cream.

'Your *inner-lath*? That is what?' asked Summy.

'We're not sure,' admitted MonSenior. 'The secrets of the Chamber have been passed from mouth to mouth through the ages – since five thousand million years before I was born . . . We believe your *inner-lath* is something to do with an inner strength. It's rumoured to be more powerful than the Surge.' His eyes tightened. 'It's eight footsteps to the end of the Plank. It's said that if your fears are equal in strength to your *inner-lath*, then you'll experience your greatest fears for the first four steps and your *inner-lath* for the final four steps of your walk along the Plank. If your fears are stronger, then during the first six steps you might experience your greatest fears and your *inner-lath* for the last two steps. Some might experience fear for all eight steps. We cannot know for certain because nobody has ever taken more than four steps on the Plank . . . because no one could endure the pain of their fears.'

If you're wondering why nobody does a long jump onto the end of the Plank, or why very tall people don't take two steps to the end of the Plank, you should know that there's a very strong force-field all around the Plank that prevents this. Inexplicably, everyone takes the same sized steps upon the Plank.

'Nobody has ever walked far enough to see their *inner-lath*,' MonSenior concluded.

'That this *inner-lath* exists, then, you cannot be certain,' said Summy.

MonSenior shook his head. 'As Masters of the Way, we can only *believe* that this *inner-lath* exists. And even then, our belief is weak. We trust the words of our ancestors, but, like them, the proof is dead.'

'I believe it,' said Rumbles.

'If you really believe,' said MonSenior, 'if you believe *completely*, then you should walk to the end of the Plank, turn so that you're facing the Steps, cross your arms across your chest, close your eyes, and fall backwards into the Abyss. They say that if you're filled with *inner-lath*, then you will be saved and you will not perish.'

Rumbles looked a little pale. 'Alright, maybe I don't believe it *that* much.'

MonSenior smiled. 'There's nothing wrong with that. No one has ever believed that much. No one has ever had the courage to try . . . It would be pretty hard to anyway, since no one has taken more than four steps.'

'Nonsense it is,' said Summy. 'Some nonsense made-up.'

'Would you like to walk along the Plank, then?'

'Eh, thank you no – a bit tired I'm feeling. Plus, a sore toe I have.'

'Well then. Who will step onto the Plank of Discovery?' said MonSenior.

'Maybe when I get a new pair of undies,' said Rumbles.

'Sure. I'll try.' Woozie bounded up the Stone Steps until he was standing beside MonSenior and smiling confidently.

'It's only from the Plank of Discovery that you can truly see into the Abyss of Visions,' explained MonSenior.

Woozie placed one foot on the Plank and immediately jumped backwards, falling down the Steps.

'Something's down there,' he yelled. 'A monster. It was trying to eat me!'

Everyone looked into the darkness, but they saw nothing.

'I'm not afraid,' said Marielle and walked past Woozie up the Steps. She placed one foot on the Plank and then stood rigid. She closed her eyes, then opened them again and stared piercingly into the darkness. Finally, she stepped back and came down the Steps very slowly.

'There's no monster down there,' she said, a little shaky. 'It was a rampaging disease spreading across thousands of people. It spread like a wind and they were writhing in agony. Dying very slowly.'

They all shuddered. Rumbles put his arm around Marielle.

'How about you, SeriousFace?' He was referring to Tommy, who was feeling concern for his two friends. 'Do you want to try?' MonSenior gestured towards the Steps.

If you're wondering what MonSenior Leebruce looked like, then think, old . . . No, no. Much older than that . . . You see, MonSenior was born before humans and iPods appeared on Earth and no longer permitted candles on his birthday cakes. He sported a bright blue bandana on his head, a few stray red hairs (dyed, allegedly) escaping from the back. His eyes were keen and emerald green, he had but three teeth, and though he was generally clean-shaven, a spiral of light-blue hair weaved from his

209

nostrils and formed a knot behind his neck. Beneath a white pyjama top, his body was brown and wizened, and hard as granite. *(It was widely held that he'd once been the InaneEgo® MilkyFed Bodybuilding Champion, but that his 'peach of a body' had shrunken to 'nothing but the stone at the core'.)* About the time humans' ancestors discovered fire, MonSenior lost all three of his legs trying to extinguish a red dwarf. Forever after, he insisted on covering 'their shadows' with a tartan rug. *(He was quoted in WIGGLEWOGGLE'S WHO'S WHO™ as saying, 'To remove the rug would be an insult to the memory of my legs.')*

When he walked up the Stone Steps and stood beside MonSenior, the Abyss still looked dark and impenetrable to Tommy. Carefully, he set one foot on the Plank.

The darkness cleared immediately and something large, round and whitey-blue sped towards him from the depths of infinity. By the time it filled the Abyss, he recognized it as his own planet – Earth. Then, without warning, the planet exploded. A raging ball of fire headed straight for his head. He closed his eyes and dodged to miss it. The sound of people screaming filled the air. He opened his eyes and saw a flying fragment of the planet on which humans were burning, cities were crumbling and children were slowly frying. The heat grew more intense and the sound of the explosion kept growing. He felt a pain and a burning sensation within his own body, as if the very suffering he saw was being transferred into his own body.

To understand the level of pain, try imagining that you're lying on a bed of nails with three sofas and a football team stacked on top of you. At the same time, there's a group of flame-throwers going bananas on either side of you – they're aiming every blast of fire at you, which is particularly annoying since you're doused in petrol. To compound matters, your shoes are three sizes too small, you're wearing a tie that some interfering auntie has tied much too tightly,

*all the way into your neck, and a very hot Indian curry isn't a bit
happy about being in your tummy. Take that level of pain and
multiply it by the age of the oldest person you know plus the number
of times any of your brothers, sisters or friends have annoyed you
in your entire life – and then you're almost there.*

Despite the pain, something – he didn't know what – made
Tommy take a second step onto the Plank. He lifted his back
foot from the top of the Steps, brought it past his lead foot
and set it firmly on the Plank. Immediately, the vision, the
noise and the heat disappeared. Everything was calm. He
looked down and now the Abyss was full of white, woolly
clouds. The only things he could hear were the distant echo
of a waterfall and a sweet twittering that might've been the
chirping of birds (since he'd never seen or heard a bird on
Earth, the pleasant noise was unfamiliar to him).

Two people melted slowly through the clouds and rose up
until they were level with the end of the Plank. A man and a
woman who looked vaguely familiar . . . But how could they
be? Surely, he'd never seen them before. The man had dark
hair and brown eyes, the woman was blonde and green-eyed.
They smiled and Tommy felt that he'd never been smiled at
like this before. It was more than a baring of teeth and a
wrinkling round the eyes. It was a beam of warmth and something else. Something stronger.

'Removeth him!' yelled a voice, a voice that Tommy
couldn't hear.

He stood enraptured and didn't hear the row ensuing not
far from his back. He was about to take one more step
forward when he was roughly grabbed by the arm and hauled
back towards the Steps. He teetered one step backwards and
the nightmarish vision of burning Earth reared into view and
a flaming comet of rock hit him across his right cheek. He

211

fainted from the impact and fell back towards something very smelly.

What Tommy had missed was Lady M entering the Uh-Oh-Doh-Joh Chamber followed by the Brillo1s.

'Henceforth, we dost be here,' said Lady M gruffly to MonSenior Leebruce. 'I hath a flashscimitar class to give.'

'We'll be finished in two minutes,' said MonSenior.

It was then that Lady M spotted Tommy standing on the Plank. He had two feet planted squarely on it. 'Fie! Removeth him from the Plank,' she yelled. 'It doth be unsafe. Only Masters of the Way canst bear it.'

'It's best to let children try as early as possible.'

'Poppycock!'

Lady M leapt up the Stone Steps and started shouting at Tommy. MonSenior blocked her path, but somehow, once the green-coated creature reared onto two legs, one of her four hands managed to get a grip on Tommy and haul him back a little. Then she lost her grip.

'Be careful, you'll kill him!' yelled MonSenior.

'Hark! I'm only trying – Fie! Fie!'

Alerted by Lady M's yell, MonSenior swivelled and caught Tommy – with a cry of 'Ophiuchus!' – before he fell down the Steps. It was the smell of Lady M's coat that brought Tommy round.

'Thou seest now of what I speaketh,' said Lady M. 'No child couldst handle the Plank of Discovery. 'Twas most irresponsible of thee, MonSenior Leebruce. I'm afeard I shallst be lodging a formal complaint.'

Tommy had to face another Felkor smirk as MonSenior and the Dream5s gathered their flashscimitars and prepared to leave. Tommy felt a pain where the comet of rock had hit his head, but it was fast disappearing.

'Soshages!' cried MonSenior and the Great Doors of the Uh-Oh-Doh-Joh Chamber opened. Then he led the Dream5s out the door, with Guttly following silently behind.

'DON'T tell anyone this Password'
(Sosh instruction manual)

Soshages literally means, the *Ages of Sosh*. Sosh was the name of a dynasty that made password-reactive doors for hundreds of millennia. They eventually dropped out of favour because the only password they ever gave their doors was (the very vain) *Soshages*, which made it easy for anybody who hadn't been jinx-double-jinxed to enter a Sosh door.

⚡ 26 ⚡

LOVE? LOVE! LOVE

Just outside the Uh-Oh-Doh-Joh Chamber is a balcony of sorts which extends into the Hall of Levels. Called the KonjugalNOT Shelf, it's a wide ledge that looks out over hundreds of floors and openings, all linked by criss-crossing stairs, glass lifts, spiral escalators and whoosh-n-plunge-Ulators.

The Dream5s were standing on the Shelf as MonSenior Leebruce gave them directions to return to the dormitory. Then, because he was running late for a hair appointment, he zipped his hoverchair forward with all the flashscimitars and disappeared into a plungeUlator.

'I do'
(punch-line to a MilkyFed joke that takes years and years to tell)

WhooshUlators are narrow columns of fast-moving air that generally travel upwards, while plungeUlators are similar, but travel downwards. Using them can be hazardous and is an acquired skill. Both of them are often set at funny angles, the most extreme being horizontal, at which point you can't tell the difference between a plungeUlator and a whooshUlator – you just need to know which way the air is travelling.

Divorce ceremonies are frequently held on the Shelf. The divorce is completed when one partner leaves on a whooshUlator, the other on a plungeUlator.

Guttly held Tommy back as the other Dream5s jumped one by one into a whooshUlator and shot upwards.

'You lost your fear after the first step, didn't you, young man?' said the bearded elder. Tommy nodded. 'I know. I saw your face. Your *inner-lath* must be much stronger than your fears.'

'I see,' said Tommy, not sure he saw anything at all.

'You know, Mr Sto– . . . *Tommy*,' said Guttly with barely contained pride. 'I've talked to a lot of MilkyFed people since we arrived here and I think I know what *inner-lath* is.'

'Really?' How strange. The Plank of Discovery was millions of years old and even the Masters of the Way were not exactly sure what *inner-lath* was.

Guttly chuckled. 'MilkyFederans are so advanced, Tommy. They're so far ahead of humans in terms of intelligence, but there's one thing they don't know about. They have everything else, but they've somehow lost this one thing.'

Now Tommy was intrigued. 'What's that?'

'Love.'

'I'm sorry?'

'Love . . . Young man, can't you see? It's like Chinese whispers. After millions of years, the words *love* or *inner love* have been lost along the way and replaced with *inner-lath* . . . Maybe MilkyFederans had a strange accent or a speech impediment at one time.'

Tommy was about to reply, but Guttly now looked sad. As though the thought or memory of love carried an unbearable weight. It lasted but a second – then he seemed to wake to the moment and banish the weight from his mind.

'You'd better get back to your dormitory, young man. Or you'll be in trouble. Big trouble. They're keeping an eye on tardiness – I don't want Earth obliterated because you were late.'

Tommy waved goodbye to Guttly and jumped into a whooshUlator. He barely noticed the floors, the rooms and the funny-looking people he shot past as he flew upwards. Without thinking, he followed MonSenior's directions exactly, leaping out of the whooshUlator and onto a spiral escalator at exactly the right moment.

He was considering Guttly's words as the escalator spiralled him diagonally up through the darkest, most shadowy corners of IGGY. *Love? Love! Love* . . . He tried saying the word in many different ways, but he wasn't completely sure of its meaning. Of course, he'd read books and seen movies that were said to feature love, but he'd never experienced it. He'd always thought it was a madey-uppy thing. And if it existed, surely the MilkyFed people would know about it. They were clever enough to know about these things. Weren't they?

He jumped off the spiral escalator onto a moving rope that carried him high up a ravine between some towering apartments reserved for IGGY's sanitation staff. It was a bit brighter here. As though a sun had just set.

Above the apartments, he passed a large statue of a giant hedgehog-like dinosaurus. A little further on, the rope came close to a jutting ledge, which he swung himself towards. At just the right moment, he let go and landed on the edge of the ledge. For a second he felt as though he was going to fall backwards, but he swung his arms round in windmill fashion and managed to regain his balance. Across the wide ravine, twenty metres below, was a statue of a badger-like dinosaurus with his mouth open. Tommy placed his toes over the edge of the ledge and stretched. Had he remembered MonSenior's directions correctly? He thought about it and told himself he was sure. Then he hesitated. How far could he dive? The ravine must've been fifty metres across. But MonSenior had clearly told them to dive.

He took a deep breath, closed his eyes and dived out as far as he could. The wind rushed past his face as he started to plummet towards the tops of the apartments. Then, as he came level with the giant hedgehogasaurus, a warm current of air caught him and sped him towards the badgersaurus. He looked back and it seemed to him that the hedgehogasaurus was blowing warm air out his mouth and it was this air that was carrying him towards the mouth of the badgersaurus. As he got closer, he saw there was a wighole in the badgersaurus' mouth. He sped in head-first and plopped out of a wighole marked *The Windy Ravine*, landing in a heap on the dormitory floor.

'What took you so long?' said Woozie who was wearing his favo-fant goggles and having a snack.

Summy and Rumbles hurried over.

'Super-nova! Lost we thought you'd got.'

'You didn't see my undies anywhere, did you? They came offskeeys on the whooshUlator.'

When they were all sitting round the table having a spot of lunch, Tommy raised the question of love.

'Never heard of it,' said Woozie.

'Is it a kind of balloon?' asked Rumbles.

'Love?' said Summy. 'Somewhere I read that 223 million to one is the probability of love in the universe existing.'

'Very clever, but do you know *what it's supposed to be*?' said Marielle, unimpressed with the winged dinosaurus' bald facts.

'Exactly, not. A type of poisonous gas it probably is. Like bakedbeanusis.'

'What about your parents?' said Tommy, trying a different

tack. He'd heard the word love associated with parents at one time. 'How do you feel about your parents?'

'I like my parents,' said Woozie. 'They're very bouncy.'

'My parents let me whack them with super-skychubb pillows,' said Rumbles proudly.

'Most intelligent are my parents,' said Summy. 'Many things they have taught me.'

'But do you *love* them?' said Tommy.

That stumped them. They didn't know what to say.

'By *love*, exactly what do you mean?' asked Summy. 'The definition we're not precisely sure of.'

Tommy tried to remember all the things he'd ever read or heard about the subject.

'I think it's when you like someone very much. So much, you trust them entirely and you'd gladly give up your life for them.'

Everyone started speaking at once.

'Super-nova! A bit strange that sounds.'

'Maybe I love Altrusian larvae eggs with Friggle sauce.'

'Red-and-white-striped undies, with pockets on the sides – I almost love *them*.'

Tommy noticed that Marielle looked a bit upset.

'You OK?' he said.

'My parents are dead,' she said with teary eyes. 'I almost said it to you last night. I—' Tommy stood in silence as Marielle searched for the right words. 'It's the only reason I'm an empress and not a princess.'

'Dead?' said Summy.

'A terrible, awful plague ravaged my planet some years ago. Our family had an escape-capsule, but my parents sent me off in it alone. They feared they might have the virus. They feared they might give it to me if they travelled with me to safety.'

'Sounds like Tommy's definition of *love*,' said Rumbles, putting her arm around Marielle.

'Most certainly it does,' said Summy.

Marielle shrugged her shoulders. 'I never heard of that word,' she said. Then she went and lay on her bunk.

No one could think of anything else to say, so Tommy climbed into the floating-bowling room above the dorm with his electric violin. There, he could look out at the stars and play in peace, without disturbing a soul.

27

THE HUMANS WHO DIDN'T WANT MORE

'Gosh, double-gosh – may I present the Urgeshaker! Yes?'

For a moment Crabble stopped puffing on his guitar-sized pipe. A double class of *Philosophy and Custard* – this is what got him excited.

'Indeed, indeed, the five who are chosen to save us from, hmmm, The TFC will need the qualities of true heroes if they are to succeed . . . The Urgeshaker pinpoints just a few of those qualities. Oh my!'

All the IGGY Cadets were sitting drowsily around five work-benches in Crabble's laboratory. There was a bench for every dorm, with the Brillo1s at the front of the class, the Dream5s at the back and the other groups in-between.

The enormous-headed tutor was pointing to a machine that looked like a huge bath with two hydraulic arms sticking out of it. On the end of each arm was a circular platform on which sat a chair (like a pilot's chair with headrest and seat-belt) with a control panel dashboard suspended in front of it.

Crabble gestured to the Dream5s' work-bench. 'Hmm, could one of you please step into the store-room and plug this contraption in, yes?'

Tommy was nearest the door at the back of the lab, so he stepped into the store-room and followed the flex from the

Urgeshaker. The small room was dimly lit and full of dusty shelves. There were lots of strange items on each shelf, but the only thing Tommy recognized was a pile of wigholes, each covered in plastic packaging.

At the far end of the room sat a very large vat of custard and Tommy realized that this must be the power source Crabble had talked about earlier. He lifted the plug on the end of the flex and dropped it into the custard.

'Spiffing! Splendid! That's it! Yes?' shouted Crabble from the far room.

Before he left the store-room, Tommy lifted up one of the plastic-covered wigholes. As soon as he did, a voice spoke that seemed to come from the plastic packaging.

'Congratulations on your purchase of a *Trustie* Wighole – made by the Trustie Thingies Corporation. We hope you will be satisfied with your wighole . . . . To get your wighole working, just remove it from this plastic packaging and then do the same with another wighole. *We only work in pairs, ho-ho.*' This last bit was sung as though it might be an advertising jingle.

The voice continued: 'Taking care to hold both wigholes with a pair of Ovun Gloves, touch the wigholes to each other so that they pass through each other. This is called the *Wighole Kiss*. Now the two wigholes are activated and will always be a pair. They will never work in a stable manner with another wighole. The wigholes can be placed wherever you wish and you may move a wighole without wearing Ovun Gloves, but always take care to hold it lightly by the edges—'

'Good Lordus, have you got lost, boy? Hmm?'

Tommy jumped when he heard Crabble's voice and threw the packaged wighole back on top of the shelf. He'd been so fascinated by the Trustie Wighole spiel that he'd quite forgotten where he was.

'No, sir,' he said as he emerged from the store-room and closed over the door.

Crabble removed a remote control from his wild electric hair and pressed a button on it. An avalanche of small, round, bright-coloured objects fell from the ceiling into the 'bath' at the centre of the Urgeshaker.

'Pleasuredrops!' yelled Marielle excitedly, waking out of her stupor.

> 'Nah-nah-nah-nah-nah! Look what I've got!'
>
> Pleasuredrops are officially the most delicious sweets in the Milky Way. They're the one thing you can't taste with favo-fant food. They're so delicious that some space-people have been known to take up to 150 years to eat a single one (because they don't want to finish it). Others find them so delicious that they eat a handful in $1\frac{1}{2}$ seconds (because they can't wait to eat them).

'Hey-ho, Miss Marielle. Indeed, they jolly well are pleasure-drops, hmmm. Now who would like to win some?'

There was a flurry of voices shouting 'Me! Me! Me!'

Crabble scanned the class. He chose Summy and a creature from the Great2s called Go-T, who had a goatish face and a human-like furry body with hooves for feet. A springboard near the bath enabled both competitors to bound onto the opposing chairs.

A large projection of one of the dashboards appeared behind the monocled tutor. It had two laser guns welded onto its opposing sides and a joystick planted in its centre, next to a large red button. Crabble pointed to the projection.

'If neither contestant presses the red button during the sixty seconds, you receive, hmmm, TEN pleasuredrops each.

If your opponent presses the red button and you don't, then they get FIFTEEN pleasuredrops and you get ZERO, yes? If you press the red button and your opponent doesn't, then you get FIFTEEN pleasuredrops and your opponent gets ZERO . . . Indeed, indeed. But if you *both* press the red button, you both get only ONE pleasuredrop each. Splendid, yes?'

Summy put up her hand. 'Excuse me. Clear I just want to be . . . If neither of us presses the red button then *ten* pleasuredrops each we get?'

'Precisely, hmmm.'

'But if the red button I press and Go-T nothing presses, then *fifteen* pleasuredrops I get and *none* he gets.'

'Precisely, precisely,' said Crabble. 'But if Go-T were to press his red button also, you'd both get just ONE pleasure-drop each, yes?'

Summy looked astonished. 'But then a very simple game it is. Happy both of us are if neither one presses the red button.'

'Yes, yes, yes!' cried Crabble, nearly toppling over with excitement. 'Now, you cannot see your opponent's dash-board, hmmm, so you never know if they have pressed the red button or not.'

'What are the guns and joystick used for?' someone shouted.

'Oh my, I've never seen them used. Never. No MilkyFederan has pressed the red button for thousands of years, yes? Theoretically, gosh, you could press the red button, shooting cream-lasers at your opponent in an effort to stop him pressing his red button, hey-ho! And the joystick? By Georgus, it moves your chair up and down and from side to side, indeed, so you can avoid the cream-lasers – jolly simple! Any questions? Yes?'

'Why do you keep saying "*yes?*"' cried a voice.

'Which has more calories?' cried a much louder (human) female voice. 'A pleasuredrop or a mouthful of Fizzalicious Overhypt Moonbeam?'

'Heavens, that depends how big your mouth is, yes?' said the round tutor (who could fit 104 litres in his mouth at one time).

The first game involving Summy was a very quiet affair. Crabble sounded a hooter and then Summy and Go–T just sat there looking at each other for forty-seven seconds. Then Crabble sounded the hooter again to signal the end of the game. (Every 'game' lasts forty-seven seconds.)

'Hey-ho, you will both receive ten pleasuredrops at the end of class,' he said.

'Such a simple game is this,' exclaimed Summy in delight when she returned to her friends. 'It, an imbecile could play.'

Four other contests ended with the same outcome, until Felkor was chosen to go against Rumbles.

'Yabbadooskies!' cried Rumbles getting up from the bench. 'I'm dying for a few pleasuredrops.'

Crabble sounded the hooter and, like everyone else, Felkor and Rumbles stared at each other quietly for the first twenty-five seconds. Rumbles had a big smile on her face and looked over at his fellow Dream5s from time to time.

Tommy, who was staring intently at Felkor's face, noticed a slight tremor and then a twitch appeared below the pale fellow's eye. Thirty-three seconds had gone when everyone began to smell a pong of rotten Brussels sprouts. Intuitively, Tommy knew that Felkor had hit his red button. The snow-coloured boy was obviously getting nervous. Rumbles stopped smiling because Felkor was now snarling at her. As soon as the smile left Rumbles' face a cream–laser shot out of

224

both Felkor's guns. Rumbles moved her joystick too late. His chair flew up in the air after two cream-lasers hit her squarely in the face.

'Ahhh! By the Hokey!' she yelled. (The Hokey is a comet that shoots past Shaggyfurmop every twenty-eight minutes.)

Until they hit their target, cream-lasers look like ordinary laser-bolts. However, they're really large helpings of a mustard-flavoured custardy substance, encased in a fine film of light. They hurt as much as being struck by a hard-hit tennis ball.

Felkor swivelled his chair and continued training his guns on Rumbles. Because Rumbles' chair was moving between Felkor and the rest of the class and because most of Felkor's shots were missing Rumbles' body, cream-lasers started raining down on all the onlookers. In a flash, everyone, including Crabble, was up on their feet and yelling.

'Super-nova!'

'My new dungarees!'

'My hair! Darlingk, my hair!'

There was an ear-splitting scream. 'AAAAGGGHHHH! I got some in my mouth! Phuhhhh-fffhghhh . . . Aaaghhh! How fattening is this custardy stuff?'

Egbert Fitchly tried to do a back-flip off his dorm's work-bench, but he slipped on his cape and landed in the bath of pleasuredrops. By this time, Rumbles had started firing his cream-lasers and although his first two hit Felkor, he was still temporarily blinded by the first cream-lasers that had hit him in the face. Unbeknownst to the charcoal mass of fur, his chair had now swivelled so that she was facing the class. Cream-lasers were hailing down on all the Cadets from every angle as Felkor started yelling like a madman and pulling on his triggers as though firing a machine-gun.

225

On average, up to half of cream-lasers do not explode on impact. In such cases, you can lift up a cream-laser and throw it at somebody – in which case it will almost certainly explode. This was precisely what most people were doing with dozens of unexploded cream-lasers littering the benches and the floor. Egbert got particularly pelted because a lot of the class thought he was trying to eat all the pleasuredrops.

Poor Mr Crabble was yelling and telling everyone to sit down, but when six cream-lasers flew into his mouth at the same time, he was left spluttering to such an extent that he didn't blow the hooter until one minute and fifty-two seconds had passed since the start of the game.

A number of cream-lasers hit Tommy on the shoulder and leg, though he succeeded in hitting Trevor the toothwolf and Brendan the furballia with a couple of cream-lasers after they started pelting the Dream5s' work-bench.

When a measure of calm was finally restored, it turned out that Rumbles had managed to press his red button 45.3 seconds into the game. The result: two red buttons pressed, so Rumbles and Felkor were due only one pleasuredrop each – the only problem being that all the pleasuredrops were now ruined. The bath was almost full of exploded cream-lasers and there was a rumour (never proven) that Egbert might've done a wee in there as well.

When order was restored, Crabble looked a little green and everyone was feeling a bit soggy.

'My Lordus, now all the pleasuredrops are ruined and no one will get any,' said Crabble angrily. Everyone groaned. 'Look at this mess, yes? There will be no more games of Urgeshaker today. No, no, no . . . Mr Stagwitch has perfectly demonstrated the behaviour of humans. Hmmm? He wasn't satisfied with getting ten pleasuredrops. Oh, no, no, no! He had to get more, more, MORE! Hmmm, that's the only thing you humans say, yes? All humans – except Bonnie and Clive. They're the only nice humans I ever met. Indeed, indeed. All the others want *more, more, more*. And don't care who they deprive to get it. Oh, no. Oh, no, no, no.'

He'd never been as furious with a class, but this didn't bother Felkor, who was giving high-fives to Trevor and Brendan (and receiving *high-fours*).

'Cripes-double-cripes,[11] now clean up this class and then go back to your dormitories, yes?' thundered Crabble. 'No more classes for today.' And with that, he threw a wighole in the air and skipped under it – disappearing as it fell to the ground.

Before he started cleaning, Tommy thought about Crabble's words. The large-headed fellow had a point. Humans always wanted more for themselves. That was their big weakness. Never satisfied with anything. Tommy even found that characteristic in himself sometimes. It was a hard one to fight . . . But who were Bonnie and Clive? They didn't have that weakness. And how had Crabble come to meet them?

He stopped thinking about these things when Rumbles patted him on the back and accidentally burst a cream-laser that had somehow stuck to his shirt.

11 This is a MilkyFed swear-word only used by adults in anger (or by kids when showing off).

227

⚡ 28 ⚡

A VERY CLOSE SHAVE

When the classroom was clean, everyone started lining up in groups behind the particular wighole that would take them back to their dormitory. Tommy felt a bit soggy and wanted to have a wash, but he knew there'd be a queue for the floating globe in the Dream5s' dormitory – and Marielle and Summy were likely to monopolize the first two time slots (in fact, they usually took so long in the floating globe, it was more likely that they'd monopolize the first *six* time slots).

So when Marielle, Summy and Rumbles jumped through the wighole, Tommy held Woozie back.

'Let's not return just yet.'

'What do you mean?' said Woozie.

'We'll just be sitting round for the rest of the day. Let's go down to the GarageZone and see if my jegg is repaired yet. And if we see Miss LeWren, I can apologize again for destroying the Blue Moon.'

It sounded like a good idea, so Woozie and Tommy set off through a series of wigholes, avoiding their dorm, before plopping out into the GarageZone.

When they scrambled to their feet, everything looked and sounded eerie, since all the lights were off. There was still no wall on the far side of the room, it just opened out to space – so the twinkling stars and bright moons provided a silvery light that threw long shadows everywhere.

'Let's go back,' said Woozie. 'No one's here.'

'OK,' said Tommy, a little disappointed. Then he had an idea. 'Why don't we take a quick look at my jegg while we're here? It'll only take a minute. Then we can go.'

Woozie was easily persuaded, so the two plodded quietly to the far end of the echoey hangar and skulked around the large silver jeggs until they found Tommy's next to a smelly beige one.

'Looks fine to me,' said Woozie.

'Yes. Maybe they've repaired it already . . . Help me up and we'll take a closer look.'

Tommy climbed onto the wing with Woozie's help, then pulled the furry fellow up after him. They were peering into the cockpit, when they heard a sound on the far side of the GarageZone. It was definitely a person or persons.

Tommy was about to call out a greeting when he recognized the voices – one of which was speaking angrily.

'Fie! Turnest not on the lights. Thou wilst only draw attention to us.'

'Sorry. Gosh, sorry.'

Tommy and Woozie thought it was definitely best to stay as still and as silent as possible. They lay down on opposite wings until they could feel their hearts beating against the cool surface (three hearts in all, since wibblewallians have two hearts).

'Yes, yes, what doth be the problem?' said Lady MuckBeff testily. 'I be taking my jegg forth for a spin, so thou hadst better not delayeth me.'

Crabble struggled to keep up with Lady M, who was striding purposefully towards the jeggs.

'Heavens, I– I . . . I think I said something . . .'

'Yes, yes! How sayest thou?'

'I– I think I said something to the Cadets that I shouldn't have, yes?'

Lady M stopped in her tracks. 'Didst thou tell them there be no such things as nairies?'

'Heavens, no. Everyone knows that nairies exist. Ho!'

Nairies are mythical creatures who are reputed to steal valuables from the bedrooms of sleeping MilkyFed children and leave hideous teeth under their pillow in compensation.

'Fie! What didst thou tell them, then?' Lady M began walking briskly again, coming directly towards Tommy and Woozie.

'Hmmm, yes, I mentioned *Bonnie and Clive*.'

Lady M nearly fell over.

'The *humans*?'

'Ye-ye-yes. Gosh, you remember them? They were lovely people. Hey-ho.'

Lady M was standing so near that Tommy began to smell a strange mix of dead fish, onion and cow-shed. Woozie, a little further away, on the opposite wing, wouldn't get the smell for another 3.2 seconds.

'Didst any of the human Cadets hear thee?'

'I-I-I'm not sure, yes?'

'Fie! *Be* thee sure! Thinkest . . . ! And cease saying "*yes?*" all the time.' Lady M was furious. 'Humans shouldst never know about Bonnie and Clive. Thou knowst how dangerous it couldst be if they found out.'

Tommy raised himself up a little on his hands so that he could see over the edge of the wing. In the silvery darkness, the back of Lady M's hooded head and the reflection of stars on Crabble's monocle were plainly visible. If Tommy had chosen to creep forward half a metre, he could easily have reached down and touched the smelly hood.

'Good Lordus, one of them was screaming, so she didn't hear a thing, no, and that Egbert chap was submerged in the bath, indeed, and that girl – ZsaZsa . . . yes, hey-ho. She was concentrating on something. Hmmm, golly, yes – forming circles with the mustard-custard, hey-ho.'

'Fine, fine! What say thee about that infernal boy?'

'Hey-ho – much too busy smirking at his friends to listen to a thing. By heavens, the idiot ruined my whole classroom, hmmm.'

'Not *that* boy! He be call'd Felkor . . . He doth be quite impressive, by the by . . . No, I talkest of the infernal creature, Master Stork or Scorn or whatsoever his damn'd name doth be.'

'Tommy Storm?'

'Yes, that be he.' And Lady M buried her nose in the flower on her lapel – as though it were smelling salts required to revive her.

'By Georgus, don't you think he looks quite like them, hmmm?'

'Like whom?'

'Bonnie and Clive – gosh, yes, Tommy Storm looks very like Bonnie and yet, he also looks very like Clive, yes?'

'Fie! Cease mentioning those names! Thou knowst how dangerous it doth be . . . I care not who lookest like whom . . . Pray tell, *to hear or not to hear?*'

Crabble was baffled. 'Hmm, I don't . . .'

Lady M sighed with exasperation. 'Didst Storm *HEAR* thee mention those foolish names . . . !? *To hear or not to hear? That is the question.*'

Crabble thought about it.

'Hmmm, I doubt he heard. No, no, there was an awful lot of mustard-custard everywhere – oh, my.'

While everyone had been cleaning up Crabble's classroom

231

earlier, Woozie spotted a relatively untouched pleasuredrop in the bath which seemed to have no mustard-custard on it. And so he placed it in his pocket. Unfortunately, the pleasuredrop chose this moment to roll out of Woozie's PancePocket and across the wing, falling onto the hard floor and under the beige jegg.

Pockets of Resistance

Wibblewallians have a number of pockets built into their furry coats – two where trouser pockets might be found (PancePockets) and one large one across their back (the DorsalPocket). Only the DorsalPocket seals naturally (there's a velcro-like substance across their shoulder-blades, between the two layers of fur) and so it's very handy for carrying documents or baking trays. A famous wibblewallian curse goes: *may hooligum* (a kind of chewing gum) *enter your DorsalPocket.*

'Hark!' Lady M drew four fingers (one from each hand) in front of her lips and Crabble obliged, by freezing. 'Didst thou hearest that?'

'Ho! What?'

'That noise . . . There doth be someone in the shadows.'

'Hmmm, there's no one in the shadows. No, no, you're imagining it. You're just jumpy. Yes?'

'Hmmm.' Lady M wasn't so sure. 'And stop saying "*yes?*"!' She took a pair of night-goggles out of a coat pocket and put them on. Everything was now as clear to her as though all the lights were on in the GarageZone. Lady M looked up and down the GarageZone, then fell onto all-sixes and peered around the jeggs.

'You see? Lordy-lordy, there's no one here,' said Crabble.

Lady M looked annoyed and started walking away from Crabble. She walked directly below Tommy, then under Woozie on the other wing and then she jumped up onto the beige jegg and climbed into the cockpit. If at that moment, she'd looked left towards Crabble, she would've seen Tommy and Woozie clinging to the wings of the adjacent jegg.

Instead, Lady M was looking straight out to space as she fiddled with the controls. Woozie and Tommy pressed themselves even more firmly onto the wings. Oblivious of Lady M's night-goggles, they felt somewhat safe in the shadows. It was his own breathing, sounding like an orchestra playing at full volume, that worried Tommy. So he held his breath and hoped that Lady M would fly off before he had to gasp for air.

Crabble walked under Tommy's jegg and continued until he was on the far side of Lady M's jegg.

'Hmmm, should I tell Wisebeardyface about this?'

Lady M looked down at the potato-like fellow. 'No! Wouldst thou be mad? Speaketh to no one of these affairs. No one. It doth be too perilous – a thousand times o'er.'

The engines of the beige jegg started to roar, but Tommy was still afraid to breathe. It felt as if a large balloon was pressing against the inside of his chest, trying to escape.

'Gosh, yes, I hear you,' said Crabble (even though he could no longer hear a thing). 'I won't say a word, yes? Ooops, said *yes* again – golly, sorry.'

Lady M scowled down at him and flew off without so much as a wave. The huge-headed man watched the jegg shrink to the size of a blackhead and lose itself in a constellation of stars, and then he walked back under Tommy's jegg. After stopping to tie his shoe-lace and picking his nose as he ambled away (his arm could fit up his nostril, almost up to the elbow), the Humpty Dumpty-shaped tutor finally jumped through a wighole and disappeared from view.

'Phewwww!' wheezed Tommy, expelling enough air to inflate a lilo.

'Sorry 'bout the pleasuredrop,' said Woozie, a little embarrassed. 'Was hoping to eat that later.'

It took some time for Tommy's breath to return to normal, but when it did, the two friends clambered off the wings of the jegg and hurried over to the wigholes. They were just about to jump through one when a silver streak blinked in and out of shadows as it fell to the ground. Immediately, the lights came on and Miss LeWren was standing before the stunned pair wearing a single rollerblade. She'd travelled down the slidey pole (thankfully, the ground at its base was now repaired).

'What are you doing here?' she demanded.

Tommy thought it best to tell the truth.

'Eh, sorry, Miss. I was hoping to find you here. We just wanted to check if my jegg had been repaired.'

'I juzt saw a jegg leave ze GarageZone. Were you trying to fly your jegg?'

'No, Miss, honest. I just wanted to see if it was OK.'

'That's the truth, Miss,' said Woozie. 'We just wanted to ask you if it had been repaired.'

'You know you shouldn't be down here on your own!' she snapped.

'We know,' said Tommy. 'We're sorry. We thought you'd be here . . . And I wanted to apologize again for . . . well, for all the damage I did the other day. I really am sorry.'

Miss LeWren appeared to soften.

'Well, neggst time, get permission first from one of ze tutors before coming down here. Ze GarageZone eez a dangerouz place and children are not allowed down here on zeir own. Zat goes for most of ze roomz in IGGY.'

'You mean like the Uh–Oh–Doh–Joh Chamber?' Woozie had no particular reason for asking this. He just had a crush on Miss LeWren and wanted to appear knowledgeable about IGGY.

'*Especially* ze Uh–Oh–Doh–Joh Chamber. Zat eez even more dangerous zan here. And far more sacred. Children are never allowed zere on zeir own. Many people haff fallen into ze Abyss and never been seen again.'

'OK,' said Woozie, troubled by the image.

'Thanks, Miss,' said Tommy. 'We'd better be going.'

'Oh, Tommy.'

'Yes, Miss?'

'I have seen ze GarageZone motion–rrecording from ze ozzer day.'

'Oh.'

Miss LeWren pointed towards a few small black globes at the edge of the GarageZone. Apparently, there were lots of similar – transparent – ones all over IGGY. 'Zose cameraz look out to space. Zey couldn't see you on ze ozzer side of ze Blue Moon before your crash, but zey picked out what you did before you disappeared behind eet.'

Tommy's heart sank. Now Miss LeWren was going to bawl him out for the dangerous manoeuvre that stopped Woozie's spin.

'I haff to say, Meester Storm, I have never seen such natural ability in one so new to ze art of jegg piloting.' Tommy blushed. 'Never haff I seen such instinctive courage, not since Cli—'

She stopped abruptly and looked uncomfortable.

'Not since what?' said Woozie.

'You'd better be going,' said Miss LeWren hurriedly. 'I juzt rremembered – I have a lot of zings to do.'

And with that, she rollerbladed off towards the jeggs.

～ 29 ～

THE GAME OF HAPPINESS

Back in the dormitory, Marielle was supervising more cleaning. During the cream-laser fight, a large number of lasers had been fired at the wall of Crabble's classroom and many had flown straight through the wighole to the Dream5s' dormitory. There was mustard-custard all over the place.

Tommy and Woozie mucked in with the cleaning. They were too relieved after the close shave with Lady M to argue with Marielle's bossing. In fact, it was quite nice to stop thinking and just clean whatever she pointed at.

When the clean-up was finished, everyone had a floating globe-bath (yes, Marielle and Summy took for ever) followed by a hearty favo-fant meal. Tommy felt a lot better – his heart rate was now back to normal after the scare in the GarageZone. Sipping a glass of Choke (really favo-fant liquid), he sat back and observed Rumbles and Summy putting on large bow-ties.

'What are you doing?' asked Tommy

'PlanetChessy,' said Summy as Rumbles opened a cupboard and rolled out a large rock-like sphere (called a *BabbaPlanet*). It was about the size of a very large TV.

'Never heard of it,' said Tommy. 'What is it?'

'Watch and learn, my furless friendskeey,' said Rumbles.

'But silent as possible please be,' added Summy. 'For

PlanetChessy concentration is required.'

When the BabbaPlanet was in the middle of the room, Rumbles pressed something on it and it opened, spilling dozens of boxes on the floor. Then the BabbaPlanet closed again. Summy carried two chairs towards Rumbles and the two creatures sat on either side of the sphere, placing both their hands on its surface. Immediately, the BabbaPlanet began to hum and became patterned with teeny, neat squares (2,346 to be exact). The squares were black, white and red, but they formed no discernible patterns. On opposite poles of the Babba, two blue patches emerged, looking like neat Arctic and Antarctic Circles.

The Babba rose until it was waist-high off the ground and then it started spinning quickly. All the squares became a blur.

'My call or yours?' said Rumbles.

'Yours,' said Summy.

Rumbles nodded and waited. Then, without warning, he yelled 'Stop!'

The Babba came to a standstill. Summy looked at the various boxes piled on the floor.

'Which species to be do you want?' she said.

'Thunderbumbles, of courskeey.'

Summy sifted through the boxes until she found a box labelled *Thunderbumbles*, which she handed to Rumbles.

'Well, kangasauri then I'll be.' (The plural of kangasaurus.)

'Ridiculous choice,' said Woozie, from where he was sitting at the dinner table beside Tommy and Marielle. 'Why don't you be the wibblewallians?'

'Thank you, no,' said Summy haughtily. 'If to be small and furry I wanted, a floating globe brush instead I'd choose to be.'

237

'Hey, what's wrong with being furry!?' cried Rumbles indignantly.

A floating globe brush is a bit like a toilet brush. Wibblewallians often get teased for looking like floating globe brushes and there are many MilkyFed jokes that make use of this fact.

Rumbles opened his box and began removing tiny moving figures from it. They looked like miniature statues of Rumbles, each doing something different. One was sitting in a spacecraft, another was in a floating globe, one was lying down and one even looked like she was blindfolded with an orange in his mouth. Rumbles placed about twenty figures on twenty different squares upon the BabbaPlanet. Summy did likewise with her kangasauri.

PlanetChessy is a game that requires the contestants to use a degree of telepathy. Once you place your pieces on the board, you're not allowed to touch them again. You just send them orders using your mind. The skill in the game is to ask them to do particular things in the *right way*, understanding that the figures have their own minds once placed on the globe and behave according to the recognized behaviour of their species. Kangasauri, for example, are very obedient and clan-oriented. It's important to remember that the pieces choose their own ways of carrying out your mental orders, that sometimes they'll misinterpret orders and, that if you stop giving orders, they'll start generating their own orders. It's been called a lazy game by some because people can place their pieces on the board and then go off to wash their space-craft, only returning when the game is over.

'Begin!' shouted Rumbles and the globe started to turn very slowly, at about five minutes per revolution.

The object of PlanetChessy is to make your players live as

happily as possible on the BabbaPlanet and you're not allowed to cheat by using a *HappinessIzzzAh* program when making moves. You can tell how happy they are by how warm the pieces are. The game lasts about two hours and ends when the Babba stops revolving. At this point, all the squares on the Babba open inwards, all the remaining pieces fall inside and the temperatures of *all* of them are measured. If *together* the pieces are very hot (and therefore very happy), the squares on the outside of the Babba go red and it looks like the sun at sunset. If the pieces are a bit cooler, the Babba looks more orangey. Cooler still and it's yellowish, even cooler and it's white, cold equals blue, freezing equals grey, absolutely frozen (very, very unhappy) equals black.

Whatever colour the Babba becomes at the end of the game, it stays that colour for a few hours and emits a level of heat that reflects its colour. It's said that PlanetChessy is played in the evening in many MilkyFed homes because families enjoy going to bed with a large red sun glowing in the bedroom.

Wham-Bam-Morning-Scram

In MilkyFed families, all members of the family tend to sleep in the same room. The bedrooms are therefore very large. Bunk-beds are popular on many planets and some wibblewallian families have bunk-beds that are up to 100 metres high (as they can have up to seventy children and always insist on one tower of bunk-beds). Those children at the top have to start climbing up the bunk-ladder about an hour before bedtime (a springboard is only used to reach the first six bunks). A big padded cushion on the floor allows kids to jump out of bed and land safely in the morning, although you've got to check above before jumping to ensure a brother or sister isn't plunging through the air already.

PlanetChessy isn't a very exciting spectator sport as Tommy soon found out. Both Summy's and Rumbles' pieces started building towns and producing food and goods. Then they began travelling towards each other and exchanging food and goods. Soon they were helping each other build better towns and started inter-marrying. These couples must've had kids, because when Tommy looked over towards the end of the game, there was over a hundred pieces and they all seemed to be laughing or dancing or singing. Tommy wasn't sure how they'd done it, but tiny little dwelling places and ornate buildings had appeared on parts of the Babba.

The singing and laughing of the pieces sounded like a distant radio to Tommy, who soon found himself in a long conversation with Woozie and Marielle. Something had been stirred in him in the last few days and he wasn't quite sure what it was. He ended up telling Woozie and Marielle about his parents, explaining that he didn't remember them, that he knew nothing of them, but that he'd begun to feel a calling from them ever since he'd thought about a trip to space.

He told them about the visions he saw on the Plank of Discovery and then they all shared their visions. It was Woozie who mentioned the close shave with Lady M to Marielle and brought up the subject of Bonnie and Clive.

'Who do you think they are?' he said.

Marielle shook her head. 'Mr Crabble said . . . What did he say?' She was trying to remember. '*All humans want more. All except Bonnie and Clive – who did not* . . . He said something like that, anyway.'

'No, no, you got it completely wrong,' said Woozie, smiling. '*Hmmm, my Lordus, all humans want more, yes? Except Bonnie and Clive, golly-gosh, yes? Hey-ho!*'

Tommy laughed, but the mystery remained. When

everyone went to bed, he lay in his bunk, enjoying the glow from the fiery-red Babba – lots of things swirling round his head. He thought about the way Wisebeardyface and the other members of the Milki Masters' Council looked at him as though they'd seen him before. About the kind couple in the Abyss of Visions and the strange connection he'd felt to them. He thought about Crabble and Lady M's conversation. Who were Bonnie and Clive? Why were they such a secret? Could they have been the pair in the Abyss of Visions?

Tommy conjured up answers to each of these questions, but none of them made sense. He'd an odd feeling about all of this. There was one possible answer to these questions that Tommy was too afraid to even contemplate. Butterflies crept into his stomach and his head began to tingle. A possible plan formed in his mind. It was one that generated fear, yet dizzy excitement within his heart. 'No, I couldn't do that,' he thought. 'I'd get myself expelled, ruin everything for the Dream5s and probably be the cause of Earth being the planet chosen for obliteration.'

Unable to sleep, he crept up to the floating-bowling room, electric violin in hand. There, he played and played and played, until he was completely spent.

— 30 —
DÉJÁ VU

Over the next few days, Tommy was too busy to think about the idea that had made him dizzy and scared at the same time. There were jegg flying lessons to be taken, science classes to be endured with Crabble and lots of other subjects besides. He learned much about the geography and history of the Milky Way and came to know many legends of the flash-scimitar. All of these skills and all of this knowledge could prove vital, they were told, to somehow averting The TFC.

MonSenior had emphasized: 'We have carefully selected the subjects and skills which will aid us in choosing which dorm should be selected for the SWIGS Mission.'

And as Lady MuckBeff had put it: 'Imagine ye, being chosen for the SWIGS Mission and ending up in a parallel universe with a clear chance to saveth the universe from The TFC – whatsoever The TFC might'st be . . . How wouldst ye feel if that chance slip'd past – thus causing billions and billions of lives to be lost – solely because ye failed to maketh use of a key fact aforetime demonstrat'd in our Milky Way?'

One of Tommy's favourite subjects was *POO*, taken by Miss LeWren. POO stands for Planetary Orbit Observations. Tommy learnt that planets generally move around stars in elliptical orbits. He was fascinated to hear that while Earth moves around the sun, at the same time,

Earth's Solar System revolves around the centre of the Milky Way, taking 225 million years to complete one orbit (which may explain why few MilkyFed postmen ever get to finish a postal round in their lifetime). Most impressively of all (because maths had never been his best subject), Tommy learnt how to calculate the precise co-ordinates necessary to fire a food parcel from a cannon on IGGY to a particular point on any planet in the Milky Way. This was a difficult calculation and the key factors you needed to take into consideration were: the speed of the food parcel (once fired), the speed of the rotation of the target planet, the speed of the planet's orbit, and whether or not you'd remembered to put the food parcel in the cannon before firing it.

Wisebeardyface took the IGGY Cadets for a number of history classes and, amongst many things, Tommy learned that a kangasaurus was a kind of dinosaurus who rarely caught the measles. (If you're wondering, a *dinosaur* is the technical term for a *dead* dinosaurus.) In the MilkyFed, dinosauri were considered to be one of the cleverest species and particularly adept at space-beach volley-ball (remarkably similar to Earth's beach volley-ball, although all participants, male or female, must wear itsy-bitsy teeny-weeny polka-dot bikinis – normally, yellow ones).

At the start of every class, the old dinosaurus used to bore them all with lines from his favourite poem (called *Comet Number 116*).

> *'Tis not what you do, 'tis how you do it.*
> *'Tis not what you say, 'tis how you say it . . .*
> *For the first shall be last.*
> *Gibbledibble blast.*

It's most important that the last line is said almost as a sneeze – otherwise the line has a completely different meaning in MilkyFed circles, a very rude meaning at that. No one would stand too close to Wisebeardyface whenever he recited the poem as fire always emitted from his nostrils whenever he sneezed or half-sneezed.

Apparently, the poem was written three million years earlier by a bearded creature called Piershakes who was allergic to sentences that didn't rhyme. Fully-fledged IGGY Knights were expected to be able to quote the poem backwards in their sleep (and I can assure you, it's quite a difficult thing to learn how to do).

One day, Wisebeardyface happened to mention Earth.

'A lot of my ancestors lived there for a while,' he said. 'There was a great deal of building work going on in their home planet, MuzeyUmm, so they moved to Earth for a few million years, until the renovations were done. I think the family kitchen was still uncompleted when they returned home, though. They were most annoyed.'

'Did they like Earth?' Tommy asked, intrigued at this news.

'Hmm, not really. There were no drive-in fast-food places back then, you know. They had to scavenge around for food . . . And day and night come and go so quickly there. Twenty-four hours, if I remember correctly. You blink your eyes and suddenly ten thousand days have gone past.'

Wisebeardyface's words might seem strange until you realize that the planet MuzeyUmm takes 202 Earth years to do a full rotation, which means that days and nights last 101 years each. This is why dinosauri are renowned (unfairly) for being so lazy. They sometimes sleep for 100 years at a time. And if they've had a particularly busy day they might have a lie-in and sleep even longer!

'Mind you,' continued the old dinosaurus, trying to

picture Earth, 'you were never sure of anything there. That is what I heard. The weather changing every day. Hot for a hundred days, then cool for another fifty. Wind, rain and changing scenery. The sky always changing colour.

'Plus, it was impossible to eat the same thing all the time. There was no favo-fant food, I can tell you. Just big trees or small tress, green trees, brown trees, red and yellow bushes, flowers of every colour.

'Nothing uniform about the land either. Mountains here, valleys there. Great oceans, flat plains, dense forests, vast deserts . . . It was just *so* varied. Much too varied. Much too easy to get lost.

'My ancestors really knew it was time to go home when apes in loincloths started writing graffiti on cave walls and throwing feeble pointy sticks at them . . . Or was that a Grow-sss-Goo movie I saw?' Wisebeardyface looked unsure.

Anjel*eek!* Jalfrezi put her hand up. No longer looking skinny, she said she'd read something about the Tyrannosaurus Rex being very fierce and eating everyone. She looked as though she might scream, but then thought better of it. Instead, she pulled a handful of favo-fant food out of her pocket and stuffed it hungrily into her mouth.

'Oh, no, not at all,' replied Wisebeardyface. 'Old Rexy was as calm as you like. Loved pottering around baking fossils and then burying them for busybodies to find.'

During one of the classes, Wisebeardyface outlined the three reasons why he'd been particularly keen to invite five humans to IGGY. They were (in no particular order):

1 He'd once been very fond of a couple from Earth (he wouldn't say who they were – but Tommy reckoned it must be Bonnie and Clive).

2 He felt some guilt about Earth being on the Possible Obliteration List and thought it only fair to enable one or more humans to survive if Earth was to be chosen.

3 He had a certain soft spot for Earth since his ancestors had lived there for a time and he'd often enjoyed watching humorous documentaries of humans visiting hilarious modern art galleries.

Lady MuckBeff WiLLyoofytus took all the Cadets for Phenomenon class – a subject that covered weird facts and anomalies of the Milky Way. The class was held in a vast, craggy, cavernous amphitheatre that served as Lady M's laboratory. Inside the enclosure, you'd never think you were inside a space-station. It was more like you'd burrowed into the centre of a mountain. Garlands of flowers dotted the walls – a grudging concession to life. Lady M stood upon the lowest level of the room while the Cadets sat upon the ascending craggy ledges.

Maybe it was because she was their jegg tutor, but Lady M clearly favoured the Brillo1s and often congratulated them for making rather obvious comments. For some reason, she seemed to dislike the Dream5s and didn't try to hide it.

After a long lecture on volcanoes that emit great quantities of lemon sherbet on the planet ToophDK, Lady M asked if there were any comments. 'Fie thee hither! madam,' she roared, when poor Summy asked whether it was possible to eat the sherbet before it cooled.

No one was entirely sure what '*fie thee hither*' meant, but it had the tone of '*ridiculous question*' or '*get lost*'.

Despite Lady M's angry demeanour, Tommy was interested in the subject matter of her class.

''Tis no coincidence that coincidences and déjà vu happen

frequently to perceptive people,' Lady M said one day. 'When iron filings jump onto a magnet, doth the iron filings sayeth, *Oh what a coincidence, we all cameth to the same place?* Why, no! 'Tis just magnetism. 'Tis the same with all coincidences. Thus, if thou art in a building and thou thinks of thy friend and they think of thee, then ye shallst become attracted – as magnets – and may henceforth bump into one other. Oft, people sayeth, *'tis a big coincidence that we bumped into one another.* Hah! What poppycock!'

Woozie whispered to Tommy: 'Lady M certainly leaves a smelly invisible trail wherever she goes. And no one wants to follow it.'

Lady M stopped speaking when she saw the pair laughing. Tommy became aware of an angry, piercing gaze. 'Master Storm, Master Wibblewoodrow! I do be having déjà vu. I canst see ye both doing extra extra homework this very eve. And on the morrow and for the rest of the week.'

This made them shut up and listen to the remainder of the lecture. Lady M started speaking about how the MilkyFed had learned to slow time. She explained that time could pass more slowly within IGGY than without, if a *Segnitia Switch* was flicked on. This technology had been developed by examining black holes.

'If ye ever fall into a black hole,' said the hooded tutor, 'time starteth to slow more and more, the further you slippeth inside. Thus, it feels like for ever for a second to pass. If ye could see out of a black hole, ye might see a spacecraft in the distance take one hundred years to travel but a centimetre. To the people in the spacecraft, 'twould feel like it hath taken but a fraction of a second to travel that same centimetre – forwhy, in truth, they wouldst be travelling at many millions of kilometres an hour.'

Tommy wasn't sure he completely understood Lady M's

explanation, but Summy had been nodding intently throughout and making occasional noises of agreement. Maybe he'd ask Summy about it later.

If you're the type of person who knows exactly how many sweets you can eat before feeling sick (it's thirty-eight for me), then you'll have guessed that a Segnitia Switch was flicked on when Tommy first met Wisebeardyface in the Ballroom. In fact, on that occasion, the 'Master' Segnitia Switch was accidentally deployed, so that time was slowed throughout IGGY rather than just in the Ballroom. This switch was absent-mindedly left switched on for some considerable period, generating a hefty power bill. This was why the other Dream5s seemed to have been in the dorm for such a long time before Tommy arrived.

Somebody asked about time travel and Lady M tut-tutted. ''Tis impossible,' she said. 'Be ye not absurd.'

'Absurd?' said a voice. It was Wisebeardyface. He'd entered the room unnoticed.

Lady M wasn't pleased with this intrusion. ''Twill forever be impossible to travel thro' time, Lord Beardedmoustached-Wiseface-oh. Physics willst not allow it.'

'What about the way the unspoken couple caused us to jump back in time?'

Lady M looked rattled. 'Speaketh not of such things, m'lord. Thou shouldst never talketh of *them*.'

'I am not mentioning any names. I am just referring to the theory of time travel. It has been shown to work in a small yet significant way.'

'Yes, yes,' said Lady M impatiently, 'but, alack, it causeth certain death and only moveth time back a minute at the very most. And only ever did it happen *once* – by happenstance, methinks.'

'Luck had nothing to do with it . . . And yes, it has not been perfected, but maybe some day it will . . . Some day, when we are long dead, Lady MuckBeff.'

When Wisebeardyface left (muttering his favourite poem, with a little fire flaring from his nostrils), Lady M looked witheringly at Tommy. It made Tommy nervous and he'd no idea what he'd done wrong.

━ 31 ━

DECISIONS DECISIONS

Some time after the discussion about time travel, Tommy made perhaps the most frightening decision of his life. The decision was made at the end of an evening like many others – one where Guttly had come to have dinner with the Dream5s.

Guttly enjoyed joining them for dinner because they were far more relaxed than the other dorms.

The Brillo1s were all very tense and serious – everyone keyed up to 'win' the contest to be made IGGY Knights (although few of them were keen on the idea of the SWIGS mission itself – it sounded a bit too dangerous).

Guttly couldn't stand eating with the Great2s because he hated the sound of Anjel*eek!*'s screams and, once she'd scoffed her own serving, she'd keep skating around the table, snatching food from everyone else's plate whenever she could. (For some reason, her skating and snatching made him think of someone playing musical chairs – someone who was frenzied and determined to win – but he wasn't sure why.)

The VGood3s were out because Egbert talked too quickly for Guttly to understand a word he was saying and, in any case, the way he kept doing back-flips during meals was most annoying (mostly because his cowboy hat kept landing on Guttly's plate).

The Alright4s weren't too bad, but Guttly was always put off his appetite when ZsaZsa started smearing her food on the table and forming intricate series of circles with the feather from her headband.

And so Guttly chose to have most of his dinners with the Dream5s and, over the course of these visits, Tommy noticed that the old man lost a little of his strict, serious air. It was like watching an iceberg gradually melt.

Sometimes Guttly regaled the group with stories of his youth. Tommy was particularly intrigued to hear stories about Earth before the Great Climate Enhancement occurred. In some ways it sounded wonderful. In other ways it sounded mad. He couldn't believe that young children paid ten times the ordinary price for shoes and sneakers if they had the 'correct' stripes on their side. It was the same with most clothes, Guttly explained. You paid a fortune for a tiny logo the size of a small coin and then the clothes came free, attached.

Woozie's interest had been aroused when he first saw the educational Grow-sss-Goo movie about planet Earth and he wanted to hear more about the strange behaviour involving TVs. A movie now and again was fine, but everyday TV-watching sounded like such a waste of time. Guttly explained that adults stopped hanging round with each other early in the 21st century. The only adults most adults interacted with were their work colleagues – and those were people they only just tolerated. To substitute for the lack of friends and chatty neighbours, people spent hours sitting in front of the TV, watching stories about the lives of *other* people. People stopped *living* their own lives and preferred *watching* other people's lives. There were always pictures of famous people in the newspapers and lots of stories about the colour of their bed linen. Ordinary adults stopped becoming participants in life and became spectators instead.

'I've never heard of a *famous* person from Earth,' said Marielle. 'Why are they famous?'

'Because they're always on TV or in the newspapers,' replied Guttly.

'Yes, yes, but they are famous *why*?' asked Summy. 'I suppose very talented?'

Guttly shook his head. 'Did you ever have any fools in your class in school who looked for attention all the time?'

'Yes.'

'QED.'

I'm an Idiot, Get Me *In* There!

From 1990 onwards, famous people on Earth became less and less talented. This coincided with the fact that MilkyFed tourists began to stop visiting Earth to plant inventions and creative ideas (see *Extra Bits no. 3*, page 421). This left an alarming vacuum, which was filled with much hot air. Yes, there were some brilliant and talented people (such as doctors, nurses, teachers, bus conductors, masseurs and musicians) who refined skills that had been left by earlier MilkyFed visitors, but they received a fraction of the attention received by loud people with large body parts or a great ability to be rude in public.

Tommy wasn't sure what *QED* meant, but he was very interested to hear about such things as double-sided sticky tape, smelly dishcloths, wonky shopping trolleys, hedgehog-flavour crisps, incessant car alarms, cramped trains, long winding queues that never moved and socks that got lost in the wash. It seemed like a different world.

'But I still love it, even though it's changed,' said Guttly. 'It's my planet and I love it warts and all. If the Milki

Masters' Council decides to destroy Earth, then I'll go back. I'd like to be with it if it goes. I am the President, after all.'

'Do you think they'll choose Earth?' asked Tommy.

'I hope not. I've been talking to all the tutors, telling them about Earth's qualities. I may have softened Wisebeardyface, because he's agreed to send a probe to Earth.'

'A probe?'

'Yes, it will fly under the clouds and take some pictures. I want Wisebeardyface to see that humans live in harmony. That we can be a decent friend to the MilkyFed . . . I've called Elsorr Maudlin, my Deputy President, and asked him to make things ready for the probe. If we can call a halt to all the wars and dishonesty for one day, perhaps the probe will bring back some positive pictures. It's our best hope.'

This was good news. Perhaps I won't be responsible for the destruction of Earth, after all, thought Tommy. 'What did Elsorr say when he heard that Earth may be destroyed?' he asked, wondering how people on Earth would react to such news.

'I didn't tell him. It's better that no one knows.'

Guttly admitted that if it were not for the threat to Earth, he'd be thoroughly enjoying the break on IGGY.

'It's nice to get away from the job for a while,' he said. 'Being the President can become a strain when you're doing it all the time. People always see you as the President, never as a person who has likes and needs and fears . . . I'm really quite unimportant here. People treat me as a normal person. It's almost like a holiday.'

Guttly mentioned in passing that his wife had died some years ago and that they never had kids. For a brief moment, tears welled in the old man's eyes and he pretended to blow his nose. When he removed the hanky his eyes were clear again. Maybe, he went on to explain, that's why he enjoyed IGGY – it gave him a chance to play granddad for a while and forget his presidential duties. Already, he found himself being less stern with every passing day. It was something he found surprisingly fun.

'Not being stern . . . Yes, it's strangely liberating . . .' he smiled, scratching his thick, grey beard.

When Tommy pressed him, Guttly admitted that the week's training given to *The Four* before they left Earth had been completely useless.

'We didn't have a clue,' said Guttly. 'We – the Grand Council – were too proud to ask.' He giggled. 'Forward rolls, sheep impressions?' And they all laughed – particularly Woozie, who fell off his chair at the idea of a forward roll competition.

'I don't know what you're laughing at,' said Tommy to his furry friend. 'You told me that the five chosen for the SWIGS mission were to become rulers of a new planet and be given free sweets and ice-cream for life.'

'But crazy, that is,' said Summy.

'I said it was a *rumour*!' exclaimed Woozie, picking himself off the floor.

The discussion was halted abruptly when a floating globe sped into view and hovered outside the window. They could see Crabble inside. He had a small ball of goo in his hand, which he threw towards them. The goo morphed through the floating globe and splattered across the outside of the window. It started bubbling and spread until it covered the entire pane and Crabble disappeared from view. Eventually, it formed this message:

```
AS OF THIS EVENING, THE STANDING OF THE IGGY CADETS IS
                      AS FOLLOWS:


  DORMS          STARS      BLACK HOLES     TOTAL
  BRILLO1S       XXXXXX          0            40
  GREAT2S        XXXXXX          00           20
  VGOOD3S        XXXXX           0            30
  ALRIGHT4S      XXX                          30
  DREAM5S        XX              000         -40
```

'So, we're joint leaders with forty points,' said Woozie.

'*Minus* forty, dumbo,' said Summy.

'Hey, my middle name might be Dumm-Beau, but I'm no dumbo.'

'So, we're in last place?' said Rumbles, knocking Guttly's glass onto his lap (luckily it was empty). 'Oops-a-dungly.'

'We got the black holes because I destroyed the Blue Moon,' said Tommy. 'It's my fault we're last.'

'Don't be silly,' said Marielle softly.

'For every star, ten points it is,' said Summy. 'And for every black hole, minus twenty points.'

Then all the print started to mix itself up and dissolve, until new letters emerged. The new screen said:

```
     PROGRAMME OF IGGY CADET TESTS AND CONTESTS


  SUBJECT           DATE           TEST TYPE        POINTS
  MILKY WAY HISTORY  BILLIEHOLLIEDAY  EXAM      (ALL)    20
  MILKY WAY GEOG     BILLIEHOLLIEDAY  EXAM      (ALL)    10
  POO               THRUSHDAY       CONTEST    (BEST)   10
  PHENOMENA         THRUSHDAY       EXAM       (ALL)    20
  FLOATING BOWLING*** DORRISSSDAY   1-1 CONTEST (BEST)  40
  PLANET CHESSY**    DORRISSSDAY    1-1 TEAMWORK (BEST) 40
  JEGG RACE         DEEDAY          GROUP RELAY (ALL)   70
  FLASHSCIMITAR     INANAMDAY       1-1 CONTEST (BEST)  90
    CONTEST**
                                               _____
                                                300
```

255

You had to read fast because soon the screen dissolved and another one had taken its place. The latest screen explained that where contest or exams had *(all)* written after them, the scores of everyone in the dorm would be added together. The dorm getting the highest score would win the points for that subject. Where contest had *(best)* written after them, the contest was about finding the best person (or *pair* in the case of PlanetChessy) out of all the IGGY Cadets. Whoever won one of these contests would win all the points in that test for their dorm.

'Three hundred looks like a lot of points,' said Guttly, 'but between five groups that averages sixty points each. If your dorm gets sixty points, your overall score will only be plus twenty . . . You'll need to do well if you want to be chosen as the IGGY Knights.'

There were a few more screens detailing times, rules and other facts concerning the tests and contests. One screen stressed the notion of fair play. It explained that Knights of the Way never cheat and show respect to opponents at all times – even when they feel cranky.

'Don't know if I understand about all the pointskeeys and all the testskeeys,' said Rumbles, when the screens disappeared.

'I wouldn't worry,' said Guttly. 'I'm sure it will all become clear once the tests begin.'

'BilliehollieDay – tomorrow that is,' said Summy. 'Tomorrow start the exams!'

'So all the contests will be over in five days from now,' said Woozie, a little disappointed.

'And then, if we're not chosen as the IGGY Knights, we'll be sent back to our own planets two days later!' said Tommy.

'So we could be back in our planets in seven days' time,'

said Marielle with a sadness in her voice. She looked over at Tommy, who tried to give a comforting smile.

'You haven't lost yet,' said Guttly. 'It's not over till the fat lady sings.'

'Who's the fat lady?' asked Rumbles, knocking over Guttly's glass again and catching it before it hit the floor. 'Oops-a-dungly!'

'It's just a saying we have on Earth. All it means is, it's never over till it's over.'

'I never heard a fat lady sing,' said Woozie. 'Not if you don't count Summy humming in the floating globe.'

'Hey!' cried Summy and smacked Woozie's bum with her tail.

A Week's a long time in Polytix
(slogan for MilkyFed calendars made by Polytix Inc.)

The MilkyFed don't have the same weekdays as Earth. A week consists of twelve days and most days are named after ancient MilkyFed presidents or types of fungal infection. ThrushDay is the only day named after neither. It's named after a bird whose miniature cousin was found on Earth before the Great Climate Enhancement. A long time ago, a dyslexic hooligan with a lisp visited Earth to plant ThrushDay in Earth's then six-day week. The result was *Thursday*.

Marielle thought of something. 'But they can't send Tommy back to Earth if they're going to destroy it!'

Guttly shook his head. 'If they decide to destroy Earth, Lord BeardedmoustachedWiseface-oh says they'll allow all the human Cadets to stay on IGGY. They'll be offered jobs in the IGGY kitchens.'

'That wouldn't be too badskeeys, Tommy, would it?' said Rumbles, patting Tommy hard on the back and making his eyes water.

Tommy made the decision as he lay in bed that night. It was something he'd wrestled with for over a week, but a number of factors had finally swayed him.

Firstly, there was Guttly saying that he'd return to Earth if it was to be destroyed. Somehow, that made Tommy realize that you have to follow your convictions. If you believe in something, if you really love something, you shouldn't abandon it because the consequences for you are bleak. Tommy had grown quite fond of the old man. He hadn't been sure when he first met Guttly, but now he was, and he respected the old fellow's wise opinions.

Secondly, Tommy knew that the odds were against the Dream5s being crowned IGGY Knights. They were in last place and some way behind. A betting person would be foolish to stake much on their chances. So if (or when) the Dream5s didn't win, Tommy would choose to return to Earth – even if it was to be destroyed. This made him think that he'd little to lose.

Thirdly, and most importantly, he felt a pull, an invisible force drawing him towards the decision. He wouldn't admit it, but he knew this invisible force was linked to all the questions about Bonnie and Clive and the couple in the Abyss of Visions. The very thought of it made him dizzy and afraid all at once. (Sometimes he wondered about the feeling he always felt on IGGY – the feeling of being watched over. And he wondered if it was somehow linked to the invisible force.)

Although he made the decision, it wasn't an easy one.

Tommy agonized over some facts that argued strongly against his choice of actions all having to do with what would happen if he got caught.

Firstly, he'd probably be expelled from IGGY.

Secondly, he'd ruin the chances of the Dream5s – they'd definitely not be crowned IGGY Knights, no matter how many points they had.

Lastly, and most importantly, it might increase the likelihood that Earth would be chosen as the planet to be destroyed.

If I get caught.

He'd fought with these issues for some days. The one about Earth made him sweat and gave him a pain in his tummy. It made him feel guilty and wrong and bad all at once, but he couldn't fight the invisible force that was drawing him. When he tried to ignore the force, he felt even worse. The pain in his tummy got stronger and he was unable to sleep. This was strange. He always thought that decisions would be simple – one choice would make you feel good, the other would make you feel bad. But he was wrong. Sometimes the right choice is the most difficult one. Sometimes you can still feel sick after you make it.

The decision itself was really quite simple. Tommy decided to sneak down to the Uh-Oh-Doh-Joh Chamber and, once again, walk along the Plank of Discovery. This time he'd walk further. He had a plan all worked out. He'd do it at night when everyone was asleep and would choose the night that gave him the least chance of getting caught.

And that was another thing . . . He might not get caught.

'I won't tell the others,' he said to himself. 'They'd only try and talk me out of it.'

It was already too late to make the expedition this evening

and, too excited to sleep, he crept up to the floating-bowling alley with his electric violin. There was some relief in having made the decision, yet he couldn't help feeling sick and more than a little afraid whenever it entered his mind.

— 32 —

TWO HAMBREROS, ONE STONE

About the time that poor Tommy was lying in bed wrestling with his decision, Elsorr Maudlin threw his sword across the President's Oblong Office and punched the air. The sword pierced the middle of a portrait of Gertrude Randolph (Guttly's late wife) and stayed two metres off the ground, swaying slightly.

'Perfect,' he said to himself. 'Perfect.'

Only a few hours earlier, Guttly Randolph had called him from IGGY. To save on telephone bills, Guttly had originally agreed not to call Elsorr unless something very important came up. Elsorr had pressed this point quite firmly because he was anxious to receive as little interference as possible from Guttly. And since the only phone on the planet that could receive calls from IGGY was in the Oblong Office, Elsorr was sure that Guttly wasn't communicating with anybody else on Earth.

Guttly had explained that the MilkyFed would send an unmanned probe to Earth in the next few days. He wouldn't explain the exact reason for this, but he told Elsorr to ensure that Earthlings were on their best behaviour. Elsorr was to command all wars to halt for a brief period, poor people were to be given some of the excess mountains of food from the city of ExtraFat, plastic garden gnomes were to be removed from stores, all forms of karaoke would be prohibited, the wearing of socks with sandals would be banned and game shows with idiotic audiences (i.e. all of them) were to be removed temporarily from Trance Screen networks.

I should explain that although there were no more gardens on Earth, some people still bought 'garden' gnomes to decorate their hallways. Also, karaoke was still popular in some cities despite the fact that songs no longer had lyrics.

Elsorr was disgusted to learn that Guttly would be returning to Earth in little over a week. He had a great deal of difficulty disguising this from the old man.

'That's marvellous,' said Elsorr, glad that the phone had no video screen attached, for Guttly would surely have recognized the disappointment in his eyes. 'We'll make Earth look just delightful for this probe and then we'll organize a big celebration when you return.'

'Married bananas are more likely to split'
(MilkyFed research institute finding no. 85,479,666)

Given the huge distance between IGGY and Earth, phone calls were quite expensive – equivalent to 350,000 floaties a second. This was particularly annoying since there was a thirty-second time delay on all calls. As the MilkyFed use bartering instead of money and as MilkyFederans are very partial to banana splits (they believe it's the best truly unaided human invention of all time), Earth would have a hefty banana and ice-cream bill to 'pay' to the MilkyFed for any calls made by Guttly.

If there are any bank robbers reading, you'll be interested to note that a floatie would be roughly equivalent to US$100 in today's money.

He was in a bad mood for quite some time after he hung up. The old fool was going to return much sooner than expected and this meant that he, Elsorr the Great, would have to give up the *acting* presidency sooner than planned. And *that* was assuming the Grand Council didn't try to have him removed as Acting President before Guttly made it home. The morons on the Council were whingeing louder than usual and were beginning to dismiss his warning that the MilkyFed wanted to conquer Earth.

When Hugo Ignominious died on the floor of the Grand Council Hall, it had given Elsorr a few days of peace. For a while, most of the Councillors seemed to believe that Hugo – a great and wise man – had died from fear of a MilkyFed invasion. But now the Council was getting restless and Elsorr was sure there were plots afoot to oust him as Acting President. Maybe he should lock someone else up in *Domesticity* to keep Helena Jadely company. That would teach them.

To try and cure his mood, Elsorr summoned a guard so that he could issue a few presidential orders to be communicated to the entire planet. The orders were:

1   All transport vehicles in cities whose names begin with a vowel should now fly on the left. All those in cities beginning with consonants should fly on the right (thereby reversing his edict of some days previous). The change-over would occur at 6.14a.m. the next morning, at the height of rush hour.

2   No right-handed drinking permitted anywhere on the planet (effective immediately). The punishment for anyone caught violating this order would be severe. They'd receive a public tickling.

Public tickling was a well-established punishment on Earth at this time, proving far more effective than convicting petty criminals and then releasing them immediately for no apparent reason. The ceremony looked very like the public executions of the Middle Ages and the tickling lasted one hour fifty-two minutes precisely (per person). The tickling itself was administered by a trained official called a *Murcyless Fahhthurr* (their formal uniform consisted of a fake pot-belly, flip-flops and a feather duster).

It always made Elsorr feel better to issue orders that would take effect throughout the planet. Amazing how powerful it made him feel, really. Almost like a god. That was the best thing about being the President – being able to order everyone around (plus always getting the best seats in the cinema).

When he stopped smiling at his own brilliance (he really liked his latest two orders), the jaundiced man prised his sword from the portrait of Gertrude Randolph and delicately tried to burst a spot on the back of his neck (with the sword's tip) while he thought about Guttly's request. *Prepare the world for a MilkyFed probe. Make Earth look as good as possible.* Why would Guttly ask such a thing? It was preposterous. Elsorr thought and thought. What a strange thing it was for the MilkyFed to send a probe.

'Yes!' he whooped suddenly, much to the astonishment of the guard who was checking the spellings in his notes (on his CP) before sending the presidential orders to all corners of the Earth. In his excitement, Elsorr burst three spots instead of one, then thumped his fist so hard on his desk that the poor guard had to start checking his spellings all over again.

'I've got it!' cried Elsorr, wiping the tip of his sword on the guard's trousers.

It was blatantly obvious. Guttly, the big-headed, pompous sneak! He was looking for some award from the MilkyFed. He must be. Probably the Medal of PompussNess or the NOBel Sickophant Prize. The fat, bald-headed git had probably made up some story for the MilkyFed just to win an honour. And now the MilkyFed was sending a probe to Earth to verify Guttly's lies. The cheeky, lying, grovelling git!

---

1 Owner. Under 60bn Light-Years on the Clock

PompussNess is a lake about the size of Loch Ness on the planet Altrusia. It's synonymous with bravery because it's so cold and so infested with second-hand spacecraft salesmen that only very brave – or very mad – people swim in it. The Medal of PompussNess is awarded for acts of great bravery, such as wedgying a wibblewallian chef *before* you order your meal.

The NOBel Sickophant Prize is a sort of teacher's pet award, bestowed by the MilkyFed on goody-goodies. It's more prestigious than the 3-Tongued Brownknows O.B.E.

That was when Elsorr threw his sword, punched the air and cried 'Perfect!' Because it *was* perfect. He suddenly saw a way to kill two hambreros with one stone (the word *birds* was dropped from this popular phrase when they became extinct).

Yes! Yes! Yes!

Here was an opportunity to wreck Guttly's stupid, vain attempt to win an award from the MilkyFed – while at the same time ensuring that he, Elsorr, was confirmed as the Permanent President of Planet Earth.

It was absolutely perfect. A simple way to guarantee that he, Elsorr the Great, finally won his rightful place in history.

What a fantastic day, he thought. And to celebrate, he dictated fifteen more presidential orders to the harried guard.

33

THOUGHTNECTAR

The CrushedVelvetGlove Hall is shaped like a giant hand, dangling downwards. It's generally reserved for 'friendship' ceremonies, such as planets signing accords or neighbours agreeing to return lawn-mowers. Known affectionately as the Glove, it's also used for intergalactic poker competitions.

The IGGY Cadets arrived through wigholes onto a balcony across the 'palm' of the Glove for the History and Geography tests. The balcony, called Palm Balcony, over-looked great drops into three fingers and two thumbs below (an extra thumb was added especially for this occasion). Tommy peered over the edge into one of the fingers and noticed that, far below, it contained a luminous, bubbly liquid.

'Alright, in you get,' cried a voice from one end of Palm Balcony. It was one of the exam supervisors. He was a wibble-wallian, sporting a large pair of headphones, flared trousers, a fluorescent chiffon shirt and platform shoes. His hair was much longer than Woozie's and he pointed the dorms in different directions.

It turned out that each dorm had to jump into a separate finger or thumb. The IndexFinger was allocated to the Dream5s.

'All hold hands,' said Marielle bossily, urging the other four towards the edge of the balcony.

Jumping off the balcony into one of the digits below was the most important aspect of friendship ceremonies held in the Glove. In poker competitions, anyone 'losing a hand' was blindfolded and spun around. They then walked blindly until they fell off Palm Balcony. If they landed in the Thumb they were allowed back into the game, but anyone landing in a finger was out of the tournament.

The Dream5s stood in a line, then leapt off the edge of the balcony like a crew of demented bungee jumpers.

'SuperNovaaaaaaaahhhhhhhhhh!'

At some point in the ten-second fall, Tommy let go of Woozie's hand and almost let go of Marielle's. It got darker and darker as they plunged, until the only light they could see came from the glow of the luminous liquid rushing up to greet them. In the far distance, Tommy heard a piercing shriek, followed by a loud splash (Anjel*eek!* had become quite chubby since arriving in IGGY). Then the liquid surface hit him.

SSSSPPPPLLLAAAAAAAASSSSSSHHHHHH!

Now Tommy was holding onto no one and he'd never been so far underwater (or under-liquid). He could feel the weight of liquid all around, pressing hard against his chest and magnifying the burning need to breathe. He couldn't see a thing, but kicked with his feet, trying to push himself upwards. He bumped into something furry, then felt something soft and warm against his head. It was still there when he cut through the surface with an involuntary whoop. His lungs thundered in and out, snatching at every ounce of oxygen in the air. The need was so great that he didn't consider for a moment why nothing was visible.

'There they are!' cried Rumbles indignantly. She must've done something, for Tommy could suddenly see her in the

267

luminous glow. 'What were you doing with my undies on your headskeey?'

Tommy shrugged and looked around. Summy was there, swishing her tail and flapping her wings.

'Some fall!' said Woozie. 'Can we do it again?'

So everyone was there – except – except Marielle!

'Marielle!' yelled Tommy and dived down into the liquid. He held his breath for as long as he could, swimming in circles, but he could see nothing. Eventually, he popped back up for air, but Marielle was nowhere to be seen. They all dived down next time, but again they popped up without Marielle. Tommy got a horrible feeling in his tummy and for the first time all day he forgot his plan about the Uh-Oh-Doh-Joh Chamber. Two more dives and still no sign. Everyone else looked as worried as he. Why had he let go of her hand?

Then, without warning, the liquid started spinning and draining away. Tommy, Woozie, Rumbles and Summy spun helplessly round the inside of the finger like flies being sucked into a plughole. In moments, the liquid was gone and they were all lying exhausted on the floor (the tip of the finger).

'What took you so long to get down here?'

It was Marielle. Tommy felt like lifting her up and hugging her, but he resisted the temptation because she looked so pleased with herself. 'I hope you didn't forget that I can breathe underwater – and under liquid. I'm an elquinine, remember?'

Tommy hadn't remembered, but he wasn't about to admit this to the cheeky-looking girl with the big smiley face. Strangely, his relief at seeing her alive had turned to anger. He felt mad that she'd made him so worried. It almost seemed impossible that he could be *that* worried. But he knew he shouldn't sound angry or she'd see how concerned he'd really been and then she'd probably think he was a fool.

'Of course we remembered. Didn't we, Woozie?' His voice was so cheery, you would've thought he was talking about somebody's birthday.

'Em . . . well,' Woozie suddenly realized why Tommy was frowning at him. 'Oh yeah, I mean. We did. Yeah. *Remember*, I mean, not *forget*. We'd never forget.'

They dried remarkably quickly and then what looked like five corduroy cement mixers appeared through a doorway and glided to the centre of the floor.

They were followed by a thunderbumble who was bigger than Rumbles and, like the other exam supervisor, was wearing flares (under a pair of striped undies), a multi-coloured chiffon shirt and platforms. His hair was very long and bright orange.

'In you get,' he said in a serious tone. 'There's a C-Tumbler for each of you.'

'What? Headfirst?' said Tommy, pointing at one of the corduroy mixers.

'Yes!'

As he climbed into the C-Tumbler, Tommy felt very silly. His legs were left sticking up in the air and a passer-by might've been forgiven for thinking he was being swallowed by a cunningly disguised furballia.

'Who owns these undies?' said the supervisor with a note of disgust. *(A thunderbumble would be even more annoyed than most creatures to find neglected undies lying on the ground and would never suspect another thunderbumble of being the owner.)*

Rumbles tried waving her legs to get the supervisor's attention, but Summy was making such a racket as she sought to squeeze her wings into the C-Tumbler that the supervisor threw the undies in on top of her.

Things I Wish I'd Never Stood On

Many academic tests in the MilkyFed are done using CerebralTumblers (commonly known as C-Tumblers). Once activated, they rotate very, very fast indeed and your thoughts 'bleed' into them (technically, copies of your thoughts are sucked out). The topic to be examined can be programmed into them using a small keypad below a tiny screen on the outside. C-Tumblers are often used in MilkyFed court cases as they're brilliant lie detectors.

In C-Tumbler clubs (very fashionable across the MilkyFed), twelve members are chosen nightly to climb into C-Tumblers and then, after a meal and drinks, copies of their thoughts are read out to the gathering. Prizes are given for those whose thoughts generate the most laughter. Favoured topics include: *My Most Embarrassing Moments*, *Old Aunties Who've Kissed Me On The Lips* and *Things I Hate About Wet Hankies*.

Tommy was vaguely aware of a spinning motion once the History exam began. His head and shoulders were supported by very comfortable cushions that pulsated bursts of light at regular intervals. No matter what he tried to think, his mind refused to budge from the topic of Milky Way History. It was impossible for any other topic to edge its way in. Since Tommy really knew relatively little Milky Way history, the same thoughts kept coming back, time and time again, like repeats of *The Simpsons*.

To the casual observer in IndexFinger, it looked like five food processors were going full blast at once. All the blurred, spinning C-Tumblers were attached by a transparent tube to what looked like a giant egg-timer in the middle. This egg-timer started off empty, but gradually filled with a thick, blue liquid that trickled from the transparent tubes attached to the five C-Tumblers.

After seven minutes, the C-Tumblers stopped, the stern thunderbumble hauled everyone to their feet and five dizzy creatures collapsed to the ground.

'Congratulations,' said the supervisor. 'None of you vomited.'

He'd just said the V-word when Tommy threw up.

'Spoke too soon,' said Woozie.

'Yeah, I doubt C-Tumblers have ever been tested on humans,' replied the supervisor with a grin.

A hambrero appeared to clean up the mess and offer Tommy a mouth rinse. The supervisor lifted up the egg-timer in the centre of the C-Tumblers and examined its contents. It was two-thirds full of the blue liquid.

'Not bad,' he said. 'There's quite a bit of ThoughtNectar here.'

Once he'd recovered, it became clear to Tommy that C-Tumblers (in exam conditions) are hooked up to a device that converts clever thoughts into a thick, blue liquid called ThoughtNectar. Repeated waffle and silly thoughts are converted into warm air and released through an exhaust pipe at the rear. That way, the amount of clever thoughts can easily be measured.

'Here, let me see,' said Rumbles, taking the glass vessel from her fellow thunderbumble and sniffing. 'Smells like stale dunglies to me.'

Dunglies, as mentioned earlier, are (allegedly) a type of flower. For some inexplicable reason, the phrase 'stale dunglies' is used by MilkyFederans to refer to awful smells in the same way that 'rotten eggs' or 'bachelor pads' are used on Earth.

'Here's another thing that like stale dunglies smells,' snapped Summy crossly.

The fiery dinosaurus hadn't enjoyed having a certain

mustard-coloured garment around her neck for the entire exam and now that she'd managed to fish them out of the C-Tumbler, she was most anxious to return them to their rightful owner. They flew out of her hand, across the air and into Rumbles' face.

A minor row ensued and somehow, when Rumbles returned the egg-timer to the supervisor, the vessel appeared only half-full and there were blue stains on the mustard undies. The supervisor just shrugged his shoulders and Tommy did his best to calm everyone down. Summy was now even more annoyed with Rumbles.

'I'm not clumskeey, you know,' said Rumbles defensively.

The supervisor emptied the vessel into a plughole in the centre of the floor where all the luminous liquid had disappeared earlier. Moments later, a projection appeared against one wall of the finger. It looked like this:

```
         RESULTS OF HISTORY EXAM

 DORMS        AMOUNT OF        POINTS     TOTAL
              THOUGHTNECTAR    WON        POINTS
 BRILLO1S     210 NFS          0          40
 GREAT2S      215 NFS          20         40
 VGOOD3S       87 NFS          0          30
 ALRIGHT4S     34 NFS          0          30
 DREAM5S      212 NFS          0         -40
```

'Told you, I did! You see?!' cried Summy. 'If the ThoughtNectar you hadn't spilt, twenty points we would've won. Then *minus twenty* in total our points would be, instead of *minus forty*.'

'Wasn't my faultskeeys,' said Rumbles meekly. 'If you hadn't thrown my undies at me.'

272

'A know-all I've always been when to history and geography it comes,' said Summy, almost crying. 'And win we still did not.'

'There's still geography to come,' said Tommy putting his arm around Rumbles. 'Let's not blame each other. We can still do alright.'

'Yes, Summy, we can win geography with your help,' said Marielle trying to pet Summy's twitching wing.

Summy calmed down eventually and, after lunch, the Dream5s won ten points for Geography (a much shorter exam than History) when they got twice the score of any other dorm – mainly, Rumbles conceded, due to the winged lady dinosaurus herself.

'I don't know the meaning of the word *sip*'
(Oh-Liver-Reeed – 'bzs' worker)

In the MilkyFed, small amounts of liquid are measured in Nectar Flies (nfs), a bit like millilitres (mls) on Earth. Nectar Flies are teeny insects that drink liquids until they're about to burst. Small amounts of liquid can thus be measured in terms of how many Nectar Flies would be needed to drink all the liquid. Larger measurements are taken in the same way, using enormous creatures that are notorious for singing the wrong lyrics to songs out of tune and then falling over. Such creatures are termed BoooZurs (bzs).

Tommy was too exhausted that night to think about venturing down to the Uh-Oh-Doh-Joh Chamber. Instead, he lay in bed and joined in the banter as everyone practised for the next day's exams, relating stories about different phenomena. Summy was no longer angry with Rumbles because she was so chuffed that they'd won the geography test by such a large margin.

'I lost my undies last month and got an eerie sense of déjà vuskeeys.'

'Don't use that story tomorrow, Rumbles,' said Woozie. 'We're trying to win points, not lose them.'

'Ha ha.'

There'd be no C-Tumblers in the Phenomenon exam. Instead, everyone would have to stand up in front of Lady MuckBeff and all the IGGY Cadets and tell an interesting story that involved a strange phenomenon. Lady M would give each person a mark and then the dorm with the highest total marks would win the twenty points.

'I didst get déjà vu when thou lost thine undies,' said Tommy, mimicking the tutor.

Rumbles smiled just as Summy smacked her with a pillow.

'Déjà vu I got when on the springboard you jumped, your bunk you missed and against the wall you slammed.'

'Very funny, dinosaurskeeys-face,' said Rumbles.

'A *dinosaurus face* – what with that is wrong!?'

What followed was a mad, yet good-natured pillow fight, which included everyone (particularly Marielle). Tommy reckoned that if the MilkyFed ever decided to make pillow fighting an official sport, he'd certainly want Marielle on his team.

34

A BETRAYAL (ALMOST)

The first exam next day was the POO contest. The Dream5s had hardly thought about this test because it was worth fewer points than the Phenomenon exam to be held in the afternoon.

The contest was held in the IGGY Galley with Miss LeWren presiding. The Galley was a long room, covered in wooden floor-boards with a series of port-holes along one wall, looking out to space. These port-holes were open and a copper-coloured cannon poked its nose out of each. (An air bubble, like that surrounding the GarageZone, was fixed outside the Galley, allowing the port-holes to remain open.)

In addition to three cream pies, each Cadet was given the statistics and co-ordinates for a planet some distance away, called Bulzii. Five differently-coloured circles, each the size of a large pizza, were painted on the surface of Bulzii and each Cadet had to try and fire the cream pies from their cannon and make them land on their dorm's allocated circle.

One Hundred and Eighty!

In the POO contest, the cream pies would travel at roughly the top speed of Fedora (over 48 million times the speed of light), taking approximately 14 minutes and 32.57 seconds to hit Bulzii. Amongst other things, the Cadets would have to factor in that Bulzii rotated on its axis every 51 seconds and moved in an elliptical orbit at 2,633 kilometres per second.

Incidentally, Masters of the Way would be expected to hit such a target blindfolded, while bouncing on a trampoline and being hit repeatedly on the head with a large turnip.

Although Tommy's POO ability would never receive the same acclaim from future historians as his many other skills, it should be noted that no one else even hit the planet Bulzii with their cream pies. In fact, due to some unnamed Cadet who was an atrocious shot, approximately 277 years later, a shower of cream pies would rain down on one of the planets of the KrayZCult Solar System in the Gullibillis Galaxy, prompting them to believe that the end of the world (their planet, Armageddonoutahere) was nigh.

Two of Tommy's three pies, however, hit the centre of the Dream5s' circle.

'Ten pointz to ze Dream5s,' cried Miss LeWren with enthusiasm. No wonder some of the Cadets started teasing Tommy that he was Miss LeWren's pet.

'Well dunskeeys,' said Rumbles, half-covered in cream pie (she'd pointed her cannon the wrong way).

'Yes, if me you ask *how* well done – *very*, I'd say,' said Summy.

When the other two clapped him on the back, Tommy allowed himself a smile. *Yeah, he'd done OK.*

During lunch, the Dream5s started discussing phenomena again and a piggyback pillow fight almost started after Woozie demonstrated his sleeping phenomenon (he could sleep anywhere, so long as he had a peg on his nose – funny smells wake him up). In a quiet moment, Tommy thought of the time – only a few weeks ago – when he'd knelt down on the floor of the Great Dining Hall at Wilchester, surrounded by broken CPs, and pleaded to an invisible power to let him be chosen to travel into space. He remembered the feeling of confidence and the strange connection he felt with a force he believed to be the spirit of his parents. Even though Felkor's name was announced only moments later, Tommy felt sure that his wish had been answered and had been responsible for him being chosen almost a week later.

That sense of his parents had only grown stronger in space, rising to a crescendo when he walked along the Plank of Discovery.

Surely, this was a phenomenon if ever there was one. Surely, this was the most incredible story Lady MuckBeff would ever hear. Tommy was sure that it was and he felt confident that it could be the most incredible phenomenon story told by an IGGY Cadet.

That afternoon, when Lady M called upon Tommy to describe a phenomenon in front of all the Cadets, Tommy changed his mind. He didn't know why, but it suddenly felt wrong to tell Lady M his precious story. Almost a betrayal of his parents.

And so Tommy described the Great Climate Enhancement that had affected planet Earth in the 21st century. It had its roots in the 20th century, but the pollution, selfishness, wilful neglect and ignorance of the people had irreversibly changed Earth's climate and brought about the extinction of millions of animals and plant forms. Now future generations would no longer enjoy the natural weather conditions or living beauty that their ancestors had cherished. What a phenomenon! Natural weather conditions for millions of years then – *BOOM!* – man changed an entire planet's climate and ecosystem in the blink of an eye.

A few people clapped when Tommy finished, but Lady M just looked at him coldly.

'Why, that proveth how stupid and short-sighted humans doth be,' she said, and took a snort from her lapel.

And Tommy did feel extremely stupid – whether it was for telling the story or whether it was felt on behalf of his species who'd ruined Earth, he wasn't sure.

Things went worse for Marielle. She started to tell a story about how her parents could predict small things in the future, including an epidemic that later ravaged her planet. The little girl in dungarees and pigtails ended up in tears, describing the final moments with her parents and lamenting their deaths.

'*Phenomen'ly* boring!' cried Felkor as she stumbled to the end of the story. And from the look on Lady M's face, she seemed to agree.

At the end of the exam, Lady M awarded the highest points to the Brillo1s, which came as a shock to most in the room.

'How can having the hardest punch in your class be a *phenomenon*?' cried Marielle angrily, when they all returned to their dorms. Felkor had got respectable marks for his ten-second story.

'And Trevor the toothwolf's story!' cried Woozie. 'What's the big deal about having a floating globe bath and then becoming twice as dirty ten minutes after you've dried off?'

'How a *phenomenon* can that be?'

'That's what I'm saying.'

'Now in the lead even further are the Brillo1s.'

'I'm sorry. I got a bit carried away about . . . well, you know,' said Marielle softly. 'I thought your story was the best, Tommy. It was definitely the most unbelievable.'

'Thanks, Marielle,' he said, putting an arm around her shoulder. When he saw that she was beyond the point of tears he removed it.

'Fie!' cried Woozie, trying to cheer everyone. 'Hark! What wouldst thou be afeard of? Methinks we canst still win.' He paused, replaying in his head what he'd just said. 'Eh, did that make sense?'

'No, but then Lady M rarely makes sense,' said Tommy.

'Nor does Woozie,' said Summy.

'Hey!'

That night, Tommy felt too annoyed about the whole Phenomenon exam to venture down to the Uh-Oh-Doh-Joh Chamber. He wanted to be in the right frame of mind for such an expedition. There was still time.

'Tomorrow night,' he told himself. 'Then I'll go. That I promise.'

And to Tommy it was more of an oath than a promise.

⚡ 35 ⚡

BEAT THE CHEAT

After the Phenomenon contest, the scores for the dorms stood as follows:

DORMS	TOTAL POINTS
BRILLO1S	60
GREAT2S	40
VGOOD3S	30
ALRIGHT4S	30
DREAM5S	-20

Since they were in last position, the Dream5s were well aware that lots of points were still up for grabs. In fact, Summy had updated the details of all the contests into a monitor at the end of her bed. After every test was completed, she'd return to the dorm and erase the test they'd just done. By now, her monitor looked like this:

REMAINING TESTS AND CONTESTS

SUBJECT	DATE	TEST TYPE		POINTS
FLOATING BOWLING***	DORRISSSDAY	1-1 CONTEST	(BEST)	40
PLANET CHESSY**	DORRISSSDAY	1-1 TEAMWORK	(BEST)	40
JEGG RACE	DEEDAY	GROUP RELAY	(ALL)	70
FLASHSCIMITAR CONTEST**	INANAMDAY	1-1 CONTEST	(BEST)	90
				240

Wherever a subject had a star next to its name, it indicated how many people a dorm must put forward for the particular contest. If there was no star, it meant everyone in the dorm would be involved. So three people would represent the Dream5s in floating-bowling, two in PlanetChessy and two in the Flashscimitar Contest.

There was a strict rule governing these particular three tests: *no person* could represent their dorm in *all three* tests and *everyone* in the dorm had to appear in *at least one*. This rule gave rise to lots of discussion between the Dream5s over meals and during rest periods. Everyone had an opinion as to who should represent the dorm in each particular test and it took a number of debates and a wighole fight before the issue was settled.

In the wighole fight, everyone grabbed a wighole off the wall and threw it at someone else, trying to 'hoop' them so they'd disappear. At one point, Summy landed into the UnstableRoom and emerged moments later looking rather green. The fight ended when Rumbles disappeared into the FutilityRoom and took two hours to find her way back to the dorm.

The floating-bowling competition was to be held almost out in space – in the enormous air bubble surrounding the GarageZone, to be precise. There were four floating-bowling alleys and after every game they returned to the mouth of the GarageZone so that contestants could climb in or out.

Miss Zohfria LeWren, MonSenior FuKung Leebruce, Mr Crabble and Lady MuckBeff WiLLyoofytus were in charge of refereeing a floating-bowling alley each. Woozie, Marielle and Tommy were representing the Dream5s against twelve other competitors from the other dorms.

After two rounds, Marielle had beaten a three-eyed camelsaurus from the VGood3s and ZsaZsa Vavannus. (ZsaZsa was disqualified for refusing to wear a blindfold because it clashed with her colouring and 'might crush the feather' in her headband.)

In his first contest, Woozie easily beat an Altrusian from the Great2s.

Just so you know, Altrusians look like oddly-shaped humans with sections of their skin resembling newspaper cuttings. When you look at an Altrusian face-on, their nose points directly left or right. All Altrusians have the same name – PKasso – which doesn't make it easy to find the right number in an Altrusian phone book.

Woozie beat Egbert Fitchly in his second contest. He was bruised after the encounter with Egbert, who'd kicked him several times (accidentally) while doing a succession of back-flips within a tap-dancing routine. Unfortunately for Egbert, it was one of the back-flips that knocked over his own skittles and lost him the game (plus his cape got torn as he climbed out of the alley).

For some reason, Lady M would never watch any contest – she'd turn her back on the proceedings and bury her face in the flower on her lapel until the game was finished. Only then would she face the bowling alley and check the result.

Tommy beat a male skychubb from the Alright4s in his first round match.

Skychubbs are voluptuous creatures from the planet Doomybumzlukbiginthis. They look very like humans, except that they have two bottoms. Adult females usually wear tight leggings, while males often work on space-station construction sites where their trousers never cover both bums, enabling them to whistle loudly (through one of the bums) at female passers-by.

In his second contest, Tommy lost a very close game with Brendan the furballia in Lady M's bowling alley.

'Behold, the victor – Brendan of the Brillo1s!' cried Lady M triumphantly as Tommy dragged himself out of the alley's trunk and peeled the blindfold from his face. Then the green-coated tutor must've realized where she was because she abruptly lowered her voice and assumed a grave tone. 'That which I meant to sayeth, was that the Brillo1 candidate did win that contest by a margin most narrow.'

'Extraordinary,' said Summy, when Tommy joined him. 'Like you had him well beaten it looked.'

But no. Brendan had clearly knocked down two of Tommy's skittles while all his own remained intact.

'Sorry,' said Tommy to Summy. 'I thought I was doing rather well, but I must've misjudged.'

When they got down to the semifinals, Marielle was up against Trevor the toothwolf and Woozie was up against Brendan (Felkor had opted not to play in the competition). Woozie's contest was in Miss LeWren's pink-tinted glass bowling alley and Marielle's was in Lady M's beige-tinted one.

Tommy was amazed at how easily Woozie beat the punk furballia. Watching closely, Tommy could see that Brendan was useless and it made him wonder how he'd lost to the snarling ball of mohican fur.

'Piece of MarreyAntwunetta,' said Woozie with a smile, when he rejoined his pals (a reference to a type of Friggle cake most often served at royal banquets) and he gave Tommy a high-four.

Behind Woozie, poor Brendan had somehow managed to get his nose safety-pin caught in the exit to the floating-bowling alley and he was yelping with pain as Miss LeWren tried to free him.

In the next contest, Marielle started having difficulties from the beginning. Whichever way she threw the ball, it never seemed to knock over Trevor's skittles. Maybe she imparted too much spin, because every time the ball would glance off the skittles and leave them standing. By the end of the game, Marielle had knocked over none of Trevor's skittles and three of her own were down.

'Fie! Victory once more to the Brillo1s!' yelled Lady M when she lifted her face from her flowered lapel to see the result.

There was to be a twinkle break (like elevenses on Earth) before the final, to give Woozie and Trevor some time to recuperate and the Cadets some time to regain their voices.

'We will see you back here at fourteen tempusfugeetz precisely,' said Miss LeWren, above the din of excited voices. 'Now, back to your dormz where new favo-fant suppliez should haff arrived. But do not eat too much. Do not rruin your lunch.'

'Hard luck, Miss Marielle,' said Miss LeWren when she passed by the Dream5s lining up to jump through their wighole. 'And you were unlucky too, Meester Storm. I sought you were doing quite well, until I saw ze final score.'

Back in the dorm, Tommy didn't feel like eating. Something wasn't right about the floating-bowling and he needed to figure out what it was.

'Marielle, in your contest with Trevor, in Lady M's alley, you chose to be the red skittles didn't you?'

Marielle nodded. 'My Corvus, absolutely no way would I be those filthy beige skittles! Uuugghh!'

Summy stepped forward. 'Red skittles too you were, Tommy, when the furballia, Brendan, you played.'

284

'Yes . . . I . . .'

'What?' said Summy, seeing an odd look cloud his friend's face.

Tommy said nothing until his eyes lit up quite suddenly.

'That's it!' he cried.

'What's *it*?' said Woozie. Why was his friend so fired up? His eyes glinting, so full of new-sprung passion – like a bottle of Fizzalicious all shaken, bursting to share his mind.

Tommy couldn't get the words out quickly enough. 'Brendan won the toss when I played him and he chose to be the grubby beige skittles. I thought it was an odd decision.'

'You mean what exactly, Tommy?' said Summy, puzzled. 'Quite strange it—'

'I saw Marielle throw the ball at Trevor's beige skittles on numerous occasions and they never budged. At the time, I thought maybe she hadn't thrown hard enough, but . . .'

'Yes?'

'The Brillo1s must've done something to the beige skittles . . . They must be . . .' *What?* 'Must be . . .' Then it came to him. 'Stuck to the ceiling!' *That was it.* 'And what's more, Lady M knows about it!'

'But she never knows who's going to win the toss before the game,' said Marielle. 'And if a non-Brillo1 Cadet won the toss they might choose to be the beige skittles.'

'That's why it's so brilliant!' cried Tommy. 'No one's going to choose to be the filthy beige skittles if they win the toss – unless you're a Brillo1 and you know about it in advance.'

'Of course,' said Marielle.

'I see too,' said Rumbles bouncing on the springboard, over-shooting her bed and slamming against the wall.

'So what do we do for the final?' said Woozie.

It was hard to know. There was no way they could sneak

down to the GarageZone, climb into the beige alley and fix the skittles.

'Let's hope it's held in one of the other three bowling alleys.'

All the Cadets were gathered in the GarageZone to watch the final. Most 'neutrals' wanted to see Woozie win for two reasons. One, he was much nicer than Trevor the toothwolf and, two, no one wanted the Brillo1s to go further into the lead. If the Dream5s won the points, it wouldn't matter too much because they'd still be in last place.

'Quiet pleaze!' said Miss LeWren sternly. 'Now, let uz see which bowling alley ze final will be held in.'

The one-legged lady dipped her hand into a small cloth bag into which four miniature floating-bowling alleys had been placed earlier. She withdrew her hand to reveal a light-blue tinted alley.

'That's my one,' said MonSenior Leebruce.

The Dream5s breathed a sigh of relief.

Lady M smiled. 'Thus your alley doth be eliminated.'

'What? That's not what it means . . . What? What?'

Using a cheap magician's trick, Lady M had whipped the cochlea-roach from MonSenior's ear and the poor man couldn't hear a word. Another cochlea-roach was sent for.

'You stole my cochlea-roach,' said MonSenior once the device was inserted.

'But surely thou art too smart and wily to alloweth a mere Dangleberry Belt such as mineself to do that without thee noticing,' said Miss M.

'Hmm,' said MonSenior.

The tutors disappeared for a conference and when they returned, Miss LeWren addressed the cadets.

'Sorry, everyone – zere waz a mix-up. Lady MuckBeff waz under ze impression that ze alleyz we *rremove* from ze bag are ze onez to be eliminated and zat ze final alley left eez ze one chozen. She haz since agreed to ze simple rrule zat ze first alley out of ze bag eez ze one chozen.'

Tommy clapped Woozie on the back. Lady M had been over-ruled.

'However,' continued Miss LeWren. 'Since Lady MuckBeff waz unaware of zis earlier, we will put ze blue alley back in ze bag and start ze process again.'

The Dream5s groaned.

'What a cheat!' said Marielle. 'She's just making that up to get another chance.'

Miss LeWren redid the choosing ceremony and this time she removed a beige alley from the bag. Tommy looked at Woozie in disbelief and it almost seemed as if a smile escaped from the inside of Lady M's shadowed hood.

'Now for ze pre-game toss,' said Miss LeWren, ushering Woozie and Trevor forward.

Since there's no money in the MilkyFed, a toss is usually done with something that won't break when it hits the ground. In this case, a small pink wibblewallian in the Great2s volunteered to be tossed.

'Heads or tails?' said MonSenior.

'Tails,' said Trevor quickly.

'What?' MonSenior tapped the side of his head.

'Tails.'

'Yes, of course . . . Sorry, these cochlea-roaches can be lazy when you first put them in.'

MonSenior threw the wibblewallian high into the air,

making him spin furiously. When he landed it sounded like a bag of potatoes hitting the floor. He was on his back, facing up into MonSenior's face.

'*Heads* it is,' said the oldest Milki Master.

There was a cheer from the Dream5s.

'So, Fuzzywibblewallian, do you choose to be the red skittles or the beige?'

'I choose . . .' Woozie looked over at his friends and winked.

'Hurry thee up,' said Lady M crossly. 'We don't haveth all day.'

'I choose . . . *beige.*'

'What?' Lady M was flabbergasted. 'Alack! Thou canst . . .'

Trevor looked pale also.

'Why can he not?' said Miss LeWren.

'Nay, I just—'

'What?'

'I just remember'd . . .'

'Yes?'

'There doth be a problem with mine alley.'

'What do you mean?'

'Eh . . . I thinkest there be a crack in the glass that doth affect the anti-gravity. 'Tis too perilous to use.'

'But people haff been uzing eet all morning.'

Lady M had no answer. She said nothing for a moment, then became very angry.

'Hie thee hither! If the final shouldst be held in the *first* alley pull'd from the bag, then it shouldst be play'd in the blue alley – be that not so, MonSenior . . . ? Thine was truly the first alley pull'd out of the bag.'

'I don't think it's worth getting into an argument about,' said MonSenior. (He'd had over three million pointless

288

debates in his long life and was determined not to hit the four million mark.)

After much huffing and puffing, it was agreed that the contest would be held in MonSenior's alley and that Woozie would be the blue skittles, Trevor the yellow ones.

Tommy never cheered so hard as he did during that final. The blue-tinted alley spun wildly just off the edge of the GarageZone, looking as if it might whirl out into space. If you weren't used to watching floating-bowling, you might as well have watched two peanuts being whisked by an electric mixer, but Tommy and all the Cadets were well used to it by now. They could make out the subtle curves Woozie put on the ball as he threw it and the way the furry fellow dived at the right time to stop a fast moving ball from hitting his skittles. Trevor looked rattled from the beginning.

When the alley finally returned to the GarageZone, only one of Woozie's skittles had been knocked down, but all Trevor's were floating aimlessly around the alley.

'Mr Cheeky Fuzzyface wins by thirteen skittles to one,' said MonSenior.

'Hey-ho, hmmm, which means the Dream5s win forty points, yes?' said Crabble.

Lady M harrumphed in disgust (though she hadn't watched the contest) and left the GarageZone without speaking to anyone. When Woozie emerged from the alley's trunk, he was lifted high in the air by Rumbles and cheered noisily by Tommy, Marielle and Summy.

'No big deal,' he said with a smile. And he looked over towards Miss LeWren to see if she was clapping.

⚡ 36 ⚡

A Smashing Game

Apart from Felkor, Brendan the furballia and Trevor the toothwolf, there were two other members of the Brillols. These two were (female) twins called ReeeRaw and RullahBullah. They were both blonde and fair-skinned down one side of their body – black haired and dark down the other. (ReeeRaw was blonde down her left side, RullahBullah blonde down her right, making them identical *mirrored* twins.) Their tails reflected their moods which were always opposite to each other – when ReeeRaw was happy, RullahBullah was sad.

ReeeRaw was generally tardy, loud and scruffy (she was disqualified from the floating-bowling competition for being late – which made RullahBullah laugh hard). RullahBullah was punctual, quiet and neat. When together, the 'Mirror Twins' spoke sentences by saying alternate words, such as:

ReeeRaw: THE
RullahBullah: Brillols
ReeeRaw: ARE
RullahBullah: easily
ReeeRaw: THE
RullahBullah: best.

Each of them was keen to be the one who finished a sentence as this often determined whether the sentence sounded joyful, distressed or boastful. They were chosen as IGGY Cadets when they (jointly) won the MilkyFed Under-12s Debatable Debating Competition.

Just after lunch, the following projection appeared in every dorm.

```
STANDINGS AFTER FLOATING-BOWLING . . .

DORMS              TOTAL POINTS

BRILLO1S                60
GREAT2S                 40
VGOOD3S                 30
ALRIGHT4S               30
DREAM5S                -20
```

'Still in last place!' cried Woozie, as Summy rushed to double-check the projection against the monitor at the end of her bed.

'Yes, but *joint first* we will be when the PlanetChessy we win,' said Summy, looking up. 'An extra forty points for grabs is up.'

'Yeah, that'd bring us up to sixty points – equal to the Brillo1s.'

'Think I'll wear my undies for good luckskeeys,' said Rumbles.

The PlanetChessy competition was to be held in a great expanse called the RushinDollGlobe (or RDG) Room. The bottom half of this room was made of glass and looked out to space, and the top half was an enormous semi-domed mirror. Suspended in the middle was the WaterWall. The WaterWall was a sphere full of water with another sphere suspended in its centre, called the Corr. The Corr, surrounded on the outside by water, had five floating globes inside it. These globes were arranged in a cluster, each housing a BabbaPlanet and two chairs upon a glass platform. A winding staircase clung like ivy to the outside of the WaterWall, affording spectators an unrestricted view of the five floating globes inside.

The finals of the MilkyFed PlanetChessy championship have been held in the RushinDollGlobe Room for 832,040 years. Like the Uh-Oh-Doh-Joh Chamber, the RDG Room is not usually housed in IGGY (it's actually in a different location for each championship). The dream of many PlanetChessy aficionados is to be in the RDG Room when five BabbaPlanets are glowing red. It's said, that if you look up at the domed mirror, the view of space is spectacularly refracted through the (crimson) WaterWall and reflected back towards you.

'There they are,' said Woozie excitedly, floating high above the WaterWall. (The gravity generator had been switched off in the RDG Room – having no effect on normal gravity inside the WaterWall and the floating globes.)

Tommy looked down and saw Rumbles and Summy taking their seats on either side of the BabbaPlanet, both sporting giant floppy bow-ties. There was a wighole in each floating globe and pairs of creatures had plopped into each of the other globes.

Wisebeardyface's voice boomed from nowhere: 'Contestants, choose your pieces. Then play to make them *happy*.'

There was a staggered start to the games – one starting five minutes after another. Summy and Rumbles started first because the Dream5s were in last place overall, and Felkor and RullahBullah started twenty minutes later because the Brillo1s were in the lead overall.

If you placed your fingers on the outside of the WaterWall you could hear everything in the closest floating globe and this is what Tommy, Woozie and Marielle did, with a clear view of their favourite pairing. The game began quietly enough. Rumbles and Summy played in much the same way as they'd done before in the dorm and only mumbled 'good move' from time to time. None of the contestants could hear anything outside their floating globes (which was a deliberate means of preventing contestants receiving tips from their colleagues), so Tommy soon gave up cheering and was glad to do so since his throat felt a little sore from the floating-bowling final.

An hour and a half into the games, Tommy noticed a group of Cadets floating around a spot that gave a clear view into Felkor's contest. Holding on to the banisters of the staircase, he pulled himself down to a position where he could see what was going on.

RullahBullah didn't look too pleased. She was playing with the *thunderbumble* pieces and Felkor had chosen the *human* ones.

'F@£#!!!' (Fishy Bobber)
– famous (censored) quote upon losing her MilkyFed *PlanetChessy* title

Thunderbumbles are always a popular choice of pieces in PlanetChessy because they're renowned for being happy. Wibblewallians can be popular too, especially amongst ventriloquists, but they're a risky choice since they have a fierce temper and can do hazardous, unpredictable things with no warning whatsoever. Professional PlanetChessy players almost never use wibblewallian pieces.

293

'Oooohhh,' gasped someone close to Tommy. 'That's gotta hurt.'

A group of human figures had crossed a line of red squares and was ransacking a thunderbumble village. Two or three thunderbumbles burst into flames.

Tommy pressed his fingers to the outside of the WaterWall just as Felkor yelled 'Gotcha!'

'This isn't how you're supposed to play the game,' cried RullahBullah almost in tears, her tail frozen. (ReeeRaw's tail was wagging with delight from her viewing spot.)

'Shut up and play,' snapped Felkor. 'It 'sabout makin' the pieces *happy*, which is what I'm doin'.'

'How?' RullahBullah was genuinely flabbergasted. Her tail started shuddering.

'When my pieces 'av conquered all yer pieces and own the BabbaPlanet for themselves, then they'll be happy.'

And before RullahBullah could answer, a platoon of human figures flew over the largest thunderbumble village and levelled all the buildings by dropping a shower of mini-bombs.

'Yer village is mine!' said Felkor, punching the air.

'We're on the same team!' cried RullahBullah, far exceeding her usual volume. 'We're supposed to be co-operating.'

But like a gambler high on addiction, Felkor was too far gone to hear. Aware only of the need to 'win' – propelled from deep inside his person.

It was when individual human figures invaded a very pretty village and started killing thunderbumbles for no apparent reason that RullahBullah completely lost her temper and her tail cracked like a whip.

'I'm not going to let you destroy all my pieces,' she said defiantly.

'We'll see about that.'

The last of her thunderbumbles crept into a human village (which was empty because all the humans had gone off to conquer other villages) and stole an arsenal of missiles and started firing them at an occupied human village, causing all hell to break loose. Bullets and mini-bombs were being fired from all angles and half the villages and trees were in flames. Certainly, the BabbaPlanet looked fiery, but it wasn't the type of fieriness the game's designers had intended.

Tommy expected the humans to crush the small handful of remaining thunderbumbles easily, but it soon became apparent that the human pieces had started arguing amongst themselves. Small groups of humans who'd taken over villages were stopping other human pieces from entering, claiming that they belonged to them alone. Then these human pieces started firing at each other, ignoring the thunderbumbles who were less of a threat.

Without making any moves, Rullahbullah's chances of keeping her remaining thunderbumbles alive started to dramatically improve.

Before Tommy had started to watch the Brillo1s – in the first seventy minutes of the game – while RullahBullah's thunderbumbles had planted trees and vegetables, Felkor's humans had carefully constructed three nuclear missiles. Felkor believed he was a good strategist and these missiles were his insurance policy against 'losing' the game to RullahBullah. Whatever else happened, Felkor was deter-mined about one thing: he wouldn't lose the game.

By the time RullahBullah's entire set of pieces was reduced to just four thunderbumbles, most of the other PlanetChessy games had finished and all the Cadets were watching the Brillo1s' game in fascination. Felkor had fourteen pieces left, but a group of five was warring with a group of six on the underside of the planet, so there was just a group of three in the village opposite RullahBullah's pieces.

Most of the bullets and bombs seemed to have run out, so Felkor reacted with consternation when a single thunderbumble emerged from the camp of remaining thunderbumbles and started walking towards the village sheltering the three humans.

RullahBullah had actually chosen to get her biggest thunderbumble to offer a truce to the humans. Maybe they could build something in the final minutes of the game and achieve a tiny bit of happiness. This was the reason that the lone walking thunderbumble held a white flag above his head.

Unfortunately for Rumbles and Summy, the great spectacle of Felkor's game meant that almost no one looked over to see them sitting contentedly on either side of their scarlet, glowing BabbaPlanet. No one even noticed the yellowy Babbas that were by now decorating the inside of three other floating globes. Although Felkor and RullahBullah were obviously going to lose this contest, there was something highly entertaining about watching the mayhem they were creating.

Only Tommy glanced over briefly and smiled to himself. Another forty points for the Dream5s, he thought cheerfully. And then he wondered why it was that the consistent, predictable happy moves made by Rumbles and Summy should be more boring to a spectator than the mad savagery of Felkor's play. It was this thought that made him feel ashamed and he chose to turn away from Felkor's game and float upwards so that he could give a congratulatory wave to his friends.

Tommy missed what was to become one of the most talked-about moves in PlanetChessy folklore. Felkor saw the thunderbumble with his white flag held up by his middle arm and thought the worst. When you're petrified of losing, you have to fear the worst, otherwise a smile or a handshake could lead to your downfall. What if the thunderbumble whacked one of his humans on the head with the flag? Then there'd only be two humans against four thunderbumbles on this side of the globe.

Maybe Felkor realized that in RullahBullah's position he'd have tried this trick, so he wasn't going to be fooled by it – oh, no. You can't fool Felkor Stagwitch, he thought with a smile. I always win.

There were only twenty-three seconds to go in the game when Felkor detonated the three mini nuclear missiles. It was a wise move, he thought, because even if the thunderbumble just wanted to shake hands, the groups of six and five humans on the underside of the globe had all killed each other, which meant, technically, that RullahBullah would then 'win' the game by four thunderbumbles to three humans.

BOOOOOOMMMMMMMMMM!

The WaterWall lurched violently sideways, throwing all the watching Cadets outwards – against the walls of the RushinDollGlobe Room. Tommy was winded and took some moments to recover before he floated downwards to check on Marielle and Woozie. In his haste, he bumped into them floating up to check on him.

'Oh, my Corvus! You're OK!' said Marielle, giving him a crushing hug.

Nothing else was said and Marielle slowly released her arms because everyone's attention was drawn to the WaterWall.

Felkor's Babba had exploded, shattering his floating globe, all the other floating globes and the glass wall of the Corr – causing the circle of water which had been outside the Corr to heave downwards and inwards. In a moment, the WaterWall became nothing but a great sphere half-full of sloshing water and debris.

All the contestants were struggling frantically in the water which started acting like a whirlpool and, for some reason, fast disappearing. Fragments of Felkor's Babba littered the spiralling water, occasionally obscuring Rumbles and Summy, who were holding on tightly to each other. Four intact Babbas swirled dangerously close to them and the other drowning cadets.

Suddenly, Miss LeWren and MonSenior Leebruce appeared from nowhere, diving headfirst through the top of the WaterWall into the water. Miss LeWren had a bouncy rope tied to her ankle and MonSenior had one tied to his hoverchair – so that when they each grabbed two contestants, they immediately shot back up towards the top of the WaterWall and disappeared. Then they appeared again in the same way, grabbing four more contestants and then disappearing out the top of the WaterWall. Just before the last of the water drained out of the WaterWall (the four Babbas had already disappeared), Miss LeWren dived in again, grabbing Rumbles and Summy.

'Put your coat on'
(Refrain of annoying mothers and slogan for Burdynumnum
PLUS™)

Although the 'glass' in the MilkyFed was very strong, some types of IGGY glass had a special coating that caused them to shatter under certain conditions, thereby allowing an explosion to 'escape'. The coating also ensured that shattered fragments of glass wouldn't cut people. After the floating globes and the walls of the Corr disintegrated, the water in the WaterWall cushioned the explosion. The wigholes that Miss LeWren and MonSenior jumped through were emergency wigholes that are sealed when the WaterWall is full of water, but which open automatically when the water-level falls.

'That was very dangerous,' said Wisebeardyface.

'He didst not breaketh the rules,' said Lady M firmly. 'There be no rules that sayeth ye cannot fire a missile.'

'Do you not think it displays a certain undesirable destructive quality, Lady MuckBeff?'

'I thinketh it displays *determination.*'

They were in the GrandKangasaurusCourt and Tommy found it far less stressful to be in the viewers' gallery than to be in the Speaker's Square where Felkor was standing with RullahBullah, fiddling with his ruffled cuffs. Once again, Wisebeardyface and the four tutors were on stilts, wearing sombreros and sunglasses. As a special concession, Guttly was also on stilts and wore a sombrero, but he wasn't wearing any sunglasses because they'd fallen onto the floor and he'd no idea how to pick them up.

Thankfully, no one had been badly hurt in the accident. Miss LeWren and MonSenior had reacted just in time to save the lives of all the contestants. The real danger had been the quintuple-decker wighole sandwich at the base of the WaterWall, formed when the wigholes from the five smashed floating globes came together like piranhas in a feeding frenzy.

Perhaps you should spare a thought for Summy here. If she was scared of double-decker things, she was absolutely petrified of quintuple-decker things.

'Wigholez rreact dangerouzly in water,' explained Miss LeWren during the court session. 'But even worse, five of zem came togezzer creating an InfinityLoopHole at ze bottom of ze WaterWall. All ze water poured into zis InfinityLoopHole and disappeared, az did ze four intact Babbaz, ze fragmentz of ze eggsploded one and ze smashed

299

floating globez. If any of ze Cadets had become sucked into eet, zey would never haff been seen again.'

'A Better Waist Disposal Service'

(Mrs Ursa Major, 1st ever client of LayZee Liposuction Inc.)

Technically, wigholes get sucked into each other to create an InfinityLoopHole (ILH). Anything else that gets sucked into an ILH enters a never-ending loop between the wigholes. ILHs are one of the most dangerous things in the Milky Way and are always disposed of by a specialist team of *Loopers*. In this case, the Loopers would seal the emergency wigholes, remove the WaterWall – intact – from IGGY and transport it to a black hole. Some of the Milky Way's black holes are now becoming full, which creates some problems for future waste-disposal, especially as no MilkyFed planet wants a new black hole located near them.

Throughout the proceedings, Felkor and RullahBullah hung their heads (and tail) in shame, avoiding Wisebeardyface's gaze. Occasionally, Felkor would look up from under his hat at the gallery – to smile at Trevor or Brendan, who'd give a victory gesture through the glass. He enjoyed seeing ReeeRaw's tail held high, quivering proudly.

'I am sorry to say,' said Wisebeardyface, summing up, 'that I cannot really punish you, Mr Stagwitch, because Lady MuckBeff is right in what she says. I can only send a strong recommendation to the makers of PlanetChessy, that they remove the human figurines from all their models. Humans really make the game far too dangerous.'

'May I say something?' said Guttly. Wisebeardyface nodded subtly (but it was easy to discern because the sombrero exaggerated any nod). 'I'd like to point out that not

300

all humans act in the way Mr Stagwitch's pieces acted today. His pieces must've been faulty.'

Guttly's speech might've found more favour, but it was interrupted by a loud raspberry sound made by Lady M who'd come to dislike the old bearded human. By putting a hand under one of her armpits, then lowering her arm so that the hand was squished violently within the armpit, Lady M could make the unpleasant noise. What's worse, with two legs occupied on stilts, she could still make two raspberry noises at once, making use of two of the four available armpits.

'I will make no more comment on humans until our probe reports back,' said Wisebeardyface. 'It reaches Earth tomorrow and will take detailed pictures of the planet over the following two days. That should be detailed enough for our purposes.'

Guttly decided to say nothing else in case it caused Wisebeardyface to cancel the probe. If Elsorr carried out his orders to the letter, then the probe should be the one thing that would guarantee the survival of Earth.

Much to the obvious dismay of Rumbles and Summy, it was decided to award no points for the PlanetChessy competition since no one had had a chance to judge the colours emanating from the Babbas at the end of the game.

'We would've wunskeeys, wouldn't we Tommy?' said Rumbles with undisguised disappointment, when they plopped back into the dorm.

'Super-nova! Easily the reddest and hottest was our Babba,' whined Summy.

Tommy agreed, but didn't feel like joining in the discussion. Instead, he lay down on his bunk while Marielle and Woozie tried to cheer up Rumbles and Summy with all the agreeing they could muster. Rumbles was most upset that her undies had been swallowed by the InfinityLoopHole. They were probably stretched over half a BabbaPlanet for the rest of eternity. (Pity the poor BabbaPlanet.)

To Tommy, the PlanetChessy fiasco suddenly seemed unimportant in the grand scheme of things. Everyone was alive and unhurt and that was the main thing. The only subject he could think about now was his plan for that night. He'd wait until everyone was asleep and then he'd sneak off quietly. Tonight was the night. The butterflies went crazy in his stomach every time he imagined walking along the Plank of Discovery.

⚡ 37 ⚡

A CUNNING PLAN

'Why have you called this *Panic Grand Council Meeting*, Elsorr?'

A number of the Councillors were annoyed about being called to a PGC meeting by Elsorr Maudlin, not least because *The Really Grate Cheese* Team-Tag-WhoseLegisthat-Twissterr Final was being shown on Trance screens that night (see *Extra Bits no. 2*, page 419 for an explanation of this sport). The next regular Grand Council meeting wasn't scheduled to take place for another three days and nine of the Councillors had already agreed amongst themselves to call a Special Vote at that meeting to remove Elsorr as Acting President.

'For a most important reason,' said Elsorr gravely. 'I received a call from Guttly Randolph and —'

'From the MilkyFed Intergalactic Space-station?'

'Yes.'

'But that must've cost a fortune. How long were you on the phone?'

I should point out that this Councillor, Octoberus Gloop, was particularly partial to banana splits and was alarmed at how much Earth might have to barter with the MilkyFed when the phone bill from IGGY arrived.

'Never mind,' said Elsorr crossly. 'I encourage Mr

Randolph to phone me as often as possible since I'm most anxious to ensure that he remains in touch with all that is happening on Earth.'

'Does he know that we plan to remove you as Acting President?'

'These calls – does he reverse the charges?'

'Silence!' These Councillors really knew how to annoy Elsorr the Great. 'Guttly Randolph called me to warn me of an imminent invasion by the MilkyFed.'

'Rubbish!'

'We won't fall for that again, you yellow-faced weasel!'

These fools were really getting far too cheeky. Once he was made Permanent President, Elsorr decided, he'd have half of them tickled to death and there'd be *gorgonzola burns* (what you might know as *Chinese burns)* for the rest of them.

The large screen floating above Elsorr's head came to life and an image of a small, odd-looking probe flashed onto it.

'This is the MilkyFed probe,' said Elsorr, pointing with his sword. 'We believe that it's fitted with powerful cameras so that it can pick out Earth's strategic weaknesses. It will show the MilkyFed where our armies are housed, where our missiles are kept and where our vulnerabilities lie. In short, it will be the spy that sends us all to our deaths.'

The Councillors went quiet as they watched the pictures of the probe travelling fast through space.

'How do we know this probe is really heading for Earth?'

'It could be going anywhere.'

'I don't expect you to believe me,' said Elsorr quietly. 'But you'll see that I'm right. It will come to Earth, circle for a few days while choosing a target and then it will unleash its weapons upon us.'

'You're right, I don't believe you.'

'Me neither, Elsorr. We're not fools, you know.'

A lot of people seemed to agree with the doubters and Elsorr waited some time until the comments petered out. It gave him time to slide his sword down his back and scratch an itchy bit. (You have to be a very skilful swordsman to do this without cutting yourself.)

'All I want to do is to protect our wonderful planet,' he said. 'All I ask is that you give yourselves and me every opportunity to defend the planet.' *Ahhh* – that felt good. The itch was disappearing.

'What do you mean?'

'Yeah, what are you getting at?'

Elsorr narrowed his eyes and removed his sword. The itch had totally gone. 'What I'm getting at is this. If I'm lying, then that will be very clear when it comes to our next Grand Council meeting in three days. If there's no sign of the probe, then I will resign as Acting President and you may vote in a successor until Guttly Randolph returns.'

The Councillors were not expecting this. They looked at each other in surprise. For once Elsorr was being very clear and honest.

'And if the probe does come to Earth?' said a Councillor timidly.

'If I'm right and the probe comes here, then you'll know immediately that we are to be attacked and that the MilkyFed plans to invade us. In that case, you must give me every power available to prevent such an invasion.'

'You mean, vote you in as *Permanent President*?' said another Councillor.

'Precisely.'

Most of the Councillors whom Elsorr had singled out for gorgonzola burns nodded sagely. Elsorr's proposition sounded fair and reasonable. The Councillors who were to be tickled to death weren't quite so sure.

Elsorr was going to say something else, but then he changed his mind. He really wasn't too bothered what any of the nincompoops thought right now. Fear can do strange things to men and women, he thought to himself.

Some of the Councillors would later argue that they saw a half-smile escape from Elsorr's lips as he licked the edge of his sword.

38

THE PLANK OF DISCOVERY

Tommy dived head-first through the wighole marked 'The Windy Ravine'. He was pretty sure that neither Woozie nor Marielle had heard him creep out of bed (Woozie was dangling upside-down, his leg hooked around the bedpost, but he did have a peg on his nose) and he was *certain* that neither Rumbles nor Summy had roused – because they were snoring very loudly. (While the HappinessIzzzAh program showed ways to stop snoring, it was probably the least observed lesson amongst ordinary MilkyFederans.) Little bursts of fire shot out of Summy's nose whenever she snored and Tommy was thankful for the extra light as he surveyed the headings over the wigholes.

Almost immediately, Tommy emerged from the mouth of the badgersaurus into the reddy-brown light of the Windy Ravine and, much to his despair, he started plummeting towards the tops of the apartments below. He half expected the giant hedgehogasaurus on the opposite side of the ravine to blow a cushion of air to whisk him towards some ledge and break his fall, but there wasn't a breath out of the sleeping giant. To be honest, he hadn't been sure how he was going to negotiate the ravine, but he felt sure the right way would be obvious. He'd already successfully travelled through this ravine once before – OK, it might've been the opposite way, but what's the big deal about a change of direction?

The tops of the apartments rushed towards him at break-neck speed. Tommy prepared for a violent impact. He closed his eyes momentarily and tried in vain to think of the Surge. Then he opened his eyes and let out a yell. Possibly, he thought, the last yell he'd ever utter.

Tommy wasn't sure if it was just before or just after he made contact with the top of the apartment block that he realized the entire roof of the block was made from a bouncy-castle substance. Instead of smashing every bone in his body, Tommy sank deep into the roof of the block and then bounced madly out into the middle of the ravine. Now he was falling between two apartment blocks, but about to crash into what looked like an enormous red satellite dish protruding from a balcony.

Thankfully, it was another bouncy-castle *node*, placed strategically to break his fall and bounce him in another direction. After bouncing off fourteen more of these rubbery nodes, Tommy landed with a jolt onto a descending spiral escalator which spiralled him away from the ravine into the dark recesses of IGGY.

The last time Tommy passed through these murky parts of IGGY, he'd paid almost no attention to his surroundings because he'd been so distracted by Guttly's earlier words about love and *inner-lath*. This time, as the spiral escalator slid noiselessly through the darkness, the ever-present orchestra of rustling and sighing noises seemed magnified to an alarming extent.

Tommy was actually passing through the AmmaZone – a rainforest in the belly of IGGY that would've been three times the size of Earth had it not been miniaturized to one millionth the size of Earth. (This rainforest generated IGGY's oxygen because, like Earthlings, most MilkyFederans require oxygen to survive – although some can survive on a gas called nudgenudgewinkwinkhowsyerfather.)

Tommy had no idea what he was passing through, but every now and again something would brush against the side of his head or the top of his shoulder, accompanied by a heightened rustle. If you've ever been blindfolded and asked to walk through the snake enclosure at your local zoo, you'll have some idea how Tommy was feeling. He'd never seen a snake, but he'd seen enough strange inhabitants of IGGY to be worried about what some hidden creatures might look like.

On top of the fear that a poisonous creature might attack him, Tommy tensed every time the spiral escalator lurched onto a different path – terrified that Wisebeardyface or some security guard might leap from the shadows. That would surely spell the end of his IGGY adventures.

The darkness was beginning to give way to a hazy blue light when Tommy made out a figure in the distance – in the path of the escalator! For a moment he panicked. What should he do? Keep going? Run for it? Lie down on the escalator? His pulse soared to over 150 beats a minute and he felt a drop of sweat trickle down his back.

You're dead. This is it. You're caught. You're Gone. You're dead.

He fought the drowning feeling. *No, no, no!* He fought the mist of horror descending through his very being. *No, you're not caught yet. You're not yet dead.* Trying to make himself believe the words, trying to find new strength in those legs of jelly. He dug deep – digging, digging – and suddenly felt his head above the mist. The bolt of fear no longer held him in its grip. Instead it powered him – like a shot of electricity.

Quick!

Soundlessly, he leapt off the escalator into the arms of a thick tree. His pulse still racing. More trickles down his back. Risking a peek through the leaves. *Oh no! This isn't good.* The figure, it looked oh-so-powerful. It was swinging through the trees. Another peek. *No, no! This is BAD!* Roaring snarls closer. A chilling menace carried with them. *Breathe, Tommy, breathe.* Another peek. *No, no – this is WORSE than BAD!* The figure – the messenger of doom – it was definitely coming his way.

Calm yourself. Stay still. Don't move. You'll be OK.

As the figure approached, its wail became clear. 'Aaghh! Thainderbumble, thainderbumble! Blood! Blood! Blood!' The roar grew louder. Tommy peeked. The figure kept stopping every five or six trees. Closer and closer, louder and louder.

'Blood! Blood! Blood!'

Tommy fought the urge to run or to jump onto the ascending escalator in an effort to make it back to the dorm. He'd be caught – dead – in an instant.

It was only when the figure stopped just five trees away that Tommy recognized its face – Lady MuckBeff WiLLyoofytus!

Quite suddenly, Lady M sprang at a branch and swung. Four trees away, three trees away, two, one . . .

FFFFFWWWHUMMMMSSSSCHHHHH!

Lady MuckBeff was there. *Right beside me!*

'Fiiieee! Thainderbumble, thainderbumble! Blood! Blood! Blood! Fiiiieeeeeeeeee!'

Her face was almost touching his, so Tommy's ears rang to the huge creature's roar. He nearly wet himself, expecting the final blow. But none came. He opened his eyes and saw closed eyelids centimetres from his own. Lady M was frantically rubbing an area of her coat, as though cleaning it. 'Blood! Blood!' she cried. Despite the dim light, Tommy could see that there was no stain, no blood. The wailing died and as a brief respite from some great pain, Lady M buried her nose in a thicket of leaves and flowers and breathed in deeply. When she breathed out (into Tommy's face), she wailed once more and leapt towards another tree.

As she swung further away, still wailing, Tommy realized why he hadn't been caught.

Lady MuckBeff WiLLyoofytus was walking (or swinging or wailing) in her sleep.

Worried about the time (and his pulse falling to a throbbing 117 beats a minute), Tommy jumped back onto the spiral escalator and descended to the point where he'd jumped from the whooshUlator some days earlier. He dived headfirst and, just as he suspected, found himself in the middle of a plungeUlator that whisked him downwards at an ever-accelerating rate.

The trick with a plungeUlator is to realize that you travel much faster in the middle of it than at the sides. Tommy was well aware of this fact (having travelled on whoosh-n-plunge-Ulators all over IGGY during training) and he somersaulted so that he was travelling feet first, then eased over towards the side of the air funnel and started to slow significantly. Some 120 metres above the required floor (IGGY Level MCMLXIX), Tommy spotted the doors to the Uh-Oh-Doh-Joh Chamber. This was remarkably impressive when you consider that at least two hundred different floors and levels were visible to Tommy, plus almost a thousand spiral escalators and whoosh-n-plunge-Ulators.

At just the right moment, Tommy lurched his body out of the whisking column of air and landed on the KonjugalNOTShelf.

The Great Doors to the Uh-Oh-Doh-Joh Chamber are

about six times the height of a human adult (unless they're wearing a chef's hat, in which case it's *four* times the height) and made from a substance so strong, that not even a flash-scimitar could scratch them. They're by far the oldest things in the Milky Way (including all stars) and have no slot to fit post through. From where he was standing, Tommy thought they could do with a lick of paint – maybe magnolia.

'Soshages,' said Tommy quietly, in case anyone might hear, but the Great Doors didn't budge. This was more than a little alarming because Tommy had no other passwords and he hadn't thought to bring a crowbar.

'Soshages!' he cried loudly, suddenly more concerned with entering the Chamber than with keeping quiet.

As soon as the word was yelled, the Great Doors opened and Tommy stepped silently through.

'Were You Born in a Barn?'
(rhetorical question used by MilkyFed chickens as a common greeting)

The Great Doors are said to have once guarded the entrance to a hallowed constellation called Nebulas B-U-L-L-S-H-one-Tea (pronounced Bewllsh-won-tea) where the goddess, O'P-Umm, was supposedly born on a mattress of nails and then visited by three pigeon-keepers, just before the Milky Way itself was born. (MilkyFederans refer to her as O'P-Umm of the Mattresses.)

The Loony Planet (a guidebook to IGGY) maintains that the Great Doors are almost always shut because 'otherwise there's a nippy draught in the Chamber'.

The Uh-Oh-Doh-Joh Chamber was cast in half-light. A moon-like glow illuminated the far side of the Chamber, but all around the entrance was darkly shadowed. For the first time on this expedition, Tommy saw images in his head of his fellow Dream5s, of Guttly, of Miss Zohfria LeWren and heard an internal voice: *What are you doing?* He tried to suppress the voice, but still some words hissed through. *Expelled. Earth. Obliteration.* For the second time, he almost turned and fled for the dorm.

Almost.

Staying in the shadows, he walked up to the BattleCircle and surveyed its surface which was bisected by gloom and half-light.

WHAMMMP!

What was that? Tommy froze when he heard the sound, half-expecting Wisebeardyface to grab his collar and fling him to the floor. When this didn't happen, he chanced a look over his shoulder and saw that the Great Doors had closed behind him. 'That's all it was,' he told himself. 'You're paranoid. Everyone's asleep.'

With the doors shut, he felt free to walk up the Stone Steps and shout without fear of waking anyone. 'Key-eye!' he yelled, and immediately the BattleCircle began to rise and the Plank extended from the top of the Steps.

The Abyss looked blacker than ever. Tommy could just about see the outline of the Plank and he breathed deeply, preparing to walk its length. For a moment, Tommy felt very alone. More alone than he'd ever felt before. Just a boy in the darkness, in the bowels of a space-station, somewhere in the infinite blackness of space.

Had he not been so fixated on his plan to walk the Plank, Tommy might've seen the figures of Woozie and Marielle silhouetted outside the Great Doors before they closed. They couldn't remember the password and, left on the Shelf, were now banging vainly on the impenetrable barriers. No matter how hard they banged or yelled, not a sound entered the Chamber.

Had Tommy not felt so convinced of his own paranoia once the Great Doors shut, he might've noticed a pair of eyes (open) in the darkness behind him. But he didn't. And they weren't about to make themselves known.

The feeling of absolute aloneness passed and Tommy knew that this was the moment he'd been waiting for. He placed a foot carefully onto the Plank.

The Abyss came to life and once again planet Earth came hurtling towards him. Before he could take a second step, the planet exploded and the heat grew so intense that it felt as if the surface of his skin were bubbling. An island of rock reared past the Plank, five figures writhing on top of it. Two were melting, one was in flames and two were covered in blood. Tommy only just recognized the five – Guttly, Woozie, Summy, Rumbles and Marielle – as his other foot touched the Plank, completing his second step, and the vision disappeared.

His skin was no longer bubbling. Suddenly, all was calm. The white clouds, the sound of birds and water – they were all the same, but there was no sign of the beautiful couple that had smiled so warmly before. Tommy took another step and then another, then another and another. Before he knew it, he was at the end of the Plank and despite the beauty of the Abyss, he felt a tinge of sadness. Perhaps the couple weren't his parents, after all. He'd been wrong and stupid. How silly of him to believe that they'd appear again.

If you could define your life in one moment, what would that moment be? If, before you die, you're allowed to relive one moment in your life, would you be able to choose that moment? This moment – on the Plank – is the one that Tommy would've chosen. He admitted it years later on his deathbed.

In the very depths of despair at the end of the Plank, Tommy remembered the oath he'd made in Wilchester. *I WILL NEVER GIVE UP*. He also thought of MonSenior Leebruce's words and merged them with Guttly's definition of *inner-lath*: 'If you really believe, if you believe *completely*, then you should walk to the end of the Plank, turn so that you are facing the Steps, cross your arms across your chest, close your eyes and fall backwards into the Abyss. They say that if you are filled with *love*, then you will be saved and you will not perish.'

And so, Tommy Storm searched in his heart for the courage to risk everything – or for a reason not to. He found one and not the other, which is often the case when you're desperate, with nothing to lose. Then he turned, crossed his arms across his chest, closed his eyes and fell backwards into the Abyss.

Tommy would never reveal much about what he experienced in the Abyss. He said that he'd met his mother and father and spent long days and nights chatting with them, eating with them and listening to their wisdom. They told him that their Earth names were Lola and Errol, but that they'd assumed new names when they were abducted from Earth and came to live with MilkyFederans – those names were Bonnie and Clive.

Some historians suggest that the three hugged for a long, long time in silence, then went for a picnic and had countless walks by a tree-lined canal. Whatever the truth, for a short time Tommy was allowed to experience paradise. It felt like months, he said, the most perfect months you could ever imagine. But to someone in the Chamber it would've seemed

315

only seconds.

And when it was over, his parents lifted him back onto the Plank and waved farewell. For no one can fall backwards into the Abyss – and be saved – more than once in their lives. It was a tearful, yet somehow contented good-bye.

39

FARCICAL

The Jegg Contest was a relay race involving all the dorms. The IGGY Cadets lined up their jeggs in five lines, just inside the semi-bubble of air (known as the *InZone*) that surrounded the opening of the GarageZone. The first jegg in each dorm would have to fly around an obstacle course and return to the InZone. As soon as this jegg entered the InZone, the next jegg from that dorm could set off. The first dorm to return all five jeggs to the InZone would be the winner.

The Dream5s lined up in the following order: Woozie first, followed by Rumbles, Summy, Tommy and Marielle.

Tommy kicked his pedals, flicking past the country music and heavy rock until he heard Rumbles' heavy breathing on the internal sound system. 'Is everyone doing OK?' he said.

'Couldn't be better,' said Woozie. 'We can win this.'

'As well, suppose I, as one could expect,' mumbled Summy sulkily.

'I'm sleepy,' said Rumbles groggily.

'Fine,' said Marielle, haughtily.

Oh, dear, thought Tommy. We'll never win with this level of teamwork.

The previous night, after his parents had waved farewell, Tommy had stepped gingerly back along the length of the

Plank. He kept expecting to see and feel the pain of a burning Earth, but it was like walking along any plank – he saw and felt no pain. It was if the Plank had been tamed and no longer held any power over him.

Having descended the Stone Steps, he yelled 'V-v-virtygoe!!' – which made the BattleCircle lower – and then yelled 'Soshages!'

He never saw the pair of eyes watching from the shadows, but he did meet Woozie and Marielle outside the Great Doors.

'Yes, I heard you get out of bed and saw you jump through a wighole,' explained Marielle.

'So she woke me up,' said Woozie. 'We thought we better go after you, in case you got into trouble. But we got delayed – had to hide in the AmmaZone from some crazy wailing creature.'

'Why would you go off without us?' said Marielle in a hurt tone.

'Yeah, what're you doing down here, Tommy?'

'It's the middle of the night. You could get us expelled.'

'I didn't ask you to follow me,' said Tommy matter-of-factly, almost immediately regretting his words.

His harsh retort stung Marielle and for a moment her eyes looked watery. Tommy's thoughts were still with his parents and so he failed to realize how much he'd hurt Marielle. She could be very sensitive at times.

They returned to the dorm in silence and without incident, Marielle angrily leading the way. Woozie overshot his bed when he bounced on the springboard and landed on top of Rumbles – who yelled, thereby waking up Summy. Summy was cross, but no one would tell her where they'd been. Rumbles was just sleepy and didn't care where anyone had been.

Tommy pulled his dormi-cover over his head. He thought about explaining things to Marielle, but he didn't much feel like talking to anyone. He'd just said goodbye to his mother and father and he couldn't think about anything – or anyone – else. The other Dream5s lay in bed in a groggy sulk, trying for some hours to get to sleep.

The floating globe containing Miss LeWren and Mr Crabble turned from lemon to violet – the start signal – and five jeggs sped out of the InZone.

'Go on, Woozkeeys!' cried Rumbles.

The Jegg Contest course involved three obstacles.

First was the *Asteroid Field*, consisting of thousands of flying asteroids. Each jegg had to enter the field between two red rocks at the start of the field and leave between two blue ones at the end of it. If you entered or exited the field by any other way, you immediately disqualified your dorm.

The *Cave-a-Saurus* was next. From a distance it looked like a giant brontosaurus – almost as big as IGGY – and each jegg had to enter the left nostril and exit through the right nostril. This sounded easy, except that the quickest route would take you all the way to the brontosaurus' tail before you could turn around and there was always the danger of taking a wrong turn and emerging back into space through the mouth or – even worse – through the brontosaurus' bottom!

Lastly, the *Hidden Maze* would provide a stern test of skill. All you could see were two ornate rings – you had to enter through the silver one, and exit through the crystal one – with an enormous space in-between. This would've been quite simple if the rings weren't openings into a 3-D

319

labyrinth whose interior and exterior walls were completely invisible.

From the InZone it was hard to see the progress of the five jeggs in the Asteroid Field. Every now and again, Tommy could just make out a yellow flash that signified that a jegg had been hit by an asteroid (the asteroids were actually full of mustard-custard and if one hit you, it would slow your jegg greatly for seventeen seconds). Woozie emerged from the field in third place and when he emerged from the Cave-a-Saurus five minutes later, he was in second.

From a spectator point of view, the great thing about the Hidden Maze was that you could easily see the jeggs inside. Woozie went around in circles for a while in the top corner, but then he found a route and flew through the crystal exit just behind Brendan the furballia. He must've put on an extra spurt of speed because they crossed into the InZone neck and neck – and immediately Rumbles and ReeeRaw sped off.

It was the delay in the Cave-a-Saurus that cost Rumbles most dearly. She handed over to poor Summy in third place.

The young kangasaurus was quite a nervous flyer. By the time she left the Asteroid Field she was in last place and remained in that position going into the Maze.

'Come on, Summy,' yelled Woozie, Rumbles and Tommy over the intercom, together. The sulkiness and grogginess seemed to have disappeared.

'You can do it,' cried Marielle tentatively.

All the IGGY Cadets were allowed to cheer whoever was flying for their dorm, but the rules were very strict – no giving advice to a pilot or to anyone who hadn't yet flown the course. A pilot could hear his dorm cheering, but, with his transmitter disabled, he couldn't speak to others while on the course.

The Maze was Summy's speciality, so she was only in fourth place when she spurted into the InZone and Tommy was off.

He pushed the throttle to maximum speed and hurtled into the Asteroid Field. Already he'd nearly caught Anjel*eek!* Jalfrezi (who'd had the seat and cockpit of her jegg enlarged in recent days). Ignoring the flying objects, Tommy continued at full speed and had just overtaken Anjel*eek!* when – *SPLATTTT!* – a mustard-custard asteroid smacked into the side of the jegg and he slowed almost to a stall. Anjel*eek!* wobbled ahead of him and into the distance.

Stupid, stupid, stupid, he thought. You can't just blast through an asteroid field at full speed!

When full power returned, he throttled up to three-quarter speed and concentrated on banking left and right, up and down, occasionally accelerating to miss an especially swift asteroid. Thankfully, he didn't get hit again and although he never saw Anjel*eek!*, somewhere along the way he must've overtaken her, for he was in third place going into the Cave-a-Saurus.

Throttling down to half-speed, he turned on his headlights and entered the left nostril. He was flying through a wet-looking tunnel and everything was cast in a dark green light. Just ahead, a furballia from the VGood3s was visible and then, quite suddenly, he disappeared. Tommy flew after him and then, from nowhere, something boomed against the top of the jegg, plunging him into a deep well-like cavity. Tommy would later learn that a ShadowMallet had hit him (it hit almost everyone – and the only way to avoid it was to slam on your brakes as soon as you entered the nostril and then flash through when the mallet was returning to the pre-hit position).

The jegg's lights failed for a few seconds and Tommy allowed himself to fall in darkness. Eventually, the cavity gave way to a huge red-lit cavern – the belly of the Cave-a-Saurus. There was no sign of the furballia, so Tommy pushed the throttle to maximum speed and aimed for the far end of the cavern. Sensing a movement to his left, he spotted a shoal of WhiteVanWingedFish swooping down towards him.

WhiteVanWingedFish (WVWFs) always fly around recklessly and enjoy bumping into things because they're under the illusion that they own MilkyFed airspace. Usually, they're very grubby and a favourite pastime of some MilkyFed children is to find sleeping WVWFs and write graffiti in the dust that covers their hard bodies.

Tommy pulled back hard on the steering wheel, soaring upwards, performing a 360-degree-inverted-turn. As he plunged back down towards the floor of the belly, the WVWFs shot past overhead and he spotted the VGood3 furballia stalled on the floor, trying to start his jegg – he'd obviously been hit earlier by the shoal.

Before he finally exited the right nostril, Tommy had to dodge a squall of flame comets and fly sideways through a narrow cave that looked like a vertical post-box slot. Entering the Hidden Maze, he saw that Trevor the toothwolf was well ahead.

There was nothing for it. He had to give it a try. After all, it had worked before – hadn't it?

Tommy flicked the lever to his side and the dashboard disappeared. He closed his eyes and tried to feel the Surge. Immediately, he could visualize the maze with extraordinary clarity and the jegg started to accelerate of its own accord.

From afar it looked like Tommy was flying mindlessly in corkscrews and figures-of-eight, but the fact was, he was gaining fast on Trevor. He finally passed the brown jegg just before the crystal exit and flashed towards the InZone.

'Yes!' cried Woozie, Summy, Rumbles and Marielle together. With all the concentration, Tommy hadn't heard a word they'd cheered for the entire race. He opened his eyes to see the scene as he raced back to the InZone. He wanted to see his friends cheering and know for sure that Marielle had forgiven him. Maybe there was more to it than that. Perhaps, he'd later concede, he wanted to revel in his own glory. He'd flown a great race, after all.

The jegg started to shudder as soon as he opened his eyes and then it veered madly, away from the InZone. He tried closing his eyes, but it did no good. He'd succumbed to the Farce and it had control of him now.

'Be calm, Tommy,' he told himself. 'Be calm.'

He opened his eyes and flicked the lever to his left. The steering wheel reattached itself to the dashboard as it swivelled back into place. He pulled hard on it and somersaulted back towards the InZone. In the distance, he could see Trevor crossing the line and Felkor setting off. At almost the same moment, the VGood3 furballia emerged from the Maze. Tommy pushed his throttle to full speed and zoomed towards the InZone. He entered it only half a jegg behind the furballia.

By the time he turned around his jegg, caught his breath and forgot about feeling ashamed, Marielle was already exiting the Asteroid Field, having overtaken Egbert Fitchly. She'd made up a lot of distance on Felkor.

Tommy sidled his jegg in beside the other Dream5s and started cheering madly.

'Come on, Marielle! You can do it! Come on!'

Tommy felt confident that Marielle would beat Felkor. She was a natural pilot and Tommy wouldn't like to have raced against her. She had a great ability to slow down to avoid obstacles instead of racing into them at top speed, the way he could. *Anticipation*, that's what she called it.

They cheered and waited. Tommy expected Felkor to get hit by the shoal of WhiteVanWingedFish and that was where Marielle would surely overtake him.

After a long wait, Egbert Fitchly emerged from the Cave-a-Saurus, followed some time later by a wibblewallian for the Great2s and a kissentell for the Alright4s. On the line, having successfully negotiated the Hidden Maze, Egbert just pipped the wibblewallian by a nose. The VGood3s had won.

'Marielle!' cried Tommy. 'Marielle?'

'Where are you? Are you alright?' called the other three.

Tommy flicked through the channels and heard the VGood3s cheering loudly. 'One hundred points!' they were chanting. Later, in the InZone, four of them lifted Egbert over their heads and carried him laughing to the wighole, still cheering as madly as ever. 'Yo, I flew the entire race with my hands totally tied behind my back,' he cried. And even though he managed to lose his cowboy hat, it was one of the happiest moments of Egbert's life.

Tommy tried to fly to the Cave-a-Saurus, but Miss LeWren was already in her jegg and ordered him back to the InZone.

Marielle and Felkor were eventually towed back to the GarageZone. They were unharmed, but both were angry.

'He fired on me!' fumed Marielle. 'In the belly of that brontosaurus. I dodged a shoal of WingedFish and then something hit me from below.'

'I never fired at yuh,' said Felkor, from under his hat.

'You did, you lying piglasaurus! Your jegg was stalled on the belly floor and you fired at me when I flew past.'

'Bull***t!' *(Censored by the Milki Masters' Council.)*

'My jegg stalled once he fired on me, Miss, but I managed to steer it towards his jegg and bang into him. Absolutely no way was I going to let him take off after shooting me down.'

'Complete tosh, Miss LeWren. I was tryin' to restart my jegg and *she* flew into *me*. It was reckless flyin'. I tell yuh. Women flyers!'

That was the wrong thing to say to Miss LeWren, who didn't take kindly to people insulting women flyers. It probably saved Marielle from getting into trouble (Miss LeWren hadn't believed Marielle's story – none of the jeggs were supposed to be armed and who'd be crazy enough to shoot someone down inside a Cave-a–Saurus?).

'Zootallore!' she said crossly. 'Back to your dormz. All of you!'

As the dorms lined up to jump through the wigholes and once Miss LeWren was out of earshot, Felkor called over to Marielle: 'Least my parents aren't dead!'

It took Rumbles, Woozie and Tommy to hold her back. They bundled her into the wighole as Trevor joined Felkor in a chant. 'Dead mum! Dead dad! Wonder why they were so bad!'

During lunch, the following projection appeared in every dorm:

```
STANDINGS AFTER THE JEGG RACE . . .


DORMS              TOTAL POINTS

BRILLO1S                60
GREAT2S                 40
VGOOD3S                100
ALRIGHT4S               30
DREAM5S                 20
```

Marielle didn't even glance at the projection. She was still smarting from Felkor's comments and seemed particularly annoyed with Tommy. Was it because he'd helped to hold her back from attacking Felkor or was she still mad at him for sneaking off to the Uh-Oh-Doh-Joh Chamber and then being rude to her? Tommy wasn't sure and now wasn't the time to ask.

'Win we still can if in the last contest we triumph,' said Summy, tapping figures into the monitor at the end of her bed.

'We'd be in the lead now if Marielle had beaten Felkor in the jegg race,' said Woozie.

'That was my fault,' said Tommy. 'If I hadn't been looking for the biggest cheer, Marielle wouldn't have started her leg in third place.'

'Don't be silly. It's no one's faultskeey.'

'No, Tommy's right,' said Marielle, suddenly joining the conversation. 'If Tommy hadn't been looking for glory, I wouldn't have been behind Felkor and he couldn't have shot me down.'

'Hey – wait a minute!'

Everyone started arguing until Tommy, avoiding Marielle's eye, called for quiet.

'Summy's right,' he said. 'We can still beat all the other dorms if we win the flashscimitar contest.'

'Precisely. Ninety points to the winning dorm will be awarded.'

'That'd put us on one hundred and . . .' Woozie was counting on his fingers. (It's harder to do sums using your hands when you've eight digits rather than ten.) '. . . One hundred and ten points! And the winners, overall.'

326

'But we have to stop arguing,' said Tommy. 'I'm happy to take the blame for the last event, but let's put it out of our minds for now. OK?'

Everyone except Marielle agreed heartily. She just nodded her head silently and avoided Tommy's gaze.

⚡ 40 ⚡

CHOOSING THE PLANET TO BE ~~OBLITERATED~~ HONOURED

'I must go,' said Guttly, wiping his lips. For old times' sake, he'd decided to taste roast turkey and vegetables during his favo-fant dinner. *Delicious.*

'Can I come with you?' said Tommy.

'No . . . I'm sorry, Tommy. They're only going to allow one person per planet to plead for mercy at this stage.' He looked anxiously at his pyramidal MilkyFed watch. 'Earlier, there was an ArmlessSensitiveskinner pleading with them not to obliterate Dust2Dust . . .' (Such creatures have a particular aversion to itching powder.) 'At the moment,' continued Guttly, 'there's a CheeeTingLothario pleading Panthurpink's case.'

'When do they make their decision?'

'Tonight – after I plead Earth's case.'

'Can't I come and watch?'

'I'm sorry, Tommy.'

Guttly patted Tommy's head apologetically, placed the wighole to the TrepidationRoom on the floor and jumped through it feet-first.

⚡

Not wanting to join in the chatter of his friends, Tommy climbed into the floating-bowling alley above the Dream5s' dorm. Playing the electric violin made him think more clearly. He thought about how beautiful Earth had once been and, perhaps, could be again. He thought of the stories his parents had told him – how there were many boys and girls on Earth like him who didn't know all the answers, who wanted to belong, who loved their family and who wanted to do something for others.

Just because adults do stupid things, doesn't mean that all people are stupid – so his parents had explained. Adults know even less than children and they only do stupid things because they follow stupid people and usually they're too scared to search for the answers themselves. But whenever adults allow themselves *to think* – to *really* think – they find incredibly intelligent answers. The problem is, they're just too lazy or scared to think very often.

And another thing . . . Just because bad things frequently happen on Earth, doesn't make everyone bad. Bad people tend to be bullies and they shout louder than anyone else. So you hear more about *one* bad thing than you do about *ten* good things. You never hear about the *million* people who travelled safely to work. You only hear about the *one* person who was shot on the way to work. News – especially on Earth – rarely involves safe, happy things. It always feeds on misery and fear.

So, really, Earth isn't as bad as people think it is. If people could overcome laziness and fear, then goodness and intelligence could thrive.

There came a point when Tommy could bear it no longer and tossed the violin aside. He had to say something. How could he just float there, fiddling, while Earth burned (or was going to burn)? How could he let things happen without him?

Woozie, Rumbles and Summy were involved in a headstand

competition below and Marielle was taking a bath. Marielle would probably be cross with him again for going off on his own, but there was no alternative. The lives of billions depended on it.

Guttly had been addressing the Milki Masters' Council for about an hour when Mr Crabble let out a yell and fell over. Guttly had explained how Earth had adapted to the Great Climate Enhancement and he was giving statistics on the number of babies born every day and the number of children under the age of seven who could spell the word *encyclopaedia* (or is it *ensighklopeedia*?).

Crabble had been standing on stilts, so he hit the ground with a thud and crumpled his sombrero. Tommy had flown through a wighole inside the GrandKangasaurusCourt and banged straight into one of Crabble's stilts.

Before any geography nerds start trying to contact me, let me explain that Tommy had come through a different wighole from the one into the viewers' gallery or into the TrepidationRoom. He'd remembered seeing a wighole for the GrandKangasaurusCourt in Crabble's lab, near the store-room – so he travelled via the lab.

'Mr Storm, yes!?' Crabble thundered. 'By Georgus, you've smashed my Moonbeambands!' (A popular make of sunglasses – or *starspex* as they're frequently called.)

'Sorry, sir. I—'

'What is the meaning of this?' boomed Wisebeardyface.

'You cannot destroy Earth!'

'Mr Storm—'

'Tommy, please, I'm handling this,' cried Guttly.

Crabble hobbled back onto his stilts as Tommy ran over to where Guttly was standing and faced the Council.

330

'I know there are rules,' he said. 'I know I shouldn't be here, but sometimes rules have to be broken. Rules have their place, but when billions of lives are at stake, I don't care how much trouble I get into.'

'Hence thou willst be pleas'd to know that thou are in *serious* trouble,' said Lady MuckBeff darkly.

'Please. Listen to me. You say you're intelligent creatures, so please listen to a child's voice . . . A voice that has something important to say.'

Tommy felt so driven and so passionate that he had no time to feel afraid. He didn't even know what he was going to say next. The words just seemed to emerge from an inner reservoir of feeling.

'Fie thee hither to thy dorm, Earthling!'

'No, Lady MuckBeff . . . let him speak,' said Wisebeardyface. 'He has a point. We are talking about the very survival of a planet here . . . Speak, boy. Are you going to give us more statistics?'

Tommy shook his head and, a little shocked, Guttly stepped aside to give Tommy the Speaker's Square to himself.

'I want to speak to you about something you've forgotten about,' said Tommy as soon as he was facing the five Masters of the Way. 'About something you think is called *inner-lath*.' MonSenior took a sharp intake of breath and Crabble stopped picking his nose.

'Yes, what you call *inner-lath*, we humans know as *love*.'

'Love?' said Wisebeardyface.

'Love,' replied Tommy. 'I love my planet. It's a part of me. It's where I'm from. Where my species is from. We may seem stupid and evil in comparison to the MilkyFed, but for all our mistakes we know how to love. And love gives us a power to rise above our failings.'

Tommy paused and was tempted to list some facts about the number of women, children and camels on Earth, but thought better of it. (There were sixteen camels actually, all of whom were a bit humped off that their relatives had died during the Great Climate Enhancement.) Before he had time to formulate another thought, a feeling swept through him and Tommy heard his own voice speaking.

'Your *HappinessIzzzAh* program has taught you to be happy in an *efficient* way, but not in the mixed-up, terrible, difficult, yet *beautiful* way we search for on Earth. We don't always find it, but we *try* . . . Without love, your happiness is empty. And if you really want to find your *inner-lath*, if you want to find out what love is, then do not destroy Earth. Because, for all its faults, it's the biggest source of love you'll ever find.'

It was quite a performance. The Milki Masters' Council had never heard such passion in a voice before. There was something stronger than logic, maybe even stronger than fear, in this young boy's voice. It was something they couldn't quite define.

Despite its brevity, Tommy felt completely exhausted at the end of the speech. It was an exhaustion he'd never felt before. He'd thrown all his energy and feelings into the words – all the love for his parents, all his hopes for Earth and all his dreams for the Dream5s. And maybe even some element of his feelings for Marielle.

The Milki Masters formed a tight huddle to consider their verdict. Wisebeardyface would later admit that he'd been intrigued to learn from Guttly that there were 3,156,777,891 waterbeds on Earth, although he was keen to stress that this had no bearing on the Council's discussion. (You see, kangasauri love waterbeds – especially vibrating ones – because they never get seasick.)

Guttly put his arm around Tommy – for which Tommy was thankful because he feared he might otherwise collapse to the floor. After a time, the Milki Masters resumed their positions and Wisebeardyface spoke.

'We *were* going to choose Earth as the planet to be honoured with obliteration – even though you gave a most insightful speech, President Randolph, and even though our probe has not yet sent us pictures from Earth . . .

'Now, however, we have changed our minds and made a decision . . . by a majority of three to two . . .'

Wisebeardyface looked sternly at Tommy. 'I should say that we do not accept every word you said, young Mr Storm, but we do believe that there may be some merit in your words. Perhaps your *love* is our *inner-lath* and perhaps there is some of this *love* on planet Earth. We will give you the benefit of the doubt . . . And so, Earth shall not be chosen as the planet to be honoured with obliteration.

'After the last of the IGGY Cadet contests tomorrow – the flashscimitar duel – we will make the formal announcement to everyone and the decision to obliterate Dust2Dust shall be ratified . . . You may not speak about this before then.'

Tommy gave a sigh of relief and felt his legs give way underneath him. Luckily, Guttly was there to hold him up and to hug him with a joy few had ever seen in the old man's eyes.

⚡ 47 ⚡
GET THE PROBE

'Do you, Elsorr Cuthbert Gary Hillary Biff Maudlin, swear to serve your planet as Permanent President in a fair and honest way, for the good of its people?'

'I do.'

'Then, with this flipper, I pronounce you *President of Planet Earth*, replacing Guttly Randolph.'

As he said these words, the eldest Councillor of the Grand Council, Eric Mkhwanazi, ceremoniously tried to put the large fluorescent flipper on Elsorr's ear, then on his left elbow, before finally placing it firmly on Elsorr's right foot.

Elsorr stood up, wearing the one flipper – his other foot bare – brandishing his ruby ring and looking up proudly at the unfeasibly large jewelled crown on his head.

The crown was known as the *WOW-Iveneverseenwunthat-bigB4 Crown*. It was as big as a beach-ball and generally only worn on ceremonial occasions or on Aintmoneyfantastic Day (a holiday for humans who could wear more than two pairs of trousers at once).

'Yes!' cried Elsorr. 'I'm now the Permanent President of planet Earth.' And he raised his sword in the air like a super-hero – or a powerful leader, at the very least.

There was no getting around it. Elsorr had been sworn in and now there were no laws that could be passed by the

Councillors that could remove Elsorr the Great from power.

It was the probe he had to be thankful for. When it flew into Earth's atmosphere and under the clouds, a tremendous fear gripped the inhabitants of Earth because Elsorr had leaked the MilkyFed invasion story to the papers and most of the Councillors came to realize that Elsorr must've spoken the truth at the Panic Grand Council Meeting.

What could they do? They had to try and defend Earth somehow, but no one except the Permanent President could order an attack on the probe and Elsorr was claiming that Guttly was too afraid to order such a move. Some feared that Guttly may have been killed already.

There was nothing for it. Earth needed a powerful, fearless leader in this time of peril. Elsorr Maudlin might lack charm, but he had strength and cunning and courage. These were the qualities most needed in times of danger. So the Council thought.

And so it was decided to swear in Elsorr as the new Permanent President and then to let him deal with the probe and with the MilkyFed as he saw fit. He was the only one, they believed, who could save their beloved planet.

'Lick my bare foot!' demanded Elsorr, still holding his sword aloft.

'What?' said Eric Mkhwanazi, aghast.

'Between the toes . . . Kneel and lick to prove your loyalty and devotion to me, Elsorr the Great. Your President.'

For many reasons – not least the fact that he was a vegetarian – Eric was reluctant to carry out this request. For one thing, it was ludicrous. For another, Elsorr had furry, corn-infested feet and their odour invited little affection.

'I'm sorry, President Elsorr. I *am* loyal, but I cannot lick between your toes. I'd better be getting back to the Majestic

Table now . . . My tea is getting cold.'

'Lick!' roared Elsorr.

'Couldn't you just use a wet face-cloth instead?'

SSSCCCHHHWUMMPPPP!

The other Councillors at the Majestic Table hardly saw the blur of shiny metal before Eric's head fell from his shoulders onto the floor, creating quite a mess.

'That's what happens to people who show disloyalty,' said Elsorr calmly, as he smeared the blood off his sword with a finger. 'Now I shall deal with this infernal MilkyFed probe.'

He turned away from the Councillors with a snort and placed a blood-covered finger in his mouth. *Mmmm*, it tasted rather good.

42

SELF-SACRIFICE

Tommy was on a high when he returned to his dorm from the GrandKangasaurusCourt and slept very soundly that night. But since good news is much easier to take for granted than bad news, it should come as no surprise to learn that when he awoke next morning, he had new concerns on his mind.

The first was the flashscimitar contest. If the Dream5s won, they'd end up with more points overall than any other dorm, so there was everything to fight for.

The second was Marielle. Tommy felt bad about the way he'd spoken to her outside the Uh-Oh-Doh-Joh Chamber a few nights earlier. His words had stung her, which was unfair. He also felt bad that he'd sneaked off in the first place and that afterwards he hadn't explained to her his reasons for doing so. He knew it might help to tell her now about his parents and his fall into the Abyss, but he felt a reluctance to do so. It wasn't that he didn't trust her. He just felt that it was private. Something more special because it was his secret alone.

And yet he didn't like seeing poor Marielle feeling hurt.

For safety reasons, the blades of the flashscimitars were coated with *Boinggg!Jelly* and contestants wore white *force field* bodysuits that covered their hands, feet and head. Together, these precautions meant that a hit from a flashscimitar would feel like a very hard smack, rather than being a mortal blow. Contestants' faces were visible because a specially designed oval, invisible force field was made to hover in front of their heads.

The contest was held in the Uh-Oh-Doh-Joh Chamber, but again, for safety reasons, it was decided that the BattleCircle should stay put, covering the Abyss. All the IGGY Cadets who weren't competing in the duel were allowed to stand around the BattleCircle and cheer. If any of them stepped into the BattleCircle during a duel, they'd disqualify their dorm from the contest.

The rules were simple. Contestants should wield the scimmy with their weaker (or weakest) hand and the first person to inflict a body-blow to their opponent would win the duel.

The morning session was called the *Slog Session* – for good reason. Everyone had to have four duels (opponents were randomly selected, but couldn't be from the same dorm) and you'd receive three points for a win, one point for a draw and no points for a loss.

At the end of the Slog Session, the four contestants with the highest number of points would go into a knockout phase called the *Crunch Session*, which would involve a semifinal and a final to decide the ultimate winner. MonSenior Leebruce explained that if too many people ended up with the same score, he'd decide who should make the semifinal, based on artistic merit marks that he'd award during the duels (the *cammPtosss*, for example, was a limp-wristed scimmy throw-and-catch movement, done in tandem with a twirl, that was worth bonus marks).

'Good luck,' said MonSenior to the contestants (two from

each dorm) before they started. 'This is your last chance to face your opponents in the other dorms . . . Look at your opponents closely because you'll not see much of them again. Either *they* will be made IGGY Knights and *you* will be sent back to your planet . . . or . . . *you* will be made an IGGY Knight and *they* will be sent back to their planets. Your destiny is in your own hands.'

At one point during this speech, Tommy thought that MonSenior looked directly at him in a strange way, but when he returned the gaze, the old man looked away.

A minor disagreement erupted before the contest even started. Technically, ReeeRaw should've represented the Brillo1s in the flashscimitar contest, since she'd not participated in the floating-bowling[12] or PlanetChessy competitions, but she claimed to have a sore tail. Felkor declared that he should take her place since the PlanetChessy competition hadn't officially counted. Eventually, he got his way.

Tommy and Marielle were representing the Dream5s and they won four contests each in the Slog Session (as did Felkor and Trevor the toothwolf), taking them through to the semifinals.

'That was great, Marielle,' said Tommy during lunch. 'You fought well.'

'Huh . . . How would someone as selfish and self-centred as you know that I fought well?'

It was Tommy's turn to feel stung. He was about to answer back when he checked himself. It wasn't easy, but he realized that a row could put them off their form later. It would be silly to let the Brillo1s win the contest because he and Marielle were upset. So he bit his lip.

'Do you think you'll beat Trevor?' asked Woozie, trying to

12 Since she was disqualified for being late.

change the subject.

'Of course,' said Marielle, 'but I wish I was fighting Felkor. I'd show him what a girl is capable of.'

<hr>

In the first semifinal, Marielle fought against Trevor the toothwolf. She was in such a ferocious mood that the contest was over in 8.4 seconds.

'Victory to Miss BossyBlondie,' said MonSenior, his voice lost amidst the cheering from the Dream5s.

Trevor shook his head in disbelief as the Brillo1s crowded round him. When they stepped back, Trevor was lying on the ground holding his belly as if he'd been punched very hard.

MonSenior hoverchaired to the far corner of the Chamber to activate a drumroll for the next contest. Felkor and Tommy stepped onto the BattleCircle and somehow Felkor 'bumped' into Marielle, sending her sprawling across the floor of the Circle. The Brillo1s laughed loudly, the sound rising above the gathering drumroll.

'Sorry,' shouted Felkor above the din as he passed within earshot of her. 'I'm awf'ly clumsy sometimes.' Then he offered her a hand up.

Marielle picked herself up smartly. 'Get lost, Felkor.'

'Oh, the poor Ickle Empress is gonna run off and tell her mummy and daddy 'bout me, innit . . . ? Oops I forgot. They're dead!'

The spectators heard none of this, they just saw Marielle look very cross and push forcefully against Tommy as he tried to hold her back. Then MonSenior appeared in the BattleCircle and indicated that Marielle should join the spectators on the sidelines.

Tommy and Felkor touched their flashscimitars to their

340

chins and the drumroll stopped abruptly – to be replaced by loud cheering from all the spectators.

The two foes circled each other gingerly for some moments. It looked like Felkor was moving his mouth, but no one could hear his words.

Tommy could hear them though. 'I've got you at last, Storm,' he was saying. 'Now yuh're mine . . . They'll never let a *darky* be an IGGY Knight.'

Tommy lashed his scimmy in a sideways motion towards Felkor, but the pale, lanky boy was too quick. He pirouetted out of the way and sent his own scimmy cutting through the air towards Tommy's shoulder.

The only way to avoid the blow was to fall backwards and this is what Tommy did, to the vocal amusement of the Brillo1s. If Tommy thought this would be an opportunity to regain his breath, he was wrong. Once again, Felkor's scimmy flashed through the air, this time coming straight for his neck. Tommy rolled sideways, then threw his legs away from himself, landed on his feet momentarily, before jumping into the air to avoid a blow that would've whipped across his shins.

'That was stupid,' he told himself as soon as he had a chance to pause and was facing Felkor again. 'Don't let yourself get angry. That's what Felkor wants. That's why he's goading you – so you become reckless and careless.'

It was the longest battle of the day and one that many of the spectators would recall in years to come. Felkor lashing at Tommy, Tommy dodging and then counter-attacking swiftly. Round and round the BattleCircle they fought. Occasionally, Tommy would fall to the floor, just sweeping his scimmy across his face in time to block a blow. Each time the noise was the same.

SSSCCHHHLASSSSTUWIZZZZZZZ!

His whole body shuddered in time to the leaping blue sparks and the metallic screech.

'He only fell cos Brendan tripped him again!' yelled Woozie to MonSenior. 'That dumb, punk furballia rolled onto the edge of the Circle!'

But the wizened Master refused to disqualify the Brillo1s because he hadn't seen the incident (he'd been distracted – ReeeRaw had pulled on his tartan rug and then apologized for the 'accident').

It was Summy who realized what it was about Felkor that was nagging in the back of her mind. Something she couldn't put her finger on for the first nine minutes of the contest. But when she realized, it was obvious.

'Super-nova! His hand!' she yelled. 'With his right hand Felkor is fighting!'

And sure enough he was. In fact, both Tommy and Felkor were fighting with their right hands, but while Summy was sure that Tommy was left-handed, she felt almost certain that Felkor had used his left hand during the Slog Session. Everyone was cheering and yelling too loudly to hear Summy, and there was no easy way to get to MonSenior, who'd hoverchaired to the far side of the BattleCircle.

As the duel built to a crescendo of leaping sparks and metallic hissing screeches, Felkor's mouth seemed to be moving even faster than before.

'Tommy Storm,' he said with derision. 'Yuh think yuh're so great now with yer spiky hair and normal voice, innit, but yuh're as pathetic as all the Dream5s. 'Specially that ugly Marielle creature.'

Tommy kept his muscles relaxed as he swivelled his scimmy to shield another blow. He did his best to ignore the bile spitting from Felkor's mouth, but what Felkor said next cut through all his best intentions.

'You're another one with dead parents, innit?'

Tommy lashed at Felkor with all his force, knocking the snowy-white boy's scimmy clean out of his hand and making him turn even paler than normal (if that were possible). Felkor's black hat fell off his head and he stepped backwards nervously, crumpling it.

What happened next is the topic of considerable debate amongst Tommy Storm historians.

Some say that Tommy's anger gave him such momentum that he fell to his knees as Felkor's scimmy rattled to the floor. This fall knocked the wind out of him and gave Felkor a chance to snatch up his scimmy and hit Tommy with a scything blow across the chest.

Others say that Tommy's anger left him as soon as he knocked Felkor's scimmy to the floor and he fell to his knees in a moment of shame – shame that he'd let anger take control of him. In that moment, he realized that *to win at all costs* was actually *to lose at every cost* and so he decided to triumph over Felkor by allowing the sneering boy to scythe him down.

Historians of the FroydyAnn persuasion claim that Tommy saw a vision of his parents at that moment. They say he 'lost' to win their honour. He was prepared to sacrifice his anger and his petty feelings, to experience the humiliation of defeat to Felkor, in order to show the undying love he felt for his parents.

The ReeahLists hold that Tommy slipped on a sliver of gherkin and then, as soon as he fell to his knees, suffered from a feverish attack of trapped wind that momentarily paralysed him.

Lastly, the SopPeee Historians believe that Tommy fell to

his knees, raised his scimmy above his head and looked over at Marielle. He didn't want to fight her in the final – he wanted to let her have the satisfaction of duelling Felkor. It was *a peace offering* to the Ickle Empress. A chance to forgo glory himself and offer it to her.

'Victory to Mr PaleSnarl,' cried MonSenior (in a disappointed tone, some would say) as Tommy fell to the floor, winded. The Brillols ran into the BattleCircle and lifted Felkor in the air, cheering loudly. In the mayhem, Tommy received a number of kicks and emerged from the scrum with a cut above his eye.

'Oooh, you're cutskeeys,' yelped Rumbles, hugging Tommy and dabbing his forehead with her third hand.

MonSenior continued to look over at the vanquished Earthling in an odd way.

'Sorry,' was all Tommy said to his friends and they were too stunned to say much in reply.

Historians would pick over many aspects of Tommy's life, but, for some reason, Tommy's 'loss' to Felkor in the flashscimitar controversy has created more controversy and bitter debate amongst nerdy historians than 'the banana debates' of human psychiatrists. Because the infighting has become so vitriolic, I'll take the time to explain something of the different schools of thought.

FroydyAnn School

This was a history college founded by Ann Grrrrr from the Planet Froydy. Miss Grrrrr believed that the actions of most creatures can be traced to quirks in their parents. She was the first person to suggest that people who remove their shoes without untying the laces were gurgled at loudly by their parents when they were infants (or else they were just wearing slip-ons).

ReeahLists

This is a cult of people who compile lists of trivia and market their products aggressively at inter-planetary duty-free shops. Their theory about Tommy's 'loss' suffers from the fact that gherkins were only found on the planet McJUNK at this time.

SopPeee Historians

These historians believe that appropriately distributed bunches of flowers and boxes of chocolates could have prevented almost every major conflict in the history of the universe. Most of their theories are recorded on Grow-sss-Goo format, accompanied by easy-listening music in the background. (*Through the Soft Fluffy Clouds of Time* is by far their most popular recording.) After much legal wrangling, the words *'peace offering'* have replaced *'love sacrifice'* in revised editions of their official account of Tommy and Felkor's duel.

⚡ 43 ⚡

THE RIDICULOUS TO THE SUBLIME

A PowerRest involves being immersed for ten seconds in a caffeinated floating globe. Felkor took three PowerRests after the duel with Tommy to prepare himself for what would surely be his most glorious hour.

Just before the blonde conqueror was about to start his duel with Marielle, Guttly appeared and asked Tommy to come with him. Tommy would've protested, but Guttly looked very serious.

'Wisebeardyface wants to see us immediately,' he said. 'He sounded very angry.'

Guttly whispered something into MonSenior's ear, realized he was talking into the 'wrong' ear, then whispered into the other one (the one with the cochlea-roach). The ancient Master nodded and Guttly walked out of the Great Doors followed by Tommy.

Just before the doors closed behind them, Tommy heard a loud *SSSCCHHHLASSSSTUWIZZZZZZZ!* above twenty-two cheers and the reflection of electric blue bolts seemed to light up the whole Chamber and spill out after him.

He followed Guttly silently into a whooshUlator and they

346

travelled upwards at a startling speed – too fast to see anything, except blurring, flickering colours. The two Earthlings started to slow when the colours faded, replaced by an impenetrable darkness. Tommy felt the air become cooler and then, quite suddenly, the whooshUlator stopped blowing and the darkness was replaced with something brighter.

He realized that he and Guttly were in a type of glass conservatory and it seemed to be perched on the very top of IGGY with a panoramic view out to space.

'This is where I come to think,' said a gravelly voice behind them. 'It's called the Eye-on-the-Universe.'

Tommy turned and saw Wisebeardyface reclining on a large sofa, smoking a strange-looking cigarette and sipping an odd-coloured liquid from a tall glass, with an umbrella and a straw sticking out of it. The umbrella was so large that it rose above Wisebeardyface's head. The straw must've been at least a metre long.

'Sometimes it pains me to think and I wish I could stop, but . . .'

The old kangasaurus didn't finish the sentence. He just puffed leisurely on his cigarette and took a long sip of the liquid, which Tommy could see inching up the long straw.

'It's not what you do, it's the way that you . . .' Again, the bearded dinosaurus failed to finish his sentence and took another sip.

'We came as quickly as we could,' said Guttly hastily. 'What is it? You sounded . . . Well, you sounded angry.'

'Yes I did, didn't I?' replied Wisebeardyface casually, releasing the straw. 'I must apologize. Sometimes I get very . . .'

'Yes?'

Wisebeardyface threw his head back and looked through the glass ceiling at a cluster of stars.

'I . . . *Irate* – that's the word I'm looking for . . .' He threw his head forwards and gazed at the far side of the room. 'Please, gentlemen . . . take a seat on the couch over there. Please. I have something to show you.'

More than a little perturbed – Wisebeardyface had never acted so weirdly before – Tommy sat down beside Guttly. Wisebeardyface took something squidgy out of his pocket and threw it at one of the glass windows. It stuck to the glass with a *SSCHMACKK!* And nothing else happened.

'Fizzlestix . . . ! I threw the wrong one. That is my . . . used chewing gum.'

Wisebeardyface fumbled in his pouch and pulled out something else gooey and lobbed it towards another window. It glanced off it and fell harmlessly to the floor. From where he was sitting, Tommy could see that it was Grow-sss-Goo, so when Wisebeardyface pointed feebly towards the purple ball of jelly, Tommy picked it up and flung it hard at the window. (Grow-sss-Goo has to be flung with a degree of force towards a flat object if it's to *MovieFy*).

An image formed on the window of a strange-looking probe gliding effortlessly over Earth's great-domed cities. The probe had been fitted with technology that could see through the domes covering floating cities and through the walls and curtains of most Earth dwelling places (such probes were often used by Peeping Tomaliens to get round the issue of curtains).

Tommy could see that the probe was a sphere made of a dark metallic substance, but it had a mane of long, bright-red hair that trailed behind it and a green and red tartan kilt. Its two shiny windows looked like twinkling eyes.

'What's that dangly thing peeking out from under the kilt?' asked Guttly innocently.

'What?' Wisebeardyface slouched forward to get a better

348

view. 'Oh, that . . . That is the transmitter.'

Then a missile streaked over the horizon and zoomed towards the probe. There was a loud explosion and the screen went black. And stayed that way.

'They attacked Paddie and destroyed him,' said Wisebeardyface with a melancholy voice.

'Paddie?' said Tommy.

'Yes, Paddie . . . My *favourite* probe.' Tommy thought he saw a tear roll down the old dinosaurus's face. 'My auntie Ethel gave him to me as a present for my 403rd birthday . . . when I was just a young lad. He was a great probe . . . Not nearly so lazy as most of them.'

'There must be an explanation,' blurted Guttly.

'Of course there is an explanation,' cried Wisebeardyface, staggering to his feet. 'Earthlings are aggressive, war-like creatures with no right to . . .'

The old dinosaurus was a bit wobbly on his feet. He let the cigarette drop from his mouth and put it out with a twist of his heavy foot. He waded towards the window and tried to remove the lump of chewing gum.

'Damn thing never tastes as good when it goes hard,' he mumbled.

'What can we do?' said Guttly forcefully, trying to rouse Wisebeardyface.

'Huh?' Wisebeardyface seemed to remember where he was. 'Do? . . . Do?' He started to shout and looked enraged all of a sudden. 'DO? DO? YOU CAN DO WHAT YOU LIKE FOR ALL I CARE!'

'But, Lord BeardedmoustachedWiseface-oh,' said Guttly placatingly. 'There must—'

'What are you doing here, boy?' cried Wisebeardyface suddenly turning on Tommy.

349

'Well, I—'

'You should be with the other Cadets! Do you think that you're more important than they?'

'Eh, no.'

'You asked me to bring him, Lord Beardedmoustached-Wiseface-oh.'

At that point, Wisebeardyface keeled forwards onto the sofa he'd been sitting on, knocked over the tall glass half-full of stripy liquid and vomited all over a set of cushions. He groaned loudly.

'I think you should go,' said Guttly to Tommy.

'But—'

'Just go, Tommy! Don't worry, I'll help him and things will be OK. There's obviously been some mix-up with the probe.'

Tommy was glad to leave the Eye-on-the-Universe (not least because it had started to smell of sick) and he leapt down a plungeUlator that took him to the Great Doors once more.

When he joined his fellow Dream5s, he was astonished to see that Marielle and Felkor were still duelling.

Not realizing quite how fond of slowing time Wisebeardyface was, Tommy hadn't noticed the Segnitia Switch flicked to the 'on' position in the Eye-on-the-Universe (which slowed time in that room only). To those in the Chamber, it seemed that Tommy had been gone only two minutes.

Tommy soon forgot about the smell of sick and the strange behaviour of Wisebeardyface as he became swept along by the emotion coursing round the Chamber.

'Come on, Marielle!'

'Felkor! Felkor! Felkor!'

Everyone was chanting something – even the neutrals.

Back and forth Marielle and Felkor slashed their scimmies with Felkor still using his right hand, leaping sideways, lunging forwards, faltering backwards. (Marielle had refused to let Summy lodge a complaint to MonSenior about Felkor's choice of hand. 'If Tommy fought Felkor's good hand, then I will too,' she'd said stubbornly.)

Occasionally, Marielle would perform a somersault over Felkor's head and each time it produced a loud 'Olé!' from the crowd, which infuriated the pale boy.

In the end, it was frustration that got the better of Felkor. Tiring badly, he gathered all his energy and flung himself at Marielle in a desperate last-ditch effort to defeat his pigtailed adversary. She back-flipped to the side (in a manoeuvre that impressed Egbert Fitchly), then whacked Felkor across the back with her scimmy as he skidded past, sending the lanky fellow sprawling face-down across the BattleCircle, his black hat sliding just ahead of him.

The Chamber went deadly silent for a moment – too stunned to comprehend what had happened. Felkor groaned and spat an obscenity as Marielle walked over to him.

'Here,' Marielle extended a hand to help the pale boy up.

Felkor smiled and swept his sword violently across the floor in an effort to chop Marielle down at her ankles. The little girl skipped slightly in the air and landed on top of Felkor's scimmy, causing him to yell with pain as a judder went up his arm.

'Here,' said Marielle again, extending her hand to Felkor.

Grudgingly, Felkor released his scimmy, took her hand and allowed himself to be helped to his feet.

'Don't you ever mention my parents in a disparaging way again,' said Marielle softly.

Felkor nodded silently, then finding her intense gaze too much to bear, he looked away and reached for his (by now very crumpled) hat.

'Victory to Miss FightingGal,' cried MonSenior after a pause, and the Dream5s ran to hug their hero.

There was a lot of loud cheering from some and gnashing of teeth from others, but all in all there was an air of relief amongst the IGGY Cadets. The training was over, the tests and the contests were finally finished.

'Super-dooper-nova!' cried Summy excitedly. 'Victorious we are!'

'I'm sorry for what I said the other day,' said Tommy, stepping back from the group hug and looking Marielle in the eye.

'I know,' replied Marielle. And for some reason her eyes became quite watery.

⚡ 44 ⚡

DOUBLE SHOCK

That evening, the Dream5s all had baths and changed into their tuxedos and ballgowns in buoyant mood. Rumbles decided to go with a yellow ballgown after deciding that a tuxedo would be too boring. Tommy helped Summy with the buttons on the back of her green gown and then he and Woozie tried to help each other with their bow-ties.

'I meant to say sorry to you, too,' said Tommy.

'Don't worry 'bout it,' said Woozie. 'I'll forgive you if you give me another game of floating-bowling some time soon.'

'Done.'

'Like that cut over your eye, by the way. Makes you look like a real hero.'

Woozie was teasing him.

'Well you look *so* rravishing,' said Tommy, 'zat I sink you juzt might get ze kissy-kissy tonight from ze rritzy Mistress of ze Way zat you like zo much.'

Woozie blushed. 'Shuttup!' And he swung a pillow at Tommy.

Before they left for the Ballroom, Guttly arrived in the dorm, wearing a very smart tux.

'Congratulations on winning the Flashscimitar Contest,' he boomed heartily. 'Where's the victorious lady herself?'

Marielle was still getting ready in the floating globe

353

bathroom, so Guttly helped Tommy with his bow-tie as Woozie had tied it wrong.

'Is Wisebeardyface alright?' asked Tommy.

'What? Oh, that? I think he'd had too much to drink, to be honest. When you left, I gave him six glasses of favo-fant liquid and told him to imagine they were black coffee. They seemed to do the trick.'

'So he stopped being angry, then?'

'Oh, yes . . . I left the old fellow to sleep off the ill-effects on a couch – not the one he vomited on.'

Tommy wasn't totally convinced.

'Is he OK about losing Paddie now? Did you find out why the probe was hit?'

'Well, I tried to call Earth – but there was no answer from the Oblong Office . . . Maybe I'll get Elsorr Maudlin tomorrow. There must be a simple explanation.'

The conversation was cut short when Marielle appeared from the bathroom. She'd removed her pigtails and replaced them with an elegant French plait. Her ballgown was light pink and stretched almost to the floor. It had a long slit up the back, a low neck-line and no sleeves. Matching satin gloves reached past her elbows, giving a regal air, and a string of bright elquinine crystals encircled her neck. She took Tommy's breath away.

'You lot ready to go yet?' she said, with a cheeky grin.

A single floating globe whisked the Dream5s and Guttly to the Ballroom. It took the same route as before, travelling into the dark tunnel on the surface of IGGY and morphing through the glass dome that covered the great room. The floating globe floated down to a small clearing in the middle of the dance floor and then a small door opened in its side.

They stepped out of the globe in pairs (Guttly taking Rumbles' arm, Woozie taking Summy's and Tommy taking Marielle's) and were announced, each in turn, by a huge thunderbumble in a waiter's outfit.

'Woozie Wibblewoodrow!' cried the thunderbumble, to polite applause.

There were hundreds of creatures seated around the room, all inhabitants of IGGY. They applauded everyone, although the loudest applause was reserved for Marielle (everyone had heard how she won the flashscimitar contest).

There was a group of five large tables just in front of the stage and the six made their way to a table beneath a floating placard with the word *Dream5s* printed neatly upon it.

After the Dream5s' globe rose into the air and disappeared, the Brillo1s' floating globe touched down and they took their seats to muted applause. All the IGGY Cadets were there in ballroom attire and a buzz of expectancy hummed around the room. (Anjel*eek!* Jalfrezi looked like a large, priceless BabbaPlanet in a spangly, gold ballgown. ZsaZsa Vavannus, her tan enhanced by a Molten-MeteoriteSession, wore a white gown, unintentionally clownish make-up and hair frizzed for the occasion – she also sported a metre-high silver feather, protruding from her headband.)

A large band at the rear of the Ballroom struck up a lively jazz number and the waiters surged forward to take people's orders. There'd be no favo-fant food today. You could order what you liked and the chefs were sure to have it in stock.

'I'll have fish-n-chipskeeys,' said Tommy, with a straight face.

'Hey, are you using my wordskeeys, now?' said Rumbles.

But when Woozie ordered *Friggletartskies*, Summy ordered mint *lambskies* and Marielle, elquinine *omeletteskeeys*, Rumbles realized that everyone was having a joke at her expense.

'That's not funneskeeys,' she said crossly. But by the time the food arrived, she was laughing with everyone else and claiming that the 'gag' had been her idea all along.

At one point in the meal, Tommy tuned out of the merriment around him. He almost seemed to be observing himself as well as everyone else. 'How happy I am,' he said to himself. And it wasn't just because the Dream5s had beaten the Brillo1s. No, it was more than that . . . Maybe it was something to do with having a great group of friends around him. He adored every one of them in their own way. OK, possibly one more especially than anyone else.

Tommy was just finishing his lemon meringue pie when Wisebeardyface waddled onto the stage to wild applause, and the music stopped.

'Thank you, thank you,' he said modestly. He seemed to have totally recovered from the weirdness and illness of earlier. (He'd actually activated a Segnitia Switch to slow time in his bedroom so that he could sleep for what seemed like three days, yet emerge from the room ten minutes after he'd entered it.)

The old dinosaurus looked down on the assembled gathering, then an air of impatience coloured his voice. 'As you know, the training and contests are over for the IGGY Cadets.' There was a loud cheer. 'Thank you . . . Tomorrow will be a rest day for all and then the investiture of the IGGY Knights will happen in the BigWig Ceremonial Hall late the following day.'

'Weh-hey! Like, totally!' yelled Egbert Fitchly enthusiastically, but he was the only one to cheer and blushed when everyone looked over at him.

'Yes, well . . .' continued Wisebeardyface. 'Unfortunately, I have to dash, but I have two quick announcements to make.'

A floating globe floated down from the ceiling and settled close to the old dinosaur.

'Firstly, I would like to confirm the final standings of the dorms after all the contests and training. This is the official, final result . . . And there will be no appeals and no change whatsoever to these standings.'

A projection appeared beside the orange kangasaurus:

```
RESULTS AFTER ALL CONTESTS AND TRAINING . . .

   DORMS            POINTS FROM          TOTAL
                    FLASHSCIMITAR        POINTS
                    CONTEST
   BRILLO1S         90                   150
   GREAT2S                                40
   VGOOD3S                               100
   ALRIGHT4S                              30
   DREAM5S                                20
```

'What?'

'Super-nova! That's incorrect! Mistaken.'

'But we won the flashscimitar contest – *you* won it Marielle.'

'How can that—?'

Soon everyone in the Ballroom joined in the consternation. They were all surprised at this turn of events.

Wisebeardyface seemed to snort, for a wisp of flame whisked from his nostrils and the room hushed. When he spoke his voice was stern.

'IGGY Cadets . . . One of you committed a certain act before the Jegg Race. As a result, we are disallowing any points that your dorm won from that time forward.'

There was a murmuring from the crowd.

'What's he saying?'

'I didn't commit any act.'

'Disallowing points? Which dorm?'

'Darlingk, where can I get some curling tongs?'

Wisebeardyface blew a spout of flame high into the air and everyone hushed. 'The dorm in question is the Dream5s.' It took another roar of flame to bring silence to the room. 'There is no effect on the points awarded for the Jegg Race, which was won by the VGood3s, but it does affect the Flashscimitar Contest. Excluding the Dream5s, I believe that Felkor Stagwitch would have won the contest. And so the ninety points go to the Brillo1s.'

There were four cheers and a boo from the Brillo1s' table.

'And so the Brillo1s end the training with the highest number of points.'

Wisebeardyface let this sink in with everyone in the room, only continuing when the cheers, boos and hisses started to wane.

'The reason for this decision?' said Wisebeardyface. 'Well, Tommy Storm sneaked down to the Uh-Oh-Doh-Joh Chamber the night after the PlanetChessy competition . . . We have it on good authority.'

Most people in the room turned to look at Tommy. At first he tried to lower his head to avoid their gaze, but when Guttly looked at him he decided to stand up.

The room went quiet.

'This is true,' said Tommy simply to Wisebeardyface. Then he bowed his head and sat down. No one at the Dream5s' table said a thing. They were too stunned at Wisebeardyface's decision.

'Secondly,' continued the old kangasaurus, 'I would like to

officially announce that the Milki Masters' Council have decided that *Earth* is to be the planet honoured with obliteration.'

This was even more horrifying. Tommy looked over at Guttly who went white.

'The decision is *irreversible*,' said Wisebeardyface. 'Something happened earlier today on Earth, involving a probe, that made up our minds and we have already started pointing the SickoWarpo Speed Runway in Earth's direction. The SWIGS Craft will pass through planet Earth on the SWIGS Mission in a little over sixty-three hours from now. We thank planet Earth for the sacrifice it is making for the benefit of the greater Milky Way.'

Before anyone could react, Wisebeardyface stepped into the floating globe by the edge of the stage and it lifted him up out of the Ballroom.

The Brillo1s broke the silence with a loud cheer (except for RullahBullah who wailed). Then someone in the VGood3s threw a crème caramel at Brendan the furballia who'd started jumping up and down on top of the Brillo1s' table. Before Tommy knew what was happening, a full-scale food fight had taken hold of the Ballroom and the jazz band started up a lively jive number.

'Guttly!' cried Marielle, jumping out of her seat, straight into the flight-path of a thunderbumblian fungus cheesecake.

Guttly had keeled backwards off his chair and was holding his chest with an agonized look. He suddenly looked even paler than Felkor.

With kangasaurian quiches, Shaggyfurmop pies and moonskunk mouse flying around the room from all directions, it was impossible to move the bearded (ex)President of Earth. (Anjel*eek!* was standing on a table in an attempt to get hit in the face as often as possible.) There was so much yelling and screaming that raising the alarm was impossible. Twice, Rumbles stood up – the first time, getting smacked in the face by an elquinine egg, the second time, receiving a resounding thump across her left shoulder (someone had thrown a furballia who was covered in food of all kinds).

The Dream5s crouched around Guttly as Tommy pressed rhythmically on the old man's chest.

'Come on, Guttly,' Tommy shouted in his ear. 'Don't slip away from us.'

The old man's face was set in a fixed expression and he'd started to look blue. Eventually, as the volume of food overhead started to thin, Tommy searched for Guttly's pulse, but couldn't find one.

'He's dead,' said Tommy. And then, despite himself, he started to weep.

~ 45 ~

A Homecoming

Known as the Bridge, Fedora's cockpit is really a large control room consisting of a main floor and two balconies – FAYS Balcony and FAYD Balcony. (FAYS standing for *Fall And You're Sore*. FAYD standing for *Fall And You're Dead*.) A ballroom globe hangs from the ceiling and the windscreen is twenty-four metres high (which might explain why Fedora has one of the biggest pairs of windscreen-wipers in the Milky Way). When in operation, the Bridge houses $21\frac{1}{2}$ officers, engineers and fumigators.

Tommy was up on FAYD Balcony as the bluey-white sphere of planet Earth sped into view. He felt a strange pang as he surveyed his planet. The 2002 picture of Earth had looked so much prettier. When the planet wasn't completely covered in a blanket of cotton wool, it looked blue *and* white, and was far more inviting. Now, in comparison, he thought it looked like a dead, slightly blue sheep floating in the middle of space – albeit a headless and legless one. But still, he couldn't help loving it. It was like seeing a friend in hospital and caring for them all the more for their misfortune.

Below him, Fedora's crew were peering into monitors and twiddling dials. Against the back wall, on the starboard side, a banner proudly proclaimed:

Fedora – the Milky Way's favourite space-line
Official transporter of the IGGY Cadets

As he gazed out at the ever-expanding vista of planet Earth, Tommy was sitting on a swing, rocking back and forth, wearing his skimming-field hover-boots (most of the seats in Fedora were swings made from small planks of wood suspended from the ceiling). Tommy's sneakers had received a number of direct hits from a Herculean pavlova the previous night and in all the excitement – if that's the right word – he forgot to put them in the chest for cleaning, so he was forced to wear something else. Luckily, you can never go far wrong with skimming-field hover-boots. If nothing else, they're always fun.

To Tommy's left lay Guttly, in an open, bright purple coffin. He looked very peaceful lying on his back with his eyes closed. Anyone would think he was merely fast asleep.

The crew of Fedora largely ignored Tommy who seemed tense and withdrawn to them. He just sat there on the swing with a small rucksack on his back that rustled whenever he made a sudden movement.

Tommy thought of his mad schedule . . . Travel to Earth today, return to IGGY later to get a night's sleep before watching the investiture of the IGGY Knights and then travel back to Earth the following day, before its obliteration. He felt a pang of sadness as he thought of saying goodbye to all his friends. What would he do now on Earth? Return to Wilchester (briefly)? Maybe a life in the kitchens of IGGY would be preferable. He might get promoted over the years and have a chance to do something else for the MilkyFed.

'Identify yourselves!' The face of Elsorr Maudlin lit up the wall behind Tommy. 'This is the President of Planet Earth. You've strayed into our airspace. Leave now or face the consequences.'

'What did he say?' said Fedora's captain (a polka-dotted skychubb). 'You do the talking, Tommy.'

Because Elsorr was never fitted with a talkie-max, none of the crew of Fedora could understand a word he was saying (they'd never learnt English). This was one of the reasons that Tommy had volunteered to accompany Guttly back to Earth.

Tommy jumped up from the swing and went to face the image of Elsorr.

'This is Tommy Storm. I'm an Earthling – one of The Five who left Earth just a few weeks ago, remember?'

'Not really,' said Elsorr. 'Now go away and take that crumpled hat of a spaceship with you – unless you want trouble.'

'I'm here to deliver the body of Guttly Randolph.'

There was a long silence before Elsorr broke into a broad smile.

'He's dead?'

'Yes. Alas, he's dead.'

Elsorr was most keen to parade the dead body of Guttly to the Grand Council, so Tommy was granted permission to descend to Earth with Guttly, while Fedora docked near the Moon. Tommy's jegg had been stowed in Fedora for just this purpose and Guttly's coffin was closed and then carefully strapped onto the jegg, directly behind the cockpit.

Once he was clear on the directions, Tommy felt strange flying his jegg through Earth's atmosphere. Here he was, just a boy, flying a craft more sophisticated than any machine on Earth. He felt like a decorated soldier returning to visit his old school.

After only a few minutes' flying, Tommy saw his destination in the distance.

ReallyReallyBig was a very small domed city reserved for

the activities of the President and the Grand Council (the name came about due to one city calling itself Big – as in *the big cheese* – and then other cities trying to outdo it). To add to the drama of the occasion, Elsorr arranged to open the city's dome and the roof of the Grand Council Hall, so that Tommy could lower his jegg onto the floor beside the Majestic Table. That way, Elsorr thought, the stupid Councillors could see for themselves that Guttly was dead and that he, Elsorr the Great, spoke the truth about the dangers of mixing with the MilkyFed.

The Grand Council was seated around the Majestic Table as Tommy carefully touched down upon the hard, sleek black floor beside it. Elsorr was standing upon an elevated platform wearing a ridiculously huge jewelled crown. He rubbed his sword against the inside of his leg while he watched Tommy climb gingerly from the cockpit, still wearing his hover-boots.

'Get that coffin onto the Majestic Table!' cried Elsorr.

A few Councillors helped Tommy untie the coffin and carry it onto a lift-panel hovering at wing-height alongside the jegg. When the lift-panel descended to the floor, the coffin was carried to the Majestic Table.

Elsorr licked the blade of his sword and allowed his platform to descend. He stepped off it and walked towards the Table.

'Behold, your dead ex-President,' he said with a smile, and lashed his sword against the fastener that held the coffin closed.

The coffin opened and the Councillors crowded closer to view their beloved ex-President. As they did so, Guttly gave a yawn, sat up and looked around brightly.

Before going any further, I believe I owe you at least a brief explanation . . .

When the food-fight finally petered out, Summy got the attention of some IGGY inhabitants at a nearby table and Guttly was brought to the Medical Centre in an IGGY Emergency Bubble.

The doctor on duty, Dr NoNo, looked very like Miss LeWren, except that he was a *he* rather than a *she* and wore a tweed outfit rather than a leather one (he also had a pair of half-moon spectacles that kept slipping down his nose).

'No, no, no . . . He's not dead-*dead*,' said Dr NoNo, once Guttly was immersed in a transparent bath of jelly. 'Of course, in Earth terms he's dead, but really he's just *gone under*, as we say in the MilkyFed. A few minutes in the heart Repairatron and then forty seconds in the microwave should see him right as piknix . . . By the looks of things, they've already made a few botched attempts to fix his heart on Earth.' The old doctor shook his head. 'By the time I'm finished, he'll be healthier than he was twenty years ago.'

It should be pointed out that MilkyFed medical science was so advanced by the time of our story that somebody could've been 'dead' for up to two weeks in Earth terms (assuming their head hadn't been munched or their vital organs sent through a meat-grinder) and still they could be revived by an experienced MilkyFed doctor. Piknix, by the way, is a quirky type of rain, which is extremely wet and found on the planet BraiiBarbie.

Once Guttly was back on his feet ('Physically, I feel super,' he said), he insisted that he should return to Earth as soon as possible. If Earth was to be destroyed, then he wanted to be with his beloved planet when it went.

Before he left IGGY, the bearded statesman made a vain attempt to persuade Wisebeardyface to change his mind

365

about obliterating Earth, but the old dinosaurus said that the matter was now out of his hands. The route of the runway had already been set.

Since Wisebeardyface clearly felt some guilt at consigning Earth to oblivion, he offered the services of Fedora to Guttly for the next few days – that way, if Guttly changed his mind, he could always flee Earth at the last minute. It was finally agreed that Tommy would accompany Guttly on his trip and return to IGGY on Fedora for the investiture ceremony.

Guttly was the one who decided to return to Earth in a coffin and pretend to be dead. 'If Elsorr has already destroyed a probe,' he explained to Tommy, 'then he'll surely attack any craft he knows is carrying me. He must've declared himself President, so he's not going to want me around unless I'm dead.'

The coffin wasn't too uncomfortable for Guttly. It gave him a good chance to get thirty winks during the journey to Earth. (The phrase *forty winks* was officially reduced to *thirty winks* on Earth in 2068 when the authorities decided that too much sleep was beginning to interfere with the average eighteen-hour working day.)

'Good afternoon, Elsorr,' said Guttly.

'You– You– You– . . .' Elsorr stared in horror at the smiling man sitting up in the coffin.

Then he closed his eyes and concentrated on squeezing Guttly's heart. He could almost feel it in his hands and he squeezed and squeezed. Now he was President, he could do this sort of thing without hiding away in a corner. He could stand there with his eyes closed if he liked – and no one could question him.

But when the jaundiced-faced man opened his eyes, Guttly was still smiling. *What was this?* The old man's heart seemed stronger than ever.

'Is that all you have to say?' said Guttly with a smile. 'I thought you'd be pleased to see me.'

Elsorr's body slumped for a moment. He looked resigned . . . And then, without warning, he lunged at Guttly with his sword. 'Die! Die! You treacherous traitor!'

The sword plunged into Guttly's midriff and it would've sunk further, except that Tommy hover-skimmed head-first into Elsorr's belly and knocked him flat on the seat of his pants, making the ridiculous crown roll across the floor.

'You– You—' Again Elsorr was stunned. 'How dare you attack the Permanent President of Earth!'

He leapt to his feet and lunged towards Tommy with his blood-stained sword. In a flash, Tommy reached over his shoulder, drew his flashscimitar and blocked the bloody sword. (Even if you're wearing a small rucksack, the best place to carry a scimmy when seated in the cockpit of a jegg, is across your back.) If the scimmy hadn't still been covered with *Boinggg!Jelly*, Elsorr's sword would've shattered into a thousand pieces, but the jelly made the scimmy as effective as an everyday Earth sword – an extremely blunt one at that.

'Drop your sword, Elsorr,' said Guttly weakly from the coffin.

'How dare you!' cried Elsorr. 'I am the rightful President. I was voted in. You've been removed.' He swung again at Tommy, but once again the swift scimmy blocked the attack. Elsorr stepped back and looked Tommy up and down with disdain. He wasn't sure of the best approach to take with this fierce young boy.

Some Councillors crowded around Guttly.

'I'm OK,' said the bearded old man. 'Don't fuss over me.'

'But now that Guttly's back . . .' ventured a Councillor who was standing away from the crowd. Her name was Salomé Jones.

'Yes?' cried Elsorr.

'Well, I think . . . Well, maybe he should be President again . . . I mean, we voted Guttly out in his absence, didn't we? We thought that maybe he was dead.'

Elsorr thought about this.

'I guess you're right,' he said finally, lowering his sword. 'Here, take the Presidential Insignia, Salomé. And give it to Guttly.'

Elsorr started to twist the ruby ring off his finger as Salomé moved towards him. Then, in the blink of an eye, he swished his sword in the air and chopped Salomé's head off.

'Oops,' he said. 'My hand must've slipped . . . Now who else thinks I should be removed of the Presidency?' And with that he lashed out at Tommy once more.

This time, Tommy wasn't going to stop when Elsorr stopped. The madman had stabbed Guttly and killed an elderly woman. If Tommy didn't stop him, who else would?

He made two blocks and then employed a few moves from the ParrrKing Offence, moving Elsorr away from the Councillors. Around the floor they fought, the harsh sound of steel ringing around the room. Elsorr jumping this way and that, Tommy gliding effortlessly in his hover-boots, taking care that Elsorr's sword never caught his rucksack (it was easy to forget it was there). Elsorr was strong and had a long reach, but he wasn't as fast as his smaller foe.

'Stop!' cried Elsorr at one point – and Tommy did, because he thought the jaundiced-faced man might be about to lay down his weapon. Instead, Elsorr licked Salomé's blood off the edge of his sword with an unseemly relish and seemed to swell with power as a result. 'I like the taste of death,' he said. 'Prepare to die, boy.'

And with that, he lashed out again at Tommy Storm, with renewed strength.

They fought around the jegg, around the Table and ended up clashing steel upon the Presidential Platform. Elsorr telepathically raised the platform in an effort to throw Tommy off balance. It worked. The platform was three metres off the ground when Tommy keeled off its edge.

'Hah-hahh!' cried Elsorr, as the platform raised higher and he peered over the edge to view the crumpled heap of boy on the floor below.

The Councillors below saw the platform rise thirty metres into the air – Elsorr leaning over the edge with his sword and Tommy standing upside-down, a bit of plastic wrapping sticking out of his rucksack. (The boy seemed to be attached to the bottom of the platform by an invisible force-field.)

'Wh– . . . Where is he?' cried Elsorr, looking alarmed.

Tommy could see Elsorr's blood-stained sword dangling over the edge and he lashed at it with his scimmy. Elsorr yelped and the sword flew out of his hand, clattering harmlessly on the floor beneath the platform. As the platform started to descend, Tommy glided around its edge, appearing behind Elsorr.

'Stop!' cried Tommy, his scimmy poking Elsorr in the back.

The platform stopped some four metres from the ground and Elsorr turned to face his little foe. He'd no idea that the scimmy held just below his neck was as blunt as a cucumber (possibly because cucumbers had become almost extinct during the Great Climate Enhancement, although they did still make occasional appearances in silly jokes and very posh sandwiches).

'OK, OK . . . I surrender,' said Elsorr, suddenly turning into a blubbering mess. 'I didn't mean anything by this friendly duel . . . And chopping off Miss Jones' head . . . that was just an accident . . . Of course Guttly can be the President. There's been a frightful misunderstanding.'

He started to twist the ruby ring off his finger. Tommy glanced over at Guttly who smiled wanly and, at that very moment, Elsorr did a back-flip towards the sword that was lying under the platform. The instant Elsorr hit the floor and snatched at his sword, the platform plummeted to the ground.

CRRRUMMMMMMPLNNCCCCHHHHHHH!

Elsorr was crushed to the thickness of a pizza beneath the platform and only his ruby-ringed hand, clutching the blood-stained sword, escaped. Together, these symbols of Elsorr's brief presidency lay alone on the floor like some relic from a horror movie.

It turned out that Guttly had lowered the platform onto Elsorr.

Confused? Well, once Elsorr gave up telepathic control of the Presidential Platform, Guttly could control it, since Elsorr had never bothered to erase Guttly's brain-wave control-access of it.

Tommy ran over to Guttly.

'You OK?'

Guttly half-nodded and looked around. 'Where's Helena Jadely?' he said weakly.

When someone explained that the poor woman was locked up in Domesticity, Guttly asked the Councillors to leave the room, only to return when they had Helena with them. He made it clear that he wanted her to take over the Presidency from Elsorr. When the last Councillor left the room, the old man clasped Tommy's hand.

'You're not OK,' said Tommy, realizing that Guttly was looking very pale. 'Quick! Let me take you up to Fedora. There's a doctor on board who—'

He stopped, obeying Guttly's determined gesture.

'Tommy,' said the old man weakly. 'I'm ready to go now . . . To be with Gerty.'[13]

What? What was Guttly saying? The old man must've been delirious.

'But you can be saved!' Frantic now, Tommy tried to put his hand under Guttly to lift him towards the jegg. But the wounded man brushed him aside. 'Don't be silly,' said Tommy with a forced breeziness. 'You're losing blood. Please, we have to be quick.'

The old man shook his head with an air of finality.

'*Please*, sir.'

Guttly fought a sudden surge of pain . . . It took some seconds for the wave to pass and then he looked at the boy before him, his voice returning.

'No.'

'But . . .' *He had to do something!* 'I can't let you die!' The cry came from the centre of Tommy's being. Beyond his control. But the old man remained unmoved. Still the words came from Tommy's mouth. 'You can live . . . *Guttly*.' It was a plea.

But again the old man shook his head. He would not be moved. 'My time has come . . . I won't cheat it again.'

Tommy felt a tear running down his cheek. He seemed to be crying too often these days.

'Don't tell the Councillors, don't tell Helena, that Earth is to be obliterated,' continued the old man softly. 'It's best not

13 A reference to his dead wife, Gertrude.

371

to know these things.' Tommy nodded and squeezed Guttly's hand. 'You can go back to IGGY and be proud of how you represented your planet . . . Don't come back after they invest the IGGY Knights . . . Stay . . . Stay on IGGY and represent humanity for a few more years, if all humans on Earth are to be destroyed.'

Now Tommy had to lean very close to the old man's lips to hear his words. His breathing had become more laboured and his voice as weak as a sparrow's song in a storm.

'I wish . . .' said the old man slowly. 'I . . . I wish that you'd been my choice to represent Earth.'

'Hush, now,' said Tommy seeing the pain tremble across Guttly's face with every word. 'Hush.'

'I wish . . . I wish that I – that Gerty and I . . . had . . . children.' The bearded man looked up at the boy before him and for the first time Tommy noticed how blue Guttly's eyes were. 'And if we'd ever had a . . . a *son* . . . I'd . . . I'd have been most proud if . . . if he turned out like . . . like you, Tommy Storm.'

The old man's lips brushed Tommy's face and pursed into a soft kiss. Afterwards, Tommy wondered if he'd imagined it. Why would Guttly kiss him with such tenderness?

And then the old man died for the very last time.

And You Think *You're* Strange?

The French Foreign Legion (which kept its name despite the abolition of countries) would later successfully lodge a request to have Elsorr's hand – still holding the bloody sword – preserved and placed in an ornamental case for display in the drawing room at the Flogzeluzerscum training-camp.

372

━ 46 ━

THE ULTIMATE SACRIFICE

After the Councillors arrived with Helena Jadely, and the Ruby Ring was removed from Elsorr's hand and ceremoniously placed on Helena's finger, Tommy climbed into the jegg, waved farewell and rose away from the scene of death. He took a quick look at the spectacle of glittering, domed cities before he disappeared into the heavy cloud-cover.

Queue is spelt funnily, but it's useful in Scrabble

Helena refused to wear the WOW-Iveneverseenwunthat-bigB4 Crown – even for her formal Swearing-In Ceremony. The enormous eyesore was eventually placed in a secure glass cabinet somewhere so that lots of boggle-eyed, gormless tourists could queue up for hours to get the chance to stare at it.

In normal circumstances, the journey to Fedora – docked close to the Moon – should've taken less than twenty seconds, but it was another three hours before Tommy flew into Fedora with his empty rucksack still strapped to his back. Fedora's crew made no comment. The boy's planet was to be destroyed in 44.324 hours precisely. Surely, he should be allowed some time to sightsee. A little time to savour the twilight hours of a doomed planet. On the return journey to IGGY, Tommy locked himself in a room in Fedora and played his beloved violin.

Tommy arrived back in IGGY less than twelve hours after he'd left. Once deposited in his dorm, he greeted his friends with a heavy heart. They had a quiet meal in memory of Guttly and then everyone packed their bags in silence. No one mentioned that they'd all have to say good-bye the next day after the investiture of the Brillo1s.

As they were packing, an apparition of Wisebeardyface appeared on the dining table.

He stared at a wall in the distance and said: 'Tommy Storm . . . I heard the sad news about Guttly Randolph . . . I wonder if you could join me briefly in the Eye-on-the-Universe.'

Then the projection disappeared.

A few minutes later, Tommy was whizzing up a whooshUlator. As he flew up the darkening shaft, he felt a little wary. Hopefully, Wisebeardyface wouldn't be as wobbly, incoherent and sick as he'd been the last time Tommy was summoned to the Eye.

Suddenly the darkness disappeared and Tommy was standing in the high conservatory.

'Expect the unexpected,' said Wisebeardyface. The old dinosaurus was standing with his back to Tommy, looking out at the stars. 'That is what I always say . . . But that does not mean you should forget the expected.'

'Good evening,' said Tommy tentatively, unsure if Wisebeardyface was talking to him.

Last time, he hadn't noticed how beautiful it was up here. You could see far more than the view from the Dream5s' dorm. A cluster of bluish stars twinkled just over Wisebeardyface's shoulder and at least four suns were setting behind a large pot-holed planet to Tommy's right. They cast the conservatory in an orange glow.

'Watch carefully,' said Wisebeardyface, pointing to a set of six moons twirling around each other. 'Three . . . two . . . one . . . Now!'

As soon as Wisebeardyface said *Now*, a swarm of fiery comets rounded the group of moons, heading straight for IGGY. They were travelling fast and some of them looked almost half the size of IGGY herself.

Instead of fear, Tommy felt a huge sense of resignation as he waited for the impact. One of the comets in particular grew larger and larger as it approached. Just before impact, Tommy closed his eyes.

Nothing happened.

Tommy opened his eyes and turned around. The swarm of comets had passed by IGGY and were flashing into the distance.

'My calculations were correct,' said Wisebeardyface. 'The closest one missed us by thirty-two centimetres.' He turned to Tommy. 'We were closer here than anywhere else on IGGY . . . That was the Inferno Comet Cluster. It passes here every 2,311 years . . . I have seen it pass by twice before. Not on IGGY of course, but from a further distance, on my planet . . . Did you feel fear?'

Tommy shook his head. Wisebeardyface continued.

'Fear is something you feel if you have any power whatso-ever to alter a situation . . . When you have no power, you just feel resignation.'

Tommy nodded.

'I am sorry to hear about Guttly . . . He was a good man.'

'Yes, he was,' said Tommy at last.

Wisebeardyface opened his arms, offering a hug and because he felt it would be rude not to, Tommy stepped forward and allowed himself to be hugged. It was a strange hug. Wisebeardyface seemed more concerned with rubbing the back of Tommy's head than anything else and when he felt a ridge of letters just above the hairline, he traced them slowly and sighed. 'Just as I thought.'

Then he released Tommy, flopped onto the couch and closed his eyes. 'Just as I thought,' he repeated slowly.

Tommy wasn't sure what to do, so he stood in silence and waited for the old dinosaurus to open his eyes.

'Tommy . . . Tommy Storm,' said Wisebeardyface eventually. He seemed unsure of how he should continue. 'I will not discuss the obliteration of Earth or the points awarded to dorms . . .' He indicated to Tommy to sit down on a couch and sighed a deep sigh. 'I feel though, that I should share something with you . . . Something about your parents.'

This made Tommy sit up. Wisebeardyface stood and poured them both a glass of favo-fant liquid.

'Do you remember when I confronted Lady MuckBeff-WiLLyoofytus about travelling back in time? When I said that we had managed to travel back in time once – just once – and only back a very short distance, maybe a minute or so.'

Tommy nodded, feeling that he knew what Wisebeardyface was going to say.

'And also . . . Maybe you noticed some people around here looking at you strangely when they first met you . . . That was inevitable, I suppose . . . Well now I am sure. I knew your parents. They were called Bonnie and Clive. We abducted them and their parents from Earth for an experiment and then we liked them so much we allowed them to stay.'

'I know,' said Tommy.

'You know?'

Tommy explained a little about meeting his parents in the

Abyss of Visions and learned some things from the old dinosaurus that he'd not gathered from his parents.

'When your parents were with us a while, we discovered that a huge meteorite, the size of planet Mars, was travelling at many times the speed of light and heading for Earth. At that time . . . maybe because of Bonnie and Clive . . . we felt a sense of protection towards your planet. We in the MilkyFed were trying to devise a strategy to save Earth and we came up with a plan to fire a very powerful missile into the comet before it entered the Milky Way.' (This missile was actually a turbo-charged cream-pie, twice the size of the Netherlands.)

Wisebeardyface looked solemn. 'The impact from the missile would knock the comet off-course and it would miss Earth and the Milky Way altogether . . . You must understand that it is very difficult to hit a comet travelling at many times the speed of light, even if it is the size of Mars.'

Tommy focused on a clutch of stars in the distance.

'On the day the meteorite was due to hit Earth, you were only a few days old and your mother had your name, *Tommy*, stencilled on the back of your head in case any harm should come to her or your father. She said that if they perished and Earth survived, we were to deliver you back to Earth with no knowledge of them or us. That way, you could live a normal life as a normal human being.'

'How did they die?' asked Tommy, wishing that Wisebeardyface would speed up the storytelling.

'For many millennia it has been said that if two people die willingly together, if they die only to save others and if they have *inner-lath* and are pure of heart, then their deaths will reverse time for a moment. Many have tried . . . and in many cases, perhaps time has been reversed by a nanosecond or two, which is a remarkable achievement when you consider the power of time . . . but it is far too small a step backwards for anyone to notice.'

Wisebeardyface paused for a second and closed his eyes. 'Your parents docked just outside your solar system, some minutes before the comet was due to impact. On the edge of the Milky Way, four Masters of the Way prepared to fire the missile into the comet . . . They were: Miss LeWren, Lady MuckBeff, Mr Crabble and MonSenior Leebruce . . . On this occasion, Lady MuckBeff was the person to fire the missile. It was a good shot, but it missed the comet by milimetres. Five seconds later, the comet slammed into Earth and destroyed it.'

'But—' Tommy had so many questions he didn't know where to start.

'Your parents,' said Wisebeardyface slowly. 'We believe they flew their spacecraft into your solar system, clasped their hands together and flew into the middle of the raging, fiery remains of Earth. They died instantly.'

Tommy put down his glass and put his face in his hands. The image was too awful to bear.

'The other day you told us that *inner-lath* is really *love*. Maybe you are right, Tommy. You made me think, *that boy, maybe he is right* . . . If you are right, then the love of your parents must have been so strong and so pure – extraordinarily so – because time reversed sixty, maybe sixty-five seconds . . . Unprecedented. It had never occurred before and it may never occur again . . . Before we knew what had happened, the comet was once again outside the Milky Way, travelling towards Earth and the four Masters of the Way were preparing to fire. This time, Miss LeWren took the shot and she hit the comet with a direct hit . . . As expected, the comet veered off-course and missed the Milky Way altogether. The rest you know . . . Earth survived.'

'But my parents!' cried Tommy. 'If time reversed, then surely they should've come back to life and appeared on the edge of the solar system?'

Wisebeardyface shook his head forlornly. 'They had to sacrifice themselves . . . That is the only way time would reverse itself. Pure love and unselfish sacrifice . . . We try not to mention their names, we try to talk of their sacrifice as little as possible . . . because it is said that idle chatter could reverse the change in time that they brought about, and wreak havoc in the universe. But I do not think that telling the son of Bonnie and Clive is idle chatter.'

Tommy shed some tears (this was beginning to get ridiculous – it felt as though he was crying every day now), and Wisebeardyface sat in silence, his eyes closed.

Before he left for the dorm, Tommy shook Wisebeardyface's hand as though it were a final farewell. In a way he believed it was. He'd be returning to Earth the next day. There was no way he wanted to stay on IGGY – no matter what Guttly had said.

'Is that why Lady MuckBeff dislikes me?' he asked, looking into the old dinosaurus' face.

Wisebeardyface shook his head. 'I don't think she *completely* dislikes you. She just hates to be reminded of that miss . . . Do you still play the World Cup on Earth?'

Tommy shook his head. He had no idea what the World Cup was, because football had long been forgotten on Earth.

'Well, if you still had the World Cup, then Lady MuckBeff's miss would be like missing a penalty in the last seconds of the final. She is really quite embarrassed . . .'

Football Hooligans have feelings too, you know

Not long into the 21st century, professional footballers on Earth were being paid $2 million a day and changing their hairstyle twice a week. Only three teams could afford this and so all other football teams went bankrupt. Ordinary people stopped playing football themselves as more and more Earthlings became spectators rather than participants in life and spent increasingly long periods of time on couches watching TV. Eventually, people lost interest in football when it became easy to predict which of the three teams would win the major competitions. The footballers remained quite famous though, as the number of TV programmes analysing their non-secret 'secrets' continued to mushroom.

'Lady MuckBeff is a perfectionist,' continued Wisebeardyface, 'and she is not very good at expressing her feelings . . . She hates failure and she does admit that she thought the Dream5s were ranked last because you hadn't *tried* hard enough . . . Maybe your resemblance to your parents particularly reminded her of her miss – her failure . . . I must say, she has never been the same since her husband died. That is when she threw herself into her beloved flower-arranging – to the detriment of all else.'

Historians claim that Lady M felt guilty about her husband's death because she pressed him hard to run for President of the MilkyFed Floating-Bowling Association.[14] *(The President is chosen on the basis of a floating blading competition – players throw a large blade rather than a ball. Thainderbumble*

14 She was said to have pressed him because of the extraordinary parking perks. ('For the rest of their natural lives' the MFFBA President and his or her family can park 'anywhere in the Milky Way that a spacecraft can remain stationary' – with complete immunity from parking tickets.)

MuckBeff was accidentally decapitated in the final by his rival, FriggleFife MuckDuff.)

'*Strictly* between you and me,' Wisebeardyface added conspiratorially, 'I don't think she should still be a Master of the Way, but the MotW Union is very strong and we can't have her removed. (*'Never Fie Thee Hither,' being the union's motto.)*

'And that coat of hers . . .' The old dinosaurus almost chuckled. 'She wears that coat because . . . because . . .' The head of the MilkyFed paused, seemingly lost in thoughts of times long passed. Eventually he remembered himself and looked down at the young man before him. 'Never mind,' he said softly. 'That's another story.'

As Tommy turned to go, Wisebeardyface looked solemn again. 'Oh, Tommy . . . I am sorry for the other day . . . For the way I behaved up here . . . Not for what I said, but for how I said it. Not for what I did, but for how I did it.' He stopped and thought. 'Actually, I am sorry too for what I did . . . I was very fond of Paddie, you know.'

'It's alright.'

'No, it is not alright . . . When I heard he had been destroyed, I became quite upset . . . I fear I smoked and drank too much that day.'

Tommy shrugged and was about to jump down the plungeUlator when Crabble appeared through the whooshUlator looking very stressed.

'Cripes-double-cripes, Lord Beardedmoustached-Wiseface-oh! Someone has stolen two wigholes! Hmmm.'

'From where?'

'From the store-room, yes? My Lordus, I fear they might be trying to sabotage the SWIGS Mission.'

Wisebeardyface went pale and immediately made an

announcement that was beamed to every room in IGGY. He warned that there was a saboteur in their midst and that everyone should be on their guard.

When Tommy made it back to the dorm, the other Dream5s were more excited than when he'd left. Everyone chatting about the possible saboteur.

'Bet it's Lady MuckBeff,' said Woozie darkly. 'There's something fishy about her.'

'And not just her coat, me dost thinkest,' said Tommy.

They all forced a laugh – a vain attempt to smother the foreboding in the air.

━ 47 ━

ALL HAIL THE IGGY KNIGHTS!

As a mark of respect to Guttly and as a symbolic gesture of unity, ZsaZsa, Felkor, Anjeleek!, Egbert and Tommy agreed to play some music together for anyone who cared to listen.

It was an hour after Tommy's meeting with Wisebeardyface and very late in the evening when The Five children of Earth gathered on the floor of the cavernous amphitheatre that served as Lady MuckBeff's laboratory. No tutors were present and the many craggy ledges that looked down on the floor were empty. To avoid squabbling and discussing distressing topics (such as Earth's pending demise), The Five had agreed that there would be no talking. This was just as well since the entire proceedings were broadcast throughout IGGY.

There was an extended period of instrument tuning while they waited for ZsaZsa to turn up – but turn up she did, with a head of fresh curls and an extra-fluffy stole. After a few false starts, the 'free-style' jam settled into a soulful sound. Anjel*eek!* sang beautifully (gliding back and forth in her skates), Felkor's guitar-playing was surprisingly good, the drums were played well by ZsaZsa (the only criticism from music aficionados was that she over-used the cymbals), but the big hit was Egbert. Some said he could tap his feet faster than he could speak. At

383

times, the music seemed to follow his stream of tapping, at others, he provided a jazzy counter-beat. (And the audience couldn't even appreciate the flamenco-like swirls of his cape!)

The electric violin didn't receive much comment from listeners. It shadowed the other sounds and instruments, giving them something to play against. Tommy did perform a wild, passionate solo towards the end of the gig, but many listeners assumed this was Felkor having switched to *electric* guitar.

IGGY's monitors suggest that the song that received most applause was *What a Wonderful Planet*.[15]

What a Wonderful Planet

I see kangasauri of green, red ones too
I see them (fire)blast for me and you
And I think to myself, what a wonderful planet
I see skies of red and holes of black
That's where we put rubbish – it never comes back
And I think to myself, what a wonderful planet
The colours of the grow–sss–goo, so pretty on the wall
Are also in the faces seated in the BigWig Hall
I see friends shakin' guggles,[16] sayin' 'How do you do?'
They're really saying, 'Do you practise Milky Foo?'
I hear thunderbumbles munching, I watch them grow
They'll eat almost anything – never say 'No'
And I think to myself, what a wonderful planet
Yes, I think to myself, what a wonderful planet
Oh yeah.

15 This song was written by two thunderbumbles about the planet Shaggyfurmop – although an alternative version subsequently found its way to Earth (and was then lost in The Great Climate Enhancement).

16 A guggle is an affectionate term for a thunderbumble's third arm.

Next morning, all the IGGY Cadets dressed in ceremonial garb quite similar to the ceremonial outfit of an officer in the navy (white, silver-buttoned suit that fastened to the neck, peaked cap, high white shirt–collar and white shoes).

'Good camouflage for Felkor,' said Woozie, displaying his bright outfit and trying to lighten the mood in the Dream5s' dorm.

Only Rumbles gave a small laugh as she pulled her undies up over her trousers.

The Bigwig Ceremonial Hall was a great hall in the centre of IGGY, with two lines of thick pillars forming a natural walkway, eight metres wide, up its middle. Everything except the wooden benches seemed to be made of light-coloured sandstone, causing the slightest sound to magnify. The roof was high with skylights at intervals, so that bright light from a cluster of nearby stars shone down illuminating everything but a few shadowy corners. Today, beautiful flowers of every size and hue adorned the Hall's floor and walls.

Tommy could see a myriad of dust particles dancing in one of the shafts of light as he took his seat in a pew alongside his fellow Dream5s. All the other dorms were seated in the pews just ahead, with a clear view up to an empty space at the top of the room. The rest of the Hall was filled with IGGY inhabitants, each dressed in extravagant ceremonial garb. It made Tommy feel that the Cadets' outfits were very plain indeed.

The bustle and chatter stopped abruptly as five figures floated down from the ceiling at the front of the Hall. Even though all five were wearing long, black feather head-dresses that fell back down to their ankles, you couldn't fail to recognize Lord BeardedmoustachedWiseface-oh, Miss Zohfria

LeWren, Lady MuckBeff WiLLyoofytus, Mr Crabble and MonSenior FuKung Leebruce. Amazingly, Lady M wasn't wearing her coat and she must've had an extra long bath because her fur looked shiny black. She was a striking – even beautiful – sight.

Once the Milki Masters touched down, a drumroll started and Tommy looked up to see a swarm of furballias flying back and forth between a set of drums housed in an anti-gravity pocket just below the ceiling.

Wisebeardyface raised his arm and the drumroll stopped. The old dinosaurus chanted his favourite poem, *Comet Number 116*, and most of the congregation joined him. Then there was silence as the flames from Wisebeardyface's nostrils died and he spoke again.

'Welcome, inhabitants of IGGY and welcome especially to the great youths of our galaxy . . . The *IGGY Cadets*.'

There was a ripple of applause plus a belch from somewhere near the back of the Hall and then the old dinosaurus continued.

'Today, one dorm of five youths will be invested as IGGY Knights. For the other four dorms, after dinner your bags shall be transported to the GarageZone. Then you will return to your own planet – except for those Earthlings who choose to take the IGGY catering option.' He cleared his throat.

'Before I forget, I would like to thank Lady MuckBeff WiLLyoofytus for looking after all the flower arrangements for today's ceremony.' Lady M bowed in response to the polite applause and Wisebeardyface continued.

'We thank those IGGY Cadets who have tried their best and who have not been chosen as IGGY Knights. Do not see it as a sign of failure. For it is not failure. You have helped us to choose the IGGY Knights whose mission it shall be to save the universe. And so you, too, have played your important

part in the continuation of our galaxy. And do not worry –
you will be given a memento of your stay on IGGY.'

He leaned towards Miss LeWren and mumbled something.
She stepped forward and brought a floating box over beside
the old dinosaurus. Then he turned to face the crowd again.

'*The Brillo1s* . . . Could you please step this way.'

To gentle applause, the Brillo1s stepped up from their pew
with broad smiles. Felkor looked back down the Hall and shot
a loaded smirk at Tommy. Then he filed up with the others as
they approached Wisebeardyface, one at a time. The orange
kangasaurus whispered to each of them as he handed them
something long and pink. Tommy couldn't quite make out
what it was, although he'd later discover it to be a stick of rock
(*ShugreLobbie Candy*, to be precise) with the word *IGGY*
imprinted through its middle.

It is alleged by historians that when the Mirror Twins
shook Wisebeardyface's hand, they said:

RullahBullah: Thank
ReeeRaw: YOU
RullahBullah: for
ReeeRaw: NOTHING.

(RullahBullah had hoped that ReeeRaw would end the
sentence with the word *everything*.)

When the Brillo1s sat down with self-satisfied smiles, the
VGood3s were called up and received the same long, pink
item from Wisebeardyface. This alarmed the Brillo1s a little
because they hadn't expected anyone else to receive the same
rewards as they. When the Great2s were called up, followed
by the Alright4s and they all received the same treatment, the
Brillo1s started muttering with annoyance.

When everyone was seated (and Anjel*eek!* had finished her

stick of rock), Wisebeardyface addressed the congregation once more.

'As IGGY Knights, it will always be important to *listen*. You learn nothing when you speak. You only learn when you listen . . . Those who really listened to me since arriving at IGGY will note that I only said two important things . . . On your first morning together, I said *expect the unexpected*. I hope you now understand what I meant.'

Light laughter trickled around the Hall.

'That PlanetChessy explosion was unexpected,' said Woozie.

'Hey, I didn't get no stick of rock,' said a voice that could only be Egbert Fitchly.

Wisebeardyface frowned. 'The other thing I said to every group when you first arrived at IGGY was, *the last shall be first* . . . This does not mean that if you try to come last, you will automatically be made the winner. But it does mean that there is something more important than trying to win at all costs. We gave you a measure to gauge your achievements . . . In this case, it was points. Points for winning contests or being the best in exams. This was never *our* measure of your abilities and achievements. The points meant nothing to us, except to see how you battled to win them. Who got the highest number of points? *Who cares?* It is not what you did, but how you did it that mattered.'

The old dinosaurus smiled at the Cadets. 'Remember *Comet Number 116* . . . ?' He paused to let this sink in. 'We had to make you believe that points were the important measure in order to see your honest efforts. Would you trample over others to get the points at all costs? Would you hold to your principles even if it meant you might lose the points . . . ?'

'These are the things we observed,' said Wisebeardyface. 'We were watching you at all times – or at least one of us was. In your dorms, as you travelled to class, after you won or lost a contest. At all times, we were observing your words and actions.'

'Does that mean they saw me doing a number sixskeeys in the loo?' whispered Rumbles in consternation.

'We know it will feel strange to learn that you have been watched, but it was necessary. The future of the universe is at stake . . . We had to be sure we chose the best group of IGGY Knights.' Wisebeardyface looked sternly at the IGGY Cadets. 'You see, some of the dorms were removed from consideration because of their cheating . . . Cheating reflects a lack of courage, a lack of integrity. How could we entrust the future of our galaxy to such feeble characters?'

There was a chorus of murmurs amongst the Cadets and, through the corner of his eye, Tommy thought he saw Felkor punch Brendan. They were silenced by Wisebeardyface's glare.

'Really, *we* never wanted to *choose* the winners. We hoped all along that they would *choose themselves* and so it has come to pass . . . They have merely been *revealed* to us . . .

389

Revealed,' boomed Wisebeardyface, 'not because of something bad others did or because of some silly points awarded for a game, but because of something positive they did themselves. Something special. Something they demonstrated to all of us. Something we can all learn from . . . Something that would make you ready to trust them with your lives and place the future of the Milky Way in their hands.'

Tommy was still unsure what Wisebeardyface was talking about.

'For one dorm showed us . . .' continued the old dinosaurus. 'They showed us what it means to be species of the Milky Way. They made us realize and understand something we had almost lost. For they revealed the true meaning of a most important word . . . Perhaps *the* most important word. The very reason our galaxy, our universe, must survive. They revealed it, not by one action – although one particular event did help us to understand – but through *their interaction* with each other.' The dinosaurus paused and looked almost dreamlike. 'The word I speak of is . . . *inner-lath*.'

'Isn't that *two* words?' said a voice from the audience.

Wisebeardyface ignored the question and gestured to Miss LeWren, who brought another floating box to the old dinosaurus. 'And so, with no further ado, I would like to call upon the Dream5s to make their way up here . . . YOU SHALL BE OUR IGGY KNIGHTS!' Wisebeardyface had to shout the last words, because the audience behind the Dream5s had leapt to their feet and were cheering madly. Almost no one heard him add: 'You shall be the ones to save the Milky Way, the universe, from the Terrible Future Calamity – I mean, The TFC.'

Rumbles reached Wisebeardyface first and the dinosaurus reached into the floating box and then placed a large necklace of flowers around the smiling thunderbumble's neck. Next, Miss LeWren placed a colourful feather head-dress on Rumbles' head (which reached down to her shoulders).

Summy was next, followed by Woozie, Marielle and then Tommy.

Like his friends, Tommy bowed to Wisebeardyface and the four tutors wearing his colourful head-dress and his garland of flowers. Miss LeWren gave them all a hug, MonSenior Leebruce gave a quick smile, Crabble just looked worried (still fretting about the missing wigholes) and Lady M gave a solemn bow, her intense eyes visible for once (mainly eyeing the flower garlands that she'd created).

The five friends linked hands and looked back at the cheering faces. Most of the Cadets were also standing and clapping and eventually, after being elbowed by RullahBullah (and kissed by ReeeRaw), Felkor stood up with a scowl and reluctantly gave a half-hearted clap.

Someone flew in the air and Tommy realized it must be Egbert Fitchly doing an excited back-flip. Unfortunately, he must've landed on Anjel*eek!* Jalfrezi, because there was a very loud scream, but she must've been OK because the cheering only got louder. Close by, ZsaZsa Vavannus was giving a startled furballia a hug. 'Kiss me, darlingk!'

'Do my undies look alright?' cried Rumbles, above the noise.

Tommy squeezed Marielle's hand, beamed at her lingeringly and then smiled over at all his friends.

'We did it!' Woozie shouted above the cheers.

'For once, right you are,' cried Summy and she fluttered her wings in excitement. 'Super-nova, right he is. It, we did!'

With all the laughter and all the cheering, anyone watching would surely have forgotten that Earth was scheduled to be destroyed in 20.989 hours, precisely. They might even have forgotten that no SWIGS Mission saboteur had yet been apprehended.

The first person to leave the BigWig Ceremonial Hall was Lady M. The cheering was still ringing loudly in her ears, but she left without saying a word to anyone.

⟿ 48 ⟿
So-Long, IGGY

The SWIGS Craft looked very like a giant, silver Spitfire and was made from the same material as a flashscimitar. It was the size of forty jeggs and was docked on the edge of the air bubble surrounding the GarageZone.

By the time the Dream5s found themselves standing in the GarageZone to view the magnificent craft for the first time, all the other Cadets had already been transported off IGGY back to their respective planets with all knowledge of The TFC erased from their memories. The offer to human IGGY Cadets to stay in IGGY's catering department had been withdrawn because another (unauthorized) food-fight occurred after Wisebeardyface left the post-Investiture dinner in the Ballroom (the room had only just been painstakingly cleaned after the food-fight two nights earlier). The fact that the fight was started unintentionally by ZsaZsa Vavannus, when she tried to create a spiral design on a neighbour's wibblewallian trifle, found no favour with the MilkyFed Council.

All thoughts of food-fights were forgotten, however, as soon as the Dream5s saw the splendour of the SWIGS Craft. They stood in awe for at least a minute before they allowed themselves to be ushered forward.

A WhiskMat, the size of three dining tables, hovered by

the edge of the GarageZone. As Tommy stepped onto it with his companions, he saw that it was made of a similar material to the small mat that had transported him around the tube in Fedora some weeks earlier.

As soon as Wisebeardyface, Miss LeWren, MonSenior Leebruce and Mr Crabble stepped (or hoverchaired) onto the WhiskMat beside the Dream5s, the great mat started to move and whisked through the air bubble towards the SWIGS Craft.

'The SWIGS Craft is a bit of a mouthful,' said Woozie, as they drew near. 'Let's call it *Swiggy*.'

No one had any objections, so the craft that would take the Dream5s (now also known as the *IGGY Knights*) to distant galaxies was officially christened.

The WhiskMat came to a halt against the side of Swiggy.

'You open the door, Rumbles,' said Wisebeardyface.

Rumbles closed her eyes and the doors opened. 'It workskeeys!' she said excitedly.

'Of course,' said Wisebeardyface. 'We have tuned in most of the controls to your brain wavelengths. Swiggy will react to all the telepathic orders of each one of you – but only one at a time.'

Miss LeWren was swift to point out that they shouldn't try to fly Swiggy telepathically until they'd been travelling for at least a few weeks.

Before the IGGY Knights stepped into Swiggy, Wisebeardyface gave each of them a vee-eye-pee toss (which was a bit scary when he was standing so close to the edge of the WhiskMat). Then, much to Woozie's embarrassment, Miss Zohfria LeWren gave each of them a kiss.

'Swiggy flize een eggzactly ze same way az ze jegg,' she told them. 'Juzt push ze throttle to *maximum* and you will reach SeekoWarpo speed. After you leave ze Milky Way, ze steering wheel will become unlocked and you will be able to move eet, but I suggest you leave eet az eet iz for a while.'

Then, one after another, MonSenior FuKung Leebruce held each IGGY Knight in his gaze, clasping their hand as he did so. When he gripped Tommy's hand, he spoke with a wondrous glaze in his eyes.

'Tommy Storm . . . Tommy Storm . . . I . . . I saw you walk along the Plank of Discovery and fall into the Abyss . . .' The ancient fellow was filled with emotion and found it difficult to find his words. 'I was born before your people, your species walked your planet and I . . . You have taught me – I mean *us* – you have taught us something valuable, something unique, something that even we, the Masters of the Way, had lost . . . And I hope some day, human, I'll have the courage to climb out of this chair and try to do the same.'

Then he turned to all the IGGY Knights. 'I . . . On Swiggy there's lots of . . . Sorry . . .' For some reason, the wizened man's eyes were all watery and he was unable to speak.

Miss LeWren stepped forward, took his arm and smiled at him in a way that said, *don't worry, no need to say anything.* And so she spoke for the oldest Milki Master.

'Swiggy eez full of cabinetz containing Grow-sss-Goo educational moviez . . . We haff also prepared souzandz of interactive lessonz and testz zat you must pass if you are to become Masters of ze Way. Zere are flashscimitar lessonz, tipz on sleeping at SeekoWarpo speed and many ozzer subjectz zat we have been unable to teach you here. Zese subjectz have been designed to help you stop Ze TFC.'

'Yes,' said Wisebeardyface. 'Even at SickoWarpo speed, it will take some months before you reach another galaxy. Your

395

real training only begins now. Swiggy will be your school and – in spirit – we will be with you all the way.'

'Indeed, hmmm,' Crabble interrupted. 'Given the extraordinary technology that has gone into the lessons, it will seem as if we're actually with you – yes? – conducting the lessons.'

Wisebeardyface looked solemn. 'The TFC is scheduled to happen in twenty-one years. That might seem like a long time to some of you, but it will pass more quickly than you can possibly imagine.'

MonSenior nodded gravely and Tommy thought he heard the word '*Ophiuchus*' pass his lips.

After a respectful pause, Crabble spoke. 'Hey-ho, I recorded everything we know – and, hmm, everything we don't know – about The TFC.' And with that he removed the enormous pipe from his mouth and started giving high-fours to anyone who'd accept. Rumbles gave him a particularly hard high-four, causing Crabble to fall over – almost off the edge of the WhiskMat. His pipe fell out of his hand and over the edge. Tommy saw it spinning into the distance.

'That was an accident,' said Rumbles quickly. 'I'm not clumskeeys, you know.'

'Good heavens, no,' said Crabble, quickly jumping to his feet. 'No, no, yes, don't worry, we'll get the pipe back later, hmmm? What was I saying? Ah, yes, all the information about The TFC is on board, hmm, plus hundreds of lessons covering scientific areas, hey-ho. There's facts on BigGalaxies plus anecdotes, hmm, about Phenomena, yes?'

'Me that reminds,' said Summy. 'Lady MuckBeff, where is she?'

'Oh . . .' said Crabble looking troubled. 'Gosh, she made her apologies, yes? Indeed, indeed, said she couldn't make it. She has, hmm, something important to do, she said.'

For some reason this explanation didn't make any of the Dream5s feel particularly comfortable. It wasn't a nice note on which to step into Swiggy, wave goodbye to the four Masters of the Way and embark on a mission to stave off The TFC.

'Our destiny is in your hands,' said Wisebeardyface before the doors closed. 'Good luck . . . Please do not fail us . . . Remember. *Expect the unexpected*.' The Dream5s had almost disappeared into Swiggy when Wisebeardyface called out. 'Oh, Tommy!'

Tommy turned towards the old dinosaurus, who suddenly looked ponderous.

'*Inner-lath* . . .' he said slowly, running his fingers through his beard and turning the word over in his mind. 'Inner-lath.' Suddenly, he snapped back to the moment with a half-smile. 'Tommy, we are going to try this *love* thing . . . Perhaps, after all, that means the legend of the *Inner-Lath Catch* is actually true. If so, who needs a Plank of Discovery?'

Before he could ask Wisebeardyface what he meant, the doors closed in front of Tommy's face and the Dream5s were shut inside Swiggy.

'YEE-HI!' cried Woozie.

'YabbadabbaWOOBLE!' yelled Rumbles, knocking over a shelf laden with toys.

For a few minutes, everyone except Tommy ran around, claiming bunk-beds, checking out the kitchen, the strange laboratory rooms and the living room which was full of cushions and cabinets stocked with entertainment Grow-sss-Goo. When they made it into the cockpit, where Tommy was looking tense, they could see that the four Masters of the Way were waving from just inside the GarageZone and Miss LeWren seemed to be giving MonSenior a kiss, while

Wisebeardyface was giving Crabble an awkward hug (the awkwardness, mainly due to their respective shapes). Hundreds of people carrying musical instruments had crowded in behind the four Masters.

Tommy flicked a dial and the sound of wild jazz music filled the cockpit.

'My Corvus! Look! Over there . . . They're dancing,' said Marielle.

Sure enough, the GarageZone now resembled the wild scene that Tommy had experienced when he first arrived in Fedora.

'The *IGGY Miles and Miles and Miles Dayviss Band*, that is,' said Summy cheerily. 'In the MilkyFed, the best band they are.'

'Hey! Miss LeWren is dancing with MonSenior – look at that hoverchair go!'

'And check out Crabble!' cried Woozie. 'Can't dance for nuts . . . I feel sorry for Wisebeardyface's toes!'

After a lot of waving and swaying to the music, the rest of the Dream5s became serious when they saw how earnestly Tommy was examining the interior of the cockpit. After a final wave to all the dancing creatures, someone flicked the dial again and the music died. Moments later, the GarageZone doors closed and IGGY's inhabitants were gone from sight.

Unbeknownst to the IGGY Knights, as soon as the doors closed, Wisebeardyface raised his arm and quietened the gathering within the GarageZone.

'They can no longer hear us,' he said.

The dancing had stopped and everyone looked sombre.

'Did we seem too happy?' said Miss LeWren.

'Perhaps.'

MonSenior Leebruce had tears in his eyes. He wanted to say something but his mouth opened, then closed without a word.

Again, Miss LeWren took his arm. 'Ze Terrible Future Calamity,' she said, addressing Wisebeardyface. 'Maybe we should haff emphasized eet more. Ze whole galaxy, ze univerze – destroyed in twenty-one yearz . . . !! We hardly mentioned eet. We acted like eet waz not dominating our soughtz every moment of every day.'

As if in response, MonSenior threw his tartan rug on the floor. If he'd suddenly burst into flames, the crowd couldn't have been more shocked.

'We did the right thing,' said Wisebeardyface recovering. 'What good would it have done us if they had been paralysed by fear?'

'Hmm, no, and the training, the classes, the tests we gave them,' said Crabble. 'No, no, we have no idea if it will be any use against The TFC, yes?'

Wisebeardyface just nodded.

'Do you think they can save us?' said a voice from the crowd.

'If anyone can, they can,' said the old kangasaurus.

'That doesn't answer the question . . . Do you think they will save the universe and all of us from The TFC?'

Wisebeardyface looked as though he was going to say something. He looked that way for a time and someone took the opportunity to replace the rug on MonSenior's hover-chair. Finally, Wisebeardyface took a funny-looking cigarette out of his pocket and lit it with a snort from his nostril. As he walked towards a wighole, the crowd parted to let him through.

'I see a drink in my future,' he said. 'If anyone needs me, I will be in the Eye-on-the-Universe.'

49

GOODBYE, EARTH

'I'll fly Swiggy for the first part of the journey.'

'No, Tommy,' said Marielle. 'You don't have to do that.'

'Why don't you lie down in your cabin?' said Woozie, settling into the pilot's chair. 'We can fly it for the first few hours and wake you after—'

'After *what*?' said Tommy, angry that everyone was avoiding the words *Earth* and *obliterated*.

'When we're out of the Milky Way, I mean.'

All of the Dream5s had noted Tommy being strangely quiet all day. Actually, he'd been quiet ever since the celebration in the BigWig Ceremonial Hall the afternoon before. If becoming an IGGY Knight was a shock to them, they knew it must be even more of a shock to Tommy. He thought he'd be returning to Earth to be there for its destruction, but now, instead, he was going to be travelling in Swiggy as she destroyed his beloved planet. Marielle and Summy had discussed things earlier and even feared that Tommy would back out of the mission. He might refuse to travel in a spacecraft that was going to destroy his own planet. That's what they would've done if it had been their planet.

'I'm flying Swiggy for the first part of the journey.' There was a determination in Tommy's voice – a steel that was almost frightening.

'Perhaps if I pilot and beside me you sit,' said Summy.

Tommy gave the dinosaurus a look that was all the answer she needed.

'Tommy, if you try to veer off course at the last moment . . .' Woozie expected some reply, but all he got was two steely eyes boring into his own. 'It was made very clear to us,' continued the wibblewallian. 'If a craft deviates from a straight line while accelerating to SickoWarpo Speed, it'll explode and turn into vapour.'

'What Woozie is saying,' said Summy, 'is that if the steering you unlock and Earth avoid, all of us you will kill, and of saving the universe from The TFC any chance will be destroyed.'

'Meaning everyone in the universe dieskeeys – *dies*, I mean – including Earthlings . . . Right?' said Rumbles, looking for confirmation.

Three of the IGGY Knights nodded.

'I'm giving you one minute to give me that seat,' said Tommy to Woozie. The words were uttered without anger.

'Are you sure you want to do this, Tommy?' said Marielle.

A strange tension filled the cockpit and Woozie looked up at the others, seeking support. One after another they shrugged (Rumbles shrugging all three shoulders at the same time). Woozie finally stood up. Without a word, Tommy brushed past him and took the pilot's seat.

An awkward silence descended on the cockpit, only dissolving as all the IGGY Knights became consumed with the task of checking dials and monitors in preparation for take-off. Every now and again someone would steal a glance at Tommy to see if he was OK. To see if the look on his face had changed. But he never acknowledged a glance and his face remained a picture of resolution.

'Summy,' said Tommy after a time, as he flicked a switch. 'Do you know what Wisebeardyface meant when he mentioned the *Inner-Lath Catch*?'

Summy laughed. 'A solar-urban-legend, that is . . . The *Inner-Lath Catch* . . .' She laughed again, then stopped when she saw Tommy's expression. 'Ahem . . . say they that if your eyes you close and backwards you fall, then if any *living* person feels *inner-lath* – or *love* – for you, then catch you will their spirit, before the floor you hit.'

'So I couldn't do it and expect my parents' spirit to catch me?'

'No. Someone *living* it has to be.'

'They say you have to keep your arms held firmly against your chest,' said Woozie. 'If you try to break your fall, their spirit won't catch you.'

'And is it true?' said Tommy. 'Do you think there's something in the solar-urban legend?'

Summy thought about it for a moment.

'Hmm . . . Precisely 38.467 million to one are the chances.'

'You can never tell,' said Woozie. 'Everyone's heard of the legend, but you always bend your legs before you hit the ground. That, or you twist and fling out your arms. They say it won't work unless you're on a hard floor. Definitely doesn't work if there's a set of cushions behind you or you do it in an anti-gravity room . . . You have to risk injuring yourself.'

'Too much trust, too much faith, needs the legend, to test fully.'

'Do you believe it?' said Marielle to Tommy.

'I don't know,' he replied. And that was the truth.

Again, the cockpit went silent. Tommy started watching the time intently and looked nervous as he revved up the engines. The steering wheel was locked in position so that

Swiggy's nose was pointing at a narrow gap between two large planets and a bright star. The unsettling and unavoidable fact was that the steering wheel would only unlock 2.6 minutes after they hit SickoWarpo Speed – long after they'd left the Milky Way and Earth had been destroyed. (This, of course, was assuming Tommy didn't kick the *Unlock* pedal while pressing the *Unlock* button on the steering wheel.)

'Watch the clock there,' said Tommy eventually to Woozie. 'Give me a countdown. We must leave the moment the needle hits the black arrow.'

Everyone took their seats. There were four of them around the pilot's seat, all with elaborate seat-belts and matching floral seat-covers.

The engines roared louder as Woozie counted out loud. 'Fourteen . . . thirteen . . . twelve . . .'

Marielle could see beads of sweat appearing on Tommy's forehead. His beloved planet would be nothing but a memory in less than two minutes and twelve seconds. She took a last look at IGGY and then fixed her eyes on a star in the distance.

'Five . . . four . . . three . . . two . . . one . . . Go! Go! Go!'

Tommy pulled the throttle back as far as it would go – past a marker with *Obscenely Fast* printed above it and into the red zone marked *SickoWarpo Speed*.

Everyone was pressed into their seats and they felt as though they were being turned inside-out – particularly since the view outside seemed to turn inside-out as well. For a few seconds, it felt as if they'd been punched very hard in the face and the flying stars were just imaginary.

Once they reached SickoWarpo Speed and the acceleration stopped, everything kept flashing by at an alarming rate outside – it looked like they were in a flashing disco – but they could remove their seat-belts.

Those of you who hate wearing seat-belts in the back of cars may find it strange to note that the Dream5s wouldn't even need their seat-belts for the impact with Earth. As mentioned earlier, it would be like a bullet travelling through an egg – having almost no effect on the bullet whatsoever.

Tommy flicked a switch and a large screen lowered just in front of him. The screen filled with an image of a slow-turning, white, woolly-looking planet that was growing gradually larger.

'Ah, the SickoWarpo Speed Viewfinder,' said Summy.

'Must be Earth,' said Woozie, pointing at the screen.

And he was right. It's almost impossible to get a clear view of anything when travelling at SickoWarpo Speed, so the best way to know what's going on is to use the SickoWarpo Speed Viewfinder. The Viewfinder allows you to pick out an image up to 93,282 light-years away and because a particular image is so far away, you seem to be travelling slowly towards it.

'Twenty-seven seconds to impact . . .' said Woozie. 'You do remember you'll kill all of us if you swerve?'

Again, Marielle noted the look of concentration on Tommy's face and more beads of sweat trickling just past his eyebrow and down the curve of his face. She thought he looked especially handsome when he was concentrating so intently. His jaw muscles were tensed and every few seconds he'd purse his lips, then softly lick the dryness away.

'Sixteen seconds to impact.'

The vision of Earth was getting larger. It filled half the screen and the Dream5s could see that the woolly substance surrounding the planet appeared, in fact, to be cloud.

'Seven seconds.'

Marielle saw Tommy place his hand on the throttle and

hold it tight. He seemed to grip it with all his force and the blood ran out of his knuckles.

'Four seconds to impact, three . . . two . . . one . . .'

Immediately, everything went black – including the screen.

It's hard to convey the contrast of this moment with the minutes that had gone before. As Swiggy flashed through space at SickoWarpo Speed, the light from stars looked like laser-bolts flashing past. Multiply one laser bolt by 60,000 million and you have an awful lot of laser bolts and an awful lot of light. Sitting in Swiggy, it felt like sitting in the middle of a fireworks display. Then all of a sudden everything went black.

It probably went black for less than a second, but it felt like an eternity. It was enough time for Woozie to feel sure that something had gone wrong and that they'd died from the impact with Earth.

Marielle thought, *This is it*, and every moment of her life flashed through her head. It made her suddenly regret the many things she'd been too afraid to say and too afraid to do. She'd always believed she'd have time to say and do them all.

Summy almost wet her seat and gave a little yelp. Rumbles leapt backwards and knocked Summy off her seat (which was the main cause of Summy's yelp).

Tommy closed his eyes and heaved an enormous sigh of relief. Woozie wasn't sure, but he thought he heard Tommy mumble, 'Thank you.'

When the dark second was over, the blackness turned itself inside-out and the flying bolts of light roared towards the cockpit window once more. They were back in the middle of the fireworks display.

'We're alive!' cried Woozie.

Summy and Marielle gave a whoop of joy.

'I'm not clumsy,' said Rumbles solemnly as he helped

Summy back onto her seat.

Then someone looked at the monitor.

'Still there it is. Still there Earth is!'

And sure enough, it was. Behind them. Somehow, the woolly, headless, legless sheep had completely survived the impact.

~~ 50 ~~

MY WAY

When he could speak again, Tommy explained how he'd stolen two wigholes from Crabble's store.

'I used all my POO training and placed the two wigholes in orbit on either side of Earth,' he said. 'I did it after I left Guttly on Earth . . . I can't tell you how frightened I've been that maybe I'd miscalculated and that we'd pass by the wighole before it revolved directly into our flight-path.'

'You mean we flew into a wighole on *that* side of Earth and came out another on *this* side?' said Woozie incredulously.

Tommy nodded.

'No wonder it went dark for so long. I thought we'd died.'

As you may realize by now, time always appears to slow greatly in a wighole. Although they must've been between wigholes for no more than a nanosecond, it of course felt much longer to the Dream5s (or IGGY Knights).

It was only at this moment that the five IGGY Knights fully registered what had happened – and they broke into a spontaneous cheer and everyone exchanged hugs.

'I say let's just enjoy this view while it lasts,' said Marielle joyfully, giving Tommy an extra-strong hug. 'We may not see the Milky Way for a very long time.'

For the next forty seconds or so, the IGGY Knights watched the fireworks display continue and admired the

Milky Way. Tommy felt a happiness mushroom inside him as the thought of Earth's survival began to sink in.

The Milky Way looked so beautiful . . . And for a moment it became more than just a random scattering of planets and stars. Like each of the IGGY Knights, he felt a sense of pride. It was more than just a Milky Way. This was *his* Way.

Just before Swiggy left the Milky Way, something gooey hit the window of the cockpit.

'Was that a moonskeey?' said Rumbles.

Before anyone could answer, the goo spread across the window, a single corvus-crocus (a type of flower)[17] stuck to one of the wind-wipers and an image of Lady MuckBeff WiLLyoofytus appeared and began to speak.

'Hear ye, hear ye . . . ! I hope this time I proveth to be a good shot. 'Tis most difficult to hit the windscreen of a craft that be travelling at SickoWarpo Speed. If I miss, then ignoreth this message and please mention naught to anyone . . . But hath I hit directly, then eventho' ye were not my first choice as IGGY Knights, knoweth that I be sitting in my jegg at the edge of the Milky Way and be ye assured that I be wishing ye success with the mission. This corvus-crocus doth be a symbol of my wish. Fail ye not. I implore ye.'

Then the goo rolled back into a ball and fell off the cockpit window.

Summy fiddled with the dials controlling the viewfinder. 'Hey, look,' she cried. She tried to improve the focus, but couldn't clarify the picture. 'Just there.'

When they strained their eyes, they could just make out a shrinking, beige object close to a cluster of moons. It could

17 Also known as a RosE – but for some reason they smell much sweeter when called a corvus-crocus. (Scientific tests have proved this to be the case.)

well have been Lady M's jegg.

'Smelly old kow,' said Woozie, flicking a switch to retrieve the corvus-crocus.

A kow is an animal that produces milkshakes from the udders on its back. Kows are notoriously smelly due to milkshake droplets dribbling onto their fur and going sour (bananakows are the worst in this regard).

'Ah, she's not that badskeeys,' said Rumbles, taking the flower and going in search of a vase.

After a time, Tommy passed the controls to Summy, went into his bedroom and closed the door. The stresses and strains of almost destroying Earth could no longer be ignored. It had been an extraordinary few days – exciting, thrilling and yet very sad at times.

Tomorrow he'd have to start learning about the SWIGS Mission and then there'd be more challenges and worries. For now, though, he put the future out of his head, closed his eyes, clasped his electric violin with one hand, the bow with the other, and lost himself in melody . . .

In the living room, Rumbles and Woozie thought they'd try out that *Inner-Lath Catch* lark.

'You're supposed to fall back without bending your legs or using your arms to break your fall,' said Woozie.

'And what? If someone loves me, then their spiritskeeys will catch me?'

'I know it's barmy, but give it a go.'

They each tried it a few times, but neither could do it without bending their legs and turning to face the floor in mid-air. Eventually, they stopped when Rumbles knocked into a cabinet and it opened, covering her in Grow-sss-Goo.

'I'm not clumskeeys, you know,' she cried and then she jumped up frantically because two balls of goo had started to stain her undies.

There were three bathrooms on Swiggy and Marielle was in the swishiest one – the floating globe. After her bath, she let the water run out into Swiggy's internal purification unit and stood on a glass platform, allowing herself to dry.

Through the walls, the strains of a strange, soothing melody carried to her and she could hear Woozie and Rumbles laughing as they vainly tried the *Inner-Lath Catch*. Twice, she changed her mind before deciding to give it a go. Then she crossed her arms across her chest, closed her eyes and fell backwards. Somehow she managed not to bend her legs.

EPILOGUE

Before Felkor, Anjel*eek!*, Egbert and ZsaZsa returned to
Earth from IGGY, all knowledge of The TFC and Earth's
pending destruction was removed from their memories by a
painless procedure involving a bendy probe. This was done
so that people on Earth wouldn't panic. (The Milki Masters'
Council had decided that it was better that Earthlings 'die in
blissful ignorance'.)

News of Tommy's elevation to the rank of IGGY
Knight spread across the globe as The Four sold their
stories to the world's press. The Grand Council publicized
Tommy's role in defeating the evil Elsorr Maudlin and
claimed that they'd never tried to hide the fact that
Tommy was one of The Five. It was just a bureaucratic
oversight, they argued, and if anyone was to blame, it was
Elsorr Maudlin. Earth went on to join the MilkyFed
although it never joined the MilkyFed's common
(bartering) currency.

Even though Earthlings were unaware that Tommy saved
their planet, Tommy was held up as a hero on Earth. Statues
were erected all over the globe, sometimes with very spiky
hair, sometimes with very floppy hair and often holding a
flashscimitar.

Even at the Wilchester Academy for Young Adults, a

statue was erected at the end of the Great Dining Hall and the little loft-room at the very top of the school was closed off and preserved for paying sightseers. The pupils were very proud indeed and groups used to argue amongst themselves, each claiming Tommy as their own. The dark kids claimed he wasn't a *whitey*, he was nearly as dark as them. The freckly kids said it was ridiculous to call him *Dusky* as Tommy wasn't that unlike them. The oriental-looking kids were sure that Tommy resembled them in almost every way. The others took delight in calling themselves mongrels ('Just like Tommy,' they claimed) and they, like all the kids, tried to style their clothes and their hair upon those of the statue at the back of the Great Dining Hall – which had floppy hair.

Old Mr Withers retired as headmaster some years later and claimed, in his widely-sold autobiography (*My Famous Pupil – Memoirs of Old Googly Eyes*), that he'd always singled out Tommy Storm for greatness. *'It was obvious from the first time I set my left eye on the boy . . .'*

The Extremely White Album
– lyrics and music by Felkor Stagwitch (2099)

Upon arriving back to Earth, the families of The Four each received $2 million (in today's money) from the Grand Council. The Four formed a band called *The Quite Fab Four* which toured Earth with some success, playing country-and-western tunes (with tap-dancing). The families had all frittered away their $2 million by the time the band broke up – due to Felkor embarking on a solo career. Unfortunately for Felkor, he couldn't sing and people never warmed to his guitar-only brand of music, so he became a (fexa-cetter) taxi driver, and lived out his days wearing a triangular hat, blaming the smell of rotten Brussels sprouts on a faulty carburettor and informing passengers what he'd have done if he'd been given his rightful chance to rule the Milky Way.[18]

Anjeleek! finally found happiness when she decided to stop dieting for ever and wrote a book – *Listen To Your Body – Or Else It Will Scream*. From then on she ate whatever her body felt like and her weight settled at 'just above average' and stayed that way for good. Having spent two years in jail on fraud charges, Egbert 'Fleet Foot' Fitchly went on to marry Anjeleek! and together they set up *The Ementhal School of Singing and Tap-Dancing*.

ZsaZsa was paid one million floaties by a national newspaper for agreeing to appear in one of their sponsored art-o-pathy competitions on the day she turned eighteen, wearing nothing but a liquorice bikini, a mink stole and a two-metre feather. She went on to make a fortune from her own line of hair products (*Darlingk Vavannus*™), married four times and lived to be 101.

18 He wrote an autobiography (*Me Me Me – innit*) in his 50s and it sold over 7,000 copies. In it (not innit), he described how his parents had always favoured his older brother, Eddie, and how his father never let him win at hide-n-seek. Felkor never married but is believed to have died leaving seventeen kids as his 'gift to the world'.

━━ EXTRA BITS NO. 1 ━━
EARTH AND THE MILKYFED

For over 6,000 years, Earth's neighbours in the Milky Way assumed that Earthlings were just not interested in communicating with them. They'd sent countless probes, spaceships and ambassadors to the planet, but in each case they were either ignored, rebuffed or rudely pointed at by locals. Many thought this proved their contention that Earth did not harbour intelligent life.

These neighbours came from a series of planets within four separate solar systems, together making up the Milky Federation (known as the MilkyFed or the Confederation).

Then, sometime in the 1950s, Earthlings began venturing into space. Over the next hundred years or so, Earthlings visited the Moon and Mars – the equivalent of Earth's doorstep, but a start nonetheless, in joining in with the rest of the galaxy.

A Very Loud *Rocket*

MilkyFederans often laughed at the primitiveness of Earthlings – *transport* being perhaps their favourite area to pick on.

It was as if every planet used Ferraris for travel, except Earthlings, who all insisted on using a faulty pair of skates. Many jokes began with the line, 'There were these three Earthlings and a rocket . . .' Part of the joke usually involved the fact that the word *rocket* sounds very like the word for *belch* in the language of at least three MilkyFed planets.

415

And so, in 2082, three years before Tommy Storm was born, a video message was sent to Earth by the MilkyFed[19] and this was followed by a meeting close to the Moon where an astronaut was given an official wuggle-hug by a skychubb. This formalized the MilkyFed's recognition of Earth and vice-versa.

Members of the MilkyFed Self-important Scientists Society have asked me to emphasize that to the MilkyFed, a video message was considered as primitive as a smoke-signal. However, it was agreed that this would be the best method of communication as all other messages had been studiously ignored.

From then on, every three years, the MilkyFed sent Earth an invitation to become the fifth Solar System Member of the MilkyFed. (The Grand Council of Earth's 2094 vote on the issue was defeated when Elsorr convinced eight Councillors that the MilkyFed would ban bendy bananas and force Earth to buy the MilkyFed's straight ones.) Earth's continuing refusal to join confirmed many MilkyFederans' belief that Earthlings were the least intelligent and least friendly species in the Milky Way.

19 Within a short time, most adults on Earth accepted that intelligent life existed on other planets. Those who didn't, flocked to the movie, The MilkyFed Conspiracy (by the acclaimed director, Stoned Olly).

Baaaahhhhd Joke
– Title of MilkyFed book dealing with the History of Earth
(5,006 BC – 2006 AD)[20]

Due to a complicated mix-up in 7,315 BC, the MilkyFed came to believe that Earthlings spoke the language of sheep. They realized their mistake 2,000 years later, but an interpreter who'd spent 1,991 years learning SheepSpeak refused to be made redundant and his union insisted that bleating noises (an exact translation of the message) be audible in the background of 'any messages sent to Earth for the rest of the interpreter's life'. (Incidentally, the interpreter had a life expectancy of 47,317 more years.) From 2082–2096, this state of affairs led Earthlings to the mistaken conclusion that anyone travelling to the MilkyFed would need to perfect a sheep impression.

---

20 BC in this case refers to Before Chocolate. AD refers to After Dynamite.

Extra Bits no. 2
Activities and High Culture on Earth (2096)

School Wurk

The essay that Tommy wrote into his CP at Wilchester (on the Great Climate Enhancement) was done using *computer word telepathy*.[21]

By the age of nine, every school kid was expected to write essays using computer word telepathy. This involved making a CP read your *word thoughts*. If you were next to your CP and pictured the word *sausage*, for example, then, all going well, the *word* sausage would appear on screen. After a while, you could make sentences appear as fast as you thought of them. Learning to spell was still important, as words came up on the screen in the way you imagined them – spell-checkers were disabled on CPs used in schools. (The name of the most popular brand of school stationery – *Duz-This-Spell-Cheque-Wurk?*™ – was a play on this fact.)

Computer *image* telepathy wasn't usually taught to students till university.

Art

At the end of the 21st century, all art classes on Earth concentrated exclusively on teaching people to draw circles

21 Tommy was 11¼ years old at this point.

on flat screens, using telepathy. The circle had to be bigger than a saucer and there were stringent controls in place to ensure that no one cheated by way of any computer or software help. A computer then measured the accuracy of the circle and awarded a mark from 1–103 (103 being the highest mark possible).

Art competitions were frequent during this period. The most lauded artist of the time, Wahndi Arhole, held the world record circle score of 94.587 (achieved at altitude) and his circles were exhibited to huge crowds around the globe. One circle sold for over 25 billion *floaties* – the common currency on Earth.

Art-o-pathy

Under the strict rules of art–o–pathy, you telepathically draw a circle on a computer screen and then telepathically colour it in, with music playing all the while. (Kids wear an antenna on their head when doing art–o–pathy, since very few kids can perform computer image 'telepathy' without such help.)

In 2096, *art-o-pathy* was taught in all schools and a pupil's rating in art–o–pathy was felt to be a much better indicator of intelligence than an IQ score. The highest possible mark is known as *pi* (3.142857). The lowest possible mark is minus 5,326.

Calculation of the mark is quite complicated and art–o–pathy judges study for up to seven years before graduating to the level of Pompuss-Referee-In-Situ.

Serious Sport

Team-Tag-WhoseLegisthat-Twissterr (TTWLT) was the only team game played in all public schools across the globe in 2096. It's very like Twister, but the mat is six times the size and you play in teams of 15. Only six members of a team can be 'on the mat' at once. If 'on-mat' players can reach 'off-mat' team-mates and 'tag', they can leave the mat. Newly tagged players begin play in the centre of the mat. The object of the game is to make your opponents so uncomfortable that all six on the mat cry, 'Cauliflower! Cauliflower!' at the same time.

The most popular brand of TTWLT equipment goes by the name of *That's-ur-Toe-IN-my-Nostril!*, and has a swollen nose as its emblem.

On the day Felkor was chosen as one of The Five, as Tommy was sitting in his loft-room in solitary confinement, two teams were playing a very tense game of TTWLT in the corridor just below – which may explain why Tommy could hear the word 'Cauliflower!' called out in occasional agonized bursts.

━━ EXTRA BITS NO. 3 ━━
CRABBLE'S FULL EXPLANATION
OF EARTH'S HISTORICAL
INVENTIONS

Crabble explained that the tradition of helping Earthlings with inventions really started when a few MilkyFederans thought it would be a laugh to build a few pyramids and sphinxes[22] in ancient Egypt. Then, during Earth's 'ancient' Greek and Roman times, mischievous MilkyFederans frequently broke MilkyFed law by popping down to Earth and leaving plans for drainage systems and what not.

Some time later (just over 2,000 years ago in Earth terms), the MilkyFed police cracked down on such space-rogues and the incursions into Earth stopped for a time. However, they started again about 600 years ago when it became something of a status symbol for MilkyFed families to leave their mark on Earth.

There was the family who whispered into Alexander Graham Bell's ear and brought about a ridiculously crude means of communication, although the one who visited the Wright brothers got teased a lot for their ridiculous airplane design. ('That was the *point*!' they claimed.) One family stayed with Albert Einstein for a week and got him drunk on favo-fant food. Another tickled Sigmund Freud for a year and kept prodding him with pointy things. Some vandals left the

22 Sphinxes are very common creatures on the planet Missingnose.

plans for an atomic bomb in someone's fridge, while a group of hooligans dropped clothes for dogs (pullovers, jackets and hats) over New York.

Tommy was amazed. It seemed that every invention – from toasters to micro-chips to resealable nappies to nylon car-seat covers – had been implanted in humans by MilkyFederans. Sometimes the MilkyFederans just left plans lying around, other times they hid near people and sent telepathic messages to the silly humans who then regurgitated the information, presuming it was some kind of divine inspiration.

The hippies from the planet Heyyehman particularly loved implanting songs and movies in the minds of humans. There was a certain cachet about laying claim to a song that became popular on Earth. One hippy got sent to prison by the MilkyFed authorities for stealing lots of MilkyFed songs and implanting them in the heads of two humans he abducted regularly. He even had the warped humour to tell them to call their band the B-Tuls.[23] Another hippie went to jail for stealing his sister's diary and giving it to George Lucas[24] and another got three months' solitary confinement for bringing *The Simpsons* and *The Muppets* to Earth.

Although the MilkyFed authorities were annoyed at space-tourists dropping inventions on Earth, what annoyed them most were the joy-riders who emerged around the 1950s. These adolescents started having parties on their spacecraft, getting very drunk and then flying to Earth and flashing their lights at

23 A B-Tul is a form of foot-odour experienced by 5-legged Addul-Essentz.

24 The girl's father, Varth Dader, was even more annoyed as his character was unfairly maligned in the diary – yes, he had a nasal problem, but he also had a regular job, was happily married with forty-eight kids and worked for the Imperial Forces' Halitosis Research Institute.

frightened humans. Some of them even went so far as to abduct Earthlings for the duration of the party, but most were caught by the authorities and the Earthlings returned to Earth (usually after a memory-cleaning procedure). When the MilkyFedPolice put an absolute ban on joy-riding (towards the end of the twentieth century), many of the youths reacted by getting drunk and visiting Earth to leave ridiculous repetitive songs with no artistic merit whatsoever. Some of them even took the songs of renowned space-families and remixed them in a crass and shallow way.

For a while, this artistic vandalism became so virulent that young hooligans would get famous human artists to 'paint' blank canvases or to 'exhibit' ridiculous things, such as an unmade bed, and then to claim it was something very significant and meaningful. The MilkyFed authorities were extremely annoyed at this because how were the poor, gullible humans who inhabited Earth supposed to know that space-people were just having a laugh at them?

The only interference on Earth that was officially sanctioned by the MilkyFed was clothes fashion. A food-fight competition was held by the MilkyFed every ten years and the winner was allowed to telepathically contact lots of humans to design clothes. Hence the dress style on Earth of the 1920s, 1930s and so on, all the way up to 2010, when the competition ended.[25]

25 The competition ended due to a lawsuit. Previous winners of the competition successfully sued the 1990–2000 and 2000–2010 winners for stealing all their ideas. Also, MilkyFederans stopped visiting Earth around 2010 because they began to feel guilty that all their inventions had created such a mess. When The Great Climate Enhancement happened some years later, ordinary humans could no longer see into the sky above the clouds and MilkyFederans began to forget about the place until a MilkyFed scientist abducted some humans in 2081 and never returned them to Earth.

The dress style chosen by the winner was usually the style of clothes they most frequently wore themselves, although the NooWavonian who won the 1980s competition[26] was said to be mad as a fedora.

Excommunicate Him!

It's believed that a criminal on the run, called Fermi Paradox, settled on Earth in the early 20th century. He was so worried about being found by the MilkyFed authorities that he made a point of convincing many Earthlings that there was no chance of life beyond Earth. He's said to have been killed by an Occam's Razor – *trust me, you don't want to know . . .*

Very few MilkyFederans are actually *known* to have made a life on Earth, although certain MilkyFed 'institutions' are thought to have eased over-crowding by making patients look like humans and depositing them on Earth. The danger with such 'impostors' is that they blurt out well-known MilkyFed knowledge that humans aren't prepared for. Some of the prime suspects include Galileo Galilei, Charles Darwin and Jim Henson.

---

26 The Fashion Food-Fight Competition started around 1919. Before that, a very uptight plumber from the planet Viktory-Ah had been the last space-person to influence clothing, maybe 100 years earlier. Previous to that, any clothes suggestions that made it to Earth were made by hooligans who just wanted to watch a good comedy at one of their space-parties. Such hooligans had particular fun with Earth's royal families.

⚡ Extra Bits no. 4 ⚡
The Terrible Future Calamity (The TFC)

All the experts agreed that The TFC was 'almost definitely' going to happen. However, they had differing theories on what exactly The TFC would be. The theories outlined below are direct extracts from just a few of the documents presented to the Milki Masters on the subject.

The Tomato Theory
(as advocated by The Purée Physics Association)

'It is likely that galaxies exist on the far side of the universe that are very, very large in comparison to the Milky Way (called BigGalaxies). These BigGalaxies are so large, they only fit in the universe because it happens to be infinitely large. It has been calculated that tomatoes would exist on BigGalaxies and we believe that one (very red one) is heading straight this way. The Milky Way would be smaller than one of the pips within this tomato, so a direct impact would spell the end of life in our galaxy.'

The Bigger Bang Theory
(as advocated by The Eridanus Eggheads)

'Imagine placing an elastic band on the very top of two fingers and then stretching it – further and further. What will happen? Correct – at some point, it will fly off one finger and give the other a nasty snap! This is exactly what's happening with our universe. It's expanding, faster and faster. But very soon it will snap in on itself, destroying all life as we know it.'

The Theo Theory
(as advocated by The Theo-Is-Really-Fab Society of Scientists)

'We believe that all MilkyFederans have an invisible friend called Theo who lives outside the universe.[27] Theo is all-powerful, all-seeing and never trims his beard.

Whenever a MilkyFederan does anything naughty, Theo writes it down in his notebook. Theo's notebook will be completely full in $21\frac{1}{2}$ years – at which point (out of rage or boredom), Theo will destroy the universe with fire, famine, disease, planetquakes and maybe some war. Although there is no basis for our theory, it is definitely true. And if you don't believe it, then that is naughty and it will go in Theo's notebook – making his notebook fill up even quicker'

As everyone was convinced that their theory was correct, a huge row threatened. In the end, the Milki Masters decided to have no official explanation for The TFC.

27 His exact address is 7th Heaven, Elysian Fields, DC 20500, Isle of Avalon.

⚡ EXTRA BITS NO. 5 ⚡
TOMMY'S FAMILY HISTORY

At the beginning of the 21st century, some scientists wondered what would happen if you mixed the major races of the world to produce one person. Would you get the best elements from every race or the worst elements? And so, four men and four women – an Asian, a West Indian, a South American, a Middle Eastern, a Celt, a Maori, an Inuit, plus a random Liverpudlian (chosen as a result of a game show phone-in competition) – were chosen to live on an island. Together they were known simply as *The Islanders*.

The island was barricaded so that no one could leave and no one could enter, although food supplies and a roll of toilet paper were dropped on a weekly basis. For the first three years of the experiment, the life of The Islanders was televised for the entertainment of ordinary people who'd nothing better to do while eating their dinners in the evening.[28]

The Islanders were Tommy's great-grandparents, their four offspring were his grandparents and, in turn, their two children were Tommy's parents. The plan was to keep this

28 By now the idea of families chatting to each other at mealtimes had been fully ditched in favour of TV. (Certainly, communal meals had been officially ridiculed in the bestselling *I'm-Quite-Famous-So-Let-Me-Tell-You-How-To-Bring-Up-Your-Children Handbook*.)

small community separated from the rest of the world for exactly one hundred years. When the Great Climate Enhancement happened, the Islanders were moved to a small floating city and they continued to be kept from other people.

Some years before the end of the experiment, Tommy's parents, Lola and Errol, disappeared mysteriously.[29] They were never seen again. Four years later, a young woman was bathing off the side of Garlicky-Cream (an up-market floating city) and found a tiny little baby boy floating among some reeds. On the back of this baby's head, almost hidden by his fluffy dark hair, was a small mark, almost like a tattoo, except that the letters were raised slightly so you could read them with your finger. The mark said *Tommy*.

Once DNA tests were done on Tommy, it was confirmed that he was the child of Lola and Errol, so he was handed over to scientists. After much analysis they concluded that Tommy wasn't very special, closing the book on The Islanders experiment. 'Better, where possible, to keep all races separated,' they concluded. The oldest scientist involved in the project, Philomena Drew, had been a little girl when The Islanders were first sent to the island and she remembered watching them on TV. She decided to give Tommy to an orphanage and because she was one of the few people who remembered the world before the Great Climate Enhancement, she decided to give him the surname *Storm* – in memory of the wonderful power and variety the weather once held.

Tommy was three when Philomena died and in her will she bequeathed a small legacy to fund his education until the age of eighteen. He should never be told about her will, she said.

29 By this time, all the original great-grandparents and grandparents had died of dysentery, bubonic plague or from DIY mishaps.

The legacy must be kept secret. Philomena stipulated that Tommy should attend the Wilchester Academy from the age of six[30] and insisted that the authorities should never tell Tommy the truth about his parents – as the news would be too traumatic. If pressed, he was to be told that his parents disappeared at the time of his birth and were presumed dead.

After a time, the scientists forgot about Tommy, and the truth about his origins eventually faded with the shredding of a roomful of dusty scientific files concerning a silly experiment started on an island almost one hundred years earlier. And so, by the time Tommy was almost eleven, even if somebody on Earth had a fit of compassion and wanted to tell him the truth about his parents and his background, they couldn't have done so.

30 It was rumoured that she chose Wilchester because she and the
    headmaster, Mr Withers, had been in love many years earlier –
    although the romance failed for vegetarian and personal hygiene
    reasons that she would never discuss. Neither of them ever
    married.